The Fabric of Choice

SELANDU TALES BOOK 3

By J. A. Komorita

The Fabric of Choice
SELANDU TALES BOOK 3

Edited by George Verongos
Cover by George Verongos
Cover concept by J. A. Komorita
Needlework by J. A. Komorita

PAPERBACK
ISBN: 979-8-9911618-4-8

EBOOK
ISBN: 979-8-9911618-5-5

Website: jakomorita.com

Acknowledgments

As always, thank you to my great editor, George Verongos, for your knowledge, hard work, and patience. Thank you for buoying me up when I needed it.

Thank you to my good friend Ginny Stern, for your eternal positivity and desire to help the world, and for handing out my books to your friends.

Thank you to George, and the joyous people who helped me in too many ways to count.

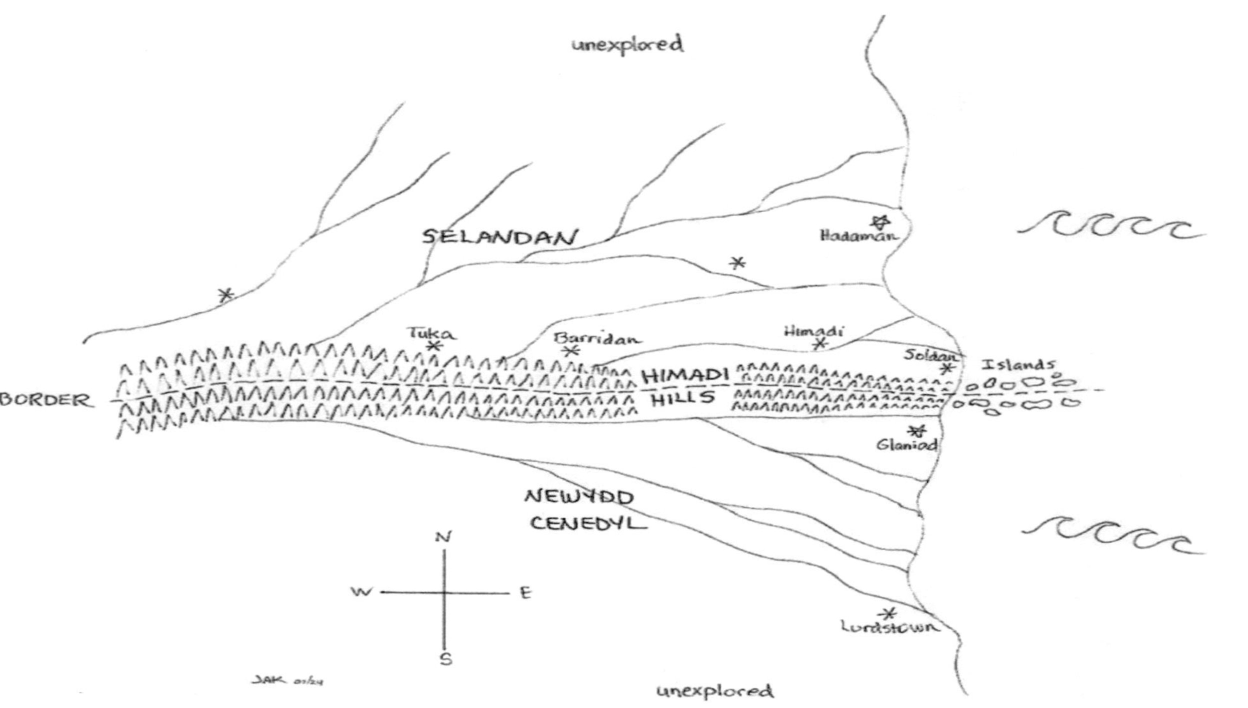

unexplored
SELANDAN
Hadaman
Tuka
Barridan
Himadi
Soldan
Islands
BORDER
HIMADI
HILLS
Glaniad
NEWYDD
CENEDYL
N
W
E
S
Lordstown
unexplored
JAK 01/24

CONTENTS

I tried so many times to fit in but I could never ever fit in. I was always like, an outcast.
—Israel Adesanya

You can't control what others think. The only thing you can control is yourself. Some people will look down on you for your choices in life, no matter what they are. You can't do anything about that. The only thing you can do is decide how to live your own life. And to hell with everybody else.
—Marie Sexton

The docks of Glaniad came into view, and it was not a welcome sight. Wooden fishing boats, sailboats, and small pleasure crafts crowded the docks. Each rocked to its own rhythm by the waves under its hull.

Cara MacLennan bent her head to the side wall of the Selandu boat. A stiff sea breeze fluttered her long hair, hair held back by a clip at her neck. Rodani had made the clip for her with the hope that she would consent to be his chosen mate. Two days ago, she'd said yes. Now they were parted, their love affair severed by bullets, blood, and death.

The boat docked with a thump. Cara looked past the Selandu sailors clad in green, past the human boats, and onto land.

Good gods of the wide deep, there was Menachem Mboto, black-haired, dark-skinned, tall and slender. As ambassador first, he was waiting, no doubt, to fill her ears with pointed questions. Next to him, in front of their mother's carriage, stood her brother, Davad. Younger than she by only two years, he had blue eyes, and brown hair that curled around his ears, courtesy of their shared father. Behind the carriage, one of only a few in the south, stood an ungainly crowd of one-room cabins, following in the distance were one- and two-story houses and sturdy buildings. Rows of workshops led from the docks, then were substituted with markets toward the heart of town. *Home?* she wondered. *No. Not really. Not since Barridan.*

Cara walked off the boat with her arms full of sacks and boxes, her heart full of grief. Davad walked up to meet her.

"What happened?" he asked, taking some of her burdens. He placed them in the carriage.

Cara clamped her eyes shut and fought back tears. She'd done almost nothing but cry since leaving Barridan. She felt both fragile and ashamed. "Just..." She took a shuddering breath. "Half of them turned against me."

Davad stared. "A hundred aliens?"

"No, no. Half the guild." She wiped her face with the back of her hand.

"So, a bunch of assassins tried to kill you. And you still live?" Incredulity and humor bled through his voice.

"No. They tried to kill my...guardian. The one who was protecting me."

"Did they?"

Cara shook her head. She collapsed into Davad's arms, sobbing.

"Whoa, whoa. You have to stop making quilts, so you fall apart?" He hugged her. "I didn't think they were *that* important to you."

She had no words for the loss that engulfed her. Even if she did, she couldn't speak them. No one wanted to hear how she'd fallen in love and in bed with an alien, or how she screamed as they'd been wrenched apart.

"Come on." Davad patted her back. "Have a drink. Have a hot meal. Teria made you meatballs. We're all invited."

Thumps and clunks erupted behind her. The tall Selandu sailors, grey-skinned and silver-haired, were offloading her belongings.

"Let's get the rest of your stuff," Davad suggested. "Repository first."

The three of them loaded the carriage, then she climbed in behind Davad and Menachem. Menachem thanked the sailors in their own language.

They wound their way through dirt and cobbled streets to the town's main storage area. Large and imposing, the repository held a cornucopia of items brought down from shipboard when it had been attacked and abandoned 75 years before. There, they dropped off the sewing machine and 'corder that Cara had borrowed seven months ago.

Menachem was quiet, dangerously so. As they drew up to her family's home, he pulled her aside. "You're going to tell me what really happened. If not tonight, then tomorrow. If not tomorrow, then Friday."

She mumbled something inaudible.

"Come by the CSC tomorrow. I'll expect you at ten."

Morose, lethargic in her grief, Cara grabbed the rest of her belongings. Her sister Teria met her at the door with her toddler daughter on her hip. Their teenage brother, Alan, stood behind her.

"Welcome home." Teria looked Cara over carefully. "I guess," she amended. Cara gave her a wan smile, and wiped a few more tears.

"Ama says you take the attic room," Alan told her.

Cara sighed and trudged up the stairs with her arms full, following Davad lugging her wooden chest. Used for storage, the attic had occasionally been rented out to relatives down on their luck. It carried a dour and forbidding air of neglect. She dropped her things on the narrow bed and stared through the small dusty window to the grass below. "Got an empty room in your cabin?" she asked Davad.

He frowned. "I don't think Merelin would like that."

"You're back together?"

"Yeah."

She sat on the bed in a graceless flop that shot feathers and goat hair out of its seams.

"What really happened?" Davad asked. His eyes, so similar to hers, stared in suspicion. He hadn't wanted her to go north. Though he traded fish and miscellany with the Selandu, his trust of the aliens didn't match his hunger for coins.

"Pretty much what I said," Cara replied. "It was a slow-motion catastrophe. Infighting, mostly."

"I'm sorry to hear it." He smiled. "But Kimi is glad you're back."

"Ama isn't, I'm sure. Where is she?"

"Ama or Kimi?"

Cara grimaced. "It doesn't take a priestess to divine where Ama is. Where's Kimi?"

"Mending nets on the beach. She'll be home shortly." He nodded. "You want to tell me about your hands?"

"Not now. Long story."

"You're full of secrets. C'mon, let's eat. Everybody's starting to gather."

His words caused another flare of anxiety. *Ama.* Cara dreaded what she knew was coming.

Despite her youngest sister's enthusiastic welcome, dinner was as painful as she thought it might be. The curious bombarded her with questions about life across the border, her hands, her muted emotions. But hiding all the things she couldn't speak of made conversations difficult, stilted. The disdainful and the sarcastic anti-alien comments, though, prodded her grief-filled tempers. Her lip curled. *Ignorant, all of them.* Even those she loved.

"What will you do now, Cara?" her mother, known as Dr. Liz, asked. The simple words wove a mat of criticism underneath. "You have no job and no home of your own."

And there it was, she thought. The beginning of the downward spiral. "I don't know yet."

"What did you do on the trip home, if not think of your future?"

Cara rested her forehead on her palm, tired of her mother already. Not because of a couple of sentences; tired of more than two decades of conflict.

"Ama," Elaine said.

"Don't you chide your mother, Elaine. That's not how I raised you." She looked around at her children. "Any of you." Her sharp gaze returned to Cara. "Are you going to answer me?"

She took a sip of wine, and swallowed heavily, leery of turning her mother's questioning into a heated argument. "At some point, yes."

Liz placed her fork on her ceramic plate. *Clink.* "And when will that be?" she asked acerbically. "Tonight? Tomorrow? Next year?"

"I have to rethink things, Ama," Cara replied in a purposely calm tone. "My removal from Barridan was quick. I didn't have time to think."

A harsh breath was Liz's only reply.

Cara's father regarded her silently from the far end of the table. She saw no anger there, just a distant but concentrated regard.

Cara poured herself a second glass of wine and nursed it as she brooded, listening to the family dynamics. Her siblings talked across the table. Grandchildren gabbled and wailed and tugged on her long hair. Her mother pontificated on the duties of her children to marry, have children, and keep the human race alive on this planet far from their origin. After a third glass, Cara rose from the table and bowed, mostly toward Teria. "Thank you for dinner. Excuse me."

The table fell silent.

"Where did those kinds of words come from?" Alan asked.

"Why'd she bow?" Kimi added.

Davad took another helping of meatballs. "Ask the ambassadors, I guess."

Cara ignored the comments and climbed the staircase. "Kimi, no," she heard her father say.

The attic room was dusty and cramped. Cloth sacks lined the slanted walls. Creeping and crawling creatures probably inhabited them. Cara laid down and let her tears flow as heartache filled her chest. Helpless against it, she cried out.

Rodani!

Square of jaw, long-limb, strong and graceful, with waist-long silver hair held back in a silver clip, or falling forward over his shoulders for her fingers to curl in. Violet eyes that had seen as much or more of the world's ills than she had, eyes that had dared to look inside her and fill her heart with joy.

Heavy footsteps worked their way into her awareness. Her father entered the room. Two steps brought him to her bedside. He tugged on a footstool and sat. "Do you want to talk?"

Cara grabbed at the sheet beneath her and wiped her eyes. "There's nothing to tell."

"Bullshit."

The word startled a memory from her, saying the same thing to Rodani. Fresh tears flowed.

"If you don't want to talk," he continued, "say so. But don't lie to me."

She heard the love behind his sharp words. "I'm sorry, Dae."

"I don't need an apology, little bit."

Oh, the childhood nickname hurt. Gods of the wide dark, she wanted to spew. Wanted to exclaim her love for her husband of two days, and the loss that stabbed her heart. *Minimize. Hide it all.*

"It started out well, then got rough toward the end."

"Why?"

"The guardians, mostly. And a few crafters. They didn't want me there."

"I thought those guardians were supposed to protect you."

"Some of them did."

"You going to tell me what happened to your hands?"

Cara stared at the scars that striped her palms and fingers. "You ever heard of a tree with bark as sharp as knives?"

Botanist, researcher, inventor of creams, potions, and elixirs, Liam raised his eyebrows. "No."

"I hadn't either."

"Must've hurt."

"Burned like fire when the doctor worked on them." *<Flash> Baldar wiping. <Flash> Rodani holding her tight. <Flash> Vomiting over them both.*

Liam shook his head. "What did you get yourself into, little bit?"

Cara rubbed her palms together slowly. "It was a lot of fun while it lasted. I didn't want to leave."

"What will you do now?"

"Okay, Ama," Cara retorted.

Her father glowered at her. "It's not an idle question."

"No shit."

Surprisingly, he smiled as he stood. "It's never easy to listen to your children talk as adults. Especially when they had a little too much wine." He patted her shoulder. "Sleep. You look like you need it."

When he left, Cara shut the door and turned up the lantern. But as she began to undress, something poked her inside the halter. *The letter! Rodani's letter! Ohgodsohgodsohgodsohgods.*

She slipped it out and unfolded it, careful not to tear it. Heart in her throat, she began to read.

Kia, my chosen,

It is with a pained heart and head that I write these words. Only hours ago, you released your hair from its confines and accepted the mating clip I offered you. Pride and fear warred within me, because I know the house guild is near to rupturing. I cannot predict when or where the shots will be fired. But I sense they are coming.

I refused to allow myself to lie to you, but neither would I tell you all the truth. I do not know when the end will come to our affinity and our life together. But end it will, and I will not steal your happiness before it does. Please forgive me.

As you are now reading these words, the worst has happened, and you have been returned to your home. I can only hope you are at least warm and dry, but I can easily imagine your distress. If it comforts at all, please know that I am similarly distraught at our separation.

Had I known the end to the path we were on, I might never have turned to it, never approached you and entreated your attentions.

But I hold out a hope to you. If I survive the punishment I will certainly face, Barridan will no longer be home to me. Kusik will make sure of it.

With a start, she remembered. Guilt flooded her. Chendal, sitting at her craft table: *"I will be ordered to flog him or kill him."*

In the following chaos, she'd stuffed the comment away. And with all the misery she was drowning in, she'd only thought of herself. *Idiot! What was happening to Rodani now? Where was he? Is there anything I could do to help him? Say something? But to whom?* Cara asked herself. She was no one. She had no pull, no power anywhere. She couldn't ask the ambassadors. And she didn't dare try to contact Barridan. Burning with remorse, she continued to read.

Here is my plan: a week in Tendiman, recovering. A week or two in Barridan, long enough to learn what abuse Kusik has in mind for me, and to prepare. Then I will leave here.

I will make my way east, to the sea, and explore the border islands by boat. The last I heard, they are uninhabited on my side. Most have no fresh water. I will be cautious on your side, and I know well how to hide.

I have pilfered Vanu's 'com, and found that I delight in Kusik's frustration at its disappearance. I packed it in your red tide bag, assuming it was less likely to be searched. On the day after the next full moon, come look for me. Turn the 'com to channel 9; its range is very short. Ride the waves between the islands. Every hand of minutes, speak my erinai once. Do not chatter, kia; others may be within range. I will be listening. When I hear you, I will reply. At that point, still your boat in the water and be silent. I will home in on your signal and find you. If I do not hear from you on that day, I will continue to listen for as many days or weeks as I can.

But I beg one promise from you, kia. If you have changed your mind, removed your clip, and made peace with your old life without me, contact Chendal in Hadaman and tell him. For my safety, I have not forewarned him, but he will understand your message. Until I hold you again, keep me close in your memories.

I remain your bonded mate.

~ Rodani

Cara flopped down on the ratty bed, helplessness crawling over her nerves and stealing her will.

"Oh, aisu, I'm sorry. I'm so sorry."

***

Shouts and orders echoed beneath her floor, the sounds of home. Someone pounded on her door. "Just a minute." She sat up in bed, bedraggled, puffy-eyed. The door opened. "Hey! What happened to privacy?"

Elaine poked her head through the doorway. "Ama says you're late. You should've been cooking breakfast an hour ago."

"Time is it?" Cara mumbled.

"8:30."

"I have to meet Menachem in an hour and a half. He'll have work for me to do, I'm sure."

"Ama says you have work here, too, if you expect to eat and sleep here."

Cara slung her legs over the side of the bed. "I don't want to be here," she whispered. But before she went downstairs, she checked her red tide bag. There it was. The 'com. *Rodani.* It was no dream.

As breakfast seemed to be over with, she grabbed a couple of meat rolls from the cold box and helped clean up the meal. Kimi jumped and swirled around her, intermingling with hugs. Her blond hair, courtesy of a different, but much-loved father, swung out around her waist. She was beginning to blossom into womanhood. She wasn't old enough to think deeply into what a small gene pool had done to traditional marriages and parenting. And not everyone was in agreement with babies purposefully conceived outside of marriage. Accidental pregnancies, multiple possible fathers, jealousy of a spouse, all could cause chaos. The commission authorized to keep track of the necessary genealogy 75 years ago, had devolved into a lackadaisical farce. And her own mother, dear Dr. Liz, was one of the most adamant of those insisting on increasing the birthrate.

Kimi stopped prancing and laid her hand on her oldest sister's arm. "I missed you so much, Cara."

"Missed you, too."

She stopped capering. "You don't look happy to be home."

Cara washed another plate. "I'm not."

"Rather be up there with the Selandu?"

"Yeah."

"You love them more than you love me?"

She had to smile at that one. "No, kidlet. But I'm going to miss crafting all day, and having my meals brought to me, my clothes cleaned, and my bed changed for me."

"Aww, you got lazy."

She smiled ruefully. "Sort of."

"Kimi!" Alan called from the porch. "Ama needs supplies!"

Thursdays were surgery days in her mother's medical practice. Her skills were highly regarded, her operating room clean and antiseptic with the help of her husband's creations. And Cara knew firsthand, she ran her practice with the iron thumb of control.

Kimi trotted out. Cara finished the dishes and wiped the table and counters. Upstairs, she dug out her notes and her diary. Her heart jolted at the sight of Rodani's precise handwriting, and his sketches of her. Made with loving detail, she reminded herself. Tears threatened again. She coughed them away and thought about what she'd say to Menachem. That was a discussion she wanted to run from and couldn't. Not if she ever wanted to set foot in the CSC again.

Ambassador Menachem ran the Cultural Studies Center. Not with a hard hand, but he took his duties seriously. He had little humor when it came to relations between the species. He'd lost an aunt, an uncle, and a set of grandparents in the River War. The CSC was the only official communication conduit between the species, the only place where Selandu customs and language were taught. Few were accepted into the training program. Fewer graduated. Cara had been, and then she hadn't. Her be-damned emotions, ever present and uncontained, had washed her out of it. Menachem hadn't wanted to let Cara go north. But a courteous and insistent request from a taso wasn't easily denied, and Cara was the only crafter who knew their language.

She headed out. The streets, the shops, the cabins and houses didn't look different. Not to her memory. But (she counted in her head, August to March) seven months in a foreign country stole the familiarity and colored it with strangeness. She had to force herself not to listen for Selandi speech, with the urge to translate. A few people nodded to her. Most were bent on their own tasks.

At the north end of town stood the CSC. The low-slung building sat on the other side of the riverbank, nestled up against the feet of the Himadi Hills. Not that the humans called them that. They were just "the hills," to most people, or "the forest."

As her gut roiled and breathing went shallow, Cara crossed the river's footbridge and walked inside. A young woman sat in the entryway at a desk, books and papers arrayed in front of her. Cara's memory of Menachem's newest employee failed her. "Ahh..."

"Lara," the girl replied sourly.

"Yes, of course." She switched to Selandi and bowed. "I'm sorry."

Lara inclined her head. The Selandu gesture brought a pang straight from her memories to her heart.

"He's waiting." Lara waved her hand.

"Thank you," Cara replied, again in Selandi, unsure of why she did so.

Menachem sat behind his own paper-cluttered desk, larger than the one in the entryway. Seeing her, he pressed a button. "Reit'u," he said.

"Sai." In a moment, Andrew Lieu, ambassador second, joined them.

They sat in a triangle, two against one. Their gaze didn't leave her face. She felt trapped in a room with two predators who might pounce if she ran. "Start from the beginning," Menachem said. "Walk to the end. We need to know what happened."

Calm, kia, she reminded herself in Rodani's voice. She kept only to the facts, the better to hide the reasons they'd berate her. Her rooms, the food, the crafting, meals in the gathering room. Reading to improve her vocabulary. Her servants. Her two guardians. One cool and remote, one a little less so.

"Did they have any problems with you?" Menachem asked.

"Well, I made mistakes, of course. Used wrong words sometimes, tried to make a few jokes that didn't translate well. The guardians were very different. One was patient, one wasn't. The impatient one left me alone while I was in my rooms. The patient one watched over me. Helped me when I needed it."

"Why were the other guardians angry?"

Cara took a breath. Where was the path? And why couldn't she tell the simple truth? *Du!* Rodani's warning echoed in her head. Just as in Barridan, she had no way of knowing which humans would be intrigued with her real story, and who would be disgusted. But here, she could guess.

"Um, they didn't like seeing me, in the halls, in the gathering room. Didn't like seeing my quilts hanging on display. Maybe even didn't like hearing me discussed in meetings. I'm not sure of the reasons."

"Did you do anything to anger them?"

"Not on purpose."

Andrew snorted. Cara bristled at the insult, turning to glare at him. "My primary guardian, the patient one, *never* had a problem with me that we couldn't solve."

"But the rest of the guild did," he judged.

"No, only half of them."

"Half? How do you know?"

<Flash> Arimeso's anteroom after the firefight. <Flash> Pools of blood. <Flash> Rodani limping, Arimeso shaken and looking lost. <Flash> Bodies on the floor.

"I was there."

"Where?"

"At the firefight. The night of the spring equinox. I didn't actually watch it. I was hidden, with Arimeso. But I saw the aftermath. Guild fought guild."

"I can't believe you're completely blameless, Cara," Menachem told her.

She looked over at him, hurting from memories that muted his disdain. "Call Arimeso a liar. I don't care. My guardian told me what she said. He was standing there when she talked to you."

"What about the man who shot you?"

Cara waved off the question with a Selandu hand toss. "Shurad. He was a Riverchild. I never even met him, let alone spoke to him."

"Let's go back," Menachem said. "When did you see the guild getting angry?"

"Not until a month or so ago."

"What did you see or hear?"

What not to say? "Umm, I noticed that my guardian wasn't taking me to the weekly gatherings with the rest of the house, anymore. And he seemed to get more...wary, I guess. More anxious? Cautious, maybe."

"Why?"

"I assume because some of the other guardians were threatening me, or bothering him somehow." Cara shifted in her chair. "You need to know, a'Reiti, that my guardians kept me ignorant of almost all the undercurrents going on in the house. They knew I could cause a problem with others, but even more, others could cause a problem for me. I was in danger, and they tried to hide it from me." She dropped her gaze to the floor between them. "Until they couldn't, anymore."

"What did you see or hear when they couldn't hide it anymore?"

"I saw bruises on my guardian."

"Bruises?"

"Yeah. And I heard him fighting someone in the hall outside my door, more than once. But he would never tell me anything."

Menachem sat back and stared at her. "Well, it was a disaster, anyway."

She stared right back, thinking, *No, it wasn't, a'Reiti. But you'll never hear it from my lips.*

"You kept notes, like I told you?"

"Yes."

"Hand them over for our review."

Oh, hell, no. "They're jumbled and messy, and some of them are private. I'll need to rewrite them."

Andrew leaned toward her, eyes narrowed. "Why did you make private comments? And why can't we see them?"

Cara grimaced, and looked him in the eyes. "Do you really need to read how I felt about my red tide, alone in an alien land?"

He blanched, waving away the rejoinder.

"Make them as complete as you can," Menachem said, "as quickly as you can. I need to decide how much of an apology you and I need to give to Arimeso and Kenimandil."

"'Kay."

She didn't want to talk to either woman. Her last look at Arimeso was when she'd thrown Cara out of her house. Politely, she'd give the woman that. But firmly. Kenimandil, she'd never seen or talked with. She ruled over all the Selandu on the planet, all two thousand or so of them, and was the employer of the ambassadors when they were in residence in Hadaman.

Cara planted herself at an empty desk and wrote until her hand cramped. But she left two drawings behind for Menachem—the sketches she'd done of Rodani and Serano the night she took Serano's herbal concoction. She didn't want a drawing of him anyway, bitter and punitive guardian that he was, and she had better ones of Rodani. Those, she promised herself, would remain private. Another wave of grief and longing welled up. *Aisu. How are you? Where are you?*

She gathered up her things and went into the CSC's comm room. Empty, thank goodness. She sat in the chair and ran her finger over the list of radio frequencies. She set the dial for Hadaman, and crossed her fingers, heart pounding in her chest.

"Hadaman."

"Pleasant day, Hadaman. May I speak to the temaso, please?"

"Who is this?"

"This is Cara, at the CSC."

She waited through an anxious silence for someone to castigate her for her audacity. Normally, it was only the ambassadors who made these calls.

But what came through was simply, "He is not here, a'sel."

She took a deep breath. *Formality, Courtesy.* "Can you tell me where he is? I would wish to ask him a question."

"I cannot."

"Do you know when he'll return?"

"I do not, a'sel."

"Thank you. Please forgive me for the interruption."

"Ninety-nine."

Well, that sign-off proved it was a guardian on the other end. Cara stood up.

"What are you doing?" The voice cut like a knife.

She flinched at Andrew's angry question, then her own frustrations and fears threatened to erupt. "Nothing worth concerning yourself with, a'sel," she replied coldly. She pushed past him in the doorway, bumping arms when he refused to move aside.

"You stay off the comm, Cara," he spat. "You cause us more trouble, I'll cause you some."

She wanted to shout. Wanted to spew her pain all over him, and to hell with secrecy. Instead, she clenched her jaw with enough force to prevent it, and an ensuing catastrophe as well.

Calm, kia, she repeated to herself. *Breathe.*

On the way home she stopped by the communications board in the town square. Notices and news snippets littered the board. Lost and founds, pleas for help, local news, recipes. Above it all was a calendar. This month, the next. Planting schedules and—ahh, there it was, the lunar cycles. She checked closely. April 17 was the next full moon. But what was today? March 32nd. Three days past the equinox, of course. A Thursday. She made careful note in her diary.

When she got back to her parents' house, her mother met her at the door wearing an expression of cold fury. She'd seen it many times in her life, and it never boded well.

"Cara, I will not put up with your disrespect."

She leaned back, away from the familiar ire. "What did I do?"

Mistake, she railed at herself, as her mother's eyebrows drew down farther. *Here it comes.*

"You need me to tell you? Have you somehow forgotten you moved out and refused to marry?"

"I—"

"You leave on some three-year-long 'ad-ven-ture', then come back in disgrace before a year is up."

The sarcasm burned Cara's ears. "But—"

"You move back here without a thank you, without a care for chores that need doing and children and grandchildren that need minding, you eat the food others cooked, and spent your night crying into the pillow you borrowed." She stamped her foot. "I will not put up with this! You carry your weight, or you will find yourself sleeping on sand dunes."

Cara swallowed the rising burn in her gut and bowed. "Yes, Ama."

"Why do you do that?"

"What?"

"That bowing thing."

Cara made the Selandu tossing motion with her hand. "Habit."

"Well, stop. It looks ridiculous."

Fuming, but knowing better than to show it, she went up to her room and hid her diary under the inner lining of her trunk lid. No one would find it there.

But in the middle of her folded clothes, something unusual poked out—a lumpy bag. It felt heavy, with something wrapped up inside. Carefully, she opened the drawstring and drew out the object. Two objects. Entwined like lovers were the metal candle holders Rodani had made for someone but never given them. Instead, he'd gifted them to her. Cara cradled them in her arms, trying not to cry again, and failing miserably. She rocked back and forth in empty comfort, huddled over her memories.

Blinking back her tears, she looked again in the trunk. There was a Selandu-style belt. Why was it there? She laid the candle holders on her clothing and pulled it out. It, too, was a little heavy, and had a note attached. Rodani's handwriting stared up at her. "Your earnings," it said.

She fiddled with the belt. It was split internally, like two halves had been glued together on one long side and left open along the other. She pried the two sides apart. Between them, carefully placed, was a hidden row of small silver coins. One for each quilt she'd made.

Her heart couldn't break into any more pieces than it already had. She brought the belt to her face and imagined Rodani's nimble fingers slipping each coin into place. Even miles and hours distant, he was still taking care of her, watching over her, remembering what she forgot.

Oh, gods, she had to see him again. *Had to.*

She replaced her treasures and locked the trunk, before hiding the key on the window frame. She went downstairs to help her younger sisters with dinner.

As they ate, her mother told the latest medical tale—a woman too long in labor. "Sometimes things just go wrong, girls." She took another bite of bread. "Sometimes there's nothing to be done." Her sisters, those with children and those without, stared at each other in consternation. Her father, decades used to the stories, simply said, "That's why I study plants."

As the others finished their meal, Cara took her dishes to the sink.

"Cara, you have to cut your hair."

She spun around to face her mother, breath caught in her throat.

"It's a way to separate your past from your future, and a waste of time and effort to care for." Dr. Liz rose from the table. "I expect to see it short at the dinner table tomorrow."

All the voices at the table went silent. Eyes stared at her, or volleyed from her to their ama. Not a person at the table was unaware of the conflicts between Cara and their mother. They were legendary within the family—and the neighborhood.

Oh no. Oh, hell no. "Ama," Cara replied slowly, warily, "my hair is mine." <*Flash*> *Rodani and Kimasa's robe.* "I can do whatever I want with it." She waited for an explosion, hoping against hope it wouldn't happen. Liz's eyes narrowed, and her mouth drew taut. *Breathe, fem,* Cara told herself. *Relax yourself.*

Her mother took a step closer, her face a cold fury. "You *will* do as I say, Cara! As long as you live under my roof, you have no right to argue!"

Behind her, Elaine grabbed her daughter and slipped out the back door. Alan followed.

And there went the deep breaths. Every muscle stiffened as Cara forced the words out. "I am an adult."

"Not when you have no job and no home of your own!" Liz shouted. "You need to grow up!"

Panicked, she retreated upstairs. "Cara!" her mother shouted. She tripped on the top step and went down on her knees. *No. No. Rodani's coming. I can't do that. I won't!*

Fumbling for her carry sack, she packed it with necessities, including the red tide bag with the 'com. She tied the coin belt around her waist, hiding it under her clothing. She'd left some money behind at the town's bank when she'd moved to Barridan. That had to stay. Who knew what the months would bring? She slumped onto the bed. Minutes passed as she willed herself to calm.

Kimi knocked on the door frame. "Cara, Ama said..." She walked in, eyeing the carry sack. "What are you doing?"

Cara stood. "Do you love me, kidlet?"

"Course I do."

"I can't stay here. Don't tell Ama I'm gone, okay?"

"You just got here!" Kimi complained, petulant. "Because of your hair? She just wants you to forget the CSC, and the Selandu."

No one else in her family called the Selandu by their species name. Only her favorite little sister. Cara held Kimi by her upper arms. "I'm not ready to forget them, Kimi. And no one should demand it of me."

"Well, you know Ama."

"Which is why I need to leave." She turned back to the trunk and locked it.

"You don't have a choice?"

"Sure. I could choose to cut my hair. I choose not to."

"I don't understand." Dejection colored Kimi's voice and set the cant of her shoulders.

"I know. And I can't explain it." She checked the lock on the trunk, then hugged her sister. "I'll be around. I'm not going back north."

"What are you going to do?"

"I don't know yet." She picked up her carry sack.

Cara followed Kimi down the stairs and snuck out the back door. She found her father in his lab, several yards behind the house. A large garden grew between them. Countless times she and her siblings had dug, weeded, watered it, and ate from it. She grabbed a few vegetables as she passed by and added them to her carry sack.

She knocked on the lab's door frame, as Kimi had done.

Liam looked up. "Hey, little bit."

She smiled, barely. "Hey."

"Ready to talk?"

She shook her head. "I need to ask you an easy but important favor."

"Why me?"

Cara regarded him across the width of his worktable. He'd never been effusive in his affection. Neither parent had. But his quiet nature had been a haven in times of strife.

"Because I trust you."

Her words brought him up short. "What favor?"

"I need a place to store my travel trunk. I can't leave it in the house, or Ama will badger everyone to let her into it. I don't want to leave it in someone else's home because I don't know that they'll care for it—and be willing to leave it alone. Your lab's my best choice."

"Where will you keep the key?"

Cara crossed her arms and grasped the opposite shirt sleeves. "I don't want to wear it. I might lose it. I would ask you if I could hide it here," she took a deep breath, "and ask you not to search for it." She stared at the floor in front of her feet, awaiting his reaction. The silence spun out between them.

"What in deep space is in this trunk of yours?"

She flung out her hands. "Sentimental things. A few childhood things. Clothes I wore in Barridan. Letters. Things I don't want anyone snooping through." She dropped her hands to her pants leg and picked at a thread anxiously. "Please, Dae."

Liam picked up a sprig of leaves, glossy green. "You're leaving again, aren't you?" He twirled it in his fingers.

Cara let out the breath she'd been holding. "The house, yeah."

He stood up, walked around his worktable, and wrapped her in a hug. "Hide the key. I'll get the trunk first chance."

"While Ama's busy," she said into his shirt.

"While everyone's busy, if I can." He left her in the lab to search its nooks and crannies.

With dusk on her heels, Cara went back to the CSC. She knocked on the door, then banged on it. No one answered.

That wasn't right. There was always someone in there, even at night. You never knew when a call would come through from across the hills. She walked around the building, but saw and heard nothing.

She kept going, east this time, and found one of the small huts skirting the edge of town. She knocked.

"Who's bothering me now?" an irascible voice filtered through. The door opened. A bearded face and dark brown eyes met hers. Gerry Canberry, drummer, drum maker, and music teacher—and more, in the past. "Heard you were back in town. C'mon in."

Cara stepped through the doorway.

"What'cha need?"

"Ger, I need a place to stay for a while. I'll do chores, help you with your drums."

"Not selling many. Make 'em too well. They last too long." He raked her up and down with his gaze. "What other chore will you help me with?"

"Not that one, Ger," she replied softly, firmly. "I can't."

"Why not? Woman gets lonely, too. Besides, it's not like I'm a stranger to you." He grinned.

She smiled back, but the corners of her mouth turned down. "I know. I need room and board. And I have to find a job."

"You check with Kanda?"

A pang erupted with the thought of her best friend, newly married. "I got a letter from her while I was away. She moved west, onto her husband's farm."

"Huh. Shows how much I notice. What about the women's hostel?"

"That's my last choice. Too little privacy, too little security against theft. And the landlord…" She shivered.

"What you got to steal?"

"Not much, but it's mine."

Gerry folded his heft down into a chair and stared at her. "Gained a few pounds."

"Fuck you."

They laughed together. "That's what happens when you sit at a sewing table for seven months," she told him.

"Didn't do any dancing there?"

"Yeah, but not much." *<Flash> Rodani, sitting in a backwards-facing chair, staring.*

Gerry waved her to a seat at the table. "Band needs a drummer. Diego got married, and his wife doesn't want him out on weekend nights anymore."

"I don't think I can play now."

His eyes widened. "Why? A little practice is all you need to tune up."

Cara held out her hands. Gerry grabbed her wrist. "The hell?"

She clenched her fists. "I don't have the strength I used to. Or the dexterity."

"You don't need to be a virtuoso to keep time. You always had rhythm." He waggled his eyebrows.

She shook her head and chuckled. "You don't stop, do you?"

"Not 'til it's dead." He let go of her wrist. "Talk to James or Jonie. If you can't drum, maybe they'll let you dance. They still play in the south square every weekend."

"Alright."

He glanced over his shoulder. "I'll put up the cot."

Cara squeezed her eyes shut. "I owe you."

"Nah. You're still a friend." He got up. "And if you change your mind, be sure you let me know."

TWO

Mind and ears reverberating with Cara's parting screams, Rodani limped his way toward Arimeso's inner sanctum. He stopped at the entrance to the anteroom. The sight of the half-sized door to the hidden corridor, and the bloodstains, caused his ears to twitch and the breath stop in his throat. Too much rage, too much death. Was it truly all his fault? Truly none of his at all? *Worthless questions*, he chided himself.

Murmurs drifted through the doorway. Chendal. His heart began to race, his fingers tingle. He turned left through the anteroom and into Arimeso's private office. His taso and the temaso stopped speaking to stare at him. Cold and remote, both of them. He knew what the next days would bring. Knew the things that might be said. He'd already heard most of it in these last painful weeks.

Cara. Grief chased his racing heartbeat, an emptiness no more unexpected than wanted.

"A'tem," Chendal said, sharp knives in his voice.

Rodani stiffened and froze, his face masked, leg shaky. "A'Temaso." *Fire and ice,* Tokennen had told him before he left for guild training more than a decade ago. *Fire and ice will keep you alive. Know when to use one, and when to use the other.*

Chendal's eyes widened at Rodani's bloody shirt. "What did you do, a'tem?"

"Obeyed my taso, a'Temaso."

Chendal took two steps and smacked Rodani across the face. "Answer the question I ask, not the one you wish to answer."

With a stinging cheek, Rodani waved his fingers in a slight motion, as if it should be both seen and unnoticed, an unspoken prevarication. "I wrote my loss onto my skin, a'Temaso."

"Nothing should be on your skin but the guild seal and scars honorably earned."

"Yes, a'Temaso." Rodani remained in frozen mien. *Do not prod the angry who outrank you.*

Chendal closed his eyes and shook his head and shoulders as a benatac shakes off flies. "You will ride with me in the morning. The guild council has been notified to expect us."

"I will not be well-healed."

"You will ride."

Rodani bowed.

"Gather what you need for the journey. Necessities only."

Chendal left the room, leaving Rodani to face his taso. He bent a knee, unsure that it would make it to the floor with the bullet wound in that leg.

"No. Sit."

He obeyed. This, in front of him, was not the taso he knew. Not the woman he'd given his allegiance to. Not the self-assured, competent leader he'd followed since his fifteenth year. She looked older, uncertain. Strained.

"I can no longer deny the guild council," she told him. "I have held them off for months while Cara was here, and they did not press me. But now I have no excuse. And they have the means to punish me as well. I cannot do without a full guild complement here. My house would not last long."

Arimeso leaned back in her chair, silent for a long minute. Her gaze flitted from her desk to Rodani's face, to the damaged anteroom, to her hands—folded and still in her lap. "Never in my imagination," she said, "had I thought to face this."

"I am abjectly sorrowed, a'Taso."

She raised her head. "Were we both fools, Rodani?"

"Not in our intentions, a'Taso."

"No?"

"I will never believe it."

Arimeso leaned forward and, to Rodani's surprise, covered her face with her hands. It was a gesture between intimates, and so clearly a human-style action that he nearly rose to comfort her as he had Cara so many times.

"I would take your sorrow from you if I could, a'Taso."

"And my dishonor? And my rage?" She slid her hands down her face. "I believe you have enough of those of your own, te'oto. Taking mine on as well might destroy you."

"This will pass, a'Taso, and you and your house will continue to prosper."

Arimeso's gaze drifted away. Then she looked back at him, her guild fifth, and back to the boy he'd once been. An image of that day flooded her mind—the shabby half-grown boy, prostrate and shaking in front of her desk.

The man he'd grown into, his strength and confidence, and yes—his willfulness—clashed and collided against his own people. And she had allowed it. Every step on the path. "And you, te'oto? Will you prosper?"

Exhaustion stole through him. "I cannot see so far as that, a'Taso."

"Come back to me when they are done with you."

Rodani bowed his head. "All honor to you, a'Taso."

***

Two benatacs stamped and snorted in the morning air. Chendal mounted his stallion with grace and practiced ease.

Rodani tied his carry sack to the saddle's harness and felt his injured thigh give way as he raised his other for the stirrup. He took a grip on his temper and another on the saddle, then heaved himself up. His thigh banged against the mare's side and an involuntary hiss erupted from his mouth. He hauled his paining leg over the saddle and seated himself gingerly.

Chendal eyed him with lowered brows.

The miles drifted under benatac hooves. The eastern sun beat on Rodani's back. But every step and jostle shot pains through his thigh. He sat back, sat forward, hung his foot outside the stirrup, even brought his lower leg up onto the beast's shoulders, in front of the saddle. Nothing eased it. Rodani bit down on every invective he longed to hurl.

Kia, he thought. Are you home? Are you well? Is there aught that can comfort you? Seek it, please, ki'tana. Do not let this cursed parting shatter you. Wait for me... Wait for me.

Early afternoon sun shone down when Chendal called a halt. Rodani recognized the area, a way-stop for travelers. A stream, a fire pit, a latrine. Chendal dismounted and rummaged in his saddlebag for travel food, and filled his canteen at the stream.

Rodani eased himself off the saddle and onto the ground. But instead of food, he withdrew a sack of powder, a small can, and a firestarter. Away from the shuffling hooves of his mount, he sat on the ground. He poured some powder into the can and lit it, then held the can to his nose and mouth, curving his hands around it to direct the smoke where he needed it.

"Rodani." Chendal came back from the stream. "You need water and food, not smoke. I should not need to remind you of basic teachings."

"A'Temaso," Rodani replied through the analgesic powder, "Baldar was adamant against me traveling so soon. If I am to keep up with you for another day, I need this." He shifted his leg into different positions, seeking relief, hands at his face and breathing the smoke.

Chendal refilled Rodani's canteen and replaced it in his pack. "Are you planning to doze in the saddle?"

"I might wish."

When the last of the powder burned to ash, Rodani put the cup, firestarter, and the rest of the powder in his bag. He reached for the pommel.

Chendal glared at him. "Eat—"

Rodani fought his way into the saddle as Chendal kicked his mount into a rapid trot, anger in the line of his spine. Rodani watched the temaso pull ahead, leaving his disgraced self to follow in the wake. He reached into his bag for a strip of dried meat.

Sleeping that night was a trial. The hard ground, the pain in his leg, the grief in his heart, and the fear of what he would face on the morrow drained all hope of rest.

The morning wore on in pain and dread. Tendiman's outer buildings came into sight as afternoon shifted into evening. They passed the Black Coat Inn, the apothecary (Rodani reminded himself of its location), and the various merchant stalls that were beginning to close up for the evening. The bar's patrons spilled out onto the walkway, while the Gentlewomen's Guild relayed their offerings across the street.

The steep and sturdy walls of the Guild of Guardians' home base rose before them. As they approached the hefty wooden gates, Rodani finally spoke.

"A'Temaso." He waited until Chendal turned back to look. "A'Temaso, if I do not survive the judgment, or my punishment, I beg you to tell Cara that I have crossed. With all the honor I still hold inside me, do not let her live her life wondering. Do not allow others to pass on the message. Radio the see-ess-see and tell her yourself. Please."

Chendal thought for a moment, then inclined his head.

They left their mounts with the door guards, passed through the double doors, and dropped their packs in the anteroom. Chendal held out his hands for Rodani's weapons. He passed them over without comment, but as always, felt bereft and exposed without them.

Chendal led the way up the massive steps to where the council waited. Rodani limped behind him. Memories of his training years fluttered in his mind as he glanced around. They made him feel too young again. But the fear he'd held at bay for the last two days began to override any other thoughts.

An excruciating flogging was the best he could wish for. A bullet to the brain was not an impossibility. As he had done to Naremit, so Chendal could do to him. It was the guild way.

"Goddess grant—" he swore as he pulled himself up the steps one by one. That comfort had faded under Cara's skeptical eye. He couldn't blame her for the sense she'd made. If his own faith hadn't been crushed in childhood, her barbed comments would have washed off him like dirt in a bath.

Demons of the deep. How many steps were there? He looked up. Chendal was disappearing into the Council of Three's inner sanctum. He pulled himself up another step, dragging his injured leg behind him. Closer and closer. To censure. Disgust. Decision. Decree. Death?

"Kia," he whispered.

At the top of the stairs, he drew a deep breath, then hobbled into the outer office. A middle-aged temichi looked him up and down, and waved him inward.

Two men and a woman watched him limp into the room. Each sat behind a desk. Chendal finished relaying their travels, then moved to the far wall and drew his hands behind him.

Rodani stopped in front of the ke'tem, Council First Hurasten. He bowed low, then began to kneel, shaky and slow with pain.

"Cease."

Rodani straightened, his face masking the horde of emotions roiling inside. *Ice*, he reminded himself. *Heat will only burn you here.*

"Rodani," Hurasten began, "you are charged with disobedience of one of the most ancient rules in the guild, which caused the deaths of five guardians and a crafter. This is no mistake," the ke'tem judged, his eyes blazing. "This is no lapse in training. This is wanton disregard of guild authority. This is unforgivable irresponsibility that could have caused a war. And all for the same pleasure you could have been gifted down the street." He leaned forward, intent. "Give me a reason why I should let you live."

Bile rose in Rodani's throat. He swallowed it, but it burned in his gut. "A'ke'Tem, when I accepted the assignment to guard an alien crafter, it was my sole intention to do my utmost to succeed at a very difficult task. My taso felt, and I agreed, that I was the only guardian in her house able to meet the requirements. The knowns of the task could fit into a teacup. The unknowns," he paused, lips pursed, "could not even be estimated.

"I had no way of knowing that the skills I would need for that duty ranged far outside my guild training, or anyone else's. Her differences were vast and unexpected. The needs of her daily life were something I was forced to learn through trial, temper, and error. It took weeks to understand what she needed—from me, from her environment, her servants, and the only companion I allowed her to have."

Rodani looked at the far wall, seeing nothing, desperately hoping his words made sense.

"My taso's instructions to me were to keep her safe, teach her our ways, rules, and courtesies, and just as importantly, make her comfortable and welcome as best as possible, so that her thoughts and energies would center on her crafting.

"I thought that would be a simple task. Food she could safely eat. Clean clothes. A soft bed. Clean facilities. Room to craft.

"What neither Arimeso nor I anticipated was the depth and breadth of her human emotions, and how closely they were tied to her ability and desire to create.

"It is difficult to describe the situation, a'ke'Tem, and I believe the temaso will support this judgment if you ask him. I was forced by circumstance to reevaluate Arimeso's instructions. Food, drink, and sleep were not enough. She needed much more instruction on courtesies, more patience than I ever thought to have, and she needed companionship. Someone to share her hours, answer her non-stop questions, listen to her concerns, comfort her troubles. I—"

"And you took it upon yourself to be that person?" Hurasten asked.

"Yes, a'ke'Tem. I was the only person who could."

"She had servants. Other guild. A houseful of artisans."

"A'ke'Tem, Serano had no patience with her and no good will. No other guardian offered to assist, and I would have counseled against forcing any of them to try. Her servants refused to cross status boundaries. Other crafters had their own duties, their own deadlines. Cara *was* my duty. I took her unexpected needs as a continuation of those duties. And I kept Arimeso apprised."

Rodani stopped, unsure of how far to carry the tale, and with what detail. He knew the council had received reports, especially as the situation devolved into violence. What Chendal and Kusik had known, the council knew.

"Carry on," Hurasten demanded.

Au, that was clear. "A'ke'Tem, I continued to meet her needs as I learned of them, even as I had concerns. Companionship shifted to comfort. Comfort shifted to desire." Rodani took a deep breath, and pushed his throbbing leg wound to the back of his awareness.

"This," he said, "is where I stumbled, because companionship cannot exist one-sided, and comfort to one is comfort shared. If this were olden days, I might say I fell under a spell. But I have no such excuse. My attempts to meet her needs uncovered my own."

Again, he halted, hoping not to continue.

Darun, Council Second, shifted in his seat. "Why did you not resign your duty? Let someone less involved meet these unexpected needs?"

"Because I was the best," he replied without boasting. "Because Serano was incapable. And because, along some unknown human path, Cara had already bonded with me. Resigning, letting someone else take over, would have thrown her off her trail, interrupted the flow of her crafts, and caused her great distress. That distress would have bled over into anyone else she spent time with, including her new guardian. I chose the path that kept her content and crafting for my taso."

"Even when it was gravely forbidden."

"Even when."

"You say nothing about your own gains from this immoral affinity," Darun continued.

"Or my losses, a'bi'Tem. I did not think it was necessary. I beg forgiveness if that was in error."

Hurasten leaned forward, mouth thinned into an angry line. "You beg forgiveness for leaving out part of your story, but not for your massive misconduct?"

Rodani took a tighter grip on his temper. "A'ke'Tem, my misconduct was a fairly direct result of my attempts to keep Cara content and working her craft. Because that, above all, was my taso's greatest concern."

Hurasten looked pointedly at Rodani's right hand. "Why do you keep your nails short on your dominant hand?"

Rodani froze, eyes wide. He closed them, then reopened them to stare at the wall above his guild leader's head. "If," he said slowly, cautiously, "the ke'tem wishes intimate details on my mate's body, I will, of course, give them. But I would prefer to do so in private."

No one spoke for several seconds. *Have I killed myself?* he thought frantically. *Why did you ask? Kia!* He hardly dared breathe. Struggling to contain raging nerves, he waited out the silence, waited to be told whether he would live or die. Waited to know whether he would ever see his chosen mate again.

"A'Tem'ai," Hurasten said into the heavy silence, "are there changes in your judgments?"

"Du," from Darun.

"Du," from Chendal.

"Sai," from Council Third Jinai. "I concur with Chendal."

Hurasten turned to stare at Jinai. She did not drop her gaze. He turned back to Rodani. "The count is thus: Kusik demands your death. Arimeso demands you be punished only as necessary, and returned to her house forthwith. Kimasa demands the same. My vote is to remove you from the guild, and forfeit your life. My second concurs. The temaso," he glanced at Chendal, "votes for punishment and a return to your taso, who is sorely in need of guardians. My third agrees.

"Rodani, although the count is four to three in your favor, it is less than equal in status. I can override your taso's demand. Tell me why I should not, and maybe I will not see your ashes scattered in the guild graveyard."

A shiver erupted from Rodani's limbs to his ears. The burning in his gut renewed itself. "A'ke'Tem, nothing I thought, and nothing I did," he paused, "was with an intent to disrespect or harm. Not myself, not the human, not my taso or keso, not the guild itself, nor my fellow guardians." He took a cautious breath. "I defended myself against their insults, against their frenzied beatings, but I never chose to attack. I kept my duty and my taso's wishes for the human firmly in mind. Throughout all the violence, all the depredations, I obeyed my taso and honored the wisdom of what she was attempting. I do not believe that merits my death."

Hurasten sat back as Rodani's gaze remained fixed on him.

"I concur, a'ke'Tem," Chendal said. "One temichi broke one ancient guild rule. Five others directly disobeyed their taso and brought mayhem and mortality to their house. We need no more deaths."

Hurasten stared out the door, his eyes hard and unwavering. But he laid his palms on his desk. "Ready the bar."

Chendal bowed and left the room.

The bar. It meant life. It meant his return to Barridan. But before those things, it meant agony.

The council muttered among themselves. Rodani stood at his place in front of them, unmoving, unwilling to be noticed until they dismissed him to his punishment. It would not be long. He heard the peal of the gong, one loud, reverberating boom that would call all instructors, students, and sundry to the great hall.

"Go," he was told.

From memory, Rodani found his way to the hall. It was as large as the gathering room in Barridan, and was already filling with black-clad people, young and old. Other colors mingled among the black. Blue for servants, brown for stable workers, grey for the healers. *Temi, grant them swift work.*

A platform stood at one end of the room. Shaking, pupils pulsing in dread, Rodani hung back near the entrance and watched Chendal, and his sister arrange the bar. Tall, thick, it rested on two upright poles. On it were two cuffs hanging down, rocking as the bar was positioned and locked in place.

The room quieted. Faces turned forward. Every person in the room knew what was coming. But only a few knew who or why.

Chendal walked to the front of the platform. Shisa circled around to the back of the hall, behind the modest crowd. "A'tem'ai, a'sel'ai," Chendal said, "you are here to witness the punishment of a temichi, who, with forethought, chose to break a guild law. The law broken was the prohibition of an affinity between a guardian and his adashi."

Heads turned and voices whispered.

"Rodani."

He pulled himself away from the wall and limped toward the bar. Chendal motioned with his hand. Rodani unbuttoned and removed his shirt. The X he had carved over his heart stood out in harsh red relief against his grey skin. He heard a few gasps, but ignored them and walked over to the bar, stopping beneath it, shivering. Having heard it before, he knew what the next order was, and what he would say.

"Speak your contrition."

Rodani lifted his chin. "I admit my guilt in the matter of an affinity with the adashi I was commanded to protect," he replied. His heart beat so fast it nearly leapt through his internal carapace. His breaths became shallow.

"Your apology!" Chendal barked.

Rodani said nothing more, only brought his hair around to hang down his chest, and reached up for the cuffs. The burning in his gut melded with the dread that dizzied him and drained the strength from his limbs. He slipped his fingers through the cuffs, then waited. *Let this be over. Let it be done.*

Chendal yanked each cuff out of Rodani's fingers and snapped them on his wrists.

"Kia," Rodani whispered again.

Chendal stood back from Rodani and pulled his belt from his pants.

Peace. You will endure, he told himself.

The first lash fell across his back in a line of fire. Then a second, and a third. His skin turned to blazing sparks as his body shook in the cuffs.

At the other end of the room, Shisa watched her brother as her partner's belt fell across his back. She knew the pain. Knew the fire. Watched as the mask over his expressions fell away and was replaced with a fierce grimace as each successive lash landed. The sharp slaps of the belt bled into her ears and, despite her anger at Rodani, into her heart. Ten. Twelve. Fifteen.

Rodani's injured leg gave out first. Eyes clamped shut, jaws clenched, his body trembled on one leg. Then it also gave way. Her brother hung by his wrists in the cuffs, his knees bent, body jerking with each new stripe. But no sound came from his mouth.

Time! Shisa shouted in her mind. *Let go!* She monitored Rodani's body carefully as the flogging continued. Then a dark spot appeared between his legs as his body went lax and his head fell forward.

Shisa drew her hand sharply over the top of her head. Chendal stopped and slid his belt around his waist as two healers ran up from the sides. They unhooked Rodani and lay him face down on a stretcher. His back was a matrix of bloody stripes and diamonds and strips of skin that had been ripped off by the leather. A copper scent hung in the air around him. The healers carried him off.

The crowd began to disperse. Shisa ignored the exclamations surrounding her. She'd heard them all before. She helped Chendal take down the bar and uprights, then made her way to the clinic.

Rodani lay prone on a bed, angled downward to ward off shock. He was either unconscious or nearly so. His eyes were still closed, and his arms hung unmoving off the sides of the bed as the physicians dealt with his wounds.

Goddess of all, she thought. She hadn't wanted to witness this, see it, hear it, be the one to watch for the bladder-release signal. But it was her duty when the order was *flog to extremis*.

If he had just kept his honor in Barridan, just thought more, felt less, walked away before he fell. If only. She could not comprehend how he let himself turn his back on all he'd been taught, and all he'd earned. He was fortunate to be alive. When she woke up this dismal morn, she wasn't sure he would be. At least she would not have to bring such news to their mother, or listen to their father rant and rail.

Rodani flinched, and his eyes fluttered. Sighing with relief, Shisa left the room.

THREE

Cara left a pot of caffee on the fire for Gerry before she left. She used to wonder why the drink didn't carry its original name from the beans on shipboard, and had asked her grandmother why. "It never tasted right," was her reply. The comment came with a curled upper lip. Neither had Cara learned to like it.

She glanced at Gerry, snoring away under a lightweight blanket. He'd always been a late-to-bed, late-to-rise person. The last time she lived with him, she'd followed his sleep/wake schedule. Anything else was difficult in cramped quarters. They'd shared their thoughts, their bodies, and their love of music. To her regret, it hadn't been enough. She locked the door behind her, leaving him sleeping in his bed.

Now, her knock on the CSC's doors was answered. Maybe Lara slept in an inner room near the radio, not by the entrance. She opened the door with a sour look on her face, blocking it with her body.

"Good morning!" Cara brushed by her. "I have to work on the dictionary."

It rested on a desk in the common room, ready for use and updates. She brought out her diary.

"Cara." Menachem stood in the doorway. "You have to be in on the calls."

She sighed and stood, packing the diary back in her carry sack. "I'd rather not say anything if I don't have to."

And there, was another sour look. "Wouldn't we all."

They went back to his office. Andrew wasn't there this time. That was a small relief. Unlike with Gerry, her relationship with Andrew had ended in acrimony that had never quite faded. She blamed it on her failure to measure up to CSC standards. He blamed it on her.

Menachem dialed up Barridan and flipped switches. "Barridan estate, this is Ambassador Menachem." He repeated the call. Static bled through.

"Barridan. Ambassador?"

Cara leaned forward, listening. She knew that voice.

"I would wish to speak with the taso, a'tem. Is she available?" Menachem asked.

"No. Not at this time."

"Serano?" she whispered.

There was silence, then: "Who is there? Cara?"

Damn. She slapped a palm across her mouth and hit her head with the heel of her other hand. Menachem stared at her.

"Cara!" Serano called out through the wires.

She slid out of her seat and jogged to the doorway, then turned back to the radio. She glared at Menachem and slashed her hand through the air in rapid waves. If Serano started lambasting her, every secret she was desperate to keep would come flooding out of his mouth in a torrent of rage.

Menachem shook his head in weary resignation. "Forgive me, a'tem," he said. "I wished only to offer my apologies to the taso, but at her convenience. Please be well."

A growl bled through the speakers. The connection went dead.

Menachem rested his elbows on the desk. "Must you make a hash of everything we try to do?"

She blew out a breath. "It shocked me. I didn't think he'd be at the comm."

"Who was that?"

"My alternate guardian. The one with no patience."

"He sounded angry."

Yeah. No, don't explain. He sort of had a right to be. "That's what his impatience sounds like." Gods, that's one Selandu she'll never miss. How many times had he knocked her to her knees with a slap? And then to importune her? Damn the man, anyway.

Menachem began to dial Hadaman. "You think about what you want to say."

Cara slouched into a chair by the door. "I think I'll sit over here."

The line went live. "Hadaman estate, this is Ambassador Menachem."

"A'Reiti," the voice replied. "How may we assist?"

"Bright morn, Tokennen. I wish to speak with the ke'taso, if she is available."

The name rang a bell in Cara's memories. Where had she heard it? What context?

"I will inquire."

"I thank you."

A few minutes went by, then a voice came on that Cara had never heard. "A'Reiti," said Kenimandil, the head of the Council of Three, the most powerful person north of the Hills.

"A'ke'Taso, I have spoken with a'Cara after her return from Barridan, and we wished to offer our apologies to you for the terrible outcome of her visit."

"Au, Mena'hem, it was not entirely unforeseen."

"My understanding is that the house guild took exception to her presence there."

"That is simplifying a complicated dynamic, a'Reiti."

"Please forgive me. I meant no offense."

"None taken. She was a magnet, brought into the house by its taso. She drew both her enemies and her defenders into her sphere of influence. If there is fault in her, it is inherent in who and what she is as a human. The fact that her presence cost lives had as much to do with our own fears and judgments as any action of hers."

"We are sorrowed for those lives lost, a'ke'Taso, and grateful for your good will."

"As the goddess wishes, a'Reiti."

"A'Cara would also wish to offer you her apologies, a'ke'Taso."

Surprise came through the radio. "She is there with you? I will speak to her."

Menachem shot Cara a look worthy of her mother. Diffident, Cara shuffled toward the radio.

"A'ke'Taso?" she began.

"A'Cara," the woman said, a lilt to her voice. "So, you are more than a phantom on paper."

Cara's eyes widened, begging Menachem to offer a reply. He waved his hand impatiently.

"Yes, a'ke'Taso. And I am," *what had Rodani said?* "...Desperately sorry for the terrible incidents at Barridan. And I am sorry for any part my presence had in them."

"Your sorrow is appreciated. Your decision was not the only one at cause."

She knew? Is that what she meant?

You need a safe goodbye. Think, stupid! "All honor to you, a'ke'Taso. Now and in years to come."

"Peace to your people," Kenimandil replied.

"And to yours, a'ke'Taso."

As the call ended, Menachem looked pointedly at her out of the corners of his eyes. "What decision?"

Cara lifted her shoulders. "My decision to go there, I assume. What other decisions did I have? What quilt to make? What to have for breakfast?"

The stare went deeper. "You're hiding something."

Her shoulders drooped, her expression one of entreaty. *Believe me, Ambassador.* "I have vocabulary to do." She inclined her head, Selandu-style. "Excuse me."

She retreated to the common room. It felt like a retreat. She had to get away from Menachem's accusing scrutiny.

Back to her diary. Words. Words. Peppered here and there on the pages, in and among her comments about life in Barridan. About her mistakes. About Rodani.

She flipped to her drawings of her lover. *Husband, now,* she reminded herself. Words annotated the drawings. Very private words for very private drawings. She smiled at the memories. Those words, she decided differently now from months ago, would *not* go into the dictionary. *Stupid, Cara. Where would they think those words had come from?*

"What's that?"

Startled, Cara shut the diary with an emphatic thump. A woman stood in the room. Young, dark hair and eyes, milk chocolate skin. "Suraya." Cara laid her hands across the diary. "I didn't hear you come in."

"Welcome back."

"Thanks."

"*The Weekly* needs an article about you."

Cara rolled her eyes. "Pfft, who cares?"

Suraya Patel sat down. "You've been around Gerry too much. Lots of people would be interested. And I'm itching to write it."

"Ama has an ointment for that."

Suraya snorted. "Be nice. Give me an exclusive. I'll make it worth your while."

"How much? I need coins. I don't have a job yet."

"I'll find out when Paolo reviews it. He'll tell me what it's worth."

"Oh, yeah, that'll work," she retorted, sarcasm dripping. The newspaper's editor was well known for penny-pinching.

Suraya studied Cara across the table. "They said you came home crying."

Cara stiffened in her chair. "Be a good fly. Buzz off."

She leaned forward. "I'll pay you out of my own funds if Paolo won't."

Cara glanced around the room. "I'm listening," she said to the younger woman. "What's your slant?"

***

Southeast side of town, near the ocean. The Wet Rag bar. Cara opened the heavy door, letting her eyes adjust to the dim light.

Nicholas Kinski looked up and smiled. "A woman, a dancer, and a drummer walk into a bar."

"'Hi,' she says," Cara answered, smiling. "That joke's older than spaceflight. And you forgot quilter."

Nick chuckled. "Ah, yes, your great adventure."

She slid onto a bar stool and rested her arms on the counter. "How you be?"

Nick slid a bottle in front of her. "New brew."

That was a typical Nick answer. "Thanks, but I can't afford it. James or Josie around?"

He opened the bottle. "This one's on the house."

"You're too good to me."

"Your swinging hips make a thirsty crowd. You've been missed."

Cara took a swig. "Nice to know. James or Josie?"

"Josie opened her shop. She's down and around on Third Street. They live on the second floor."

"Aww, she did it."

"Yup." Nick smiled again. He had a nice one. There were a few wrinkles at the corners of his hazel eyes, and a sprinkle of grey in his well-groomed beard. But at forty-one, he was still handsome.

"What's the news?" she asked.

"Well, Emmie graced me with a daughter."

"I heard. Congratulations."

"What's one more baby?"

"It's a lot if it's yours. I'm surprised her husband let her."

"She already had her two with him. 'It's the law,'" he intoned.

It was, indeed. No couple was to have more than two children together. Later children had to be conceived by other fathers, and were automatically adopted into the marriage. But not every man was comfortable with the idea. Nor some women. In a small genetic pool, biology edged out culture, and jealousy was forced to take a back seat. That didn't always happen, however.

"How many do you have, now?"

"Four, but none under my roof. How many do you have?"

Cara covered her eyes. "Don't remind me."

"It's a good thing they decided not to penalize women for childlessness."

"You can't pay if you have no money."

"Jail's no fun, either."

She shook her head angrily. "It was stupid, the whole idea. Even if you don't have them—or can't, you can help others raise them."

"Preaching to the choir," he said, grinning.

Cara grabbed the bottle and began to slide off the stool. "Can I take this with me?"

"On one condition."

She stopped mid-slide. "What?"

"Come back when you've talked to them. I have something to ask."

Surprise spread across her face. "Sure."

Around the corner on Third Street, Josie's Skirts and Slacks sat between Alma's Candles and The Leatherworks. There were no lights on downstairs, but the second floor shimmered in flickering yellow.

One more knock on a door.

"Who is it?" a male voice called down, a shadow at the window.

"James, it's Cara. Got a min?"

"Hold up." The shadow moved. Steps pounded behind the door, then it opened to a red-haired, green-eyed beanpole. "Hey there, swish!"

Cara blushed. "Good gods, James. I hoped you'd forgotten that."

"Never. Your tush is legendary. Come on up. Josie's feeding the baby."

Cara followed him up the narrow stairway. "I heard Diego quit drumming."

He looked over his shoulder. "Figured that's why you were here."

Upset baby noises turned into screaming. Cara's eardrums reverberated in sympathetic pain as they entered the room.

"Cara!" Josie passed the baby to James, then hugged her.

Cara looked at the baby. "Lungs work."

"Ha ha. So does the other end. Sit down."

Cara lifted the bottle of brew. "I would offer, but..."

"Yeah, but." Josie sighed. "Give me some months, then offer."

"I will." She looked around at the cramped, but neat, one-bedroom apartment. "How's the band?"

"Minus one drummer."

"Want another?"

Josie regarded her skeptically. "You gonna stick around?"

Cara sighed and ducked her head. "That hurts, but I hear you. Barridan was an offer I couldn't turn down."

Some communication passed between Josie and James, but Cara couldn't interpret it. She waited as James bounced and patted the baby. Josie turned back to her.

"We have a few new songs. Can you practice with James tomorrow?"

Her eyes lit up. "I will. Thank you! Now I know I can buy food."

"Stop by the shop first, see if there's a skirt you like. You gotta dance, too."

Cara hugged them both. "You guys are life jackets."

"Glub," said the baby.

The sun had set, and the street lanterns were lit. Nick still held the reins. It was Friday, and the bar was getting crowded. Cara walked up to him. "Do you want to talk now, or some other time?"

Nick looked around at his patrons. "Let me ask you now, and depending on your answer, we can talk later. Chucko!" He waited for his helper, then led her to a back room. It held a small table, a couple of chairs, and a cot. It looked like the one she slept on at Gerry's.

Nick sat down and waved her into the other chair. "I hope you won't turn me down. I've been thinking of this for a while."

"Play your cards." <*Flash*> *Rodani shuffling with a bandaged thumb.*

Nick bumped his chair closer to the table, intent on his thoughts. "You've heard about that new place that's being built up north, right? Where both humans and aliens will live?"

"Himadi House."

"Yeah." He glanced down at his hands. "Cara, I want to open a bar there. And I need your help to get the job."

She looked at him quizzically. "Me?"

"Do you have any say as to who goes there?"

"I'm sure not. It'll be Menachem and Andrew, and the Selandu in Hadaman."

"What will get me in the door?" he asked eagerly. "How much money do I need? Who should I talk to, and what should I say?"

"You're serious?"

He responded with a serious look. "You bet."

Cara scratched her head. "How are you going to wait on patrons who don't speak your language?"

"Oh," Nick leaned forward in anticipation. "I've got that figured out. I learn just enough words that have to do with bartending, and make a few signs they can point to. I don't need to carry on conversations. You could teach me."

<*Flash*> *"Teach me your language, Cara."*

Laughter bubbled up from the tables out front.

"Considering my circumstances, I'd want you to pay me a little for each lesson. For my time and effort."

"I'll pay if you take me to talk to Menachem when we're done, and tell me what I should say."

"Deal. Buy some heavy paper. We'll need cards." <*Flash*> *Rodani, head bent over a stack of cards in his hands.*

Nick smiled and slapped the table. "I knew I could count on you. Tomorrow?"

"It'll have to be morning. I practice with James in the afternoon and expect to play tomorrow night."

"Ten?"

"Yeah, okay."

She drifted out. Since James and Jonie were not yet on the stage at the opposite corner outside of the bar, she stopped at the bakery next door.

Gerry met her at the door of his cabin to let her inside. He played a ratamacue with his fingers on the back of his chair, grinning. "You change your mind?"

"No. But I brought you food." She laid it on the small table. "Peace offering."

***

Suraya stepped back from the community board and smiled. She'd had to write quickly, but the words had come without effort this time.

All Does Not Always End Well
That something ends in difficulty doesn't negate its worth.

Seven months ago, Cara MacLennan traveled over the Himadi Hills to a houseful of aliens. A couple hundred seven-foot-tall Selandu spend their days and nights there, living by their rules, their courtesies, their culture and mores. Then a human moved in, by way of a curious taso who decided to lead her people down a slightly different path.

Not everyone wanted her there. For weeks, stares and mutters followed Cara everywhere she went. She was escorted at every step outside her rooms. Group dinners, meetings with the taso, occasional jaunts outside the house, at least one black-clad guild guardian walked at her side every minute. And even in her rooms, there was always someone close by. Someone within calling distance. Someone who, if they wished, could hear every sound she made. Privacy was non-existent from the very first hour.

She did most of what she wanted to do. Live in a Selandu manor house. Craft all day. Use the language she spent years learning. Meet new and different people.

None of us know all the rules of this northern culture. Not a day went by that she didn't accidentally say a wrong word, mistake a facial expression (yes, they have them), offend with a jest or, in turn, receive an offense.

Imagine not being allowed to open a window in your room or step outside your door without permission and escort. Imagine hearing comments that you can't interpret with any surety. Were they laughing at her? Insulting her? Asking inappropriate questions? She couldn't know, unless her guardians would take the time to explain.

How do you know, in another culture, if you're being told the truth? How do you know, in an emotionally reserved culture, if you're liked or disliked? Polished, or uncouth? Laughed with, or laughed at?

And what do you do with your ignorance? How do you handle it? The unknown, the pressure to conform, the daily apologies, the entreaties to be taught? Ego and pride won't play here. They can't. Not if you want to fit in.

And even when you try, some will never accept you. Deadly someones.

Cara tried to play by the rules. Respected her servants. Praised other crafters and the work they did. Obeyed the security instructions of her guardians. Obeyed the taso, and sold every quilt she created.

But it couldn't be enough. Not to those who feared the unknown and hated the different. They took their fear and their hate and put it back on her—and her guardians. She paid the price, and so did they.

Bloodshed ended it. Ended her journey into a contrasting and conflicted household of aliens, an adventure in happiness and pain.

Welcome home, Cara.

FOUR

Rodani woke abruptly and reared up in pain.

"Du!" A hand pressed down on his head. "Cease, a'tem. Calm." Someone put a smoke pot under his nose. "Breathe. Slowly, deeply."

"Yes, yes," he muttered. His back burned from shoulders to waist. Every movement hurt. Every breath provoked a deluge of pain. *Demons haunt you, Chendal. You are too exacting in your duty.*

The room held only lantern light. There were no windows in the security-conscious guild house. "What time is it?"

"It is the next morning, a'tem."

Rodani lay on his chest, head to the side, legs slightly elevated, nether regions covered only by a towel. A young man in grey clothing stood in front of him.

"A'tem," said a different voice, "we must turn you on your side. Your thigh wound needs treatment." Several hands pushed and pulled on him, rolling him. Rodani bit down on the guardian-specific curses that shuffled through his mind. His back felt like molten fire. His fists grabbed the sheets as they turned him, his fierce grip a silent cry of pain.

Deft fingers prodded his bullet wound. "It is healing, but you should not lay on it more than necessary. Pillows," the healer ordered.

Several were shoved between the bed and his chest and groin. A hand gently pulled his knee forward, laying it on the mattress at an angle. The healer opened a jar of cream and rubbed some on the wound. One by one, they left his room. "Rest, a'tem," the last one said.

Gods of the deep night, he thought, using one of Cara's favorite oaths. This wasn't the first flogging he'd endured, but it was by far the worst. He still hadn't decided if he deserved it or not. Chendal's words scrolled through his memory. *One temichi broke one ancient guild rule. Five others directly disobeyed their taso and brought mayhem and mortality to their house.*

He had to honor the temaso for that one. It may have been the remark that saved his life.

Kia. Where was she? Was she raining or smiling? What would she do with her days? He hoped she'd read his letter, taken it into her heart. And forgiven him, as well, for hiding a part of the truth that he himself had resisted acknowledging.

Fool. Double fool. Triple fool. Falling into an alien's arms. Falling afoul of his guild's proscriptions. Failing to barricade them both against a handful of other fools who refused to see reason.

The smoke worked its magic, and he fell into an uneasy doze.

***

"The bigger problem, a'ke'Tem," Chendal argued, "is not a temichi/adashi affinity, but half of a house guild trying to kill the other half—and against the explicit orders of their taso and keso."

"Much as I disapprove of my brother's scandalous lapse," Shisa added, "I must agree."

Hurasten's face held a stony expression. "Rodani began the turmoil, Chendal. His was the original cause."

"But we are not discussing Rodani at the moment, a'ke'Tem. It is the training program we must review. Especially with the walls of Himadi House nearly risen." Chendal crossed one leg over the other in an attempt to relax. "A'Cara is not the first human to pass over the border, nor will she be the last. How many in Himadi will fall prey to curiosity and desire? Hadaman is decreeing years of residence, not three-month stints as the ambassadors cycle through now."

"I care not what scientists and engineers do."

"But guardians harbor the same desires as everyone else," Chendal reminded him. "Some may look to the different, as Rodani did, and others may take fatal offense, as Imal and the rest who aligned with him did.

"A'ke'Tem," he continued, "I am not against reiterating the prohibition between temichi and adashi. I am, however, forced to believe we must teach that cross-species trysts and affinities are not a matter for murder. That dogmatic belief will do far more damage. We have already been forced to see it. I am not looking at the morality of the problem, I am looking at the results of not addressing it."

Hurasten turned his head away. *From a truth he did not wish to hear*, Chendal thought.

"What is your suggestion?"

"Begin, now," Chendal answered him, "to speak to all trainees and all instructors. Remind them of the fact that humans are people, with agency and desires and fears that are not so different from ours. Explain, in detail if necessary, the difference between the disapproval of an act, and the choice to break rules to punish it. Remind them that, above all, it is the taso who sets the rules *for her house*, and she must be obeyed. And if a temichi has an urgent question about any taso's orders that fall away from guild teachings, he may call on me to discuss it."

Hurasten again refused to meet Chendal's eyes. "You will spend your time," he said with care for each word, "sitting at a radio, fielding calls from dawn to dawn."

"At first, that may be. And at the first sign of this type of trouble in Himadi, I should be there to quell it. But Shisa and I should also travel to the estates, especially the nearby ones, to explain this adjusted thinking. We cannot expect new knives to retrain their superiors when assigned to a House."

"And one item." Shisa raised a finger. "How many guardians will be needed at Himadi, and who do we send?"

"You will not send Rodani," Hurasten growled.

***

Hours must have passed. Rodani fidgeted in bed, torn between utmost tedium and the pain that shot through him with every muscle twitch. He shifted his head and eyed the facilities. Close enough, he thought. Finger-width by finger-width, he moved off the bed. First one body part, then another. But with both leg and back pain, there was hardly a muscle that didn't cause agony. Slowly, he pushed himself off the bed and shuffled to the facilities.

Task done, Rodani eyed the bed with trepidation. Maybe he could walk a bit, limber up, let some of the stiffness fade. He searched for any article of clothing that might hide his nakedness. But the loose healer's pants folded in a drawer were difficult to climb into when he couldn't bend over. He circled the room, the ambient temperature slightly cool against his raw skin. The limp was still there, but not as pronounced. At least something was healing.

He missed Cara with a pain inside that nearly matched his surface miseries. He could hear her voice in his head. *I'm sorry, aisu. What can I do for you? What can I get you? I'd stop them if I could.*

His pupils expanded at the memory. So little power she had in their world, but she harbored a caring nature to match any priestess in the Enclave. Kimasa included, he amended. And, he thought, a surprisingly protective one. An image of the scarred fireplace mantle appeared in his memory.

A physician entered the room. Dark grey stripes on the sides of his clothing denoted his status as the master healer, and dark stripes in his hair, his age. "A'tem," he chided Rodani. "You should still be resting."

"A'Simandil," Rodani greeted him. "I remember you."

"Yes, yes, I am still here. I am quite sure I will cross over here, also, and my ashes will drift and eddy with those already outside. But not for a while longer, the goddess wills." He walked over to the bed. "Lie down."

"I tire of lying down," Rodani replied to the order.

The master healer eyed him critically. "And from where did this first-year student attitude emerge?"

A bit chastised, Rodani waved his hand and lowered himself— ever so cautiously—back onto the bed. Simandil lit another pot of the soothing smoke. "Breathe," he ordered.

"What time is it?"

Simandil peeled back a corner of the bandage that covered Rodani's back. "Not quite dinnertime."

"I need to begin my three days."

"I forbid it. You are not ready."

"The sooner I stand for my censures, the sooner I can leave."

"I will release you when you are well enough, a'tem, and not before." He pulled another corner of the bandage, checking the wounds below. "Do not test my temper. Besides," he said after a moment. "If you begin tonight, you will leave in the afternoon of the third day, and spend two nights on the ground. Is that what you wish?"

Rodani rubbed his forehead. He wasn't thinking clearly yet, that was clearly so.

"Make haste more slowly, te'oto," the master healer told him.

***

"We may have trouble finding enough guardians willing to move to Himadi," Shisa said. The instructors' common room held a handful of tables. Currently they were covered in trays of food and drink. Award plaques and trophies lined the walls. Several of them had Chendal's name inscribed on them.

"Yes, I have thought of that, and I have an idea."

Shisa held out her empty hand to her partner in entreaty, the other one holding a piece of bread. Two guild instructors sat with them at the table.

"We suggest to Hadaman that some human authority figures should also lodge there to control the human citizens," Chendal said, "rather than expecting the guild to command their obedience."

"So, a minimum of each might be acceptable," she offered.

"We may hope."

"Who do you have in mind, a'Temaso?" the tracking master asked him.

"That is one of the things I will determine while I am here. I will need to speak to the third-year students, one by one."

"It will be done," the weapons master replied. "Tell me when."

"Andreh' is to head the House?" Chendal asked his partner.

"I believe that is still the decision."

"And who of the Selandu in Himadi will offer him their allegiance?" the tracking master asked. "He is not a taso."

"That is as yet unanswered," Shisa replied.

Chendal pursed his lips and looked off into the distance.

***

Rodani woke the next morning with a growling stomach. An empty smoke bowl lay near his head, with a dinner tray next to the bed. He attempted to lift his body from the crumpled sheets.

The burning on his back had eased but a bare minimum. With a shaky hand he reached for the glass of water that waited on the tray and promptly knocked it on its side.

"Demons blast," he grumbled under his breath. He drew his legs off the bed, sat up, and walked carefully to the facilities, holding his back as stiffly as he could. He grabbed a towel and tossed it on the water that lay in a puddle and trickled along the floor. Subdued, he reached for the invalid's pants in the drawer, sat on the bed, and managed to pull them on.

Slowly, cautiously, he made his way out and down to the dining hall. A few early-rising students sat at tables, eating. He looked more closely. No, not early-risers, judging by the half-closed eyes. They must have had overnight training.

He took his place at the entrance to the hall, in guild parade rest. He'd seen more than a handful of guardians, students and graduates both, stand where he placed himself this morn. Instead of one walk-past censure after a punishment, this kind was piecemeal. Stared at, questioned, snickered and sneered at, he was a warning of what would happen if one ran afoul of guild laws. This was the first of three days he would stand during mealtimes.

A middle-aged temichi stopped to consider him. "Rodani," he said.

"Melee Master," he replied. It warmed him to be remembered years later.

"I confess I am not completely surprised to see you here," he said. "You were the best ground fighter I ever trained."

With some effort, Rodani kept a smile off his face. "I still am."

Three students entered the room and stood behind their fighting instructor, listening.

"But you invariably looked for ways around the rules," the instructor said.

"I remember your wallops."

"They do not seem to have kept you on the path."

"Not entirely, Master," Rodani inclined his head in respect. "But more than you might think."

"Heal well."

As his favorite instructor turned toward breakfast, the students crowded around him. Au, they seemed young. Hardly old enough to begin training. No, he'd never been that young, that eager, that wide-eyed and open. Rodani regarded them steadily. He might be in censure, but he was far above these younglings in experience, status...and loss.

"Geimachi," one sniggered. It was a crude term for someone who engaged in immoral joinings. Rodani ignored it as beneath his slightly damaged dignity.

"Why did you do it?" asked another.

That was a question one was ordered to answer. "It was my duty to meet her needs," he said. "My taso did not gainsay it."

"Tasos cannot tell us to break guild rules," he replied, sure of his newfound knowledge.

"They can," Rodani countered. "We have a choice to do so, or not."

"And pay the price," the third student countered.

Rodani stared at the boy. "And I accepted that." He raised an eyebrow. *Would you, little man?*

Another handful of youngsters, including one woman, passed by and eyed him suspiciously. He regarded them steadily, without pride, but without shame as well. That was one emotion he refused to let himself feel.

Another boy, a third year by the arrogant set of his shoulders, swaggered up—and slapped Rodani between his shoulders. "You—"

Back pain flaring, Rodani spun and grabbed the boy by his neck, slamming him against the wall and jamming his knee into his groin. He pulled his other forearm up to his chest, ready for a counterattack. Heads turned, but he ignored them in favor of the fool in front of him. "*That* is against the rules as well."

The boy's eyes went wide as an open sky.

Rodani bared his teeth and snapped them shut. "Do not assume an injured man is a harmless one."

"Yes," the boy answered faintly.

"What do you say to me?" he asked, shaking the youth.

He swallowed past Rodani's tight grasp at his throat. "Forgive me, a'tem."

From a seat at a table, the melee master smiled.

***

Rodani walked down the steps of the guild house a week after he walked up them. Chin high, back straight, he stared into the morning sun. The smell of benatacs invaded his nostrils. Clomping feet padded around the corner of the house, led by a stablehand.

Behind him, Shisa stood with her arms crossed. His sister carried anger in the stiffness of her bearing. They'd had more than one difficult talk this past week. There was still a barrier between them that hadn't existed before he fell afoul of guild law. But it wasn't quite as high, as deep, as wide as it had been.

He couldn't count on that remaining true. Only to one person had he told his plans.

Kia.

He pulled himself up in the saddle with less pain than he had the trip west. The bullet wound in his thigh was healing well. His back was still striped with wounds, but the pain no longer claimed his full focus.

"Inform the taso we'll send the new knives along as soon as the decision is made," Shisa told him.

"Yes."

He gave a short bow to his sister. He rode the streets slowly, in no hurry to return to a grieving guilt-filled taso and her abusive keso.

Kusik. Only to himself, Rodani wished it had been the security first who had died in the firefight, not the second. Timan had been rational and thoughtful. Kusik was a one-armed stalking, growling poridi with a penchant for cruelty.

Rodani sighed and stopped at the apothecary. He bought a large bundle of the smoke powder and a similarly large batch of varigestra tea, provoking a raised eyebrow from the druggist.

He kept half an eye open for both toothy hunters and food on his way back to Barridan. A cloven-hoofed malik strapped to the back of his mount might calm a bit of anger as it filled depleted coffers in the kitchen. But his two-day trip was boring and uneventful. Ruminations on the near future took up most of his thoughts.

As the estate of Barridan came into view on the eve of the second day, Rodani mused on his options. Seek a bed first, bypassing painful reunions? Avoid Kusik at all cost? He couldn't avoid Arimeso. She'd voted to save his life. But the guilt and grief they both carried for their losses made any meeting a painful one.

Rodani left the benatac at the stables and walked across the field to the garage. He took a back way to the taso's quarters. Despite attempts to break his habit of pleading with the goddess, he bent his head. *Please let Kusik be elsewhere.*

The comm room held only young Deneban. His eyes widened at Rodani's entrance.

"Kusik?" Rodani asked.

"Clinic."

"The taso?"

Deneban inclined his head to the doorway. Rodani walked through. He took a firm rein on his labile emotions and tapped on the door frame.

Arimeso looked up from her desk. "A'tem," she said softly.

Now, with no wounds great enough to prevent it, Rodani went to his knees before her. He waited for a word or some other sign of recognition. Because of her, he had a home when he had left his own behind. Because of her, he was a crafter as his young heart had wished. Because of her, he'd been allowed to petition the guild for entrance. Because of her, he had met, bedded, and mated the human woman who held his heart in her five-fingered hands.

"Sit, te'oto."

He rose stiffly and sat, hands in his lap, still-healing back straight and eyes clear.

"You look better," she said.

Rodani pursed his lips, considering. "If it would not offend, a'Taso, you do as well."

She waved his comment away.

He relayed Shisa's statement first.

"Is she or the temaso coming with them?"

"She did not say, a'Taso. I am sorry."

Arimeso looked off to the side, unhappy.

"The keso?" Rodani asked, in the hope that he was masking his trepidations.

"Healing."

"Lanata runs the day-to-day?"

"Yes."

"I owe you a debt for your directive to Tendiman, a'Taso. You helped keep me alive."

"It was the least I could do, Rodani, as it was my decision to offer Cara a place here that began the chaos."

His ears twitched at his chosen mate's name. He closed his eyes against the pain.

Arimeso waved her fingers. "Eat, te'oto. Rest. We can speak another time."

Rodani stood and bowed. He made his way through the back hallways and stairs to the rooms he had shared with Cara. He walked up to the door slowly, staring at it. How many times, how many times had he walked through that door to see Cara's welcoming smile? He'd not been in her rooms since before the final shootout.

The rooms are empty, he told himself. She is not there. Nothing resides inside but memories. Walk away.

Instead, he slipped his key in the door and went into the workroom. Her table was there, but no sewing machine whirred on top of it. The shelves sat to his left, but they were empty of fabric. The oil lamp remained unlit, adding to the gloom. He turned left.

Her bedroom. It drew him, almost against his will. The bed lay empty. Only a few pillows rested on top. Rodani could hear her laughter, her whispers, smell the scent of her body. He sat on the edge of the bed and ran his hand over the sheets. Slowly he drifted downward. He laid on his side and drew up his legs, not even deigning to remove his boots.

Kia. The erinai had become his mantra, every repeat of it a balm to his aching soul. He pulled a pillow under his arm and tucked it to his chest as he had seen Cara do on countless occasions.

To his astonishment, he realized why she had done so.

He shut his eyes. For the first time in nearly a decade he released his emotions in full. His mind filled with the pain of his loss, his mistakes, his ignorance—willful or not. His body shook in spasms. Deep, repetitive coughs erupted from his chest. He retched. His hands clenched spasmodically as his body convulsed and his back burned.

If he could have seen himself, heard himself, he would have been aware of the similarities between his own breakdown and one of Cara's. But he was sunk too deeply to see it. The biggest difference was his eyes that did not rain.

***

Serano walked the corridors. He checked doors and alcoves, eyed the artisans who strolled the halls from one place to another. He checked in with the Enclave, inquiring on the priestesses and acolytes to see if there was any worry to be considered among them. He strode into the festive room and checked with the bartenders for anything amiss their sharp eyes might have caught. But tonight was quiet.

The taso had told him to expect Rodani's return this evening. But he'd seen not a hair on his former partner's head. Unfortunate, he thought, as he had things he wished to say. Not the kind of words he'd used a month ago. No, those words still hung in the air, clouding his memories with a haze of anger and regret. He shoved them aside.

This walk-around had been one of Timan's tasks, an assay of the house and its people. With Timan dead and Kusik still healing, such tasks fell to lesser guardians.

Serano wound his way to the front doors and walked out into the evening. The sun was just above the horizon as he peered west, hoping for a rider to be approaching. Impatient, he walked around to the back doors and did the same. Nothing.

Maybe Rodani was already here. Serano headed back inside, to the out-of-the-way corridor where so much had happened in the last seven months. He let himself into his and Rodani's rooms. No one was there. No travel pack or saddle bag. No boots lying at the foot of the other bed.

Serano walked back out and closed the door behind him. He stared at the doors across the hall.

No, he wouldn't.

Serano considered it a moment, then opened the workroom door and looked in. Aiming to be thorough, he took a few steps into the room. In the bedroom to his left, a body dressed in black lay on the bed. Panic flooded Serano's mind. He ran toward the body, reaching to touch the carapace under the skin, at the shoulder where an artery lies.

Rodani opened his eyes.

"Tem'u!" Serano shouted to block his momentary fear.

Rodani closed his eyes again. "You have none."

Serano recoiled visibly, his own words now flung back in his face. "Rodani."

His ex-partner made no move.

Serano seated his hindquarters cautiously on the bed. "I am pleased you have returned safely."

Rodani only ducked his chin.

"You have paid for your errors and regained your honor." Serano tapped Rodani's boots at the foot of the bed. "Reunite with your guild. Come down to the festive room, as we used to."

A glitter of reflection appeared in Rodani's eyes, then he shut them again.

Serano slid off the bed and paced the room. "You remind me of Cara, Rodani. When she was told you had chosen reassignment." He looked back at the body on the bed. "The same lethargy. The same refusal to respond. The same empty look on your face."

Rodani lay still.

"This does you no good, tem'u. Only ill. Get up. Restart your life. You are not helpless as she was."

Eyes still shut, he replied, "You turned your back to me in my critical need."

"I turned my back to you because you ignored the cliff edge you were headed for."

"You still do not understand, Serano," Rodani said from his place on the bed. "For all the women you have had, for all the receptive times you have been through, you have never had what I had. You have no idea of the loss I feel."

Serano took a step forward. "I felt the loss of my partner."

Slowly, Rodani sat up, his eyes ablaze. "You rejected *me*, when my life was on fire. And hers," he added slowly.

"I rejected the dangerous path you were walking with your lawbreaking."

Rodani bared his teeth. "And by doing that, you left me to the mercy of those who had none."

Serano swallowed heavily. "I regret that, tem'u. Will you forgive me?"

Rodani laid back down, feeling as if his body weighed as much as a benatac. His eyelids lowered to half-mast.

Serano waited for an answer, but none seemed to be forthcoming. "You are not even here anymore, are you?"

No reply.

"Shall I call for Kimasa and her healers? It did not work for Cara, but it might for you. She wishes to speak with you, anyway."

Rodani blinked his eyes and let his gaze rest on the door to the facilities.

"She wishes to confine you to the Enclave for reeducation."

Rodani's eyes went wide. Thoroughly alarmed, he slipped off the bed and faced Serano. "She said this?" Reeducation, he had heard, was less about teaching, and more about browbeating, intimidation, physical discipline that left no marks, and threats from the afterlife.

"Yes. And I agree with her. You need reminding that the goddess and consort guide you, not your injured heart."

Rodani sat back on the edge of the bed, staring at the floor.

"Now that you've returned," Serano continued, "Kusik will call a guild meeting."

"He is still in the clinic. Deneban said."

"He is in and out. Ambulatory and petulant. Still healing."

Rodani's face went to mask. He lay back down in the same position as before. "I need to rest."

"In your own bed," Serano argued. "It is waiting for you."

Rodani closed his eyes, interlaced his fingers, and folded his hands to his forehead as if it pained him. He refused all the rest of his ex-partner's entreaties.

Serano left the room with many a backward glance. *Goddess of all. This is Cara all over again. Are her insanities really catching?*

FIVE

The next morning Cara ran from one side of the village to the other, passing shops, houses, cabins and huts. And people. Human people. Not a strand of long silver hair or a hair clip in sight. Dressed in normal human clothes and shoes. People she knew, people who knew her. And her family. And her reputation. Nick was waiting in the back room of his bar.

"I thought you'd forgotten."

"Nope," Cara said, taking deep breaths. *Out of shape, fem.*

Nick eyed her. "You gonna manage tonight?"

"Yeah. I won't be dancing continuously. Or I don't plan to. I've asked Jonie and James to intermingle their play list for me, at least some."

Nick pulled out a stack of cut paper. "This do?"

Cara fingered the pieces. "Yeah."

"So where do we start? Wine? Rotgut?"

She laughed. "Let's start with some basic words and courtesies."

He cocked his eyebrow. "Courtesies?"

"They're important. Trust me."

"You're the boss on this one."

"After the months I just had, that's nice to know."

Nick tapped the edges of the cards on his table. "I heard about Suraya's article. It's up on the board."

Cara just shook her head. She didn't want to know what the journalist had said. Suraya was a graduate of the CSC, as Cara was not, and was equally fluent in Selandi. Maybe more. She'd wanted to be the one to go to Barridan, but had no craft skills to use.

"We'll start with yes, no, please, and thank you." She pointed to his pen. "Write those down on the first four cards."

He did so.

"Now write on the back of each: 'sai', 'du', 'ashi', and 'verelin.'"

"Spell 'em."

She did.

"The next thing to remember is they don't nod or shake their head for yes and no."

"They don't?"

"Well, my guardian and servants did learn them after a while. But they have their own types of non-verbal communications that you probably don't need to know. At least not for now."

"Like what?"

"Worry about those later. What's the word for 'yes'?"

"Umm," he looked at the card. "Sai."

"And 'no'?"

Another look. "Du."

She ran through the other two, then started asking questions.

"Do you want me to continue teaching you?"

"Sure."

"Selandi, ashi, a'sel."

Puzzlement flashed across his face. "What?"

"I said, 'Selandi, please, respected person.' Do you want me to continue teaching you?"

"Ahh," he shuffled the cards. "Sai."

"Do you want a drink?"

"Du."

"Add courtesy, a'sel."

He rearranged the cards again. "Du, verelin."

"Do you want me to dance tonight, so you'll sell more drinks?"

His eyes lit up. He glanced at the cards. "Sai."

"Courtesy."

"Sai, ashi."

Cara folded her hands on the table. "Let me think how many alcohol names I can remember."

"Good. That's about all I'll need then. Right?"

Cara laughed. "Oh, you sweet, naïve old man."

Surprised, he leaned back. "What?"

"I don't want to see what your face looks like after you've called a temichi 'a'sel.'"

"A what? And why?"

"Because you'd be reducing him, or her, in status. A temichi is an assassin. A guardian. You don't want to diminish them to the level of an average, everyday person. You'd call them 'a'tem.'"

"So, what would they do if I called them that other term?"

"Depends on the temichi. Anything from an offended stare to a slap across the face."

Nick's expression made Cara laugh again. "And if they're only staring at you, you'd better be apologizing and calling them the correct honorific."

He drew a breath and let it out in a noisy huff.

"And then there are the plurals. A'sel'ai. A'tem'ai. And tasos and ambassadors. A'Taso, a'Reiti. Young man. Young woman. Te'oto, and te'ono. Respected man and woman. A'oto, a'ono."

Nick raised his hands in surrender. "Hold up. Hold up. I really need to know all those?"

"Ideally, yes. The more words you know, and the more courtesies you say, the more Selandu will drink in your bar, because they'll feel welcome there."

He leaned back in his chair. It cracked and popped beneath him. "How do I know a guardian from anybody else?"

"Easy. They're almost always dressed in black. Shirt, pants, belt, boots. And if they're not dressed in black, they probably won't expect you to know they're guild.

"I know it's overwhelming at first. But you're right in that you don't need to converse. At least not for a while. How much else you want to learn will probably be up to you. And no one will expect you to be perfect. But the more you try, and humble yourself with apologies for mistakes, and bow in respect, and try again, the more respect you'll earn for yourself."

He crossed his arms onto the table. "They attacked you, where you were."

"I don't think you'll have to worry about that. Himadi should be all volunteers."

Nick pushed blank cards at her. "Do all those other words, too, will you?"

She smiled. "What's the magic word?"

He looked through them again. "Ashi!"

***

"Not a bad article, Su," Bethamy said. She sipped her caffee while it was warm, watching her office mate pour over her latest article.

"Thanks, I think," Suraya said.

"It made her trip sound interesting, not boring."

"I never thought it would be boring. I wanted to go."

"How many times have I heard that since she was picked?"

Suraya slumped down into her chair and tapped her pen on her desk. Forgotten for the moment was the fact that the nib was full of ink.

"Wanted to get away from your brothers?"

Suraya eyed the older woman. "If you had my brothers, you'd want to get away, too."

"Are they still trying to convince your parents to join their new sect?"

"Yeah, but they're not obliging. They say it's too restrictive."

"Thank the gods of the galaxy for that."

"I don't know why they're turning so hateful, so controlling."

Bethamy smiled. "Usually means they're scared of something."

"I agree. But when I asked Ahsan that, you'd think I shot him full of arrows."

"Maybe they've been listening to that crazy preacher down in Lordstown."

Suraya leaned forward, avoiding the ink splatters. "Who is that?"

"Some guy wandering the town ranting about whores and angels, contraceptives and hellfire."

"You'd think someone would shut him down."

"I think they're scared of him."

Suraya blew raspberries.

"Might make a good article. An important one."

"Maybe."

Suraya took her notepad, left her ink-spattered desk, and headed to the center of town. She bypassed the huts and cabins and made her way to the two-story physician's house. She knocked on Dr. MacLennan's front door. Elaine answered it.

Suraya smiled, winningly—she hoped. "Cara home?"

"She moved out," her sister said.

Her eyes widened. "Where?"

"I don't know. She was here the first day, gone the second."

"Does Kimi know?"

Elaine shook her head. "Try Davad, if you really hope to know."

But Davad wasn't home. Nor was Merelin, his fiancée. Suraya checked the docks. His fishing boat was gone. She'd have to check back tonight.

A face peered out of a cabin. "Looking for someone?"

"Ahh, Cara, actually. Seen her?"

"I heard she's staying with Gerry."

Suraya nodded. "Thanks. Appreciate it." She started for the drummer's cabin just west of the docks, then stopped. Maybe it was too soon. Maybe she should back off?

But backing off wasn't the job of a journalist. She knocked on the door. Gerry opened it and glared at her. "What?"

"Just wondering if Cara was here."

"No."

"Where'd she go?"

"Why should I tell you?"

Suraya smiled again. It was one of her better weapons. "You're so personable, Ger. It's a wonder anyone can stay away from you."

He grumbled and started to close the door. She put her hand out.

"Can you at least give me a direction?"

He glared at her. "South."

"Thank you!"

She found them in the square, Cara and James, practicing with drums and guitar. She watched from the other side of the bar entrance, where a sign proclaimed Cara's return to the stage. Why was she so downcast? Suraya remembered the woman she used to be, before Barridan. Before the Selandu surrounded her. Usually happy, occasionally bubbly, acerbic at times, reclusive at others. Not this reserved, dour replacement. What in the world had happened to her?

Suraya watched until she got bored with watching, and made her way back to *The Weekly's* small offices. Bethamy had left. Suraya sat at her now dry desk and thought. An image of Cara's notebook at the CSC drifted into her mind. What had she seen? What had Cara drawn? Just the glimpse she'd gotten had been enough to goad her curiosity. It had looked like someone's body. But surely the Selandu didn't pose nude for artists, let alone quilters. It was a puzzle she wanted to solve.

***

Kimi MacLennan looked around the kitchen. Dishes, done. Floor, swept. Trash, removed. Cabinet doors, shut. Stove, banked. Quietly, she left the house, careful not to let the door slam. Dressed in her best blouse and slacks, she made her way to the south square. She'd waited months for this moment, this stolen freedom.

Her favorite sister was going to play tonight, and dance. She waited eagerly at the edge of the gathering crowd. The bar was emptying out, patrons with glasses and bottles and mugs in their hands. The majority of the bar crowd was men. *Of course,* she sneered. Ama had taught her the evils of alcohol, and what it could do to one's morals—and liver.

Suddenly the rat-a-tat of a snare drum drew her attention back to the stage. There she was! Oh, she looked good. But, Kimi thought, still not too happy.

The trio began a song, an older one that Kimi recognized. She swayed to the music as others stamped and raised their glasses in salute. She wound her way through the crowd and watched Jonie sing. She had such a wonderful voice. Strong, but not overwhelming. Clear and resonant. Cara had taught her those terms, and what they meant.

As the song ended, cheers went up along with cries of "Dance!" "Dance!"

"Patience my friends," James called from the stage. "We have a set to play. You'll get your due."

Another song, and a third. Then Cara rose from behind her drums and stood at the front corner of the stage. The audience gathered around her, shouting.

James began to play, and Cara began to dance. Whistles and words erupted from the people in front of her, but Cara seemed not to hear them. She danced as if she had cork in her ears and blinders on her eyes. Kimi found herself jealous of the grace and agility she saw that seemed to be missing from her own talents. At the end of the song, Cara bowed to the audience and went back to the drums. Three more songs went by that Kimi nodded and stamped in rhythm with. Then it was time for another dance.

This one was faster. Cara skipped and pattered across her half of the stage, keeping exquisite time with the guitar. Her hair spun out and swayed with the music. But why did she keep that clip in? It would fan out better if she didn't. It was another question that Cara gave no answer to.

As the dance wound down, Kimi felt someone grab her arm in a fierce grip. She tried to wrench it away, turning to see who had assaulted her.

Ama.

Her face was livid. "What do you think you're doing here?" she whispered, seething. People turned to look. Dr. Liz shook Kimi's arm, rattling her head on her shoulders. "Who gave you permission to hang around with this crowd?"

"I wanted to watch Cara!"

"Well, you can't. You don't belong here."

"Ama!" Kimi fought a losing battle.

"When I get you home..." Her mother dragged her out of the crowd.

From her place on the stage, Cara watched the short-lived tussle wind down. She hadn't known Kimi was in the crowd. She was too busy making sure she didn't drop the drumsticks. Appalled and angry for her sister, Cara turned her back to the tumult and sat at her drums. Her scarred hands were getting sore from the repeated pressure and friction of the sticks. But she gritted her teeth. She would not let her band mates down.

By the end of the two hours her legs were shaky, and her scars inflamed. As the crowd dispersed, she sat on the stool and stared at her hands. They burned. Someone came up the steps behind her, onto the stage, and peered over her shoulder.

Gerry ran a surprisingly gentle finger over one of the scars. "That looks nasty."

"And feels just as bad," Cara replied.

Gerry looked past her shoulder. "Here comes your mother. Ask her for some hand cream."

"Shit," she whispered.

Dr. Liz marched up to the side of the stage. "Cara, get down here!"

She glanced at Gerry and rolled her eyes, then turned to her mother. "Just a minute. Gotta get these drums down."

"Now."

Cara gritted her teeth and whispered her way down the steps. "Are you freaking kidding me?" *Hand me that priestess robe, Rodani. I need it again.* Tired, wanting this over with, she leaned against the stage wall. Staring at her mother was a provocation in itself, but she'd used up all the energy she had entertaining.

"Explain yourself," Liz said.

Uhh, nope. Not going to open myself up like that. Too many options for her to choose from. "You start first, please," she countered.

"Did you know Kimi was in the audience?"

"Not until you pulled her away." *And made a big scene.*

"She doesn't belong here," Liz said, adamant.

"That's between you and her, Ama. Not me."

Liz stared at her daughter, anger and frustration in every line of her countenance. "Do you know what an attractive nuisance is?"

Cara's eyes widened in surprise. She stared at the ground to her left and thought. "Uh, no, but I can kind of guess."

"Well, you are one," Liz said, with every word sharply edged. "Music is fine to listen to once in a while, but we have more important, *necessary*, things to do for ourselves. And you're ignoring those things. You make noise, you flaunt yourself, you urge others to drink and debauch. And your actions tease your little sister into joining in." She jammed her fists onto her hips. "What actual good have you done for your people?" And stomped her foot. "Point to it! Now!"

Cara closed her eyes as a heavy weight dragged at her body. She wondered what—if anything—she could say. Not to satisfy her mother. That was impossible. But to shut her up? Nearly the same. "Ama," she replied with a hopeless mien, "You're smart. You *could* understand that entertainment is a necessity, not an option—if you let yourself. But you don't. Your life is a straight line. Straight is good. But so is curvy. So is jagged. So is looped." She turned away, toward the stage stairs.

"Cara, I'm tired of you walking away from me, instead of answering my questions."

She glanced back. "I do answer. You just don't like them. And I'm tired of you trying to force me to be who you want me to be." She dragged herself up the stairs, head down, exhaustion pouring out of every pore. The swish and rasp of her mother's clothes as she stomped away filled Cara's ears.

"No hand cream?" Gerry teased.

"I'd better not get within a thousand yards of her for a while. Poor Kimi." She lifted a drum. When Ger got a look at her carrying one of his babies between her forearms instead of hands, he reached over to help. Startled to see them still there, Cara thanked Jonie and James for a good performance, and walked with Ger back to his cabin, drums tied onto his rolling cart.

She thanked him once, twice, refused his intimate entreaties, and crawled onto the cot in the corner. Her hands smoldered. With nothing else to concentrate on, she wished desperately for a Selandu smoke canopy. *<Flash> Rodani attaching a canopy to her bed and lighting the powder. <Flash> Rodani holding a yellow ball between his fingers, watching her.*

She turned on her side and shut her eyes. Three weeks. Could she wait that long?

SIX

"Four, Five. Four, Five."

With 'com in hand, Rodani sat on the edge of Cara's bed. The skin on his back was stiff, and pulled and ached with every movement. Shooting pains erupted if he moved in certain ways.

As the windows were still bricked up against attacks, only the timepiece told him what part of morning it was.

The empty bed matched the emptiness in his heart. He'd bonded with a woman before. He'd been chaste until his third year of guild training when a fellow student had first gifted him her attentions. He'd thought that bond was strong, but it was a piece of twine next to the hardwood tree he carried within him now.

Cara's rooms were not home anymore. His old room across the hall, shared with Serano for nearly a decade, was not home. Thanks mostly to Kusik, Barridan itself had lost its ability to be a stable home base, and it also meant his allegiance to Arimeso was shaky. Now it was a temporary shelter. That was another uncomfortable truth he was reluctant to admit. A guardian without a taso was considered an unpredictable and unwelcome drifter in most towns and estates, his honor considered untrustworthy. Chendal's allegiance to the guild as a whole was the only exception.

Where was Lanata? Was she still in charge of the guild while Kusik healed? She hadn't answered his call.

Rodani checked the armoire. Yes, it still held his clothing. He washed and changed, then pulled out a belt. List in his head, he set out to make some arrangements before Kusik found him. There was no avoiding any meeting that his keso called. Not unless he wished to leave Barridan now. At the thought, he halted at the door to the hallway. No, he still had tasks to accomplish before abandoning his old life.

The house accountants laid claim to a suite of rooms and a locked vault, halfway between the taso's quarters and the Enclave. In the outer room sat a woman at a desk, a woman with a familiar face.

Hamman's daughter, the first girl he had desired enough to pursue. She was mated now, and visibly carrying a child.

"Hammalita."

She looked up from her calculations and smiled. "A'tem."

Rodani sat down in the chair before her desk. "Tell me truly you have forgotten my name."

"Truly, a'tem, I have forgotten your name is Rodani."

He smiled in return, the first for more days than he wished to remember. "May the goddess protect you and keep you both safe."

She inclined her head in acceptance. "I leave an offering every morning and night. What may I assist you with?"

"I wish to withdraw my earnings."

"All of it?" Surprise lilted her voice, but her expression went to mask.

Rodani waved his hand. "I have some debts to pay and items to buy. I will bring back any I do not use."

Hammalita pulled a folder from a stack behind her desk. She leafed through the immaculate records. "Twelve gold, seventeen silver, nine copper. You are sure you wish it all?"

"Yes. Are the rules of privacy still in place?"

She nodded to the larger office behind her. "Except for Danit. Do you need a belt or lock box?"

"No, I thank you."

Hammalita took a key from the inner office and walked to the vault, her abdomen leading the way. She brought back a small bag and counted Rodani's earnings in front of him.

He tucked the bag into a hidden pocket in his guild jacket, and laid a hand on Hammalita's. Then he placed two fingers against his lips. "I do not wish others to know how much damage I have done by ill-thought wagering."

His next stop was the reuse room. In it was a myriad of used, dented, chipped, or cast-off items the denizens of the house no longer needed. Rodani checked the clothing bins. Shirts, long pants and short ones, and a pair of worn but serviceable outdoor shoes that fit his feet, he gathered them up in a bag.

As he left the reuse room, he saw Serano turn the corner into the Enclave. Rodani assumed his ex-partner was looking for his bedmate, so he took the opportunity to slip into his old room to fill the coin belt and push the bag of clothing into a back corner of his armoire.

"Five, Four. Five, Four."

Rodani pulled out his 'com. "Five."

"I was on the radio with Tendiman," Lanata said. "Meet me in the comm room."

"Ninety-nine."

Lanata was a half-head shorter than Rodani, and her hair was a half-shade darker—like silver that had begun to tarnish. When he'd met her, Rodani had thought her middle-aged, or possibly sickly. But it was simply genetics—like his dark eyes. It brought an inner, but unremarked-upon, empathy for her. Being different was forever a trial.

She crossed her arms. "At what percentage are you?"

"It depends upon the tasks I am set to, a'tem. I would not wish to run races or scrub floors, but for ordinary tasks I would estimate 80%."

"Well—"

A rasp of boots against stone was no warning in a guild room, but Lanata's quick switch to formal demeanor was.

Rodani turned to see Kusik behind him. The slap was quick, as was the follow-up backhand. Cheeks stinging, Rodani blanked his face and waited.

The keso looked past him. "Lanata, call a meeting." He walked out of the comm room.

After her call, Rodani followed Lanata to the meeting room. "Are there any warnings I should hear?" he asked. She didn't reply.

As they entered the guild room, Rodani's first thought was on its emptiness. Only half the guardians he'd known so well still lived and it was, he forced himself to admit, partly his fault.

Kusik stood on the left end of the long table as usual, but no one stood on the right. Timan's absence was a cold spot in his heart, and in the room. At Kusik's right (and only) hand, Lanata sat next to Serano. Misheiki sat further down. All but one sat with their backs to him, by order of status. Toward the far end sat Deneban, last of the newer recruits, the only one who fought for the taso instead of against.

Rodani walked behind Kusik to his place across from Serano, and put out a hand to grab the chair back.

But there was no chair.

Rodani blanked his expression and pulled himself to attention, hands on his thighs. Serano's face, he noted, was also a mask, as was Lanata's. Kusik shot his arm out and pointed to the far corner of the table where the lowest rank guardian would sit.

Without comment, Rodani made his way around to that end of the table. Kusik followed. Rodani pulled the chair out to sit, then heard the rustle of fabric behind him. Kusik's fist hit him near the base of his skull. His arms flew out and he fell forward onto the table. Another strike hit in the center of his back. A cough of pain escaped his lips, and his half-healed wounds began to burn. He heard his keso's boot steps walk back to the head of the table. Demoted and even more disturbed, Rodani took his new seat slowly and stiffly. He stared straight ahead over Deneban's shoulder. *This is how it begins*, he thought.

"The temaso," Kusik said, "has promised us some graduates soon. We should expect them within a week. Lanata, Serano, and I will instruct them in the *proper* way to be a guardian in this house. At that time, Misheiki will make the rounds of the house with Deneban, and will trade off on comm duty." Kusik paused. "Rodani will move the furniture out of his former adashi's rooms, and scrub the walls and floors. I will have no scent of that human left in the rooms when it is done."

Rodani kept his body frozen in stasis as if he were a kumiri being hunted.

"Now, a'tem!" Kusik snarled at him.

Rodani stood up and took a few steps toward the door. As he did, Kusik turned toward him. Rodani's heartbeat rocketed upwards, but he forced himself to keep moving, as he must. Kusik walked up and kicked his feet out from under him. As Rodani went down on his hands and knees, Kusik raked his back with his fingernails. Then he landed a savage kick to Rodani's abdomen. An audible crack filled the room. Rodani doubled over in pain, falling onto his side.

"Disperse," Kusik called out to the rest of his guardians. They filed past in silence. Kusik followed them out.

Rodani lay on the floor gasping, unable to decide which part of him hurt worse—his back or his midsection. After a few minutes he tried to roll onto his hands and knees, but radiating pains near his waist stole his breath. He dare not roll onto his back. It still blazed.

Orders. Do not let him find you here, fool.

He took as deep a breath as he could, and pulled his knees underneath him, forearms on the floor. His forehead rested on his arms.

More than one pair of footsteps came running down the corridor. Not boots. Please.

Grey pants and indoor shoes surrounded him. "A'tem? Where are you hurt, a'tem?"

"Back. Abdomen." He waved his hand around, panting in pain. *Thank you*, he thought, to whoever called the healers.

They guided his body sideways and down onto the stretcher. One more trip to a clinic. One more block of days with healers' hands prodding him nearly past endurance. His body bounced painfully as they carried the stretcher through the corridors.

"What caused this, a'tem?" Baldar asked as Rodani was shifted to a bed.

Shallow breaths were all he could take. "Guild matters."

"Who?" Baldar demanded as he took Rodani's shirt off of him. Another healer carefully removed his weapons belt and pulled off his pants. Baldar felt across Rodani's carapace. He let out a gasp as the physician poked it.

"Cracked," Rodani told him. "I heard it."

"I feel it. It will need to be bound." Baldar walked around behind him and stopped. "You were flogged."

"Yes," was all he would say.

"Simandil did not release you in this state. Someone reopened the wounds." He studied the bloody marks in the center of the scabbed back.

"Yes."

"That is still against guild law, is it not?"

"Yes."

Rodani dug deep into his guild training for what pain control he still had as Baldar and his healers went to work. The last dozen days had depleted most of his reserves. Unfortunately, Kusik's reserve of rage had not diminished. It was time to reevaluate his scheduled departure. In two weeks, he might be finding out the permanent way if Sela truly existed or not.

With his back patched and his entire midsection wrapped taut as a drum, the healers lined padding along the front and back of his body. Not that he had any intention of rolling over. Someone set up a smoke canopy over his head. An image flipped into his mind of Cara in bed as he set a canopy over her, her mutilated hands held out, stiff and swollen.

Au, Sela, why would— But he stopped. Those questions had never been answered in his childhood. They would not be answered now. As the smoke took hold in his brain, he shut off all thoughts and tried to rest his wounded body.

***

Deneban walked into the festive room, but not with the pride he usually wore. He found Lanata and Misheiki where he had hoped they'd be, at a small table in the corner where only the bravest of non-temichin would dare to sit.

"A'tem'ai," he said, both a formal address and a question in his voice. Lanata kicked a chair out for him to take.

"Where is your bottle," she asked as he sat.

"I think I should not drink tonight." Deneban folded his hands on the table in front of his chest. He saw the other two guardians exchange glances.

"One bottle?" Misheiki offered.

"No, a'tem, thank you. I believe I need to keep my reflexes sharp."

Lanata drew her hand down between them in negation. "Kusik has no reason to take his furies out on you, te'tem. You were innocent of all that went down."

Deneban rested his gaze on his clasped hands. "I thought I had left that kind of treatment behind when I graduated."

"He was not always that way."

"When did it begin?"

Lanata took a drink from her bottle. "When the taso decided to bring a human here. Before she ever arrived."

"It worsened," Misheiki added, "when Rodani agreed to be her guardian."

"They could not have known what would happen," Deneban said.

"Not the details. But Kusik and Arimeso were ever on opposite sides of the attempt."

"What happens now?"

"The same as every day since the carnage, and before. Follow orders, one at a time."

***

A clatter of earthenware woke Rodani, a kitchen servant with a tray. Four healers followed him in.

"You must be turned to your other side, a'tem," one said. They crowded around him, pushing and pulling. He grimaced as he was rolled onto his back, and again as they drew him over to his opposite side. One healer peeled the bandage, a part of it that wasn't covered by the stiff wrap.

"It will heal, a'tem. Eat. Rest."

"Smoke," Rodani demanded.

"Eat first. I will return in half an hour."

"Quarter."

The healer laid his hand on Rodani's shoulder. "A'tem," he said with a scold in his voice.

Rodani picked up a spoon.

Maintaining his promise, the healer returned in less than half an hour with more smoke powder. The smoke and canopy were beginning to be a second talisman to Rodani in his weakened state. A ten day ago he was strong, powerful, protective. Now he was bereft of both health and safety.

Fool. Should he even seek after Cara? Would he ruin her life there as he had nearly ruined his own, here? That was another emptiness within him: surety. What kind of life would they have there? He wasn't ignorant of living outside civilization. Guild training had prepared him for that. He knew many plants that were edible, and how to hunt and trap. He knew how to build a smokeless fire and protect himself from the elements. How to dig a latrine. But would Cara be happy in such a coarse state of existence? Or would she yearn for her town's amenities instead? Au, such a provider he was.

He began to make another mental list, one he would need to fulfill in Endolan, the village just north of the port town of Soldan. A small boat. Map of the islands. Lantern. Candles. Another set or two of clothes, seaside-style. He needed to let go his armor of guild black, needed to blend in.

But what would he do with his dark eyes? They were a calling card left for anyone who came hunting him. Musing on an immutable dilemma, he fell asleep.

Shouting blasted his ears. Orders! *Feet on the floor, caldazon!* A hard hand struck his head. A training course? Where was he? Stunned and disoriented, Rodani tried to rise.

"Obey me or pay the price!" came the shout.

He opened his eyes to find a dim clinic room and Kusik in his face, enraged. A slurry of curse words fell from his keso's mouth.

"State your orders!" he demanded.

Rodani put his palms on the bed and tried again to sit up.

Kusik shoved him onto his back against the padding. "Your orders!"

Smoke brain. Think, fool! The center of his back flared with pain. "My orders were—"

Healers rushed into the room. Behind them strode Baldar, arranging a shirt over his chest. "Who disturbs my clinic?" he said, forceful in contained outrage. Then he recognized the visitor. "A'Keso?"

Heart pounding, Rodani watched the two men—in fright and in gratitude—as Kusik spun to face the master healer.

"A'Keso, this man is under my care," Baldar stated, his voice sharp. "He is in no shape to take orders, except from me. By whose right do you come in here in the dark of night, shouting and waking my patients up and down the hall?"

Kusik drew himself up to his full height and breadth. "I am keso," he growled. "And I will speak to disobedient guardians as I see fit."

"And I am your equal as it relates to healing. Your right to dominate your guild stops where my authority starts."

"Never!"

Baldar slid his tall body between Kusik and the bed. "You will leave my clinic, and forebear from abusing my patient."

Rage blossomed across Kusik's face. "You dare give me orders? I will have you dismissed from this house!"

Baldar pulled a 'com from his pants pocket, and pushed a button. "This is the master healer. I require—"

Baring his teeth, Kusik grabbed for the physician's 'com. Baldar pulled it away. Bedridden, Rodani waited for Kusik to take the physician down to the floor, but the keso backed off.

"—I require security presence in the clinic, second hall. Now!" Baldar shut off the 'com. Healers began to move around the little room, crowding the snarling pair.

"That is not necessary," Kusik snapped.

"Leave my clinic."

"With my temichi."

"I forbid it."

"You have no power to forbid me anything, Baldar." Kusik reached around the physician for Rodani.

Baldar moved between them again. "Du!"

Rodani froze in the bed, waiting to be grabbed, waiting for his wounds to be mauled by his keso. Serano, Lanata, and Misheiki, all in various states of undress, pushed their way into the room. They stared at the scene of chaos and rage. It looked to Rodani as if they weren't sure who they were allowed to tackle and cuff, and were waiting for someone to tell them.

Baldar glanced at the three. "This is my domain. The keso needs to leave it."

Lanata cleared her throat. "A'ke—" she began, then stopped as Kusik swiveled around to her in a full body spin.

Serano pulled his 'com. "Deneban, wake the taso and bring her to the clinic. Escort her to the second hall. Immediately!"

A gasp came through the 'com. "A'tem...yes, a'tem."

Then Kusik pulled his 'com. "Deneban," was all he got out before Baldar ripped it from his hand. Kusik punched the physician in the jaw. Baldar's head rocked back, but he didn't fall. The other guardians stepped between their keso and their much-respected master healer. It was, Rodani thought, all they could do. He couldn't see Baldar's face, but his demeanor was very much as frozen and stiff as Kusik's. Rodani had a ringside seat to a confrontation as grave as he'd ever seen between two high-ranking people.

"I will leave the clinic, Baldar. But I will take Rodani with me. He can sleep in his own bed."

Baldar didn't move. Nor did the three lower rank guardians. Nor did Rodani. His back throbbed in time with his cracked casing, but he wasn't going to ask anyone in this grim tableau to shift him.

"Rodani, get up," Kusik ordered him.

"A'tem, keep still," Baldar responded.

Au, this was a replay of his last fight with Cara, with himself as the child, Ikemi. Of a sudden he knew how the boy had felt, and why he had chosen to run. Through Kusik's persecution, Rodani saw himself as Cara had seen him—harsh and unyielding.

Kia, I am sorry.

Arimeso walked in. All eyes turned to her. "Explain this." A growl could be heard at the base of her words, drawing out a middle-of-the-night temper on edge.

"A'Taso," Kusik stepped in, "I chastised Rodani in our meeting, and ordered him to clean out the human's rooms. When I went to check tonight, I found the rooms just as they had been left. After searching, I found him here, smoke-addled."

Almost, Rodani shouted out his defense. But he clenched his teeth together and waited.

"Why is he here, a'Baldar?" she asked.

"Because my staff was called to his aid. They brought him here for treatment."

"What—" Arimeso began.

Kusik shoved his guardians out of the way and leaned into Baldar's face. "Who 'commed?"

Now Arimeso grabbed her keso and pushed him to face her. "You will let me speak," she said, cold. Hand on his arm, she turned back to Baldar. "What was the treatment for?"

"His back wounds have been reopened and his carapace is cracked. He would not tell me why."

Arimeso glanced down at Rodani. He blanked his expressions, mortified by his helplessness and being the cause of so much disruption in so many lives.

"A'Taso," he whispered.

"How many days will you keep him here, a'Baldar?"

He waved his fingers. "Four days, five. When he believes he can return to duty, I will release him." Then he turned to Kusik. "To light duty."

Arimeso swept her arm over the room's crowd. "Everyone out except necessary healers." The trio of guardians headed out first. She waited for Kusik to move, then followed him out. Neither held an expression Rodani wanted to see.

Baldar stared at Rodani, then sighed and headed for the door. "Lock the room," he told his healers.

SEVEN

The days rolled by like a skiff in a languid river. But Cara's mind was not so calm. She begged some healing cream from her father in his cluttered lab, and asked about Kimi.

Liam shook his head. "Did you tell her to go watch you play?"

"No way."

"Well, her ears are still echoing from her mother's shouting, and she has chores enough to see her through to her sixteenth birthday."

Cara kicked the leg of his worktable. "It's not like I was stripping!"

Liam grimaced and looked away. "Please, little bit."

She sighed. "The older Kimi gets, the worse Ama gets."

"It's because she sees you in her."

Cara's eyes widened. "What?"

"You don't see it?"

She tried to think, tried to see it, but her mind remained a blank. She shook her head.

"You're too close to it," he told her.

Cara slid onto the stool opposite her father. "Explain?"

Liam set aside the mortar and pestle he was using. *<Flash> Serano grinding up the hallucinogenic herb at his table.*

"She is interested in everything, but focuses deeply on nothing. She cares little for babies and children, but treats each with a gentle good humor instead of discipline. She wants to be someone, but doesn't know what. She wants to follow in your footsteps, but doesn't know where you're going or where you'll end up." He rubbed leaf driblets off his fingers and smiled ruefully. "Of course, we all wonder that. And," he took the jar of cream from her hand and opened it for her. "She whispered to me that she wants you to teach her that alien language, just as you're teaching Nick."

Cara bent her head and pressed a few fingers into the cream, then began rubbing it into her scars. "Every bloody person in the whole town must know where I go and what I do."

"And if her mother finds out..."

"It won't come from me."

Liam studied his biological daughter. "You never told me what happened in the north."

Cara looked away.

"Keep your secrets, then. I know you're good at it. I don't know why."

She blew a breath through her lips. "How many years have you been with Ama, now?"

They sat in their respective silences as Cara tended each reddened, sore scar. At the end, she closed up the jar and slipped it into a pocket.

"Thank you, Dae."

"Any time, little bit."

She gave her hands a few days to rest, concentrating on working with Nick. They sat in the flickering light of his office behind the bar. In the outer room, a few patrons lingered over a long lunch.

"You sure I need all this?" he asked. The stack of flash cards was becoming unwieldy.

"You want your best chance at getting the position?"

Nick sighed.

"How much does this cost?" she asked.

He flipped a card over. "Ene und hal aosa?"

"I want five of those."

Another card. "A grat drin he hael."

"Try to stutter your tongue on the 'r' in *grat*. G-dh-at."

"Guh-dha-t."

"A little faster, tongue a little farther back when it touches."

Nick rubbed his forehead.

"Changing your mind?"

"No," he said in a clipped tone. "Will there be anyone else there who knows both languages besides Andrew?"

"I have no clue. But unless he's taking a student, or Suraya, probably not."

"What happened to all the other CSC graduates?"

Cara grimaced. "All eight of them? Life. More important things to do."

Nick sat back in his chair and stretched his legs out. "Would I come back from there as subdued as you are?"

"What?"

"You heard me. You're not the same person you were."

Cara waved her hands in front of her face. "It was an eye-opening experience, that's all."

"Right."

She heard the sarcasm. "Let's go back over the easier ones again."

***

Half of the days on Tuesday, Wednesday, Thursday, Cara practiced drumming. Gerry played metronome, or drummed with her. Cara slathered her hands with salve and covered each drumstick with a wide strip of fur.

For the other half, she'd purchased some embroidery cloth, threads of various colors, and one needle. One only. They'd been brought down from the ship, and no one in Newydd Cenedyl yet knew how to make more of any similar quality. She had sketched a pattern onto a piece of paper, silently ruing the lack of bright colors, hoping somebody in Himadi House could invent some. Stitching helped while away the hours, and days, before she could see her husband again.

On Friday, the crowd in front of the stage was every bit as large, and every bit as noisy. Saturday proved the same.

The hidden coins in her hidden belt increased, despite paying Ger for a corner of his cabin, and for food. He asked her again to share his bed. She refused, gently.

Kimi remained incommunicado. Cara and her mother stayed on opposite sides of the town. Ger began to clench his jaw when he looked at her.

The next week was more of the same.

The moon waxed toward full.

Cara and Nick made their way to the CSC to talk to Menachem. "I've never been in here," Nick said.

"It's nothing special to look at. But the knowledge is important."

"He knows we're coming?"

"Yes. You remember your talking points?"

"Pretty sure."

Cara led him into the hallway and headed toward Menachem's office. She knocked on the door frame.

"Haji," came the reply.

Cara waved toward Nick. Menachem regarded them both with a dour silence. Cara bowed, properly. She motioned to Nick. He repeated the bow, properly.

"Sai?"

She nudged him. Nick took a deep breath. "Ambassador, I'd like to be allowed to open a bar in Himadi House."

Menachem raised one black eyebrow. His dark face swung from one visitor to the other. "How long have you been on this tack?"

Nick glanced at Cara.

"Three hard-working weeks, a'Reiti," she said.

"How do you think this would work?" he asked Nick.

"I've been learning the language. The basics, at least."

He glared at Cara. "You decided to tutor him all on your own?" The tone of his words fell into displeasure.

"A'Reiti, I was not usurping your role. Nick wants very much to try his hand in Himadi. He asked me to help."

Menachem turned back to Nick. "And why did you not ask me?"

"I...thought she would have more time to work with me."

"And you thought she would be more amenable."

Nick's eyes went wide. "That wasn't my first thought, Ambassador." He glanced at his shoes like an errant schoolboy. "This is the chance of a lifetime," he lifted his chin, "and I am already past my prime. Please let me try."

"Sit."

He sat.

"Cara, you can go."

She tried to mask her expression, and bowed. "I hope you'll give him the chance."

"It's not solely up to me."

Cara left the CSC and walked back to Nick's bar. Inside was cool and dim. She bought a mug of beer from Chucko and sat at a table in the corner. Three rough-looking men crowded a table across the room. She knew them, remotely. Ne'er-do-wells and troublemakers. Haters of anyone they felt beneath them, especially the Selandu. She'd heard enough of their repulsive comments before she left for Barridan last year. They stared at her, spoke to each other in muttered tones, then stared again. One got up and came over.

"Cara," he said as he stood on the other side of the two-top.

"Mack," she replied, trying to sound courteous without being friendly. That wasn't an easy task.

"I want to buy a dance from you."

She shook her head, a slight movement from left to right and back, and pursed her lips. "I don't do private dances. Sorry."

He threw some coins down on the table and sat across from her. "Yeah, you will. For enough money, you will."

She pushed them back at him. "No."

"Bet you danced for those damned aliens across the hills. How much did they pay you?"

Cara sipped her drink slowly. Several replies crossed her mind. None of them sounded safe to say to this man. She stuck with the simple. "I crafted. That's what they paid me to do."

"I know where you live."

Suspicion crawled up her spine. She lifted her gaze to his face. It wasn't an ugly face, but his expression held an underlying grimness. He smiled, a cruel one, and it scared her.

"You can get what you need from other women, Mack."

"I've heard for years how easy you are."

Cara grabbed her temper before it exploded. "Those were nothing but rumors, just because I dance."

He leaned over the table, way too near to her. "Did you lay down with those devils? Did you fuck 'em, Cara? Do they have dicks? Do they know how to use 'em?"

Cara stood up, fury in every line of her face. "This conversation is over."

Mack leered at her. "I could do you better than they did."

She didn't dare answer. It might get her assaulted—or worse. Heart hammering, she left the bar with a dire hope he'd go back to his fellow assholes. What those men did for a living was anyone's guess, but every one of them had spent time in the sheriff's lockups. With shaking hands, she glanced behind her several times, heading east. She ended up at the docks, watching the sea birds dive. Eventually she calmed.

Where would Rodani be? There were more than a dozen islands slanting out into the ocean, plus undersea hills that matched the ones above water. And that was just on the human side. Nearly that many sat beyond the Selandu boundary line.

She made her way to the marina and checked the weather reports. Calm with a mild breeze. Good. She knew the basics of sailing. Everyone did, but she wasn't the master that Davad was. She tried to memorize the layout of the islands on the marina's map. It was Friday, and the full moon was next Wednesday. Thursday... Thursday, she would borrow her parents' seldom-used boat and listen for the voice of her husband.

The thought cheered her on her way to the southside stage. She played and danced with all the enthusiasm she could muster, for the coins and her band mates if nothing else. When they took their bows, she packed the drums onto the cart. Gerry wasn't there.

But Mack was. He stared at her from the bar's doorway, easily seen when the crowd cleared. As she sat on the bicycle to take the cart back to Ger's hut, he called to her. "Tell me about the grey devils, Cara! Are they as hard to kill as people say?" He mimicked notching an arrow in a bow. "Where's their heart, Cara?"

<Flash> Rodani, lying next to her in bed after their first time. "I have decided it no longer matters."

Archery became a common skill once their stock of guns had been captured by the Selandu early on. But they could be equally lethal. A chill crawled up Cara's back.

As she rode, she watched to see if Mack would follow. He only stared. Cara towed the drums back to Gerry's. She almost called it *home*. But it wasn't. He nagged for her attentions every few days, fortunately without Mack's coarse intimidation. But she rolled them off her back with a regretful smile. He didn't argue.

Wednesday dawned rainy, and the forecast showed continued rain through Friday.

Now, there was a dilemma. What would Rodani expect? Would he wait for her call in the rain? Or huddle in the hammock or a tent until it was over? She hated the thought of him sitting, listening, listening, and hearing nothing but silence.

Maybe tomorrow would be clear.

Cara puttered around the wood stove, heating a broth with pieces of meat and a few vegetables she'd bought from a local shop, making them into a stew. She wiped her hands on a rag and stared out the door. Ger sat in a corner of the cabin under a hanging lantern, composing, she assumed.

She sat at the table, thinking of her husband, out there in the rain somewhere. Which island was he on? Where should she start looking? When should she leave? First thing in the morning? Or wait to see if the weather cleared later? What was a little rain compared to the arms of the man she loved? That was the easiest answer of all.

Again, she went to the door, grabbed her umbrella, and stepped out to check the horizon for any break in the clouds. But it was a uniform, dreary, drippy grey, so different from Rodani's grey gleaming skin. The image of his unusual dark eyes appeared as she closed her own against the slanting rain.

Rain. That's what the Selandu always called her tears. Their eyes could water from irritation or injury, but never from emotion. She envied the lack. Too often in her life she'd been shamed for being emotional in the face of anger or criticism. She needed a bit of Selandu reserve.

Under the door overhang she shook out the umbrella, and stepped back inside Ger's cabin.

"What is wrong with you?"

Cara turned her head to look at him. "Do you think you're the first person who's asked me that?"

"You've gotten even worse the last week."

She tossed the comment with a Selandu hand wave that he wouldn't even recognize.

Ger leaned back in his chair and crossed his arms. "Why won't you go to bed with me?"

Cara sighed and sat in the kitchen chair. "We talked about this. I can't."

Ger stood up sharply, his chair scraping the wood floor. "We haven't discussed anything. What have I said or done to make you reject me? We used to have a nice little relationship, and I'd like to have it back again."

"It's nothing you did."

"Oh, I've heard that before. 'It's not you, it's me.'" He came over to the table.

"Sometimes that's true, Ger."

He waved his arms in the air. "What did that place do to you? Did they abuse you, or something?"

"No." She drew inward, freezing her body in the face of his anger, movement in her eyes only.

Now he slapped his hands on his waist. "Do you know how hard it is for me to watch you sleep in that cot every night, and keep my hands off you?"

Cara stared down at the tabletop. "I'm sorry. I didn't know."

Ger kicked the nearest chair. "That's all you can say?"

She bit at her lips and sighed heavily, wondering how far this would go. "I'm sorry I can't give you what you want."

"Then I want you to leave." His eyebrows were drawn inward, his lips pursed in a thin line, his jaw jutted.

Now she unfroze. "What? Why?"

"Because I can't stand to be around you nearly every hour of every day and not be with you." He stormed back to the desk in the corner, among his papers and pens.

She laid her elbows on the table, fists on her forehead. Sometimes she hated her life. Sometimes it deserved to be hated. "All right. As soon as I can find another place."

"No," Ger said. "Today. I won't spend another night staring across the room at you while you sleep."

"I have no place to go!"

"You can afford the hostel."

A skimpy, dirty room with a greedy landlord who couldn't keep his hands to himself.

She stood up. "You can give me a little while. I deserve that for doing most of the cooking and cleaning while I've been here." She lifted the still-wet umbrella.

"I'll give you the small conga drum."

Wind whipped the rain past the door. "Thank you," she managed to say. "I'll need the tall one, too."

"Make me an offer."

"Ten coppers."

"Fifteen."

"Twelve."

"Fifteen."

Cara sighed and stared out into the wet gloom. "Fine." *Damn him.* Where could she go? Where could she store the drums during the week? Where would she practice? Jonie first. See what she suggests.

She made her way along the main street's wet walkway to the other side of town. Her pants dripped with water, her shoes splashed in mud as she crossed from one street to the next. She pounded on the door. James opened it up from the store side. He took one look at her and ushered her in among the clothing for sale.

"What's up?"

Jonie stood up from her sewing machine and came over, eyeing her bedraggled clothes. "James, get her a chair. She can't be walking around the clothing racks in that state."

James brought a chair, and Cara sat down. A few tears fell.

Jonie crossed her arms. "Spill it."

"Ger kicked me out."

"Why?"

She looked away as shame and anger battled inside her mind. "I wouldn't have sex with him."

"Was that part of the deal?" James asked.

"No. I told him that before he ever let me stay the first night." Water dripped from her pants legs onto the floor. "But he kept asking."

"Did he threaten you?"

"No. He just now said he couldn't stand for me to be there, sleep there anymore, if he couldn't have access to me."

Jonie stomped away as James stared at Cara.

"There's no room for you here," James said gently.

Cara shook her head. "I know. I was just wondering if you had a place where I could keep two conga drums. That's all I'll have to play on, now."

"We really don't. I tuck my guitar into a corner of the armoire, among Jonie's shoes and baby clothes."

Cara rose. "Okay. Thanks, anyway." She walked out into the rain and mud, and wondered where she and her drums would spend the night.

She toured the town, knocking on doors. The CSC? "No," Menachem said. "This is not a hotel, and you don't work here."

Davad? "Still no."

Dae's lab behind the house? "There's no room, little bit."

Her sister Emmie's home? "Sure, if you want to babysit every day. I can put a cot on the back porch."

With evening drawing near, she trudged into Nick's bar, morose. She didn't know which she needed more: a beer, dry clothes, or a bed to sleep on.

He turned to her. "You look like you fell into a goat pen and got gnawed on."

She slumped onto a bar stool.

"Did I miss a lesson?"

Cara shook her head for the umpteenth time that day.

Nick folded his arms on the gleaming bar that stretched between them, and waited. As a bartender, he was good at patience. *Almost as good as Rodani*, she thought. *Aisu. Will I see you tomorrow?*

"Nick," she began, pushing away the hope, "if I stop charging you for your lessons, will you let me stay here the two nights I play?"

He rested his chin on his hand. "What happened to you and Gerry?"

"He kicked me out."

"Why?"

The litany was getting old. She gave the same answer.

And the answer came back as it did the other times. "Did you say you would?"

Cara slapped the bar, making her scarred palm sting. "No. I specifically did not. And I had to remind him over and over, since he kept asking."

He smiled. "You know how men are."

"I know how men are, Nick. But a *no* is a *no*, dammit. I wouldn't do that to a man, and they shouldn't do it to me."

"No argument," he admitted. "But I'm only here for another four or five weeks before Himadi House opens."

She looked up in surprise. "Menachem said yes?"

"Yep." His smile was something worthy of witnessing.

"Well, congratulations. Keep studying."

"Keep teaching me. I'll let you stay here. But when my ex-wife takes over after I leave, all bets are off."

"That'll do for now. Thanks, Nick. You saved me from being groped, or worse, at the women's hostel."

Nick grabbed the bar rag and began to wipe the already clean counter. "That place should be closed down."

"No argument."

With her wallet fifteen coppers lighter, Cara pedaled Nick's smallest delivery cart back from Ger's, the drums covered with the umbrella and everything else she could think of to use. She stored them in his shed behind the bar, then climbed the back staircase and into a small room over the bar's kitchen.

Drenched, she toweled off and crawled into bed. She was asleep within minutes.

EIGHT

For four days, the door to Rodani's clinic room stayed locked. Healers came and went with their keys, and Baldar monitored his healing each day.

But each day, at some point, the door to his room was tested. Heavy boots on the stone floor, a hard shake at the handle, and then boot steps disappearing into the distance.

On the fifth day, Baldar ordered the door unlocked, and Rodani was free to return to his guild duties, chest still wrapped in tight bandages. But a 'com call to Lanata found not the light duty the physician had ordered, but a repeat command to scrub the floors of Cara's rooms. He knew better than to complain to Baldar. Ignoring or fighting Kusik could be a death sentence. Both dejected and angry, Rodani made his way down to the maintenance room for a bucket, scrub brush, and soap. He borrowed a hand truck and went to the rooms that had held his heart.

Those rooms were completely empty now. No tables, couch...or bed. Nothing was left but bare stone floors. Empty rooms, empty heart.

He started at the far corner of the study, on hands and knees. It was hard work. The position aggravated both his wounds. His knees became bruised, then raw. His shoulders ached, his hand cramped, his abdomen was a constant drum of pain. The soap proved an effective skin irritant that added to his inner and outer miseries.

A whisper of indoor slippers came through the servants' rooms and into Cara's empty study.

"Rodani," the voice said, sharp with ire. "Why have you not reported to me? I demanded your presence in the Enclave days ago!"

Rodani closed his eyes and whispered a plea for patience. He shuffled to his feet and stretched his aching muscles. "A'Selaso."

The silence filled the distance between them.

"And?" Kimasa asked.

"A'Selaso, I have been under the care of the master healer, and now I am following the keso's orders. No one ordered me to the Enclave."

The high priestess thrust out her hand and raised her chin. "But you must! You need reeducation. Your close proximity to the human contaminated you and caused corruption of your faith! You must be healed." She nodded at the soapy floor and cleaning brushes. "Leave this now, follow me."

"I dare not, a'Selaso. I am sorry." He began to kneel down.

"You dare deny me?" The question came out in a screech that made Rodani's ears twitch. "You cannot!"

"A'Selaso, between a direct order from my keso and a direct order from you, I must obey him. I am guild, not an acolyte."

Kimasa strode up to his crouching body. "You *will* allow me to reignite your faith, Rodani. A few weeks of discipline while sequestered in the Enclave will heal you and rekindle Her flame within you. I will *not* be gainsaid!"

Rodani pushed his body upward. "And I refuse."

Her eyes went wide. "You will not," she whispered.

"But I do. Reeducation of the type you are demanding is for criminals and the mind-sick. I am neither." He lifted his chin just a bit. "I paid my debt to the guild. That is all that was required."

"Just the fact that you have lost your faith proves you are mind-sick, Rodani! You deny what is standing in front of me."

"I never said I lost my faith, a'Selaso. If someone told you that, they were telling falsities."

"But you have lost it."

"A'Selaso, please do me the courtesy of not telling me what is in my own mind."

Kimasa pointed her finger at Rodani's nose. "And that is human-speak! I heard her myself! You repeat her own words to me but deny their meaning? You *are* sick!"

Rodani sighed deeply and bowed his head. "Please forgive my discourtesy, a'Selaso. I am in great physical pain. That is not the kind of hurt the Enclave heals. And I must continue my task, or Kusik will find me slacking."

She stamped her slippered foot and continued to berate him as he bent to his scrubbing. But his silence and cold shoulder won him a temporary reprieve.

Kimasa turned and walked out. "You will not refuse the goddess, Rodani. I will see to it."

By evening he had finished the study and was midway through the center workroom. Past ready to call a halt, he slipped in and out of the kitchen for food from the ever-helpful chef, Cassig, and ate in Cara's bedroom on the floor. He pushed his shoulder pack over to the wall where the bed had stood and laid down, resting his head on the pack. At least Kusik had left him alone today. Maybe the keso was back in the clinic. Or maybe not, he thought, remembering the heated argument Kusik had waged with Baldar.

Rodani's eyes closed down. Muscles ached against the hard stone floor.

A key rattled in the study door. Rodani sat up and attempted to rise, but his internal carapace complained of the abrupt movement. He sat back down as Serano walked in.

"Are you determined to play the fool?" he snapped. "Kusik is waging war on you, and you choose here to sleep?" He gave Rodani's pack a savage kick. "Get up before he finds you. I am beginning to think you wish for his abuse. What do you gain from this suffering?"

Rodani clamped his jaws shut, took his pack across the hall, and fell into bed. Serano slammed every door he walked through, then stuck his head into Rodani's room. "This," he said in a rage, "is the damnable double-bond!" Then he slammed the last door.

A bellowing voice woke both of them in the dark of night. Serano rolled out and turned up his lantern. Across the living room he could see into the other bedroom, where Kusik was shouting orders at a bleary-eyed Rodani. Calisthenics that he worked to keep up with, and pain he attempted to keep off his face. Guild rules shouted at him that he was forced to repeat back at full voice. Slaps and blows punctuated Kusik's commands.

Serano crawled back in bed, but there was no sleep to be had with guild retraining taking place thirty feet away.

After nearly an hour, the shouting quieted to a guttural, irregular tone that went on for several more minutes. Then boot steps stomped past and the door to the hall opened and closed.

He thought of going to check on his ex-partner, but—truly—the man deserved some of what he was receiving. He needed his head cleared of the Cara-fog that still resided in him, and their keso was more than adept with a verbal broom. Serano hoped it worked.

Morning found Rodani back at his task. Kusik had made it clear that he needed to finish, and scrub again the places where Cara spent the most time: in front of the fireplace, where she sat at her craft table, where she slept.

Where they had slept.

Kia.

He shook his head. Tomorrow, he was ordered to scrub the taso's anteroom clean of the bloodstains that still remained. But today was one more day, one day closer to the point of escape.

But to live as an outcast? And for how long? How long could he stay south of the border without being seen? Without being caught? A month? A year? A week? And how long would Cara be content to live that way? It was a question he couldn't answer, and it wouldn't go away. It stuck in his mind like stable sweepings to a bootheel.

He wished he could have discussed it with her before she was sent home, but there'd been too much uncertainty and too little quiet time. As well, he forced himself to admit, he couldn't have predicted how Cara would react to the idea. Was it cowardice to have waited and given her the note? Or expediency?

No. He was no coward. That was nonsense. The scars on his back proved that, and the obvious fact of his and Cara's survival of the last three months.

But what was he waiting for? The question halted him mid-scrub. What was the rationale behind his timetable? *Two weeks in Barridan*, he had written. Why, when he already knew what kind of post-Cara life Kusik was going to provide him? Arimeso was too caught up in more significant issues to show much sympathy for his predicament. Kimasa's idea of reeducation frightened him. And he couldn't hide in the clinic.

Baldar. A follow-up visit was due, and Rodani had forgotten. He eased up off his hands and knees, feeling every pain from the last week and the terrible night he'd just had. He dumped the scrub brush in the bucket and went to seek out the master healer.

He was seen first by an assistant, who watched Rodani's painful stride then demanded he strip off his clothes. The healer took one look front and back, head to feet, and called for his master.

Baldar took that same walk-around, but more slowly. He pushed at the wrap that covered Rodani's cracked casing. It provoked a gasp of air and flinch. He unwrapped it and studied the flogged back, the bruised and bleeding knees, the raw hands, the new marks on Rodani's face and arms.

"What duties since I saw you last, a'tem?"

"Scrubbing floors, a'ke."

The physician crossed his arms and narrowed his eyes. "And does your esteemed keso believe that floor scrubbing is light duty? And when does floor scrubbing put bruises on your face and upper body?"

"I cannot say, a'ke."

Baldar flung his arms down at his sides and turned to the door. He muttered orders to his assistant and left the room. Rodani waited while his chest was re-wrapped, then made his way to the kitchen with a jar of healing cream.

It was time.

He found Cassig by the wine racks and drew him aside. "A'sel, I am being sent on a secret multi-day courier assignment. I need a large supply of travel food, and your silence. May I depend upon you?"

The chef bent low. "Of course, a'tem. Right away."

Rodani tucked himself into a dim corner while Cassig hunted his requirements, grateful for the man's loyalty. When he returned, Rodani took two sacks from him and laid a hand on his arm. "Thank you for all you did for Cara and me."

Cassig bowed again. "I was pleased to, a'tem, and hope to do so again in the future."

Rodani stole through the back corridors to his room and packed quickly. The sun was beginning to set. There wouldn't be a more suitable time to pretend a legitimate errand. He 'commed a request to the stablemaster, again asking for discretion. He made his way to the stables where Domendi handed him a gentle mare.

"I thank you, a'ke," Rodani said, bowing. With a few winces and an intake of breath, he took his seat in the saddle and headed northwest toward town. When he was out of sight of the manor, he turned east and spurred the benatac into a speed that pushed right up to the limits of his riding ability.

He didn't look back.

***

"Six, One! Six, One!"

Serano woke up with a start, as did Larisi beside him. He grabbed his 'com. "Six."

"Where is Rodani?!"

Serano pulled the 'com away from his ear in an attempt to save his hearing. "I do not know, a'Keso."

"Check his bed. Did you hear him last night?"

"I was not in my own bed, a'Keso."

"Well, he is not here scrubbing the taso's anteroom, and he refuses to answer his call. Find him. Send him to me. Now!"

"A'Keso." He turned to Larisi. "Sleep."

She glared at him in mock ill-humor. "Yes, of course." She flung the covers back. "I could assist you, beba."

Serano considered it. "Check the Enclave and the clinic. I will check guild areas."

"And Cara's rooms."

Serano hung his head, then raised it. "Yes, but he will not be there. It worries me he is refusing to answer."

"He could be in the forest again," Larisi said.

"Then it will be long before we find him."

Rodani was not in the Enclave, or the clinic, or the kitchens. He was not in his bedroom, nor had the bed been slept in. Cara's rooms were empty. The library, the target room, the gathering room, the festive room, the garage, even the roof, all were empty of the now security twelfth.

Serano strode into Arimeso's office. "Roda—" He stopped and pulled himself to attention. Chendal, Shisa, Kusik, and Arimeso all turned to him.

Kusik bore down on him. "Where is he?"

"I do not know, a'Keso," Serano said, wary of repercussions. "I cannot find him in the manor, and his 'com does not broadcast."

Chendal walked up. "Where should he be?"

Kusik flung out his hand. "Scrubbing this floor!"

"That is what you have for his tasks?" Chendal's voice went cold.

"That is what needs doing, a'Temaso. That is what is appropriate for a demoted guardian." He turned back to Serano. "Where have you *not* looked?"

"The stables. The forest."

"Why not the stables?"

"Because he avoids the beasts, a'Keso. He prefers to drive."

Kusik pulled his 'com. "Stablemaster."

"Domendi," came the belated reply.

"Have you seen Rodani in the last day?"

Domendi hesitated. "A'Keso, he borrowed a mare last night."

Kusik gripped the 'com with a rigid, shaky hand. "What did he say? What excuse did he give you?"

"That he had been given a courier assignment, a'Keso."

"Where?" Kusik's voice rose in rage with each answer given.

"He did not say, a'Keso," the stablemaster replied calmly. "He asked me to keep the assignment quiet."

"When?!" came the shout.

"At dusk last night."

"What direction?!"

"Northwest, I believe, a'Keso, but I did not watch for long. I had other duties."

Kusik shut off his 'com with a punch of his thumb and swore vehemently.

"A'Keso," Serano ventured into the angry silence. "There is one more place I could check...to verify."

"Where?" His lips pulled back in a snarl.

"When he went to Tendiman, he left something behind in a drawer. I should see if it is still there."

Kusik stormed out of the office. Serano followed him out, with Chendal and Shisa silent behind them. Inside Rodani's bedroom, Kusik pulled out every drawer and tossed the meager contents on the floor and bed, as Shisa did the same with the armoire. Serano shuffled through them.

"What do we look for?" Chendal asked into the chaos.

"A drawing," Serano answered. "Of Cara." He shook out every piece of clothing. "I do not see it here." He stared at the floor, not daring to face his superiors. "Now, I believe he is gone."

From the corner of his eye, Serano saw Kusik's fist swing. It struck his jaw with a heavy crack and knocked him to his knees.

"Why did you not know?" Kusik resumed shouting. "Did he give you no warning? Did he talk to you? Did you listen? Did you watch his body language?"

Serano pulled himself off the floor and back onto his feet. In a moment, he was down again with the wind knocked out of him.

Chendal sliced his hand downward between them. "Cease. Allow him to answer."

Serano stood and lifted his chin, but chose to face the temaso. It seemed temporarily safer. The room felt small with four irate or bitter guardians in it, surrounded by the detritus of a man's former life.

"He said very little to me, a'Keso. What he said, I heard. His demeanor was of a man sick at heart. I did not know he was also desperate. He gave me no warning of any plans to leave."

Shisa slammed the door of the armoire. It bounced back open and smacked her knee. "Where else would he go, Serano?"

"It would depend on his intentions, a'tem. There are many places here to hide. Your parents' cabin. Or places he visited with Cara: the storage cave, the forest where he and Cara spent a week, the falls, the cliffside, the stand of trees that grow the nuts he sent you. Or…" Serano shifted his weight, cautious of where the next blow would land.

"Or?" Chendal prompted.

"Or, he could be on his way to Himadi House."

Kusik growled. His single fist clenched rhythmically. He scanned the room, then stalked out in a boiling temper. As he followed, Serano glanced at the shelves in the living room, where Rodani's candlesticks had once stood.

"Himadi is forbidden to him, Serano," Chendal told him.

"So was Cara."

The reminder caused a moment of quiet.

"Shisa," Chendal said behind them, "go tend to the new knives. I will find you when this is settled."

Shisa's pupils pulsed. "Settled?"

***

Arimeso was alone at her desk. One more task finished, Kusik strode in and stopped in front of her, eyes narrowed with heat. "Rodani has left your house. Again."

"Again?"

"I will not repeat myself." Kusik paced back and forth in front of her desk. "I am certain you will miss him."

She set aside the pen in her hand. "What is your meaning, my keso?"

"Maybe if you had made him a special as you wished, he might have stayed."

Arimeso rose from her chair. "How dare you?" she said in a hot voice. "How dare you insinuate—"

"You can lie to me, tisal, or hide from me, but I will know it."

"Now you race from rage to absurd jealousy?"

A flutter of gold interrupted their exchange. "Where is Rodani, a'Taso?"

Arimeso let herself sigh. An imperious priestess was not what she needed right now. "A'Selaso?"

Kimasa stepped in, seemingly oblivious to the emotions running rampant in the room. "You promised I would have him for reeducation. He has not sought me, and refused my command to enter the Enclave. Why?"

Kusik settled himself into a corner chair, away from the flames he knew were coming.

"He seems to have left the house, a'Selaso," Arimeso said.

Kimasa straightened, stiff in indignation. "Left? Well, someone must find him and bring him back. He is in dire need of my ministrations!"

"We might. If we knew where he went."

"You must find him. The goddess demands it. The human's presence doused Sela's light within him, and it needs to be reignited."

"Kimasa," Arimeso said resignedly, "you do know how large this land is, do you not?"

The selaso raised her hands upwards. "You have guardians. Trackers. Hunters. They must go out!"

"I have five guardians where I used to have twelve. Now, with thanks to the guild and my coffers, I have three new graduates who need orientation and guidance." Arimeso leaned forward. "No."

Kimasa was beginning to resemble a rabid poridi. Her eyes flashed as she tugged at her golden robes. "A'Taso, I cannot countenance you ignoring the goddess or the Enclave's needs. You have done so repeatedly on the issue of Rodani and the human. He would never have left if I had re-instilled the Teachings! The goddess knows, a'Taso. She knows all. And she knows how to punish, as well."

"I believe he has been punished enough, Kimasa."

"And have you?"

Arimeso's pupils pulsed as she came around her desk. "Excuse you?"

Kimasa took a step backward, eyes wide. "A'Taso, I only meant—"

"I have eaten enough censure to keep me full for years, a'Selaso. You do yourself no favors to make an enemy of me."

"I would never—"

"You nearly did."

"A'Taso—"

"Cease this. Let him go. And leave my office."

Kimasa blinked. And blinked again. She took a deep breath and spun around, only to face the master healer in the doorway. She pushed her way past him, even as he stepped aside in courtesy.

Kusik let the corners of his mouth turn up. That was entertainment at its finest. The goddess must have smiled on him at last.

Baldar waited for a signal. Eventually, Arimeso waved her hand. He stood in front of her desk, waiting, as so many people had in the last weeks.

"Talk, a'ke."

"A'Taso, I must speak to you alone."

Kusik's smile failed. Alarm bells jangled in his head.

Arimeso pursed her lips. She turned to her husband. "A'Keso."

He shot the physician a look that would have left the man bloody, then withdrew from the room.

"A'Taso," Baldar began, "if it would not offend, may I sit?"

She waved to a chair. "Are you ill?"

"No, a'Taso. At least, not in the body."

Arimeso let surprise fill her face. "My ears are empty, Baldar."

He laid his hands on his thighs, stiff with ill ease. "A'Taso, I am decades used to seeing artists and crafters show up in my clinic with minor wounds. Stablehands with bites and claw marks. Kitchen staff with burns. Rashes, gashes, illnesses. These do not distress me. What does, a'Taso," he paused for a second, "is the number of times lately that I have ministered to a guardian from wounds at the hands of the keso."

Surprise turned to confusion. "Rodani had been attacked several times by other guardians, a'ke."

"I mean recently."

"I do not understand."

Baldar took a breath, then another. "A'Taso, within one day of Rodani's return from Tendiman, Kusik reopened his back wounds and cracked his carapace with a kick when he was down. Yesterday, Rodani returned for an evaluation, and more wounds had appeared. He refused to name Kusik as the perpetrator, but his words told enough. Today, I find both Serano and Lanata in adjoining rooms with similar wounds from a beating. Neither would reveal anything except that it was guild business." Baldar leaned forward, his voice heavy, deep. "When three of your keso's highest placed guardians come in needing healing, I know where to look for the cause."

Arimeso swallowed a lump in her throat, and swept her hands across her desk. "I was aware of the first, a'Baldar, because you 'commed me. But not of the others."

"A'Taso, I deal mostly with ills of the body, not the mind. But there is something dire happening with the keso. I understand discipline, punishment, rules, and oaths taken. But I cannot countenance the abuse that is hovering over your guild."

"I will look into it, a'ke. That I promise you."

Baldar clasped his hands in his lap. "It is not to me you must promise, a'Taso. I am resigning my place in your house and will be relocating to Himadi when it is open."

"Baldar," Arimeso whispered. "A'ke, this...this is an aberration. It was short-lived and is ending. You need not go."

"You are blinded by your bond, a'Taso, though it pains me to say such an offensive thing to one I respect. Kusik's abuse of his guild is far from new. It has simply gained strength since you allowed a'Cara to reside. I do not see it waning."

"But Cara is gone. And now, so is Rodani."

"Yes, I was told. But Kusik's depredations are the last bag on the saddle. I find myself looking for a different path, new skills, and new knowledge. I believe I will find what I seek there." He stood and bowed, low and long. "I will not leave tonight. I will spend another month here, and a month or two with the healers in Hadaman. By that time, Himadi should be open."

Arimeso collapsed back into her chair as Baldar left the room. In a few minutes, Kusik returned. She held up her hand.

"Leave me alone."

***

Rodani rode his benatac late into the night and nearly into a frothing fit. As the sky began to lighten, he offloaded his bags, turned the mare toward home, and tapped her rump. There was water nearby, and the beasts had noses as sharp as their teeth. She would find her way home. *He* would have to nurse his wounds.

He'd chosen his stopping place with some care. Just an hour or two further east was the hamlet of Endolan, a sleepy village that provided Soldan with birds and small game and clothing made of leather. There was no guild. Boats could be bought for a fireside tale. *Oh, the tales I could tell.*

By the time he made it into the village, the sun was up and warming his face. How long had it been since he'd seen a sunrise? Ages, it felt like. Somewhere along this morning's walk, a weight had dropped from his shoulders. He couldn't truthfully say danger had passed, but it had receded into a distance that allowed Rodani to breathe more easily than he had in many months. Surely, no guardians would look this far afield for him, despite his unusual eye coloring. Surely no one would bother to remark upon it.

A small general store stood near the village center. Rodani walked in. Maintaining propriety, he placed his own bags on the floor in front of the shop's counter, then trod the narrow aisles. There wasn't much he needed, having raided the re-use room and his facilities for body and clothing care. He still had the analgesic smoke powder and varigestra from Tendiman's apothecary. He had plenty of travel food, thanks to Cassig's generosity. Now, boating shoes would be welcome. Specially made not to disintegrate in sea water, with a pebbly sole, it might keep him from a broken leg—or worse.

He lifted a pair and held them up to his feet. That would do. And a long strip of gauzy fabric that worked to dim the sun's glare on water. He remembered that from training. And, of course, a few fishing supplies. *And do not forget a map of the islands, fool.* He paid with two copper coins. A few other coins hung from a bag on his belt. The rest of his life's savings hugged his waist in the coin belt under the shirt he wore.

It seemed strange to be wearing non-guild clothes, held up with a non-guild belt, and wearing simple shoes instead of boots. Only a knife hung from his waist. That raised no eyebrows here, twitched no ears. Fish could not be gutted quickly with fingernails. His other weapons were stored in a smaller bag.

"A'sel," he addressed the shopkeeper, "I am in need of a small boat, a used one in decent condition. Nothing for deep water, just coastal use."

"Au, you must see the fishmonger on the pier, a'sel. He will have something for you."

Rodani bowed, grabbed his package and bags, and found the entrance to the pier at the water's edge.

"Yes, yes, a'sel, over here," the fishmonger urged him toward a rickety dock. "I have one right here. Perfect for coastline fishing. Newly refurbished and ready to ride the waves." A small, powered boat rocked at dock. Twice his height in length, nothing to be proud of. Seaworthy?

Rodani looked it over, cudgeling his brain to remember what was important. "Is there a way to see the bottom of the boat?"

The man tapped his chest with his fist. "Au, a'sel, you wound me. Would I tell you untruths? The goddess take me now if I would do such a dishonorable deed to a man such as you."

Tired with more than the need for sleep, Rodani rubbed his eyes. "If it is as worthy as you say it is, a'sel, I will come back with an extra copper for you. If it leaks or breaks, I will come back for just recompense." He glanced at the boat and back to the man. "Do we understand each other?"

"Truly we do, a'sel. Unquestionably." The seller bobbed up and down on his toes. "Two silver, please, honorable." Rodani handed them over. "Shall I assist you?"

"I must see what I can do for myself, first. But I thank you."

Rodani stepped gingerly into the boat and found, as expected, that he had no sea legs. Wellaway, they would appear—or they would not. He started the boat and turned to watch the propeller spin. It moved easily, without fits or starts. He ran his fingers along the boat's seams at the bottom that he could see. They were dry. The shipwrights and metalworkers earned their coins, it seemed. And it was well his people still had cartons left of the energy cells made on their home planet. Those tiny miracles powered their 'coms, their radios, and the carriages bought from humans. And boats.

Rodani pulled out his map. "Would you tell me where the best fishing is among the islands, a'sel?"

The fishmonger's eyes went wide. "I do not give out secrets, a'oto," he said, scandalized. "I keep them!"

Rodani stopped and thought, refolding his map. He inclined his head. "Please forgive me for my offense, a'sel. I withdraw the question." He bowed. "Your integrity is a great gift from Sela."

The man bowed in return. "You honor me, a'sel. I wish you good fortune."

"And you as well."

Rodani backed the boat out of the tiny harbor and turned east. It was still a hand of days or so before the full moon. He had time to watch for where others congregated at dawn and dusk, alerting him to areas he should avoid.

NINE

Three days it took him to find an island that would suit. South of the border, it sat a little aside of the rest of the island chain, the better to avoid the fishhunters' routes. A trickle of fresh water ran from an underground stream near the north end of the island, under the deep cover of trees.

Rodani sat crouched in the rain this morn. The fire wouldn't light, even under its makeshift canopy of leaves and tree limbs. Last night's full moon kept him awake with apprehension of what today would bring. He kept falling back to his guild training, but nothing eased the burn in his stomach or the hands that wanted to clench. His ears twitched with every snap and rustle in the soggy trees that surrounded him.

So far, his 'com remained obstinately silent this morning. He placed it on a log, then carried it around, then clipped it to his belt, then tucked it inside his bag as a squall of rain passed over him. As he waited, a small furry animal poked its nose out from under a bush. Rodani tossed it a piece of fish. Skittish and wary, the animal crawled forward, grabbed it, and ran off.

Did she know today was the first day after the larger moon's full phase? Surely, she would remember the letter he'd sent home with her. Would she seek him out today, as he had told her? *Maybe not,* he thought morosely. Assuredly, she was resting indoors somewhere, a cup of hot tea at her elbow and a book in her hand, as he had seen her so many times in her study at Barridan. Surely, she was waiting for more pleasant weather before wandering the islands in an open boat.

He nibbled on the fish he'd caught and cooked the night before and chewed on a piece of dried meat from his travel bag. He double- and triple-checked the channel his 'com was set on. Nine, he had written in his letter. She would remember, he declared to himself. As the rain lightened to a mild patter, he stretched out his legs,

105

unwrapped the binding Baldar had put on his chest, and considered climbing the tree and into his covered hammock for a nap.

Rodani hadn't realized how exhausted he'd become in the last few months. From the changes she'd wrought in his life, his double-bond, the rage of his guild cohorts, and the havoc and pain they had caused him (and Cara, he reminded himself). And the punishment due, and the knowledge that it was inescapable if he wished to remain in his world. Yes, it took a toll on his health, mental and physical. Even in Cara's arms after one of their exquisite joinings, the future had hovered about his ears and skittered through the fears that lay uneasy in the back of his mind.

These handful of days among the islands had calmed him, allowed him a measure of rest and healing. Allowed him to enjoy the hope that replaced the rising angst of Barridan. But today it was back. Today was the first day that he might hear Cara's voice whisper to him from his 'com.

She may be busy. It may be tomorrow. Or the next day. Or the one after that. What if she couldn't find a boat? What if she couldn't afford one? What if the 'com had been broken in transit or afterwards? What if it had been stolen from her...or confiscated? What, he thought with a deepening dread, if she had notified Chendal that she'd changed her mind, but the message had missed him?

Cease, fool. Wipe the sprinkles from your face and gather the remnants of your patience.

He prodded at the dead fire and clicked his firestarter. Behind its telltale rasp he heard a second sound. He froze.

Did his ears trick him? He ran back to the 'com and grabbed it in trembling fingers. Was it Cara, calling for him? Did he miss it? He waited, breathless, watching for six minutes to pass. Five. Four. Three. Two. One. Zero.

"Aisu."

He stared at the 'com in his hand, then ran to the cove, heedless of creeping vines and tree roots, heedless of the raindrops that splattered down from the leaves he brushed by. Undid the boat's rope. Tossed it in. Climbed in. Started the motor. Swept aside the camouflage net he'd made to hide it. More sprinkles.

Out in the water, he scanned the coast with his 'com, searching for a signal.

"Aisu."

Hands shaking, he flipped a switch. "Kia." *Au*, that he could say the erinai, knowing she would hear! *Au*, that all the pieces of his plan had held together, and she was soon within his reach. Would she do as he'd asked? Still the boat and wait, silent? It didn't seem to be in her nature to sit quietly while others moved.

But she was out there. The 'com beeped. He noted the readout and headed west toward land. Straight ahead? No, slightly north. On the Selandu side of the chain of islands?

His heart beat rapidly behind his sore carapace as he fought against the waves. The boat rocked in tandem with them, making him lurch from side to side. Rain created concentric circles around him in the water.

Where are you, ki'tana?

He checked the readout, jogged north, then west again. Was that a boat? He wiped his face. It was nothing much but a speck on the misty horizon. He checked the 'com again. Correct direction. Must be her. Will be her. Has to be her.

He drove his boat closer as waves crashed into the prow. Flipped the switch again. "Look east."

A minute passed. The 'com spat back at him. "Is that you?"

He knew that voice. Now it came clearly through the airwaves. The accent. The lilt of happiness. He even heard the breathless expectancy. Now, he could see her standing. Sea spray splashed him as the boat raced toward her. As he neared, he yanked at the steering wheel and brought his boat side-by-side to hers.

She was as wet and bedraggled as he, but her smile stretched from ear to ear. She bobbed on her toes as he roped the two boats together. When he jumped over to her, she threw her arms out.

"Aisu! Aisu! It's you!"

Rodani swept her up in his arms and held her cold, sopping body to his.

"Kia, my mate," he whispered.

"You're here. You're here! Oh, gods!" She squeezed him tightly and wrapped her legs around his waist. "I'm going to rain, Rodani," she said, laughing.

"If I could, kia, I would," he replied into her hair. His hand reached for the nape of her neck. Yes, there was the clip he'd made. His fingers recognized the shapes.

In the wet, in the rain, in the rocking, drifting boat, Rodani had never felt happier in his life.

His life.

It was right there in his arms, whispering words he hadn't yet learned.

"You still wear the earrings I made you."

"Oh, yes," Cara said into the side of his face. "Every day."

The rain continued to sprinkle over them as the boat rocked beneath Rodani's feet.

"Shall we get dry?" he asked.

Cara loosened her arms and looked at him. "Where?"

"Follow me."

She smiled. "Anywhere."

Rodani climbed back and unroped their boats. As they sped east, he looked behind repeatedly to see that she kept up. Almost, it was a dream. He had to keep reassuring himself that he was awake. This was not a child's story of daring-do, or a young man's fantasy. This was reality, and he'd paid for it with fresh scars, the loss of his guild partner, his duty, house, and taso, as well as a damaged relationship with his sister. He looked back one last time before they entered the cove. "Worth the price," he whispered.

Rodani lifted the netting for Cara to maneuver her smaller boat alongside. There was room, barely, for them both in the curving shallows.

Cara studied the net. "You made this?"

"Yes. I thought it was necessary."

She turned to him. "You made the hammock yourself, too, didn't you?"

He smiled. It felt good to his face. "You did not know?"

"No, but I shouldn't be surprised."

Rodani studied the sky before leading her inward to his small camp. "There is more rain to come."

"Yes. The forecast said it would rain all tonight and into the morning." She dropped her bag on top of a log.

Rodani perched his rear on a stump, and without asking, Cara crawled into his lap to straddle him. "I'm sorry, aisu," she said, her voice breaking. "I'm going to fall apart. Give me a little time, please." She wrapped her arms around him as far as they would go and began to rain in earnest. Her great sobs broke his heart, but he held her through each of them and out the other side, all the while ignoring the shivers borne of his own emotions.

Good goddess and Temi's knives, it felt right for her to be here, held tight to his chest. How many times had they sat together, clinging to each other as the world clawed at them? And never for a better reason. He spoke no words, having learned that sometimes none were necessary and, equally, sometimes were ineffective. He simply sat with patience and waited with her as his own anticipatory nerves calmed as well.

After a time, she quieted and chuckled into his shirt. "Now if the sky would just stop raining." She released her tight grip and stared up at the trees, then down around their feet.

He waved a dismissive gesture at the dripping fire pit. "I hope you ate before your search."

His bonded mate grinned up at him. "I'm not hungry for food."

His eyes pulsed with lascivious expectations, and his ears twitched. "What do you hunger for, ki'tana?"

"Oh, whatever you have waiting, ready to go."

"Go where?"

She placed her palm on his face. "Where it belongs, aisu."

Cara followed him up the tree he climbed and into the hammock and under its canopy. Rodani stroked her face, then reached for her blouse. She stopped him and began to unbutton his shirt.

"Let me...first. Like you did me our first time."

He lowered his arms and waited. Cara undressed him one button at a time, with an occasional glance at his face. His pupils were already pulsing, slowly. She tugged on his sleeves so that he could pull his arms out. She laid the shirt over a branch. She'd learned the hard way that resting clothes on the top or bottom cords of the hammock before lovemaking made for an unnecessary trip down to retrieve them afterwards.

Rodani shifted around so that she could pull off his pants. She laid them on the branch without looking, so intent she was on his bare body. He had to grab them to keep them from falling off. But he only smiled as she reached for him. For his skin. For his warmth. For those magical hands.

He peeled her clothes off as she explored him. When she leaned back, he buried his face in her breasts. Cara wrapped her arms around his head, running her hands down his hair and over his broad shoulders.

He lifted his chest and ran his palms down her neck, over her breasts, and down across her abdomen. Chills ran up her body at his touch. His fingers meandered through her triangle of hair and down between her thighs in a touch that was almost a tickle. He lifted her knee and kissed her inner thigh in several places. He knew more was allowed in her culture, but early Enclave teachings were difficult to ignore. Instead, he used his palm and fingers to tease, to please, to entice.

Cara caressed everything within reach, and started to move toward more, to return some of the pleasure he was giving her. But he splayed his hand on her stomach and gently pushed her back down. He leaned over and kissed her lips, then eased a knee between her legs.

She opened for him, and he positioned himself at her entrance, raising up and locking his arms. He gazed into her eyes as he pushed, slowly, slowly.

"Aisu. Gods." She clutched at his waist, his hips, urging him to move. He resisted her entreaty, breathing heavily.

His pupils continued to pulse as he drew out of her channel and back in. Out and in. Out and in.

Warmth and friction created waves of desire through her body. His mouth closed and opened as he pushed against her, his breath audible in her ears.

"Did you think of me at night?" he asked, as he continued to move.

"Every night, every morning, every afternoon."

He began to smile, but it turned into a rictus of pleasure as he pressed hard and held still. "What did you do for your desires?" He moved again, a little faster. "Did you pleasure yourself?"

How could she answer, while feeling what he was doing for her? He knew; she was breathing as deeply as he. But he waited, listening, never stopping the exquisite internal strokes he was giving her.

"Yes," she said finally. "A couple of times. Mostly, I waited for you."

Rodani dropped down on one elbow and placed his thumb on her sweet spot, circling.

Warmth, powerful. "Not too much, not too soon," she pleaded as he watched her. "Ride me, please. Faster."

He removed his thumb and rested on both arms, increasing his speed a little, and a little more, and a lot more, until the hammock shook and swayed with their frantic movements. Enveloped in their mutual lust, Cara couldn't keep quiet. And Rodani, normally reticent until the end, gasped and groaned above her.

Rodani slowed his motion, panting. "Goddess above," he swore.

Cara ran her hands over his chest, then reached down and plied her fingers along his shaft. He hissed and closed his eyes.

"You can reach the top first, if you need to," Cara offered. "I won't mind."

"No," he replied, pressing his pelvic bone against hers. "Not this time." He moved his hips up and down against her, pressing firmly, right where that pressure needed to be.

"Ohhh." It wasn't a gasp. It wasn't a moan. It was a large helping of nirvana. An itch, that wonderful itch, began to form. Her legs spasmed.

Rodani sped up at this familiar signal, keeping his hips at the correct angle as he swung into and out of her. She began to scream in staccato cries. Her music in his ears brought his own crest to rush through his body with growls and man-sized cries of his own.

And they fell quiet, clutching at each other while their pleasures faded and love caught up to lust, then surpassed it.

Eyes closed, Cara whispered to him. "I don't think that ride will ever be repeated, aisu."

He bent his head to hers. "Shall we try?"

***

The rising sun filtered through the treetops. Cara clambered out of the hammock, silently lamenting her lack of grace in the act. As she climbed down the tree, her thighs stretched and twinged, reminding her of the night's activities. She stopped to smile and look below at the arrangement of the camp Rodani had made for them. Logs for seats. A fire pit. Mats, dishes, utensils. A fishing pole, a few tools, a blanket hanging from a branch to dry. A long length of loosely woven fabric.

She dropped to the ground and made use of the latrine several feet away. The ground was damp from dew and yesterday's rain. The trees swayed in languid waves of winds, dancing to their own inner rhythms. The sea breeze blew her hair around her face in wisps. The smell of fish surrounded her.

A noise behind her interrupted her musings. Rodani walked up and laid his fishing pole against a tree. The morning's meal was already gutted and headless. Cara pulled a couple of potatoes from her carry sack and cut them into slices, laying them across a grid of wires he'd found somewhere. She arranged them on the fire with the fish next to it.

"What will you do today?" she asked.

"Drink the varigestra tea."

"Ooops!"

He smiled at her. "I expected it. And fish for our dinner. Sit with you and hear your stories. Nap with you in the breezes."

Cara stirred the fire and added a handful of twigs. "Rodani, I'll have to go back to land for a couple of days."

Rodani sat himself on a nearby stump. "Why?"

"To earn money. I have a job that I do on rest-days."

"What do you do?"

She tossed the question as if her next answer were nothing important. "Dance. Drum. A local couple plays music south of town, and I help them."

"For what do you need money? We have what we need. And I can hunt."

"Not south of the border, you can't. And what will we do for vegetables? And bread?" She shook the wire grid and used a knife to shift the fish and potato. "Aisu, there are hunters and farmers and children everywhere beyond the town. You can't hide from someone you don't know is there. They'll see you."

"Then I will go north to hunt when we need meat."

Confused, her face drew taut. "And be away from me while you do. I can accept that. But also, for the two days I perform, I will be away from you and earn the money for other things we need. We can both contribute."

Rodani stared into the fire, hands between his knees. "I did not know you could drum."

Cara smiled, but his demeanor set some flags waving. "You saw me tap my hands along with music more than once in Barridan. I'm not great at it. I'm better at other things. But I can keep a rhythm going."

Rodani's hands clenched and twisted together. "You dance for others."

"I dance for whatever audience shows up."

Now he looked away. "Men watch you dance."

And it came to her. "Men, women, and children, Rodani. And now I know why you don't want me earning."

Here was the genesis of his pique. Jealousy. It really was a new dawn. A new set of expectations and boundaries to be set. *'Ware the minefield, fem. Don't blow it up.*

"I danced in the gatherings in Barridan, aisu. Next to Serano. Remember? Everyone watched me."

He glanced at her, then his gaze slid away. "I was there to watch over you."

Cara locked her arms about her waist. "Aisu, I was dancing for food money before I ever met you. I'll dance for it now. I don't have another way to earn money at this point. Not in any way that I would wish to."

"You could quilt."

"I could. But I have no place like my rooms in Barridan to work in. I have only one small room. And if I did it for money, I would have to spend five or six days out of seven, working."

Rodani's eyes drifted over the fire, the greenery around them, the small items strewn around their feet.

"Is that what you wish?" she continued. "For me to be away from you six days, and with you, one? Or, with you five days, and away, two? Which is better for us?"

"I disapprove of men watching you dance."

"You disapprove of human men watching me dance."

"Human men are more likely to approach you for your attentions."

"And I'll refuse them, just as I did Serano and Litelon."

Rodani's face went to mask. It seemed the mere mention of those two men brought up memories he'd rather not face. Not that she blamed him.

"Rodani, I've already refused one man several times, just since I've returned."

His eyes went wide, eyebrows lifted. "Who?" He leaned forward.

She sliced her hand downward slowly in the guild *cease* gesture. "Someone I used to have an affinity with. He wished to restart it. But I'm your bonded mate, not his woman to play with."

He took a heavy breath.

"Why do you worry so?"

"Because it is in the front of my face now, kia, not in the back of my mind."

"Two days out of seven, aisu. That seems a good deal to me. Money for food, for drink, for medicines we might need. For rope. For netting to fish with. For replacement clothes."

His mouth thinned into a line, his protruding lower lip disappearing in front of his teeth.

Cara knelt in front of him. "Trust me, aisu."

Rodani pulled her to his chest and wrapped his arms around her. "It is my duty to protect you, kia."

"But you can't, here. Not very well."

He fell silent. His fingers curled into the hair on her scalp.

"Rodani, I wish you to know something about my dancing."

The silence continued, then he drew a breath. "My ears are empty."

"When I dance, I don't see my audience. I don't listen to anything they say. All I'm aware of is the movement of my body and the rhythm of the music." She placed one hand on the side of his neck, and rubbed her cheek against his shirt. "I'm sure there are men who watch me dance the same way you watch me. And have similar thoughts. But I don't dance for *them*. I dance for me. For me, and the coins I earn."

She felt his chin lift from the top of her head, where it had rested. "Coins earned because men desire you."

"Coins earned because I entertain my audience. And it helps earn my companion musicians' money, too, so they can feed their baby. It's a group project. I don't dance every song, either. Only about one in four. I think you exaggerate some, aisu."

"If I saw this display, maybe I would think differently of it."

"And how would you do that?"

"Hide in the trees."

"The trees are too far away to afford you enough detail to tell much. And the only light is some lanterns. Half of what they see when I dance is in their imaginations."

"Do you dance in that skirt you had at Barridan?"

"No. That skirt is only for you, aisu. Only for you."

Rodani released some of the grip of his arms and looked sideways into the trees.

Cara held him under his arms and shook him, just a little of that solid mass. "Should I be offended at that look? Do you wish me to keep the skirt on this island, so you'll be certain? So that you know I don't lie?"

He turned back to her, looked down to her, with an expression that tightened her gut. "I wish you would take my concerns seriously. I wish you would refrain from dancing."

Now, she caressed his face. "Aisu, I give no one the right to touch me but you. You are my mate, and access to me is your privilege—my gift to you. No one else has my consent."

His face warped into something near a snarl. "And what if someone takes without your consent?"

"Then that's a crime. Rodani, that could happen to any woman— or man—at any time of day, on any day of their lives. It has little to nothing to do with dancing."

Rodani stood up, forcing her to slide off his lap. Stunned, she watched as he walked away.

"Aisu?"

He stood looking out to sea, back straight, silent.

"Rodani?" Should she go to him? Stay back? Give him space, or touch him?

After a frightful few minutes, he returned. "When do you leave?"

She looked for the sun's position in the sky. "A few hours. Before lunch, I teach the town's bartender to speak Selandi."

"Why?"

"Because he's moving to Himadi. I'm helping him do that."

Rodani looked at the fire at his feet, and let his arms drop to his sides. "I have no wish to argue after such a reunion as we just had. Do what you planned, kia, but I do not promise I will be silent on the subject."

Cara stepped forward and lifted her arms. He picked her up. "When I'm back in two days," she said, "then we can nap in the breezes and exchange stories. I want to hear everything that happened to you while I was gone." She stroked his face with her fingertips. "There are more scars on your back."

"That is not something I wish to discuss."

"I have to know what they did to you, aisu."

"No. You do not."

Rodani leaned up against a tree and crossed his arms, watching Cara's boat fade toward the coastline. Already, he felt bereft, despite her assurances. Was he being stubborn? Or was she? He ached to follow, to hold her back in safety. Who knew what the men who watched her dance thought in the dark of their hearts. But what safety could he give her, skulking around the peripheries?

Anger washed through him. *Control, fool. You have not been deserted.* No, it only felt as if he had.

Not deserted, but demoted. That was the word. He understood promises, and the need to keep them. He understood that their situation had changed. But his weapons lay unused in their camp, and his urge to protect had no focus, now. It was a new feeling, and it ached.

Unsettled, uneasy, without an immediate goal, Rodani turned back to the fire and his solitary vigil. From his pack, he retrieved pen and paper. A menagerie of thoughts swarmed through his mind. What lay north. What lay in front of him. What lay in his past. What the future held in store for him. The jumbled notions wiggled like worms in the dirt and would not rest. He began to write.

Arimeso, most esteemed taso,

I truly regret my absence from your House. I beg you to forgive me, though I will understand if you do not. As your keso made it his duty to punish me every day, it was a necessary parting. He made a mockery of my guild status and a misery of my life in Barridan. His anger became not only a daily trial, but a danger to my life. Despite his wishes to the contrary, I am not ready to cross over.

Please know that I am forever indebted to you for granting me a place in your home and the opportunity to earn what respect and status I gained there. Be assured that I will speak of your wisdom, your far sight, and your good will at every occasion that presents itself. If ever we meet

in the future, I hope you may afford me some measure of consideration
for the duty and service my skills provided you.
I will honor you forever.
~ Rodani

He folded up the note and slipped it into a mail pouch he'd brought from home. Behind him, the small, furred creature padded up to the fire. It stared at Rodani expectantly.

He managed a smile. "Pleasant morn, little hunter. Have you caught anything today?"

It crept forward as Rodani held out his hand. "I am pleased you returned. Did you find yesterday's food tasty?" Carefully, he reached into his pack and brought out a bit of dried meat. The bewhiskered animal sniffed the air in front of Rodani's fingers and took a few small steps.

He clicked his tongue and moved his hand a little closer, then tossed the meat toward the animal. It bent its head and began to eat.

***

Cara let the waves take her into dock, tied off, and climbed out. Was it better that the docks were busy today? Everyone intent on their own business might keep them out of hers. Not much she could do about it either way. Just saunter. Nothing to notice here. Just some woman going about her day. She'd check a few things off her to-do list and find a corner of Nick's bar to relax in before she hauled her drums to the stage.

Unfortunately, the local irritant was already there. Mack looked up when she walked in and followed her with his eyes as she crossed to the wet bar.

"Hey, Chucko."

"Cara. How was life in the north?"

"Complicated."

He set a glass of her favorite on top of the bar. "Here comes Mack," he said under his breath.

"Oh, gods."

Mack heaved his bulk up on the stool next to her. "Where you been?"

Cara looked down at her drink, feigning ignorance.

"Can't talk? I'm just trying to be friendly."

"I know. I just need quiet time before the show. Thanks, anyway."

"Thanks for what? I haven't done anything yet." He nudged her.

Cara leaned away, resting her arm on the bar.

"Why you so cold?"

"Because I'm not in the mood for whatever you have in mind."

"What d'you mean what I have in mind? You think you know me? You read minds?"

"No, I read body language, tone of speech, and facial expressions." She glanced his way, then turned aside. "Not to mention what you said the last time you approached me."

Mack was silent for a moment. "Aww, c'mon. That was just joking."

Cara caught Chucko's glance and made a face. *Help*, it said.

Chucko bellied up behind the bar. "She's not interested, Mack. Go back to your corner. I'll bring you a mug."

Mack clenched his fist, then slid off his stool. "You better."

Cara rested her head in her hand as Mack stomped away. "I owe you one. Thanks a lot."

Chucko wiped the bar with a rag. "What did he say to you last time?"

She shook her head. "Made some nasty comment about what I might have done with Selandu men in my spare time. Said he could do me better."

"He can barely shine his own rod, let alone do better for a woman."

The sun sank. The crowd gathered. In front of only two drums, Cara rubbed her hands on her thighs in anticipation of the long haul and the drain on her energies. She had time for one last thought of Rodani before James tapped his foot to set the beat.

Drum. Dance. Drum. Dance. The crowd fell into and out of her consciousness as she focused on the music and on the movements of her body. *Entertain. Earn your keep. Go the distance,* she told herself as her palms began to burn and her feet ache. *You can do this.*

As the last song ended and Josie's voice faded out, Cara slumped her shoulders, tired and feeling guilty.

Josie caught the motion. "You get to go to bed. I have to go home and feed the baby."

Cara tossed the comment with a Selandu hand wave. *At least you didn't leave your husband to sleep alone*, she thought.

Drums safely stored behind the bar building, Cara collapsed at a table. Nick handed her a sandwich he'd saved from the evening. "Many thanks," she said.

"Tonight's take was better than last week."

"Yours or ours?"

He smiled. "Both. Tomorrow's lesson still on?"

"Sure. Gotta pay for my room."

His smile turned flat as he slipped into a chair across from her. "Chucko tells me Mack is bothering you."

Cara sipped her beer. "Yeah."

"I saw him at the edges of the crowd. I didn't like the look on his face."

"Do we ever?"

"You don't want that man after you, Cara."

She took a bite and chewed. "How do I stop him?"

Nick stretched his legs out to the side of the table, a table marred with names and dates carved by three generations of drunks.

<Flash> *Rodani in her bedroom chair, long legs within her reach. Rodani in the study, drink in hand.*

"Try Graeme," he told her. "While you were away, he got promoted to deputy sheriff. Maybe he'll listen."

Cara took another sip. "People like Mack don't listen to others."

"You need to alert them."

She sighed, letting it out slowly. "Yeah."

***

Morning found her back at the table, a glass of water her only companion. The bar wasn't officially open; no drinks were being served. But the doors were unlocked for those needing a place to congregate. Cara glanced up as a dark-haired, dark-skinned form closed in.

Suraya waved at a chair. "May I?"

"Not real talkative right now. Still half asleep."

"Is that a yes or a no?"

Cara rolled her fingers out and opened her palm, a Selandu gesture Suraya would be sure to understand.

The journalist sat down and drew out a piece of paper and pen. Cara sat back and eyed it with trepidation.

"Didn't you weasel everything out of me last time?"

"Change is the only constant, a'sel."

The unexpected term jolted her. Wrong time, wrong place.

Suraya grinned. "I saw the drawings you did of your guardians in Barridan."

Cara tossed the comment, Selandu-style.

"How did that come about?" Suraya continued.

"We were sitting around one evening, and they let me sketch them."

"No security concern for that?"

Cara cocked her head. "I guess they never thought the sketches would end up at the CSC. I don't know."

Suraya drew her palm across her paper. "I caught a glimpse of other drawings in your little notebook. What were those?"

Now a shrug of her shoulders. "Just other stuff."

"Oh, I doubt that," Suraya responded. "I'd love to see them."

Cara's gaze roamed the room. She shook her head.

"Why?"

Another head shake.

Suraya leaned forward. "What in the deep sea did they do to you?"

No answer.

"Did they hurt you?"

"No. Not at all."

Suraya studied her with a doubtful expression. "Well, something happened."

"Lots of things happened. I was there for seven months."

"Tell me, please. I want to know."

Cara glanced at her under lowered brows.

"Whatever you're willing to tell me. That's all."

"Cara?"

She looked up to see Nick leaning against the wet bar, flash cards in hand. Turning to Suraya, she said, "Gotta go."

Suraya strolled up to the bar as Cara and Nick went into his office.

She turned to Chucko, who was prepping cheeses and meats for the lunch crowd. "What's that about?" She nodded her head at the door.

"Nothing to do with you."

Suraya raised an eyebrow. "I thought he just had another kid."

"He's got plenty. No need for more."

"So, what's up?"

Chucko laid the knife down and glared at her. "Haul sail."

***

A cramped group of offices in an unassuming east-side one-story building held the human version of guild guardians. Sheriffs held the only guns still owned by humans, kept order, and knocked heads when necessary. But knowing what Cara knew now, there was no real comparison between the two.

Graeme Wilson bit into his sandwich. Brown-haired, green-eyed, stocky, with muscles that bulged on his arms, he pointed to the chair in front of his desk.

"Congratulations on your upgrade," Cara ventured into his silence.

He chewed thoughtfully. "What's on your mind?"

"Mack."

Graeme rolled his eyes and put his sandwich on a plate. "What's he done now?"

"Nothing terrible. Yet. But he said some very rude things to me some days ago and tried to cozy up to me yesterday afternoon. Chucko had to run him off. Nick said he was watching me pretty closely last night."

"Lots of men do," he said with a grin.

"Not men like Mack."

"True enough. What do you expect me to do?"

Cara shrugged. "Nick said to tell you. So you could be on the lookout. Let the other sheriffs know."

"Not much I can do about it 'til he breaks a law."

Cara stared at him, eyes narrowed. "Yeah. I know. I'm a woman."

"Women aren't the only people he bothers." Graeme answered with a dismissive shrug.

Cara took a deep breath. "Please?"

Graeme leaned forward and picked up his sandwich. "You keep dancing. I'll keep an eye out."

"Thanks."

ELEVEN

Rodani awoke with a start and leaned over the edge of his hammock. His eyes adjusted to the semi-dark as his ears caught the sound of movement. Down below was a shadow making its way toward the fire pit. Senses on high, he studied the shadow. *Yes.*

As he climbed down, the shadow poked at the banked fire, then turned as he reached the ground.

"Kia."

"Aisu." She held her hands up to him.

The cold that had held him in its grip for two days melted away in the warmth of her embrace.

"I missed you," she whispered.

Rodani felt her heartbeat against his chest, and her breath tickled the sensitive hairs at his ear tips.

"Are you still angry?"

He ran his hands up and down her back, comfort for himself as well as her. "Yes. But I thank all the deep dark gods you swear by that you returned safely."

"Nothing bad happened."

"And if it had?"

"What could you have done, hiding in the trees on the periphery of town?"

Rodani set her down and pulled his hands behind his back. There was the conundrum. He had to trust others to protect her. His mind searched for dangers with empty hands, and they shook when he dwelled on it.

Cara laid out a blanket. "Sit with me, please, aisu." She folded herself downward and patted the rough wool.

"I see you have more to say." Rodani sat across from her, a little space between them.

Cara scooted closer and took his hand in hers. "Yes. And I need to say it. And you need to listen, listen with our bond in mind." She began to caress his hand, as she had done in Barridan after they had been reunited by Arimeso.

"It's about boundaries, aisu. What I can expect from you, and you from me. It's not about intimacies. Not about respect or honor. Those stay the same as we had in Barridan. Those promises we made to each other." She brought his hand to her lips, then rested it on her leg. "In Barridan, you had a status high above me, and were in charge of my safety. Here, our status is on the same level. In fact, we might say neither of us has any status at all, in relation to the people on the mainland."

Rodani's face went to mask.

"No, no, aisu, wait. That's not a bad thing. It means no one tells us what to do. No one forces us." She glanced out at the trees surrounding them. "In Barridan, you gave me orders, and I accepted your right to give them because of who and what I was and who and what you were."

His pupils constricted. "I am still guild." A growl hovered in his voice.

"Yes." She clenched his hand. "Of course you are, and you always will be, aisu. But circumstances change. You're not under any orders from a taso or keso. There is no one trying to kill me here. It's just you and me. You no longer have an automatic right to give me orders. And I'm no longer required to take them. You haven't changed, aisu. I haven't changed. But the rules have.

"Remember our bond, Rodani. You can always tell me of your concerns. What they are, why you have them, and what I might do to lessen them. I'll make myself listen and take them into account. And we compromise, just like you told me when I accepted your clip. Then I'll make my decisions, and accept whatever consequences come."

"And I am forced to accept them as well. Yes?"

Caught out, she stopped to think. "Yes...just as I had to do in Barridan with your consequences."

Silence enveloped them. Then Rodani stood.

"I will walk the beach."

Cara started to rise.

He glanced at her. "No."

Her eyes widened. "No, *please*."

He didn't like the correction. That, at least, was clear on his face. She sat back and watched him disappear through the trees and into the distance. *I will not cry. I will not cry. I've done enough of that to last a lifetime.* This time, it was his change in power to eat, not hers.

The sun was over the horizon now. Cara hoped the fishing boats had gone out already. They didn't need to see a tall alien meandering across the sand as they passed by. She stoked the fire and settled a pan over it, adding a thin layer of water before covering the pan. Then she washed and sliced a melon and a spice root she'd brought back from the market and dumped them in the water.

She heard Rodani's footsteps as he returned. Angry? Accepting? It was hard to tell from sound only. *Please, aisu.*

He crossed over to the other side of the fire and knelt down, lifting the lid for a quick look. His face held no anger she could see, but he wouldn't meet her eyes. She went over to him and sat facing his side. She stroked his thigh. *<Flash> Barridan's stables after their first joining.*

"I know this is hard for you. It probably goes against everything you've spent the last thirteen years doing." She rested her other hand on his shoulder. "But for whatever peace you can find in this, I thank you."

Rodani closed his eyes, but held her hand on his thigh. She took it back and wrapped her arms around his neck. "My bonded mate," she whispered. "^I love you^."

He pulled her into his lap, and watched the fire.

***

Suraya opened the door to the bar and walked into the dim light. "Good morning," she offered.

Nick sat at a table shuffling flash cards. He turned to see who had come in. "Morning."

"Is Cara around?"

Nick rested his arm on the chair back. "No. She said she wouldn't stay here during the week."

"Why? Where does she go?"

"No idea."

"Which way did she go when she left?"

"I don't know." He looked at her from the corner of his eye. "Why?"

She shrugged. "I still have a few questions."

"You'll have to wait 'til the weekend."

"Thanks."

Suraya turned to go, then turned back and approached him. "She spent a lot of time here this weekend. Did she talk about anything?"

Nick tapped the edge of the card deck on the table. "Nothing that needs to be displayed on the community board, Suraya. Talk to her."

"What's on your flash cards?"

"You're becoming a pest. Do what I asked, or you're gonna get swatted."

Suraya smiled. "You're not a hitter. You're a lover. Is that what you two are about? Working your way through the sisters?"

Nick stood so fast his chair hit the one behind him. His eyes flashed. "No, and no. The tavern is closed. There," he pointed, "is the door."

She reared back against his heat. "No hard feelings, Nick, please. I'm just doing my job."

"Go do it elsewhere."

Suraya made her way back to her cabin. It sat, tiny and neat, at the north end of town between the news office near the sea and the CSC to the west. When she looked out her window, she could see the Himadi Hills. A familiar longing to cross them filled her heart. She loved her parents and adored her job, but her dearest dream was to live among the Selandu. She envied Cara with a guilty fervor. But the abrupt departure her fellow student had been forced to make put a damper on her dreams.

Andrew had already told her she wasn't going to Himadi House. Nor did Menachem allow her a turn in Hadaman. She sometimes wondered why she'd so diligently studied at the CSC.

A knock on her door interrupted her musings. She opened it and found herself facing her oldest brother Ahsan's taut expression.

"What's wrong?"

Ahsan brushed past her and into the room. "Shut the door."

Suraya closed it behind her, eyeing her brother warily. He stood both stiff and shaking.

"Why were you in the bar this morning?" he asked with a stare that didn't waver.

"I was looking for Cara. Were you following me?"

"You stay out of that place. It's full of evil."

Suraya knew better than to roll her eyes in front of him. "Please. The only thing it's full of is liquor, and I don't drink."

"You had better not. The gods will punish you for polluting your body with it."

She rubbed her forehead. "Ahsan..."

"If you walk into that place again, I'll demand that father order you to go to our meetings. Your soul and your place in the next world are in peril!"

"Ahsan, you can't force me into your religious sect. The town charter forbids it. You know that."

"I know what's right better than the town's founders did."

"Maybe." She opened the door again. "But the charter stands. Thank you for thinking of me."

Ahsan glared at her for one long moment, then stalked out. Suraya followed him, heading toward the news office. She collapsed in her chair and threw her notepad on the desk.

Bethamy glanced at her. "Find Cara?"

"No. She's not around."

"Why do you want her?"

"She has more stories to tell, Beth. I know she does. I want them."

"You should pay more attention to what's happening in town."

Suraya shifted her attention, leaning on her desk. "Speaking of, did you know Mack's been following Cara?"

"Just give him a wide berth."

"Is that what you'd tell her? Mack needs to do the same."

"My cousin doesn't listen to women."

"I know."

***

Rodani sat on the blanket, cleaning his knives as the furry animal sat and watched.

"What's it doing?" Cara asked. "I've never seen it before." It was maybe nine inches long, she decided as she studied it. Fuzzy, round, red-brown ears, with an equally furry body shaped like a loaf of her grandmother's bread as the animal crouched on folded back legs. It sniffed the air with a quivering nose, its eyes scanning the area for danger. Its forepaws clawed at the dirt.

"I do not know the species," Rodani told her. "It comes to visit me when I am quiet."

"Why?"

"It is looking for food."

"And you feed it?"

"Yes." He reached into the dried food bag and brought out a bit of meat. The animal crept up and snatched it from his fingers, then scampered off to the base of a nearby tree.

"Can I try?"

Wordlessly, Rodani gave her a couple of pieces of the meat. Cara held it out in enticement.

Slowly, slowly, advancing and retreating, it sniffed its way to her fingertips. Cara clicked her tongue and whispered to it. With hunched shoulders, it crept, its whiskers quivering in agitation as it neared. Cara held her breath. "Come on, little one. Come on."

Leery, the animal inched closer. She hardly dared to breathe. It pushed its nose forward, then snapped the morsel out of her palm and retreated to the greenery that surrounded their camp.

"Have you named it?" Cara asked.

"No."

She looked after it, contemplating. "I can think of a name for it."

Rodani glanced at her. "And that is?"

"Fuzz."

Rodani pursed his lips. "Fuss."

"Fuuuzz," she corrected him. "Fuzz."

"Fussss."

She smiled. "Almost."

The little hunter finished the piece of meat and waited to see if more was forthcoming, but Cara turned back to Rodani with more than skittish animals on her mind.

She slipped into his lap, careful to dodge his weapons. She reached around his neck and unhooked the clip that held his hair back from his face. Slowly, she pulled the strands over his shoulders and ran her fingers down through them. Silky, soft, silvery. She grasped one hank and ran the ends under his nostrils. He wrinkled his nose.

"Ready to exchange stories?" she asked.

"If you wish." He placed his knives behind him on the blanket.

"I do wish. So, what happened after Serano pulled me away from you?"

"There is nothing worth telling."

Cara swatted his nearest hand. "Don't tell me things you know are untrue. It hurts."

The silence built. Rodani shifted on the blanket. "I am reproved, kia. But there is nothing I wish to speak of." His breath fluttered the unruly curls on her head. "And you?"

She dragged the silence out further. "Nothing."

"Is that punishment?"

^Tit for tat.^

"And what is that?"

"I give you what you give me."

The silence spun into an uneasy détente. Rodani patted her off his lap. "Let us eat what you cooked, and I will consider your titfor."

They filled their plates, then their stomachs. Or whatever passed for a stomach in a Selandu.

Cara gestured with her fork. "Maybe the hammock would be more restful. Might induce you to tell your tale."

"Do you really wish details on my punishment, kia?" Disapproval lingered in his words.

"I already know Chendal flogged you. When he and Shisa explained the double-bond, he told me he would either flog or kill you in the end." Unblinking, she stared at his chest. "You're still here. And I know what scars you had on your back. And I've seen the crossed lines on your chest." She bent her head. "Did you know you would live?"

Rodani took a deep breath and set his plate aside. "No."

"I would have forever wondered."

"I asked Chendal to call the see-ess-see and tell you, if I did not."

"Thank you," she said softly. She reached across their painful divide and took his hand—again. "I'm glad you're here." He raised his eyes to hers, finally. She continued. "Did you begin our affinity knowing you'd get that kind of punishment?"

"I had some hope I would not, but knew very well that I could face the lash. I never thought about death, because I did not foresee what happened at the end."

"Did Kusik survive?"

"Yes."

"Tell me he treated you better."

"You told me to tell you no lies, kia."

She paused. "Arimeso?"

"Still grieving when I saw her last."

"Serano?"

He paused, lost in though—-or in feeling. "He tried to mend the breach when I returned from Tendiman. But I was too deep in the well to respond."

"The well?"

"Of my own grief. That, coupled with Kusik's renewed abuse, left me with little but breath in my body. I had nothing for any else."

"Did you visit Ikemi?"

"No. I left that issue for Hamman."

"How long were you there after Tendiman, before leaving?"

He tossed the question. "A ten-day or less."

"And Shisa?" she said softly.

His lips pursed as he looked aside. "Things are not as they were before you arrived. Likely, they never will be. But I will abide."

"What do you think they did when they found you gone?"

He smiled, finally. A small one. "Now that, I would have liked to see."

"What did you do when you left?"

"Rode a benatac east. Let it go when I thought I was close enough to my destination."

"Where was that?"

"A small village north of Soldan. I bought some supplies and the boat and went hunting for a home among the islands."

"Do you think they looked for you?"

"Nearby, probably. Farther? Likely, I was not worth the trouble or expense."

"Did you worry that I wouldn't try to find you?"

He tilted his head and looked off into the distance. "I would rather have assumed you would."

Cara drew the hand she was still holding up to her cheek. She thought back to that night at the fireplace, where Rodani had admitted his desire. "Aisu, you'll never know how I felt when I read your note. When I knew there was hope."

He placed his free hand on her knee. "You will never know the depth of pain and height of hope I felt when writing it."

"When did you write it?"

"An hour after you accepted my clip."

"Oh. Did you know it would end so soon?"

"Not until I learned an attack was imminent. Then I knew, though I still held hope for a better outcome."

"Was it worse for you before I left, or after?"

After a moment's consideration, he spoke. "Before, it was worse with the other guardians. Afterwards, those guardians were gone, but Kusik became vicious. If I had stayed, he would have killed me, or contrived my death. He blamed me for Timan. For it all, actually."

"Always in the wrong. Always. Oh," she said, leaning back. "I found out who alerted the Enclave."

An eyebrow raised. "How?"

"Litelon drove the cart we rode in. Serano mentioned it to him, and I overheard."

"What did Serano say?"

"Something about what happened was partially Litelon's fault because of what he did."

"And his reaction?"

She shook her head. "I didn't see it. I was in the back, raining my eyes out."

"Now, there is a surprise." And that brought a welcome laugh. "Your story, now, kia."

"There really isn't much to tell. I rained all the way to Soldan and most of the way home to Glaniad. My brother and Ambassador Menachem met me there. I spent the night at my parents' house, and left the next day when my mother told me to cut my hair."

Two eyebrows raised at that admission. "Would you have?"

"Not after I read your note, no. Absolutely not. I'd sleep on the beach before I did that."

"Where *did* you sleep?"

"That man whom I'd had an affinity with before allowed me to sleep on a cot in his cabin."

"And...?"

"He wished to continue it. Asked many times. I turned him down many times. Finally, the day before you and I found each other, he threw me out."

Rodani sat up straighter. "Threw you?"

Cara waved her hands in front of him. "No, no, bad interpreting on my part, aisu. He made me leave. Right away. In the rain."

"Where did you go?"

"There's a bar across from where we perform on weekends. The bartender has a couple of rooms over the bar. I'll be staying there the two nights a week that I'm on the mainland."

"Are you safe there?"

"Yes."

"From the bartender you are teaching, as well?"

"Yes," she said emphatically. She stared at the fire, which was burning down to embers. "Oh, I forgot! Your candlesticks, aisu! And the money belt. You put them in my trunk. Thank you!"

Rodani paled into embarrassment and poked at the embers. "You keep them at the bar?"

"No. They're too important for that. I left the candlesticks in my trunk. My father is keeping it safe for me."

"And you wear the belt every day?"

"Yes. But most of the coins I left in the trunk. There were too many to carry around. I put some of my own earnings in the belt now. How did you know to put them in the trunk? You didn't have time after Arimeso told us."

"Dire anticipation, kia."

Cara pulled on his hand. "Hold me again. Please?"

"I suggest the hammock. I need to do more than hold you."

Need was not a word he used often for himself. She stood up, taking his hand with her.

Up high, swaying with their movements, Rodani cradled her tightly before he let his hands roam. And glued himself to her at the end as their racing hearts slowed. Too much change, too much insecurity, could topple even a guardian's equanimity. The last months at Barridan had proved it to him, and Glaniad was proving it anew. He felt Cara's arms tighten around him and knew he was not the only one storm-tossed.

TWELVE

As Cara's boat headed toward the shore for a second time, Rodani's eyes roamed over their meager belongings. But his mind lay elsewhere. He remembered Cara's tales of some young men, their high mating drives, their drunken revelries, and her dismay at the treatment she sometimes received at their hands. If the beach lands were forbidden to him, how could he protect her? There were no safe rooms to hide her in, no windows to brick up. There was no chance of stalking the streets of her town, secure in his guild status and the weapons he openly carried. His task, it seems, was to either hide in the trees of their island home or hide in the trees at beachside, watching her dance and drum, waiting for a hungry reprobate to paw at her and suggest things he couldn't bear to think of.

He was no good at being helpless. Or pretending to be. His childhood had taught him the futility of that. He walked through his memories of guild training, searching for a viable weapon. One that could be learned quickly.

He climbed into his boat and dropped a few items on the bench, then began his own trip to the coast. He went north first, the better to avoid any humans, then turned west. Just a ramble out in the Selandu-side islands, that is all. No notice, no problems. *Please, no problems.*

A dot that was the dock at Endolan came into view, transforming into a motley row of wooden slats that bobbed in the waves. Rodani berthed his boat and stepped out as the fishmonger strode down to meet him.

"Au, a'sel," the man greeted him. "And how is the boat? The fishing? Have you enjoyed your time away from civilization?" He waved his arm past the small village as if it were Hadaman at its finest.

"I have, thank you. And here is the coin I promised you. May I know your name?"

The man didn't hesitate. "Mandai, a'sel. And yours, if it would not offend?"

Rodani stiffened. *Fool*, he thought. *Now, what do you do?* "My name is Aldano." *Remember it, lest you make yourself a larger fool.*

"And may I serve you, today, a'Aldano?"

"I am seeking supplies. Travel food, mainly. Fresh, also, if it is available."

"Au, I have more fish than you could eat in a lifetime, a'sel. Here for your choosing." He led the way to a canopy that kept the morning sun off barrels of fish, some fresh, some dried.

Rodani pulled a small sack from his pocket. "Fill this, please. Dried fish. I will visit the general store for other food items."

Mandai bowed. Rodani took the path to the village. The store looked as it had earlier. Various and sundry items useful for the villagers, and a short wall of those a traveler might need. Rodani made quick work of his choices, preferring not to linger where he might be noticed. But he searched the traveler's bins and shelves more carefully. No. What he sought could not be found here. Not unexpected, but it meant seeking help. Trusting someone.

Rodani paid the grocer and made his way back to the fishmonger's stall.

"Honored Mandai," he began, "I am in need of your assistance, if you would consent."

"A'sel." Mandai straightened and lifted his chin.

"I am in need of a certain…item. One that I cannot search for myself. It may be found in Soldan…if an enterprising man might visit a specific shop that I name."

"My ears are empty, a'sel."

"It is a weapon I need. A simple one, not too expensive, not one that would be much remarked upon if this man were to purchase it. I would, of course, pay for its cost and for the trouble of procuring it."

"A weapon."

"Sai. A telescoping baton, about this long when closed." Rodani spread his hands a foot apart. "Heavy for its size. Useful in a fight when one wishes to remain somewhat distant from the attacker."

Mandai stared at Rodani with renewed interest. "A'sel," he replied slowly, reticent. "I must be bold for a moment. I beg you not to take offense."

Rodani's pupils constricted, but he waited.

"Are you in trouble, a'Aldano?"

He stiffened in reaction, his senses in high alert. "Why do you ask?"

"There has been a stranger in black seeking you. Dark eyes, he said. The bearing of a guardian, he said, but likely dressed in common clothing. Coin was offered for your whereabouts, a'tem."

A'tem. Rodani froze for an instant. "And you said?"

Mandai bowed his head. "Not a word, a'tem. But I knew of whom he spoke."

Breathe. "Why did you not say?"

"I am no fool, a'tem. I know evil when I see it, smell it. It is not in you. Your life is your own to live."

His expressions closed down into a mask. "When was this?" *Panic is not the way. Calm. Calm.*

"Two days ago."

"The grocer. Did he speak to the grocer?"

Mandai pulled out a stool and sat. "There is a reason no one in this village will speak of you, a'tem. Temichi from Soldan have visited here more than thrice. Each time, they mock our people, our simple lives here. Twice, a woman has been attacked, a'tem, in a most abominable way. We hold no respect for those who would plunder what little we have. We cannot stop them, nor will we ever assist them."

Rodani glanced at the village outskirts. "I am sorrowed for the lack of honor they have shown you, a'Mandai. I would stop them if I could, but it would take more power than I have."

"And I can see that you have the honor and courtesy they lack. They will not learn of you from us. Walk safely, here."

He closed his eyes and bowed deeply. "I owe you a debt I cannot repay, a'sel."

"No one will ask for it." Mandai shifted on his stool. "And this weapon I need find?"

Rodani pulled out a silver coin and a copper one. "Another copper awaits you, if you return with it."

Mandai pocketed the coins. "I will endeavor."

"When should I return?"

"Two days. I have an errand in Soldan, myself. The name of the shop?"

"Marketta's."

***

Cara tied her boat at the southernmost dock, wanting the relative privacy of the ass-end of the chaos that were the Glaniad docks. She grabbed her weekend bag and slipped into the line of trees along the beach.

Nick was at the bar, as expected. He waved her inward. "You found a bed this week?"

"Oh, such as it was, yeah."

"Where?"

Damn the man's curiosity. Cara waved him off and headed up the stairs to her cramped room with a very welcome lock on it. She dumped her clothes and drumsticks on the bed, then crawled onto the mattress.

Rodani. She could still feel her husband's arms around her, his body inside hers, his warm breath on her face. How she'd missed him.

But, oh, he wasn't happy, that had been clear. Even if he did expect her to stay with him every minute of every day, that was hardly possible. No more than the opposite could have been in Barridan. He had spent hours and hours away from her at times, off doing guardian things and weapon things and meeting things and who-knows-what things while she sat in her rooms to quilt. Now the sandal was on the other foot, and he would have to wear it, despite the guilt she felt for disappointing him.

Tired from their pre-weekend intimate activities, Cara dozed on the bed until later, when there was a rap on the door.

"Crowd's gathering."

"Thanks, Nick," she mumbled, then stumbled into a quick wash and change of clothes. It wouldn't do to dance in raggedy shorts. Rodani wouldn't care so much what she wore when she was with him. But her slavering horde of admirers would.

Once again, she borrowed Nick's cart to roll her drums to the stage. Once again, she hefted them up the steps and settled in behind James and Josie. This time, Cara tapped out the tempo, and James picked an intricate tune on his acoustic strings. Josie took a deep breath.

Almost idly, Cara looked around the crowd. She knew most everyone by face, a large number by name. No Kimi, she noticed, and felt bad for her littlest sister. She should take time to talk to her. But how to get her away from the house? Maybe Nick or Chucko would have some ideas.

When it came time to dance, she imagined herself back in Barridan, in her study in front of the fire. A bit of melancholy drifted into her mind.

When the dance ended, cheers and claps shook her out of it. *No, this is better.* Fewer rules. Room to move. Familiar faces and colors, scents and sounds. And Rodani was safe. At least as long as he kept hidden.

And there was Mack, off to the side. She kept her eye on him, surreptitiously. He kept his eye on her, but kept his distance as well.

Late the next morning brought Cara out of her slumber and down into the bar, a sack in her hand. Chucko nodded a greeting. As she reached for the door to go out, it opened in front of her.

"Just the woman I was looking for." Suraya smiled.

Cara stopped in her tracks. "Bright morn," she said in Selandi. Maybe it was time to brighten her own morn. She was safe, had coins in her pockets, her husband waited for her not a mile away, and the sun shone brightly.

"And to you, a'sel," the journalist replied. "Are you feeling better?"

"Maybe."

"Maybe that maybe will get me another interview. Maybe?"

Cara snorted. It wasn't a bad thing for another to enjoy word games. She knew too few who appreciated them. "And maybe you're a stone in my shoe or maybe a trial on my patience." But she smiled in return to take the sting from her words. "What are you bugging me about, now?"

"Ah! There's Gerry again."

"I just got up," she said, emphasizing every other word.

"It's noooon." Suraya drew out the word as if it were water from a desert well.

"And it takes time for the post-performing adrenaline to fade at night, too."

Suraya looked down the street they were walking, and behind them. "Oh. Where are you headed?"

"Laundromat."

"Um, did you know Mack was back there?"

Cara's gut clenched, and a chill ran up her spine. "Good gods and Temi's knives," she managed to whisper. She couldn't risk a peek. "Is he following?"

"I don't dare look again."

"Shit."

"Will you tell me a story? It'll get your mind off him."

Cara regarded her out of the corner of one eye. "If you stay with me while he's nearby. And if you help me with my clothes."

"I can't wash and write," Suraya said with humor.

"You have a good memory. Write it up after and let me look at it next time. I'll correct it."

"Sai. Verelin."

They entered the laundry facility and took a place at one of the wringer hand-wash machines. Cara opened her bag.

"So, what story do you have for me?" Suraya asked, filling the tub with water.

She stared down at her dirty clothes. "Let me tell you about Ikemi."

***

Two days had not crawled by so slowly in years. *No*, he amended, only since his trip to Tendiman with Chendal. At least now he was not facing his possible death.

When Cara's boat pulled into the cove in the early morning, half the anxiety Rodani had borne fell away. His chest expanded with her return, safe in the haven he'd cobbled together. Cara lifted two bags and handed them over to him.

"Did anyone see you leave?"

"It's hard to tell, aisu. If I stand around looking for people who are watching me, people will watch me. I have to act naturally, which means I can't be seen acting suspiciously." They headed for the fire.

"Were there any other concerns during your days?"

Cara opened her mouth to speak, then shut it.

Au, yes, he thought. *Concerns.* They were written on her face. "Kia?"

She sat on the upturned stump Rodani had set for her comfort. "Do you know what a can of worms is?"

"No."

"It's something noxious inside a container, like stable sweepings. You don't want to open it because it will be a mess when you do."

"And did you fall into this mess?" he asked, when she paused.

"Not yet. But my honesty with you will open it."

Another pause. "Play your cards, kia."

"How is your patience?"

Rodani tossed the question with the Selandu gesture.

"Then sit, please. I don't want you to stare down at me."

He sat, not without some trepidation.

She closed her eyes, pursed her lips, and took a deep breath.

Composure, a'tem, Rodani told himself. *You know this look. This language in her body.*

"There is someone who's bothering me." She began to rock to and fro.

"And?"

"He follows me. Right at the edge of my sight. I know he's there, and he knows I know." She crossed her arms on her thighs and bent forward. "He's spoken to me before. Covert suggestions. Offensive questions. Outright rude suggestions."

"When did this begin?"

"Before you arrived."

Rodani's face went to mask. "And you only tell me now?"

"Aisu," she said, taking his hand. She hoped it was a balm to his worries as it was to her. "Many women receive such offensive attentions because there are more than just a few men who have no courtesy and no honor when it comes to women. It isn't unusual."

"I do not like your men."

Cara's eyes went wide. "No, no, no. We have many good men. Should I distrust all guardians because of Kusik?"

He looked aside. "I dislike that you make a point."

"Well, at first, I thought he was just being a rude man. I thought I could ignore him, and he would leave me alone. It wasn't until this weekend that I saw more."

"What did you see?"

Cara looked anywhere but Rodani's face. "Now I open the can of worms."

"I believe the can is already open, kia."

"Well." She flung her hand upward. "Let me toss them around."

He waited, body still. Waited to hear his fears come true.

"He's stalking me, aisu. Follows me from place to place. Watching. Waiting for what, I don't know." She bent her head to her chest and lifted her shoulders. "It feels like he's hunting me."

Rodani shot off his seat and paced around the fire. *And I cannot set rules for her security? Temi's knives, no!* What sort of temichi, what sort of mate would he be if he let her walk blindly into danger?

"You cannot return. I do not permit it."

Cara sighed heavily. "And there is the rest of the worms." She raised her head to look at him. "I don't give you permission to order me, aisu. I have obligations. I've made promises."

"Promises can be broken for safety reasons. You will break these promises."

"You're still ordering me. I talked to the deputy sheriff. He agreed to keep an eye on me and on Mack. I'm not in the danger you think I am."

"And this eye is sufficient?"

"It has to be. Because you can't be there."

"Then neither will you be."

She shook her head. "Rodani, you're making me sorry I told you."

"You would lie to me?" His voice went low.

"No, just withhold information, like you did to me many times in Barridan." She cocked an eyebrow. "Yes?"

Rodani resumed his pacing. *Deepest dark hells and gibbering demons. This is unconscionable.* "I am guild, kia. You cannot expect me to ignore this."

"I'm not expecting you to ignore it. I'm expecting you to stay safely away from the mainland so that you don't get captured."

"And your aggressor?"

"The sheriff watches."

"He has my skills?"

"No. But he's what I have."

"Unacceptable."

Cara scrunched her shoulders and laid her head in her hands. Rodani watched too many expressions flow across her face. Far too many to interpret.

"I see no compromise here, aisu," she said to the ground at her feet.

Rodani crossed his arms and stared down at his adashi. *No*, he thought. *She was correct on that trail. Not adashi. Mate.* Pacing again. But wouldn't any mate of a guardian know what to expect of him here? Know that he could not turn his back when she was in danger? Promises mean nothing. Coins mean nothing. Not when injury or death lay in the balance.

She shifted her feet. "One of us has to give way. One of us has to back off." She looked up and met his gaze. "I had to give in, in Barridan. Every day. It's your turn," she said gently.

He stared back, stared into an expression he rarely saw on her.

"I have an errand." He turned toward the cove.

Cara jumped up and started to follow. "Where are you going?"

"To fetch your compromise," he said, short and sharp.

Now it was Cara's turn to watch her mate sail away. Patience, kia, she heard in her head. At least they hadn't shouted at each other. Gods of the dark space, keep it that way. You're not a willing captive here, fem. Show him you can be an adult in more than the bedroom.

She looked around the camp. *Something to do. Something to do. Keep your hands busy.* Opening one of her bags, she pulled out a piece of fabric, the needle she'd acquired, and threads of varying colors. Following that came a piece of paper she'd worked on in Nick's bar— a geometric pattern she could stitch.

Light. She needed light to work on it. Taking the blanket with her, she settled into a patch of sun at the edge of the north-side trees. Stitch and watch for Rodani to come back. That would do. Go into a flow state and calm down.

Perfect. *Sort of*, she corrected herself.

As she stitched, she took the time to notice the things around her: the breeze, the swaying of branches in the wind, their shivering leaves, the waves lapping onto the beach, and the smell of sea salt. At the peripheries of her vision, the little hunter waited, eyes fixed on her. Its fur ruffled in the ocean breeze, and its nose wiggled from the scent of Rodani's breakfast. She called to it, but this time, it remained aloof. They stared at each other for a minute or two before Cara bent to her stitching. Eventually, it retreated to the woods behind her.

The sun was past noon when Rodani returned, puttering into the cove and under the veil of vines he'd created. When he neared her position at the tree line, she laid her stitching aside.

"Aisu." She greeted him with a smile. *See, I'm calm. Nothing wrong here, a'tem. No cause for tempers.*

"Kia." He tilted his head. "What is that?"

"Needlework. I had to have something to do with my hands besides use them on you."

Rodani's face paled, and his eyes pulsed once, twice. He laid aside a sack he'd brought from the boat. "I had time to think, while I sailed. And I believe that at one point I was unfair to you."

"Really," came the droll reply. "What point?"

"When I asked you why you did not tell me of this man earlier." He paused. "There has been an issue in Selandan, also." Another pause.

Her anxiety shot up again, now with a different focus. "Yes?"

He looked down at his hands. "Someone from the guild was looking for me. In the town I visited, and in Soldan."

"What?" Her breath caught in her throat. "I mean...who?"

"I do not know. The man who told me did not give a name. He may not have known it."

She shoved her needlework to the side. "You can't let them take you, aisu!"

He waved it away. "Today, I spoke to the man who told me. He said someone wishing to report me must go to Soldan and speak to the guild or harbor master there. He led me to believe no one in town will go to the trouble."

"There's a lot riding on that belief."

He turned full on to her. "And on yours."

"Well, we're equal, now, at least."

"Only in danger, kia, not in defensive skills."

She sighed, heavily.

"Fortunately, I have brought you something that may alleviate that." He lifted the bag and drew out a hard wooden rod that was a little shorter than his forearm.

Cara felt the far end of it with her fingers and shook it up and down as he held it. "What do I do with this?"

"Watch." Rodani stood up, drew his arm back, and whipped it out and down. In a flash, the rod was three times as long.

Her eyes grew round. "Whaaat?"

He walked to the nearest tree, lifting his arm. With a massive sideways pull, he cracked the rod against the tree trunk. Bark flew off, leaving a hefty gouge.

Cara came over and inspected the tree. She held out her hand for the weapon. Rodani pushed the extension back into the hollow core and relinquished it.

She drew her arm back and forward again, in an attempt to mimic Rodani. The rod flew out of her damaged hand and into the sand ahead of her. She ran, grabbed it, and ran back. "What's it called?"

"A baton. An extensible baton."

Neither was a word she was familiar with. She made a mental note to write it down for the CSC's dictionary, then tried again to extend it. It remained stubbornly closed.

"I can do this. I can do this." She tried again. And again. She got mad and threw her body into the arm motion. <Sssshhhp> She examined the rod from grip to tip, then turned to the tree. Smacked it with all her strength. The baton rebounded off the tree. The grip abraded her hand from the edge of the palm to the tips of her fingers.

"Ow, ow, ow!" She switched hands and flapped the sore one as Rodani reached to inspect it.

"You may need gloves, kia."

"Wrapping it would be better. That's what Gerry and I did with my drumsticks." She flexed her fingers. "Leather gloves are expensive, and cloth wouldn't protect it well enough. A simple wrap might do."

Rodani walked back to the camp and returned with a rag. "Hold this, please."

With three hands available to him, he cut it into strips.

"What's it made of?"

"Animal hide, softened. I use it to wipe down my gun. But as I do not anticipate firing it here, the rag is available for other purposes." He wrapped the baton's grip, knotted the end, and trimmed it. "Try now."

She whacked a few tree limbs. "It's better, thank you."

"Come." Rodani walked past the blanket and onto the sand. He turned to face her, waiting as she approached. "Try to hit me."

Cara curled her fingers in her hair and grimaced. "Rodani."

"Try," he coaxed.

"Fine." She swung. He stepped out of reach, neatly avoiding the wooden rod.

"Again." Swing and a sidestep.

"Again." Swing. Backstep.

"Again." Swing. Rodani grabbed the baton and yanked it out of her grip. He lifted an eyebrow. "Now you are in trouble."

Cara crossed her arms. "How do I prevent that?"

"A stronger grip, a faster swing, and learn to take it back instead of letting it go."

"Show me."

They worked their way up the beach and back, then took a break for dinner. Afterward, they returned to the blanket. Cara sat and flexed her arms and hands. "They're sore."

"They should be." Rodani grasped the nearest one and began to massage it with his fingers.

She hissed. "Ow."

Rodani lightened his touch.

After a few minutes, Cara glanced at her arm and back up to the face of her husband. "Ow?"

He lightened his touch further, and smiled.

"Ow," she whispered, and winked.

Rodani pushed her back on the blanket and leaned over her, hovering. "Are there any other places needing a massage?"

She linked her fingers in his hair. "I can think of one or two."

"Tell me where."

"I'd rather show you."

"Please."

Show him, she did. In all her glory.

Rodani stripped off his clothing and explored anew her private places. Palms, fingers, mouth, tongue. Nearly everything went nearly everywhere.

Cara tried to return the favor, but winced in pain. Rodani took her hands and set them above her head. "Let them rest."

He delighted in her curves, in her shadowed and moonlit areas, in her flat and mounded skin. When his fingers told him she was ready, he rose over her and dove into her softness. His growl matched her gasp. Hands pressed against the top of her head, he drove her with more abandon than he was wont to do, needing release from his earlier tempers. She took what he gave her, and returned all she could.

The slap of their bodies filled the night air. The crest of the hill neared. She rode with him, he knew. Her telltale signs were inscribed in his memories. Soon, her staccato cries poured into his ears and over his nerves, bringing him along. He growled and emptied himself into her, his own sounds of pleasure mixing with hers.

Satiated, satisfied, Rodani's awareness returned to him. Cara's body lay limp beneath him, but her channel still pulsed from the ride he'd given her. It sent waves through his body and up to his twitching ear tips.

"Kia," he whispered, nearly breathless.

She only managed a sigh, but opened her eyes.

He boosted himself on his elbows, the better to see her expression. Their height disparity made face-to-face rides problematic, but sound and touch made up the difference. It had ceased to disturb him long ago.

"As always, thank you, aisu."

"And as always, there is no need." Rodani withdrew himself from her body and pulled her to his chest.

"I hope," Cara said, her voice muffled in his embrace, "that no boats were going by."

"It is dark, kia, in case you had not noticed." He ran his fingers through her hair. "We are off the main travel lane, as well."

"Sound carries over water."

"So, we entertained the fishes and the richu."

"Oh, please, none of those claws near our sensitive places."

"I believe strenuous activities would keep them at bay."

She laughed against his skin.

THIRTEEN

As Rodani had been the one to fish this Monday morning, Cara cleaned up after breakfast. It hadn't been difficult for them to fall into an egalitarian pattern of chores. When Rodani didn't initiate a task, Cara did, and the other followed up. Fairness, as best understood by two different species, was a trait they both shared. Fortunately. Cara's personality didn't commend her to an unpaid servant's position. Nor did Rodani's. His duty in Barridan had often included fetch and carry and assist, but those had been part of a much larger security task that he'd been assigned—and paid for. Guardians didn't come cheap.

"Are you bored, aisu?"

He looked up from his place on the blanket. "Why do you ask?"

"Oh, you always had plenty to do in Barridan. Here, you don't."

Silent for a moment, he replied. "It might be important for me to learn more of your language, kia."

"It might. We should do that." Cara pulled her stitching out of her carry sack and sat next to him. "I'll think about it."

Rodani glanced at the cloth and the pile of assorted threads next to her.

She noted his glance. "Do you wish to try?"

"It would seem a little too tedious for my taste."

"You won't know until you try. Here." She held it out to him, a needle between her fingers.

He took a few tentative stitches, then passed it back. "Thank you, no." Instead, he threw a piece of dried meat out in front of them...and waited.

"What do you miss most?" she asked him.

The silence went on a little too long. "My fellow guardians. Before you arrived." He glanced toward her, then away.

"Serano?" she ventured in a quiet voice.

"Yes."

The silence reappeared. Cara wondered whether to ask more, but didn't want to open old wounds. And she didn't notice he hadn't returned the question. Then she heard rustling.

The little hunter poked its nose out from the surrounding growth. Rodani nudged Cara, and tilted his head. Fuzz, as he was now called, crept toward the meat, and snatched it off the ground.

"Oooh. I'll try, too." She delved for the meat and held it out with a coo and tongue clicks. "Come here, Fuzz. No one will hurt you."

As if considering her words, the animal cocked its head and crept forward. As it nosed at Cara's food hand, she reached with her other and touched its cheek. It shied away, but the lure of food brought it back. Again, she touched its fur.

The animal lunged for the meat and scampered back into the forest.

"What will you do to keep busy when Fuzz isn't around?" she asked.

"I have an idea."

He stood and walked into the trees, then returned quickly, with a handful of sticks. He sat back down, pulled out a knife, and began to slice across one of the sticks.

"What will you make?"

His hands jerked as the knife caught and slipped against the bark. "At this point, nothing. I am letting my hands remember twenty years ago."

"Before you apprenticed, then."

"Yes."

"What did you make?"

He tossed the question, Selandu style. "Nothings. Faces. Trees and leaves. A flower. Other inconsequential things. I was a child."

"What did your parents think of what you made?"

"I hid them."

Cara leaned back in surprise. "Why?"

He waited a moment, his hands still scraping the bark from the stick. "My father forbade his children from having weapons."

"What if you were out and needed to defend yourself?"

"I carried a large stick."

"Which is where you got the idea for the baton for me?"

He stared out into the distance, then back at his knife. "Essentially. You are not capable of fighting with a knife, and a knife is equally dangerous to a gun at close quarters."

Intent on their own activities, they sat quietly for some minutes before Cara again broke the silence.

"Aisu, will you tell me the names of the common Selandu drinks?"

"Why?"

"Nick wants to know."

"Who is Nick?"

"The bartender I'm teaching Selandi. Remember? The one who's going to Himadi House. He'll need to know what he's serving."

"I believe you did not tell me his name."

"Oh. I'm sorry. Um...names?"

"Yours and mine: Shigeli and eisenico. Chendal's: Yolaro. Chint. Senta."

"Wait, wait. I need to write them down." She grabbed her notebook and scribbled quickly. "Go ahead, please." He named a few more. "What do they taste like?"

"He should taste them, himself, when he arrives."

"How much in a serving?"

Rodani continued to whittle at the stick. The tip was becoming sharper by the moment. "It varies by name. There are measuring cups."

"Will there be some there when he arrives? And glasses, or mugs?"

"If they are building a space for a bar, they will likely supply it with the basics in the beginning. He will need to know how to resupply."

"And the cost?"

"A quarter copper is typical. A more expensive one will have a smaller serving, a lesser one will be larger. Then they will be priced the same."

"How are they ordered?"

"He will make a list of needs and amounts, then give the list to the purchaser."

"Who will that be?"

"I have no knowledge of who will be there."

"I mean, where will they be found? In the house?"

"They will be an assistant to the accountant."

Cara flipped her pencil in her fingers, thinking. "He will need to bring human drinks with him, too."

"I would assume."

"It will all have to go through Soldan, won't it? Not over the hills."

"Through Soldan, yes."

"I need to tell Davad! He could offer one of his boats for that. He's always looking to expand his business."

"He must discuss it with the ambassadors."

She thought for a moment, of proprieties. Chain of command. Influence. "Yes, okay."

"While we are riding the question trail, I have a few for you."

"What ones?"

"Where do you sleep?"

Cara pushed her needle into the cloth for safeguarding. "Right now, over the bar."

"In a loft? As in a barn?"

"No. The building is two stories. There are two bedrooms above the bar itself."

"Then you are in one room. Who is in the other?"

"Nick. He lives there. It's common for owners to sleep in the same place as their businesses."

"He sleeps alone?"

She chuckled. "I don't know. His sex life is none of my concern."

"Has he approached you?"

"For joining? No. We're...casual companions, aisu. That's all. Since I'm teaching him some Selandi, and he earns more money from my dancing, he is returning the favor by letting me stay there on weekends."

Rodani turned his gaze on her. "How does he earn money from your dancing?"

"Nothing you would disapprove of. The stage is across the street, across from the bar. People buy a drink, come outside and watch us, and go back in for another drink. He was pleased that I returned from Barridan so soon." She picked at the thread in her lap. "He was probably the only one who was. Besides my youngest sister."

"Where is this bar?"

"Why?"

Rodani dropped the stick in his lap, knife still clenched in his hand. "Because I need to image in my mind where you go and where you dance and where you sleep. And where you clean your clothes, and where the sheh-riff's office is, and the see-ess-see. I need to know. Draw me a map."

Cara reached up to touch his shoulder, to curl her fingers in his long hair. "I'm sorry. I know this is difficult for you, like your security restrictions were difficult for me. But you'll manage, just as I did." She smiled. "Eventually."

Rodani tossed his knife on the blanket and stood. "Fetch the baton, kia."

"Agh. Now?"

He turned a steady, firm gaze on her. "Please." He waited a beat, then, "it will help me *manage.*"

^Fine.^

"I recognize that tone. You have a new word to teach me."

Cara retrieved the hardwood rod, remembering Mack Cornyn's fixed and heavy gaze. She wondered if he would actually frighten her enough to use what rested in her scarred hand.

Rodani interrupted her troublesome thoughts. "Human men are stronger than the women, yes?"

"Oh, yes."

"You must hit harder than before."

"I did the best I could." She shrugged. "Wish I could use a gun."

"I would give you the Kishata if I could, kia. But would your sheh-riffs allow it?"

"Not if I had to use it. And it's very likely someone would want to steal it if they saw it."

"And how accurately would you aim in the midst of an attack? Without years of practice, fear steals your skills."

"Good point. But won't that be the same with this?" She hefted the rod in her hand.

"Some. But it is a more natural movement, is it not? Would not a hit on any part of his body wound him?"

"Yes, and might enrage him, too."

"We must work together on this. Begin."

Nearly an hour later, Cara called a halt. Her palms were burning with a vengeance, and her arms and shoulders were sore. Rodani had proved again to be as exacting a taskmaster as her mother. Granted, her safety was at stake here, instead of a spotless kitchen and smoothed sheets, but she'd had enough. She groaned and swiveled her head on her shoulders, hearing the pops and cracks. She dug her father's healing cream out of the carry sack and dropped into a sit on the blanket. But before she could open it, Rodani plucked it from her hand, pulled out the cork stopper, dug a finger into the cream, and began to massage her hands.

She held her breath as memories flooded her. Sitting on her bed in Barridan after their fight, rubbing his palms as she gazed at his thumb she'd bitten. Sitting on the couch after Arimeso had reunited them, emotions strong enough to choke them as she had caressed his hands and arms. The uncounted times she had kissed those nimble fingers after they'd pleasured her body. And, at his table, right before their first joining. She closed her eyes.

He must have missed her every bit as much as she'd missed him. What had he felt as Serano pulled her away? Her own vision had been blurred by tears, and a shriek had risen from her throat. What had he faced in the aftermath? She knew what Chendal had done to him. It made her cringe. What had Kusik done? The keso must have been livid. Had Arimeso intervened? Had Kimasa? His earlier answers had barely quenched her curiosity.

Rodani took another swipe of cream and continued his ministrations.

"I never asked you about Kimasa."

Rodani glanced at her, then back down. "About her?"

"How she reacted to the firefight, and what she said to you after I was gone."

He stopped rubbing her hands. "Kia, why do you wish to know about possibly painful experiences?"

Damn, damn, damn. "I'm sorry. Don't stop. Please."

"I did not ask for an apology."

"But I offended you."

"And I asked for an explanation."

Cara shook her head rapidly, back and forth, denying her stupidity, denying what she'd just done. "I'm not sure why. I was thinking about Barridan. My imagination runs wild, and I'd rather fill the gaps in our past with facts."

"I would prefer you look to the future."

She bent over and brought their hands to her forehead. "What kind of future do we have, aisu?"

He dropped her hands and pulled away. "What has brought this to the fore? How displeased are you, here with me?"

Now, she waved her hands between them, her eyes watering. "Can we just forget all this, forget my original question?"

"Why are you distraught?"

"I don't know. Demons of deep space! I interrupted a quiet, peaceful moment with an inappropriate question and ruined the peace."

"And I ask again, kia, do you know peace?"

Another memory flooded her. "I don't know. Please. Don't let me ruin the moment."

"I hear Arimeso in my head. I tire of 'I don't know.'"

"And it's even more true to you than it was to her. I knew why I was raining in front of her after we returned from the falls, but I couldn't tell her. I don't have an answer for you."

His eyes widened, and his pupils expanded. "Why *were* you raining?"

"Now you're asking me about my pain. Do I answer?"

Rodani's jaws clamped shut. He turned away. "I am reproved."

She held her hand out in mute conciliation. "I'll answer this time. It's because I was already bonding with you, but I didn't think it would ever come to anything."

"What does that mean? 'Come to anything'?"

"I wanted you to bond with me as I was doing with you." She tapped her heart. "I didn't think you could. Or would, because I'm alien. I thought I would be hungry and empty for the rest of my time there. I couldn't tell her that. And I wanted to join with you. But I didn't know if we could."

Rodani stared at her, open-mouthed as he rarely was. "And you could not tell me that."

"Yes."

"Why?"

She goggled at him. "I thought you would laugh at me or be disgusted. Like Serano was. I thought I would lose everything, even your companionship. I couldn't let that happen." She reached for his hand. "I would rather have had just a piece of you than not have you there at all."

"Temi's knives, what a tangle." He curled his fingers around hers. "I have thought at times that I pressured you too much that night. That you truly did not wish for what we did."

"No, aisu," she said quickly. "I was just a little frightened of the unknown. You did the right thing. You were the brave one. You let yourself be vulnerable first."

"I doubt vulnerability was what was driving me."

A welcome laugh erupted. "No, but you had to be vulnerable to ask for it."

"It was my home. My world. That made it feel less risky."

She covered his hands with hers and pressed them together. "You gave up your whole life for me."

"Do not sorrow for me, kia. I would rather be in the sand and trees with you than under Kusik's tender care."

"So would I. See, we agree!"

"Usually." Now he smiled. "Eventually."

FOURTEEN

Determined not to be left behind for a third weekend, Rodani packed his boat. He waited until dusk to head toward shore, then let the boat nose its way into the tall beach grass that hugged the shoreline. He tied it to the nearest tree, grabbed his saddlebag, and walked into the narrow strip of woods that lined the shore between sand and town.

Instant darkness caused his pupils to expand into circles. He listened closely to the night songs of amphibians and insects as he made his way inward. He stopped behind each tree he came to and waited to hear anything else that might inhabit the woods.

Taking each step cautiously, he was brought to mind of the forest south of Barridan where he and Cara had dwelled while he healed from a beating, and his attempts to teach her a few stealth techniques. He smiled as he crept forward. In a short while, he reached the other side of the woods and peered out at the backsides of cabins and one-room huts that sat scattered around. Each rested on one or more rows of logs, lifting them up off the land.

South, Rodani reminded himself. *Find the stage. Explore later.* He took a few steps back and turned left, following the tree line.

Eventually, he heard voices. He flipped his long hair down the back of his shirt and covered his head with a dark cap of cloth. He had yet to think of a way to darken his grey skin except to cover it with mud, but that solution was a little too foul for him to accept at this early point.

He continued left and soon saw the glitter of lanterns and torches. There, just beyond them, was the stage. Empty. As he spotted a convenient tree to climb, a heady scent reached him. It wasn't wine. Something stronger, more pungent. He wrinkled his nose at the unpleasant odor, then began to climb. Behind him, voices cheered, and hands clapped. Now the strum of a stringed instrument of some kind, and the clump of something heavy being set down on wood. A rat-a-tat followed, and more cheers erupted, punctuated with words he didn't know. He moved out on a limb and held aside a branch of leaves.

There she was, and her hair was held back from her face. She must still be wearing his clip. It eased just a bit of the concern he held in his heart, a concern that she had turned back to her own people more than he might have wished.

They began to play. Rodani watched with some fascination as Cara pattered away at the drumheads with a skill he didn't realize she had.

The other woman on stage opened her mouth and began to make music with her voice. *Singing*, he thought. It had a different quality than he remembered from weeks ago, the last time he heard Cara sing. A pang of nostalgia ruffled his emotions.

As the first song ended and the second began, Rodani interrupted his musing to scan the crowd. Expressions were hard to discern in the dim light, even with Selandu eyesight. More than one human man stood stiffly on the peripheries, refusing the draw of the music. But Rodani could see no obvious enemy. Several people, men and women, came and went from the door to the building across from him. In little time he realized it was likely the tavern Cara had mentioned. Few came out empty-handed. Most of the other buildings to its north remained mysteries in the dark.

After climbing down from the tree, he crept inward and took a closer look at the bar. Two stories, the bottom one lit, the top one black in the night. He made a mental note to examine the building more closely after the crowd dispersed. His gaze returned to the audience.

A cheer went up. Cara stood front and center, quietly accepting the accolade. As the stringed instrument began to sound, Cara started to sway.

Rodani watched raptly as his bonded mate danced for her own people instead of for him. *Calm*, he told himself. Watch and verify that what she had told him was truth.

She did not tease the crowd. She did not taunt them or fling her hair. She did not hold her hands out to anyone or approach too close to the edge of the stage. The enticements he'd seen from the gentlewomen in Tendiman were absent from Cara's display. He watched her wind down the dance, then return to her conga drums and pick up the sticks. Somewhat placated out of his jealousy, Rodani relaxed.

The entertainment continued. He observed the stage and the audience by turns. Only when a man curved round the back of the crowd and stood near the trees did Rodani center his attention.

Broad back, thick arms and thighs, stocky, light-colored hair cut short, the man crossed his arms and stood stiffly as Cara once again took center stage. He neither whistled nor clapped as the others did, nor did he sway or bounce to the music.

Rodani crept to his left in an attempt to see the man's face. As the lights flickered, he realized the man stood in the exact place where a light would shine on him. Hair grew out of his chin, Rodani noted with a touch of surprise, as he hadn't seen that before. He couldn't tell the eye color, but the set of the man's mouth suggested to Rodani he wasn't pleased with what he saw and heard.

Rodani took a careful few steps closer, to better judge the man's height and breadth. Quite a bit shorter than he was, Rodani thought, but then who wasn't, here in the south? But the man was nearly as broad as he was. This grim man would tower over Cara, and could do whatever he wished with her if he chose.

Was this the man? Was this human his new enemy? *Patience*, he bid himself. He returned to his former position and watched both the man and Cara as she finished playing. But his patience turned to alarm as the man walked up to her on stage. What could he do? Nothing! Where is the baton he gave her? He ground his teeth together as they talked. Cara shook her head, denying the man whatever he had asked. She carried her drums down the steps and onto the cart. *There it is.* The baton now hung from the belt at her waist. Would she draw it?

Cara rolled her cart toward the bar, then dropped the handle to speak to another man. The burly man, the watcher who raised Rodani's hackles, stared at the two then walked off to the north. He disappeared into the darkness.

Cara and this new man walked into the shop, and after a few minutes, they walked back out with food. They spoke, then parted ways. Rodani watched until Cara was safely ensconced in the tavern's upper floor and the south side window was lit. He moved back from the tree line and waited for the last stragglers to clear the area.

An hour after, Rodani emerged from the cover of trees and circled the stage. He probed for hidden doors and found nothing. He crossed the short distance to the southeast corner of the tavern and studied its outline. He tested the windows and doors. All were safely locked. He stole around to the south side, but nothing except a blank wall met his eyes on the first floor. On the second, one window shone in the moonlight. No lights flickered behind the curtains. Behind the tavern was another door and a staircase leading to the second floor.

Easy access.

Not pleased, Rodani tested the first step. It creaked beneath his weight. *Later*, he told himself and turned away. *No*, some other part of his mind replied. *Now*. He removed his shoes and placed one foot at the far edge of the step where it met its vertical support, then shifted his weight. It remained silent. He placed his other foot at the other end of the step and put his full weight on the wood. No sound.

Ever so slowly, he made his way upward. At the top, he gripped the door handle and turned it.

Locked. She was as safe as she could be in this strange land.

He sighed, turned, and worked his way back to the packed dirt at the base of the stairs. Shoes back on, he paced his way down the alley, checking gates, bins, boxes, and the occasional door. As he neared the north end of the alley, an animal made a repetitive sound, almost like the cough of a torac, but loud and insistent. Rodani retreated several paces, then fled into a nearby shadow as a light appeared in the window. He held his breath and hoped that the unknown animal would cease its noisy warnings and return to sleep.

A man stuck his head out the window and looked around, but seeing nothing disturbing, pulled it back in and snuffed the light. Rodani crept back down the alleyway and headed for the tree line. Hidden under a mat of leaves, he dozed until dawn, then climbed a likely tree.

***

Suraya shuffled and straightened the papers in her hands and sat back to contemplate a distressing lack of focus. Her desk was awash in notes, scribbled and scratched out. A cup of caffee sat forlorn and cold, out of the way of the chaos.

"You're restless today," Bethamy said from her corner of the office.

"Am I?"

Bethamy shook her head and raised an eyebrow.

"I keep wanting more stories from Cara, but I don't know what to do with them."

"Paolo won't publish them?"

Suraya grimaced in frustration. "Not enough interest, he said. Old news. I hate that term."

"If you relate it to her dancing, he might allow it."

"Oh, that's all she needs. Right. And three more Macks come out of the trees to stalk her."

"He won't harm her."

Suraya's eyes widened. Suspicion and doubt enveloped her face. "Get that in writing, will you? That time he came up behind us scared me enough. I hate to think what Cara feels. Maybe I should write about obsession. Use him as my example."

"You could use yourself, too."

Suraya looked over at her coworker, confusion now on her face.

Bethamy laughed. "You don't see it, do you? Are you mirrored? I'm pretty sure she goes for men."

"It's not Cara I'm obsessed with, Beth. It's the Selandu."

"If you say so. I don't see a lot of difference."

"Then you're not looking hard enough. I'm dogging her footsteps because the ambassadors keep their mouths shut. I haven't learned anything about the species from them since I graduated."

"Maybe you can make a serial out of your stories. You know, chapters. To be continued. That type of thing."

"He still won't publish."

"Then you're writing a book, aren't you?"

Suraya stared at her hands, brown against the beige paper beneath them. "Huh."

Outside, she wandered the town, checking Cara's usual haunts. Not in the bar. Not in the laundromat. Not in the library. Not at her parents' house. And no, she was told, not at the CSC. Not for weeks. She wasn't needed there, spoken with *not welcome* as the underlying message. As a last stop, she visited the repository, winding her way between cabinets and shelves under the watchful eye of the archivist. She still marveled at the number of items her grandparents and great-grands had salvaged from their spaceship. Anything from pencils and sewing needles to history and music cubes and their readers, to quality metal tools, and to the precious long-life battery cells that powered them and the weather station that still communicated with the ship. It was a closely guarded secret how many of the batteries were left, how long they would last, and what machines deserved to get one. Bicycles outnumbered carriages by a very wide margin, and more than one person lamented that their great-grandparents decided against bringing horses onto their spaceship.

And there she was, Suraya thought. Cara's head was bent over the music 'corder she'd taken to Barridan. Her body swayed with the tunes only she could hear through the ear fixtures. Her hair was still held back in a clip, Selandu style. Why she kept it was a puzzle Suraya had yet to solve. Cara waved off the subject whenever Suraya got close to it.

She slipped into a chair next to Cara's table and plopped her notebook on it, then pulled out a sheaf of papers. The motion alerted Cara, who unlinked herself from the 'corder with a frown.

"What?"

Suraya grimaced. "If your admirers ever learned how pleasant you are, Cara, you'd never lack for attention."

She had the grace to be embarrassed. "Sorry."

"Speaking of attention, how's Mack?"

"Still stalking, but I think Graeme had a talk with him."

"Good." She picked up her papers and held them out. "I wrote your story on Ikemi."

"Oh, yeah?" Cara took them and began to read.

Suraya waited patiently, toying with the music cubes stacked on the table. She watched Cara's expressions as they flowed across her face. Amusement. Dismay. A soft smile.

Cara handed them back. "I like. Good job. You have talent."

"Thanks. I can't dance, though."

"Hell, your brothers would kill you if you did."

"And you think you exaggerate."

"Actually, I don't think I do." Cara leaned back in her chair. "Did you know Mandeep cornered me not long after I came back?"

Suraya leaned forward. Her voice went low. "What did he say?"

Cara waved her hand in the Selandu dismissal gesture. "I suspect you could imagine what he said."

"Tell me. Please."

"Oh," she sighed, "the aliens are wicked. They worship a false deity. You have been contaminated with their heresies, and you need to be cleansed," she said, sarcasm front and center. "Your soul won't move on after death but dissolve into nothingness. Come with me and be free of their negative influence before you pay a high price. I don't remember it all."

"I'm sorry."

"Not your fault they're creating a cult. He was very earnest and trying hard to convince me to join, for my soul's sake. But I demurred. The last thing I need is religious indoctrination. I got enough of the secular type from my mother."

Suraya chuckled. "Nah, she wouldn't do that."

A tranquil hush fell between them with their rapport. Some things needed no further explanation.

"Maybe," Cara said into the silence, "some day I can tell you about Kimasa, the high priestess."

Suraya inhaled a quick breath. "Tell me now!"

"Another time." Cara fiddled with the 'corder. To forestall her, Suraya laid her palm on the table. "Please. Before you immerse yourself again."

Cara thought for a minute. "I'll tell you about my guardian and his knives."

Suraya's eyes lit up. Her note-taking flowed fast and fierce as she listened intently. And at the end, "So you never learned who he was thinking of when he threw those knives at the trees?"

"No. There were occasions I would ask something a second time, and other times his refusals were curt enough I knew not to. That was one of those times."

"Were you ever scared he'd use those knives on you?"

"Not really. We did have a fight, though."

"Did he hurt you?"

"He did, but not too badly. And I hurt him—less badly."

"So, you had a knock-down drag-out fight?"

Cara bent her head to her chest and chuckled through her words. "Pretty much."

"Aaaaand..."

She put her head in her hands and shook it back and forth. "I can't. I'm sorry. I wish you hadn't asked the question."

"Awww, fem. Don't do this to me."

"Maybe someday in the future I can tell you. When it's not so close. Maybe." She looked up. "Go write the story I already gave you. Please."

***

Another Sunday morning in town. *Way early morning*, Cara thought as she yawned. It was a good thing she had an alarm on the 'com Rodani had sent home with her, or she'd never get up before noon, let alone before dawn. She locked the back door behind her and carefully made her way down the staircase to the alley. No stars twinkled above. The sky was overcast. She made her way east, behind the stage, to the stand of trees that ran behind the last row of cabins. Maybe Mack, if he were up and about, wouldn't see her. *Please.*

The docks were dark except for a few lanterns hanging on support poles. It was a little too soon for the fishing boats to go out, though Davad and his crew might be awake. She settled into her boat and took off south, the better to leave a false trail. She glanced at the black shoreline as she went by but saw nothing to worry her. All was quiet.

After a short time, she turned left and followed the line of islands—undersea mountains, she reminded herself—toward home. Toward camp. Toward Rodani.

The sea was a bit choppy, and the wind was up. A storm coming? Well, it was a good excuse to crawl into the hammock with her husband and pull the covers over them. She smiled in anticipation.

As the southernmost island came into view, she swung the boat around it and entered the north-side cove.

It was empty. Where was he? Fishing? It was a little early for that. Not quite dawn.

"Kia."

She spun around. It sounded like he was in her boat. But no, she realized. It came from the 'com. She plucked it out of the pocket of her carry sack. "Aisu? Where are you?"

"Turn around."

She turned and looked across the water, but it was still too dark. "Are you out there? I don't see anything." The prow of her boat ran up on sand. She tied off and jumped out. By the time she looked again, Rodani had sailed up next to her. She waited for him.

"Cara, we should talk."

His hands, empty of fish, slipped into his pockets. So, he wasn't particularly angry since his arms weren't crossed, and his voice sounded normal.

"Where were you?" she began, softly. They began to walk.

Rodani turned on the light in his 'com so they could see the ground. "When?"

"What? What do you mean, when? This morning. You weren't here, asleep."

"I was on shore in my boat, watching for you to leave."

Cara glanced up past the com's light and toward his voice in the dark. "Why? I'm safe enough."

"Did you bring food again?"

"Yes."

"Let us eat. I am hungry."

Rodani built up the fire while Cara rummaged in her carry sack.

"Some meat, veggies. Berries. Bread." She shook their water can. "You didn't fill it. I'll do it after sunrise."

"It will wait."

They began to eat. Rodani broke the loaf of bread and gave her the smaller half.

"So, what's wrong?"

He shifted his weight on the blanket. "I spent your ^weekend^ in the trees on shore. I watched you play. And dance. I tested the lock on the second-floor door near your room. I watched the men watch you."

Several seconds of silence crawled by while Cara's heartbeat soared.

"Rodani, I thought we agreed—"

"No. If you remember, there was little to nothing we agreed upon. And I did say I was not finished discussing it."

Another silence.

"Well, spit it out."

"Occasionally, your crudities disturb me," he replied, scolding her.

"Then, occasionally, I'll apologize. And?"

"I needed to know, kia. I needed to see where you spent your time. Where you slept and ate. Who you talked to."

Her eyes widened as the realization hit her. "You spied on me."

"If you wish to call it that. I prefer to consider it watching over my bonded mate to see how she lives her life when she leaves me behind for two days of seven, and displays her skills for a crowd of people I know nothing about."

"So we're back to jealousy?"

Rodani glanced down at his plate and back up. "No, that has lessened because I saw nothing in your drumming or dancing other than what you described to me."

"I didn't lie."

"I did not say you did. I know your thoughts on the subject of lies. But we do not always see ourselves as clearly as others see us."

^Okay.^

"Describe this man who frightens you."

She thought for a bit and took another bite of food. "More than a head taller than me. Broad shoulders. Muscular build. Short sandy hair and blue eyes. A crooked nose from being broken in a fight."

"Do you remember what he wore the first night?"

"What's the name of that day?"

He pursed his lips at the quiz. "Friday," he replied in a clipped tone. "Do you remember?"

"No, sorry."

"I believe I saw him. Please make note next week of what he wears and where he stands."

"Why?"

"So I will know who to watch, Cara." His voice rose.

As did hers. "Why, when there's nothing you can do?"

Rodani toyed with the remnants of his breakfast on the plate. "Kia, before Kusik was punished, you told Chendal you were not able to explain why you ran from the Enclave. That it was not a logical decision, but an emotional one. I am similarly...caught...with no logic, though it embarrasses me to say so. I cannot explain, and I cannot deny it. It is something I must do."

"The double-bond?"

He sighed and rubbed his fingers over his forehead and into the hairline. "That is one way to view it."

"So you're going to continue following me."

"Yes."

"And what happens if you're seen?" she asked, eyebrow raised.

"I will run. Hide."

"And when someone figures you out and they confront me?"

"You deny."

Cara bent her head and interlaced her fingers, clutching tight. "I don't like having to lie for you."

Rodani tossed his plate and vaulted up from the ground. He didn't quite stomp. He paced the area around the fire with his hands clasped behind him. "But you will, to keep me safe."

"If I have to, yes. And what if you're captured?"

He stopped and stared through the trees, out over the water. "Can you rescue me?"

"Not from the jail. And I would need help to free you from someone else. Who would I ask? Who would I ask to put their own freedom in danger for breaking the laws I've broken?"

Another silence stole between them, a barrier she couldn't cross.

"I do not like your questions, kia."

"You ride in my saddle," she said, her voice dropping deep. "And if you were in jail, the chief sheriff would tell the mayor, and the mayor would tell Ambassador Menachem, and Menachem would tell Hadaman. How long before Chendal comes to take you back north? And what punishment would you face?"

"I see no clear end to this discussion."

"And no baton will help."

Rodani stood still in the dawn light, his face masked of emotion. "I need sleep." He turned toward her. "Wash the dishes. Please," he amended.

Afterward, they crawled into the hammock and wrapped their arms around each other.

***

Noon heat woke Cara. She glanced at the empty place beside her, then remembered Rodani had climbed down earlier. She leaned over the side, and found him whittling sticks and trying to fit them together. He murmured Cene'l vocabulary words as he carved. She climbed down to greet him.

"What are you making?"

"A cage."

Her eyebrows drew together as she considered. "For Fuzz?"

"Yes."

"You're going to try to keep him in that?"

"Occasionally. I wish to train him to accept it."

Cara shook her head. "He won't like it."

"We shall see."

She got up to check the fire. "Lunch?"

"No," he replied, standing up. "Fetch your baton."

She stared at him over her shoulder.

"Please," he amended.

"More practice?"

"Do you deny you need it?"

"Oh, probably not."

Rodani looked out through the trees. "Today I will chase you, attack you. You will need to engender some ferocity if you are to fight me off, kia. I will not coddle you."

Her brows drew together as she turned his way. "I have ferocity?"

"Surely you have not forgotten our first fight."

"Oh." The memory of Suraya's question made her cringe. "Meaning you're going to frighten me out of my wits and try to make me rage at you."

"Essentially." He laid a palm on her shoulder. "Just as in any kind of fighting, with guns or fists or aught else, practice never allows you to sense the immediacy of real danger. You need to feel it, as best I can contrive. You need to react to it and learn to use it to protect yourself. Otherwise, the baton is simply a stick. An encumbrance."

Cara pulled her baton from the carry sack while Rodani reached behind a nearby tree. In his hand was a branch nearly half his height and as thick as his wrist. It had been shorn of offshoots and leaves.

"You're going to hit me with that?"

"I will try. You will prevent me. Open the baton."

She gave it a hard shake. It extended with a quiet scrape.

Rodani posed, arms and branch raised, his face masked. "Defend yourself." He swung.

Cara yelped and jumped back, ending up on the ground.

He stood over her, branch resting on his shoulder. "That was not a defense."

^No shit.^ Cara scrambled up, brushing dirt and leaves from her pants.

"Are you convinced yet that I am serious?"

"Yeah."

He raised the branch. Cara matched his stance.

"Defend yourself."

He swung. So did Cara. Wood and wood met with a bang that shook her whole body. The baton flipped out of her hands.

"Now you are free to be beaten, or worse."

Cara picked up the weapon and gritted her teeth. "Again."

They swung. This time, Cara kept her grip.

"Now move." He took a step forward.

She looked around. "Where?"

Rodani pursed his lips and glared. "Where you must." He raised the branch.

She stepped back.

He advanced. Swung.

Barely, she met it with a parry.

Through the trees, over roots and lumps of dirt, past the latrine. Strike and parry. Repeat. Repeat.

"Cease," he said. "You need to do more than defend. You need to attack me. Any man who means you harm will outlast you if you do not."

Cara dropped her arms and gasped for breath. "I never got a chance."

"You must go on the offensive."

"I don't really know how. I've never done this." She glanced at her red-striped, pulsing palms.

"Look at me as you would Mack," he said, his voice sharp. "Is he relaxed or stiff?"

"Rodani..."

"What is his expression? Where are his arms?!" He spat out the words. "Did he make fists?!"

"Rodani!"

"Is he standing or walking toward you? How far away is he?" He made a fist and pumped it. "Anticipate!"

Supremely aggravated, Cara swung at her husband.

He parried it. "Again."

She did.

"Step forward. Make me retreat."

Shoulders sore and hands stinging, she complied. Rodani parried it easily.

"Again!" he demanded. "Do not stop."

Finally, something in her brain flipped. She took a death grip on the baton and pounded the damnable branch that threatened her. Over and over, from one side, from the other, from the top, she beat at it until her arms were ready to fall from their sockets. Rodani continued to back up, taunting her with threats and insults, meeting each movement with one of his own.

Dimly, she noticed they were near the camp. "Enough!" she shouted and threw the baton aside. Completely drained, she fell onto the edge of the blanket and turned on her side, dragging breaths into her starving lungs. Her palms burned, and every muscle in her arms and shoulders throbbed. She felt more than heard Rodani sit down behind her.

He laid his hand on her arm, but she yanked it away.

"Yes, you are angry," he said to the back of her head. "That is better than how you would feel if this were real. Cara, you are a sleeping victim; unaware. You are helpless against anyone who wishes you ill. You poke and prod me for my training, but you will not spend the time you need to become proficient. 'Teach me to shoot. Teach me to throw. Teach me to ground fight. Teach me your hand language.' And I have, in small bites. But nothing I have taught you is adequate to keep you alive. You ignore the most basic precautions you should already know to take. Did you learn nothing in your months at Barridan?"

Painfully stung by the truths she heard, she said, "Well, I won't ask you for any more training."

"You walked past my point, Cara. I understand your curiosity, and I indulge it. But your safety skills remain those of a child. You treat this as a game, and it is *not* one."

Still with her back to him, she looked out into the trees. "I know it isn't. Teach me more."

"But you act as if it is. And you just contradicted yourself. Did you notice?" He clasped his hands in his lap. "I believe it would not be worth my time and energy to teach more. Or yours."

"But it would help relieve your worry."

Rodani had no answer to that.

"What would you teach me if it were worth it?"

"Basic, everyday security," he told her. "Door locks, window latches, light and darkness, stealth, patience, constant awareness of your surroundings; who is *friend*; who is enemy. The need to forget how you lived when you were here before. To learn to see it as I do, a new land, one full of dangers.

"Are you still angry?" he asked.

Cara rubbed her aching arms. "I'm trying not to be."

"I thank you."

"I don't like being angry at you. It feels terrible. Hurts."

"It does," came the soft reply.

She rolled over to look up at him. "How did you feel after we fought about Ikemi?"

"When you threatened to bar me from your bed?"

She looked away, embarrassed at the memory. "Yes."

"As if you had knocked me to my knees and thrown me down a well to drown."

FIFTEEN

Cara woke, disoriented, for a moment. *Bed, not hammock.* Town, not island. No Rodani next to her, or dappled sunshine in her eyes. Weekdays versus weekends were slicing her life in halves and made her feel like two people existed inside her body. The two cultures were intermixing in her mind more and more as the months went by. Sometimes, she wasn't sure how to respond to a simple gesture or word without reorienting, without remembering where she was and who, exactly, she was talking to. Incline her head, or nod? Bow, or not? Be circumspect, or bold? So many times she got it wrong. So many times she saw people side-eye her. It was uncomfortable, like a scratchy shirt she couldn't fix—or even remove. Anymore, she didn't feel exactly at home in either frame of mind—Selandu or human. A sore thumb in both places.

She washed and dressed, then bent over the bed and tied her carry sack closed. She slung it over her shoulder and headed out as Nick opened his own door. "Morning."

Nick squinted in the sunlight coming through the window. "Is it?" he asked, groggy. "What day is it?"

Cara smiled. "Saturday."

"Thanks for the pastries last night," he said.

"You're welcome. You and Graeme help keep me safe." She went down the stairs and out the door on the way to her least favorite chore, wondering if Suraya would catch up to her today. She hadn't taken three steps before a burly form came up beside her.

"Where you going?"

The rough voice grated in her ears. She stopped in her tracks.

"I saw you walk in the bakery last night. You bought that sheriff some goodies."

Cara kept her eyes glued on the street ahead. "Mack, that same sheriff told you to leave me alone. I suggest you do that."

"Why do you pay attention to him and not me?"

"Because he helps me."

"You won't let me help you."

"I don't need your help, and you have ulterior motives."

He was silent for a moment. "What are those?"

She rolled her eyes, but attempted to keep her voice calm. "It means you offer help because you want something from me that I don't want to give."

"But you give it to him."

She glanced over at his shoes. It was as near as she wished to look. "Who?"

"Graeme! I know he watches me for you. And I know what coin you pay him for it."

"Yeah. Sweetbread."

"No. Sex. You spread it for him, but you won't for me."

A chill flew down her spine. "Mack, you need to get off the subject."

He grabbed her arm with a painful grip. "If you're not fucking him, you're fucking Nick. Your type doesn't breathe without a man to do your bidding."

"Let go of me!"

"No." He began to pull her. "You're staying with me until I get the answer I want."

Cara let out a scream that came from her toes and reached for the baton at her waist. Mack grabbed her other arm.

Shandar, the baker, ran out of his shop. Behind them, Chucko dashed out from the bar, with Nick not far behind. The three men tackled Mack, taking both him and Cara to the ground. Arms, legs, elbows, knees, oaths, and swearing erupted from the mass of bodies. Feeling Mack let go, Cara crawled away and stood, shaking. She put her hand on the baton but feared she would hit someone undeserving if she swung it. She could only watch.

In a few moments, it was over. Mack, bedraggled and fuming, was frog-marched to the sheriff's office with Cara trailing behind. He'd barely set foot in the office before he began ranting. Cara stopped outside the door and turned to the tree line. She bowed and made a hand signal to the man she loved, who was certainly watching with opinions she had no wish to hear. She waited at the door.

"I wasn't going to do anything to her!"

Graeme heard the commotion and stepped into the room.

"They kidnapped me! Arrest them!"

Graeme studied the tableau before him. "Sit him down."

Shandar and Chucko hustled Mack into the farthest chair. Nick turned to leave.

"No. I need all of you. Cara, come inside."

Mack's lip curled into a snarl. "I said I didn't do anything."

Graeme pointed at Cara. "You start."

Cara waved a hand at her carry sack, now speckled with dirt. "I was walking out of Nick's with my dirty clothes, heading for the laundry. Mack comes up behind me and starts walking next to me, which he shouldn't have done because you told him to stay away from me. He said he'd seen you and me go into the bakery last night after the show and accused me—very rudely—of having an affair with you. I told him I wasn't and to please leave me alone. He then accused me, again rudely, of doing the same with Nick. I told him I wasn't doing that, either. He then said—"

"I wasn't rude. She's lying!"

Graeme held a hand out. "Stop, Mack."

"So then he said, 'I don't believe you. A woman like you doesn't live without a man to leech on.' And he grabbed my arms. He started to say something about hiding me away until he got an answer he liked. That's when I screamed for him to let me go. He started to drag me off when Shandar and Chucko ran out and tackled him. Then Nick came out. Then we came here."

"I heard him," said Shandar. "She's got that right. And the rest."

Mack stood up. "Now you're lying. You couldn't've heard me."

"Your voice travels," the baker continued. "I heard you very well. And I heard Cara's reply about Nick."

"Sit down, Mack," the sheriff ordered.

Graeme turned to Nick. "Are you having an affair with her?"

Nick shook his head.

"Graeme, that's not the point," Cara said. "The point is Mack accosted me in the street against your orders, grabbed me, and would have kidnapped me if I hadn't been rescued!"

Graeme studied her. "Point taken. Chucko?"

The barback shuffled his feet. "I heard the first part of Mack's questions and her scream. I didn't hear the rest, but I saw his shadow cross the window. I knew he was out there."

"Nick?"

"I didn't hear anything but the scream, but I knew who it was. I saw her walk downstairs with the laundry bag."

Mack stood up again. "Then it's Shandar she's bangin'."

Shandar stiffened, and his eyes widened. "You dare shame me? My faith is stronger than that."

"It's gotta be someone. Don't you see what she is?"

Graeme stood to face him. "C'mon, Mack." He nodded his head toward the cells behind him.

Mack's face burned with fury as he turned to stare at Cara.

"Look at him. Look!" she shouted. Fear crawled down her nerves. "He'd rape and kill me if he had the chance!"

"Don't make it worse with exaggeration, Cara." Graeme pulled Mack down the hall and opened the doors to the jail cells.

Astonishment flooded her. She looked at her three rescuers in turn. "Exaggeration?"

"He's wrong," Nick admitted.

Shandar raised his chin and looked down his nose at Cara. "Mack is right about one thing. If you weren't dancing in public, you wouldn't have this problem."

"That's not true, Shandar," she countered. "Mack began to fixate on me when he found out I was moving north. He only uses my dancing as an excuse to be a predator—of women and aliens."

"Nevertheless, you should treat your body more circumspectly. Then people wouldn't have bad opinions of you."

"No, Shandar." Chucko shook his head. "Men and women have been dancing for hundreds of thousands of years. The problem is with Mack, not Cara."

"Thank you, Chucko," she said. "And thank all of you for stopping him. I could be dead right now. Or worse," she added.

***

Tired from more than drumming and dancing, Cara climbed the stairs to her room across the hall from Nick's. At least she was safe for a while with Mack behind bars. The ball of anxiety that had lain in her stomach for three weekends and more had mercifully dissipated. She shoved the hall door open, closed it behind her, then did the same to her room door. She lit the lantern and collapsed on the bed, inspecting her sore palms. The skin was shiny from the constant rubbing, and the scars were brighter—as they were each night after she played. Intent on her wounds and memories, she hardly heard the sound of something falling on the first floor.

Outside her door, she heard Nick retrace his steps down the stairs. Thumps and bumps and muffled swearing floated up from below. Cara slid off the bed and pulled out her baton, flinging it into its extended position. She opened the door to peer out into the darkened stairwell. A heavy tread clumped its way up the stairs. A jumble of arms and legs appeared in her view. She barely had time to recognize it before it shouldered its way into her room. She stumbled back and pulled the baton behind her.

Rodani released Nick and pushed him across the narrow room, then shut the door and fell against it, pupils wide. Nick, stiff in shock and mouth agape, stared at the grey alien across from him. Cara held her hands out between the two men in an attempt to forestall violence.

^Wait, wait.^ She glanced quickly between the two. ^It's okay,^ she said to Nick. ^It's okay.^

She shifted her body to Rodani. "What in Temi's name are you doing here?"

"I had to see you," he replied with some heat. "To see that you are well and safe." He glanced from the bartender to the bed. "He does not sleep here."

It wasn't even a question, Cara noted. "No, he doesn't. I've told you that. And I'm fine, as you can see."

^That,^ Nick said, breathless, ^is a Selandu.^

She turned to him. ^Well done,^ she replied, deadpanned.

^Male or female?^

^It's a man.^

^Why is he here?^

^In the south, or in your bar?^

Nick dragged his gaze away from Rodani and fixed it on Cara. ^Both.^

^It's a long story.^

^I'm not sleeping for a while.^

^Sit down, please.^

Nick crossed his arms. ^I will when he does.^

Cara sat at the foot of the bed and patted the mattress beside her. "Sit down, aisu. Nick deserves an explanation."

"That is the man who is going to Himadi, yes?"

"We'd both be in trouble if he weren't. You took a big chance."

"Your safety is still my priority, kia. I heard you shouting earlier and watched that man grab you!"

She patted the bed again and closed the baton. Rodani took a seat, gingerly. When Cara turned to Nick, he did the same, pulling a chair out from the tiny table under the window.

Cara took a deep breath and motioned to Nick. ^Nick, I would like to present to you my husband, Rodani.^ She swung her hand in the opposite direction and switched to Selandi. "Rodani, this is Nick, the man who will be bartending in Himadi House." She turned back. ^...Nick?^

Nick clamped his jaws shut and ran a hand over his mouth and beard. His gaze flicked from one to another, the short and the tall, the familiar and the alien. Eventually, he found his voice.

^You have got to be shitting me.^

Cara laughed softly, as much from relief as humor. ^Nope. No shitting here.^

^You mean the word 'husband' specifically?^

^Yes.^

He stared a little longer. ^I didn't know that was possible.^

A wide grin spread across her face. ^Neither did I until the time came.^

^And how did that...time...manage to come?^

^How about just asking how we got together?^ His steady regard worried her.

^Okay. I'm up for a story. A true one,^ he amended.

Cara glanced between the two of them. ^Nick, how about a round of drinks first? I'll pay.^

Nick tilted his head. ^Nooo, this round's on me. What does he drink?^

She turned to her mate, who was silent and waiting. "He's offering a drink. What kind of taste do you prefer?"

"Does he have something that doesn't offend the nose? Something semi-sweet, if he has it."

She relayed the request. ^It seems he doesn't like the smell of ale.^

^I'll find something. And for you?^

^That new one you let me try when I first came back, please.^

^Give me a few.^ He left the room, not without a side-eye to the grey form on the bed.

"Rodani," she said heatedly as Nick went down the stairs, "where has your sense of caution gone?"

"I had to verify your safety, Cara, after you were attacked. I cannot stress enough its importance to me." He reached around her and pulled her into an embrace. "You cannot know how difficult it was for me to watch you be accosted and not rush to save you." He buried his fingers in her hair. "To allow others to rescue you."

"Be pleased they did."

"And if they had not?"

She felt the force of his question throughout her body, and had no answer. "He's in jail now."

"What is ^jail^?"

"Remember that room in the Enclave with bars on the window and locks on the wrong side of the door?"

"Yes."

"Like that."

"And will he be freed?"

"The sheriff said he would be there for at least two weeks."

"Then we will revisit this discussion before this second rest-day arrives."

^Yes, dear.^

"And what is that meaning?"

"Grudging acceptance."

They drew apart when Nick could be heard on the stairs.

^You two look guilty.^

^And you know what guilt looks like on a Selandu face?^

He held out a tray with three drinks.

Cara smiled. ^Just a reassuring hug.^ She handed Rodani's to him and took her own. She saw his nostrils flare as he brought the glass to his lips. He took a sip, considered, and took another.

"Well enough?"

"Yes." He inclined his head to Nick. "Verelin."

Nick hesitated, and Cara cleared her throat, eyes wide, gesturing him to reply.

^Um....^

^Just bow your head in a tilt. Like I showed you.^

Nick bowed and took his seat. ^Talk.^

^Let me get through the story before you ask questions. I'll try to keep it short.^

^Okay.^

She took a drink and began. The setting. The people. The rules. The encroaching loneliness. The companionship trials. Tasos and Temichin. Knives and Guns. Music. The maze. Serano's herb. Onana. The falls. The poridi. The approach, and a hint of its sweet end. Shurad. The Enclave. Her abortive flight. The first firefight. Rodani's perils. The second firefight. The sundering.

She took a long swallow as Nick digested the tale.

^And you came home crying.^

She huffed. ^Does everyone know that?^

^And his presence here?^

^Oh. He left Barridan a few weeks later. We met up, reunited.^

^And where do you stay now?^

Cara hesitated.

^Please. Don't you trust me?^

^Yes, but why do you need to know?^

Nick began to answer, then shut his mouth. ^Never mind.^

She took another sip. ^Can he stay here tonight?^

His lips thinned in thought. ^We'll all be in trouble if he's found. And I may not get to Himadi if he is.^

^He'll be gone before it gets light.^

Nick glanced around the room, then back to the waiting pair. ^Tonight only. I'll think about tomorrow, tomorrow.^

^Thanks, Nick. And for today, too.^

He strolled to the door, then turned. ^The bed squeaks.^

She grinned. ^I know.^

***

The next night, Rodani 'commed his location to Cara. He slipped in the back door that she held open. Behind her in the hallway, Nick frowned. ^There are people awake at night, you know. This is the last time. I'm not jeopardizing my move north.^

^I understand,^ Cara said.

Rodani bowed to the bartender and went into the bedroom. The other two followed, sitting where they had the night before.

^Ready to play interpreter?^ Nick asked.

^Yes.^

He looked at Rodani. ^I'm allowing you to stay here tonight with the trade-off that I get to ask you questions. And you answer them. Cara agreed.^

She turned to Rodani and translated Nick's comments. Rodani inclined his head and turned his hand over, palm up. "Up until the point I betray my people."

"He won't ask that. Not on purpose. And you don't have to answer if he does."

She turned back to Nick. ^Did you note his head movement? His hand?^

^I saw his head move. Not his hand.^

^It's best to watch both if you can. The head dip meant he agrees. The hand movement means, basically, 'go ahead.' And he said he'll answer questions up until the point where he'd put his own people in danger. I reassured him neither you nor I would allow that.^

^No, I won't. It would also put me in danger, wouldn't it?^

^Most likely.^

Nick shifted in his chair and took a sip of wine. ^So, I take a boat to that town over the border. Then what happens?^

^The town's called Soldan.^ She translated and listened to Rodani's reply. ^He said someone will inspect the things you brought and confiscate any weapons. Then someone will escort you to a wagon, pile your belongings in it, and take you to Himadi. There may or may not be another wagon meeting you halfway. If so, they'll transfer you from the one to the other, and you continue to the house.^

^What happens if I need a bathroom?^

She turned to Rodani and asked, then turned back. ^There are facilities you can use in Soldan. I'll make you a flash card you can show them to make your request. If you need to stop on the way, you'll have to relieve yourself behind the wagon.^

^How long is the trip from Soldan to Himadi? And what happens when I get there^

She checked with Rodani. ^About four hours. Andrew should already be there, but he may be busy. If he's not, he'll probably take you to your rooms and show you the bar. You can ask for him. If he's busy, someone else will show you to your rooms. I'll make a card for those, too.^

^Where will I go to eat?^

Cara dug her notebook out. ^There'll be a first-floor gathering room with tables, chairs, and a buffet. I need to make a list of cards for your questions.^ She scribbled them down.

^Does each set of rooms have a toilet and shower, or are those communal?^

She interpreted for Rodani and waited while he answered. ^The better rooms, for Andrew, you, and the researchers, should have them. There are smaller rooms for servants, cooks, housekeeping, etc., that may not. They'll use communal.^

^What do I do with the money at the end of the night?^

^You can ask Andrew that.^

^Will there be assassins there?^

^Guardians. Let me ask.^ She checked and turned back. ^Yes.^

^Can they be trusted to escort me to the bank each night?^

^Yes.^ She made another note.

^What if there's a fight between Selandu, or between the two species? Will a guardian be there each night I'm open, or do I have to hire a Selandu bouncer?^

^Hmmm.^ She checked with Rodani. ^Other patrons usually stopped fights in Barridan. Guild were there sometimes, but not usually as bouncers or security. They could be called though if the fight got too bad.^

Nick let his gaze roam over Rodani. ^It wouldn't take but seconds for a human to get killed.^

Cara turned, and they talked in Selandi back-and-forth for a few minutes. ^Couple of things,^ she told Nick. ^If he hasn't already, Andrew needs to tell the Selandu there how to deal with angry humans, especially drunk ones. They need to understand their relative strength and the inadvisability of deaths between the species. Second, you might be able to hire someone on your busiest nights. Either with a free drink and a coin or two...or more than a couple of coins. You'd have to talk to Andrew to set that up.^

^Will there be musicians?^

She checked again. ^Maybe. Probably Selandu ones. Instrumental music. That's the only kind they do. No singing.^

^Who pays them?^

She asked. ^In Barridan, the cost was shared between the bartender and the taso's house accounts.^

^Doctors? Nurses?^

^Huh. I haven't heard. Surely someone would be there. Barridan had its own clinic, but they were all Selandu. I wonder who would go.^

^Not Dr. Liz, I assume,^ he said with some humor.

^No. She wouldn't leave her own patients for a handful or two across the border. Besides, she's not done molding Kimi into the shape she expects.^

Nick drained his mug. ^Well, I'm tired. And I'm sure you are, too. See you next week? Just you?^ he amended.

^Yeah.^

He rose and gave Rodani the same bow he'd received in the hallway, then shut the door behind him.

Cara wrapped her arms around her husband. "Thank you, aisu. I appreciate you and your patience."

"It seems my earlier concerns were unnecessary." He joined her in the hug. "You should make those cards for him before you sleep so he can review them during the week."

She spread her hands and looked around. "He has the blanks. It'll have to wait."

"Then we sleep."

***

Monday afternoon, Suraya left the newspaper's office and made her way south to the bar. Nick and Chucko stood behind the long bar top, deep in conversation. She stopped just inside the door.

"I don't think I can stay here when Dottie takes over, Nick."

"Just tell her you know what you're doing, and to leave you alone."

Chucko made a rude noise. "Like that worked for you? She's gonna run this place into the ground."

"She might. And I'm sorry. She was the only one to accept my offer. The only one who'd pay me what it's worth."

"Wish I could have bought it."

Nick put a hand on his shoulder. "Me, too. Let me know in Himadi if you do leave. I'll send you a severance."

"Right. How am I supposed to contact you there?"

"Through the CSC, of course." He turned to the door. "Suraya."

She took it as an offer, and walked toward the men with a polite smile on her face. "Congrats," she said to Nick. "I envy you. Got a place for me there?"

"Not unless you want to be a bouncer."

"Any new news from Cara? Did she give you any advice about Himadi?"

He rolled his eyes, and his voice dropped deep. "No."

"I'm still trying to find out where she goes during the week."

"Why don't you leave her her privacy instead?"

"I don't mean her any harm."

"Doesn't mean you can't cause it."

Suraya froze. "What do you mean?"

"Just what I said."

"What do you know that I don't? Is she in trouble?"

"Not that I'm aware of. But she must have her reasons for staying away from all the sharp-tongued busy bodies who follow her." Nick leaned forward and raised his eyebrows. "That sound like anyone you know?"

Suraya turned to the barback. "Do you know anything, Chucko?"

He shook his head.

"Well, if you learn anything..."

"I'll get right on that." The sarcasm dripped.

Back to Nick. "When does she leave? In what direction?"

Nick walked around the bar top and took Suraya's arm in a firm grip. "I believe you've forgotten where the door is."

Ejected and dejected, Suraya made her way to Davad's cabin.

"He's down at the docks," Merelin said with barely disguised discourtesy. *Pregnant women must have an extra aversion to former lovers,* Suraya thought, shrugging. It wasn't like Davad was still interested in her.

And there he was. She made her way over to his fishing boat, where he scrubbed and scraped. "Hey, Dav."

Cara's brother turned his head. "Su."

"Got a minute?"

"Not really. Unless I can work and talk."

"You can." She watched him for a moment, as she had Nick and Chucko. "Have you seen a difference in Cara since she returned?"

"I did. She got over it. Why?"

"Is she really over it?"

"What's this about?"

"Do you ever wonder why she disappears every week? Do you know where she goes?"

He looked at her, confusion on his face. "Why should I care?"

"Because she's your big sister? Because you guys are close?"

"She knows what she's about. She doesn't need me mothering her. Or smothering her, as the case may be." He went back to scraping.

"Nick gave me the impression she might be in some trouble."

"I heard about Mack. Won't be the first time some loser paid her too much attention. She can ask for my help if she needs it."

"Will she?"

Silence.

Sensing another obstruction, Suraya turned away. She left Davad's boat, with him wondering if it mattered—and why.

Cara had acted weirdly when she first came back, Davad admitted to himself. But he hadn't seen her since then. He'd given up drinking as a promise to Merelin when she found out she'd conceived. So, he hadn't bothered to watch Cara's performances.

Is she in trouble? More trouble than just Mack? He didn't see any reason for her to be, though he had to admit some level of ignorance on the subject. Where did she stay during the week?

Is it any of my business? Not really.

He went back to cleaning.

***

Three days later, Cara lay still and somnolent on the blanket, Rodani beside her. His forearms rested on his flat belly, fingers entwined and lax.

A little bit of nirvana, she thought. *Valhalla. Elysium. Whatever. Shut up, brain.* She laid a hand on Rodani's arm, and heard a rustle. Feet, claws, something she didn't recognize. She opened her eyes to see a red and black pseudo-lizard hop on Rodani's shirt. It crept toward his bare arm.

"Aisu!" she hissed. "Freeze!"

Rodani's eyes shot open, and his body jerked in reaction. Also startled, the lizard clamped his jaws on Rodani's arm. As Cara let out a scream, Rodani swore and yanked it off, which took a patch of his skin with it. When the creature landed, he stabbed it.

"That's a death's head!" She reached for him and started rocking in dread when he pulled away.

Rodani glanced up from the bleeding wound in his forearm. "What do you mean?"

"It's venomous! It's going to kill you!"

"It will not kill me. I recognize it under a different name."

"Yes, it will!" She reached for him, shaking. "Every person who's been bitten has died! Oh gods, Rodani! I don't want you to die!" *Nothing to do! Nothing to say. He's dead already and doesn't believe it!*

"They do not kill us, kia."

Rodani stood and inspected the bite. Already it was swelling, cutting off the blood flow. As he made his way to the latrine, Cara followed, babbling in shock and despair.

"Are you sure, aisu? Are you sure it won't kill you? I didn't even know they were here on the island." She stumbled over roots and crashed into dead branches. "Oh, gods, I'm so sorry!"

At the latrine, Rodani divested himself of his weapons belt, laying it on the ground nearby. Then he stripped off his clothes. "I am going to be very sick soon," he told her. "I can feel it coming. You need to go back to the camp and wait."

She threw out her hands. "I'm not leaving you!"

Rodani drew an arm over his stomach and winced. "Kia, I am going to be spewing from both ends. Please leave me my privacy."

She stared, uncomprehending. "You wouldn't leave *me*."

Rodani stared at the ground in front of his bare feet. "Please," he said in a whisper.

She ran off, panic and rejection stealing her courtesy as she yelled. "I'm going to stay close enough to hear you call for me, Rodani. Don't tell me I can't!" A last glance showed him dropping to his hands and knees.

Frantic, swearing, she circled the camp, looking for whatever might help. Water barrel. Wash rags. Mug to rinse his mouth. Oh, gods, this was as bad as the poridi attack on Kusik! He won't be able to move far. He's gonna collapse. Blanket and the woven mat

186

underneath. Clean clothes? No. Food? Gods, no. Medicines? We hardly have any. His smoke and umbrella? Maybe, maybe. Soap, fool. Who knows how badly he'll spatter himself? Water, for the gods' sake!

She might need a change of clothes if she were going to clean him up. *Strip down to underthings if you do, fem. What else? What else?*

She stared at the remnants of the death's head. How much venom lay mixed in with the expelled innards? She didn't dare touch it. Or use a utensil they ate with. *Forget it. Bury it later.*

Everything but the heavy water barrel went into a pile in the middle of the blanket. At the last moment, she grabbed her carry sack for something to keep her busy while she waited. The bundle was unwieldy, but she stumbled her way back toward the latrine, listening for sounds she didn't want to hear.

Then she did hear. Explosive body sounds that invaded her ears and ripped gouges in her heart. "Oh, aisu," she whispered. "Please be right. I can't lose you."

She went back for the mat and the water barrel, then flopped down on the blanket. The sounds continued, interrupted with intermittent silences. Cara rocked back and forth as the minutes passed. How long did a human last before dying? An hour? A half-hour? *I don't remember. I don't remember. Why can't I remember?*

But the sounds emanating from Rodani's body seemed to go on for longer than expected. She couldn't judge the time. Little by little, she calmed. Maybe he was right. Gods of dark space, please let him be right. She couldn't live without him. Not and be happy.

She stood, sat, wandered the spot, sat again. Drew out her stitching, but stuffed it back in the sack. Opened her notebook and translated Nick's questions for the weekend. Sketched a plant, a leaf, a stick.

Eventually, there were more silences than sounds, then no sounds at all.

An effluvium assaulted her nose as she crept forward. *What did you expect, fem? Perfume?* Rodani lay on his side next to the latrine, his back to her. He didn't move. "No. Nonononono," she muttered, fear creeping upward. A few more steps. "Aisu?"

Fingers that rested on his hip waggled for a second. He muttered something. She ran forward, heedless of the smell, and crouched down behind his back. "What did you say? What do you need, aisu?"

"Let me rest," he whispered.

"Will you rinse your mouth?"

"I do not think I can sit."

"Can I wash you while you rest? Whatever I can reach."

"Later."

She sat down where she crouched and laid a hand on his arm. "I'm here. I brought what you might need. We can spend the night here if necessary."

Silence, then: "Thank you."

Cara dragged the blanket over next to him, and lay down. Hours inched by. The sun hit its zenith and began its descent.

Rodani moved his head. "Kia?"

Cara jolted awake. "Aisu?"

"Water, please."

She ran to get it. Barrel. Filled his mug. Ran back. "Can you sit up?"

"I believe." He shifted parts of his body in turn, and put a hand on the ground to push upward. "Au," he groaned. His left hand and lower arm were swollen to twice its size. He rolled into a sit as they both stared at it.

"Rodani, you need to go to that town. Now. Didn't you say you were safe, there?"

"No. Yes. It is safe. No, I will not." His normal hand waved aimlessly. "Water?"

"Here." She handed him the mug, leaving her hand near his just in case. She watched him empty it, then refilled it—twice, before he stopped.

"But your hand. Your arm."

"It will shrink. I remember the lesson."

"Let me wash you."

Rodani cleaned his own face and privates, Cara took on the rest, including the ends of his hair that had fallen forward into the muck. When they finished, Cara started to move the mat forward.

"Du. I need away from this smell."

"How far can you walk?"

"We will discover." He rolled onto his hand and knees, and crawled to the nearest tree. With more effort than she thought he had in him, he made it to his feet, shaking and pale. He shuffled north between the trees, Cara following with the mat and blanket. When the smell had faded into the background, Rodani stopped.

"Here?" Cara asked.

"Yes."

"How much pain are you in? Do you need the smoke powder?"

He considered for a moment. "Yes."

She made his bed, grabbed the powder and umbrella, and set it up for him. While he lay under it, she went back for the rest of their belongings. By the time she finished, he had moved the umbrella aside and was flat on his back on the blanket, still naked, mouth open and motionless. He wanted only water, refusing even a mug of broth. There, they spent the night.

She stayed by his side all Friday while the sun was up, plying him with liquids and soft foods. He napped, washed a little more, managed to dress himself, and napped again. As the sky began to darken, he sat up.

"Are you not going to perform tonight?"

"Yeah, I will. But I wanted to stay with you as long as possible."

"I will manage."

"You only have one hand."

Rodani raised his injured one and studied it in the firelight. "I may not need more than that. For now."

"I'll come back tonight."

He gave her a long look. "That is not necessary, kia. I will abide."

"And I'll abide better if I'm here rather than lying sleepless in that room over the bar."

Cara crawled around to his good side and wrapped her arms around him. She still couldn't quite believe he was alive and moving and talking to her. She thanked all the nonexistent gods she'd fallen in love with a Selandu, not a human. She'd be a widow, otherwise. It made her sick to think about.

She was going to be late, and she didn't give a good goddamn. Her husband was all that mattered. She'd left him still on the blanket, wan and shaky, unable to climb to his hammock. At least he'd eaten something, but he refused again to go to that village to see a doctor. His hand and arm looked like stuffed sausages, and it frightened her.

Cara looked around the camp. Water and food nearby. Blanket if he wanted it, and the mat. She refilled the umbrella cup with more smoke powder. It was so little, but it was the best she could do.

She docked her boat and made no attempt to be circumspect. A pox on anyone who cared what she did or where she went. She speed-walked to Nick's shed behind the bar and grabbed her conga drums. Revelers were already congregating, and Jonie and James were waiting onstage.

Nick met her at the shed doors, looking her over carefully. "You okay?"

"Barely."

"Allow me." He picked up the larger drum. "What happened?"

"He got bit by a death's head yesterday."

Nick set the drum down, eyes wide. "He died?"

"No, he survived. But gods, he was sick, and not just his mouth. He's still weak. I hated to leave him."

He lifted the drum again and put it in the cart. "He got really lucky." Behind him, Cara did the same with the smaller drum.

"Yeah, do I know it. I thought for sure he was gonna die right in front of me. I panicked, bad."

Nick pulled the cart, then carried the larger drum up onto the stage. He reached for the smaller one as Cara climbed the steps.

"You're a good human, Nick. Thank you."

He smiled. "I could say the same about you. Take care of him," he whispered as he walked past.

Cara took several deep breaths as she settled herself in front of the drums. She held her drumsticks up, looking to James for the start sign. He gave it, eyeing her at the same time.

At the end of the evening, he walked back to her. "You were late. Problem?"

"Handled."

"Mack?"

"No. He's still in jail."

"Family?"

She picked up the small drum. "You could say that."

James rested his arms on the top side of his guitar. "You got something going with Nick?"

Cara scrunched her eyes and grimaced. "Are you kidding me? Really?"

"I've never seen him help you before."

"He knew I was late. Like you did! My dancing helps him earn money, James, just like it does you and me." She turned toward the stairs. "Get off my back."

"Just making sure we know where we stand."

Davad stood at the bottom of the stairs, looking up into the confrontation. "Need a hand?"

"I'm all right. Thanks. Don't usually see you here."

He tilted his head. "You sure you're okay?"

"Yep." She saw the hesitation in his face, but decided it was better to ignore it. She wasn't up to more dissembling. Her patience was already at low-tide levels, and she didn't want to cause strife with her best ally.

Cara bid him good night, put the drums away, and sped back to the docks.

Rodani was where she left him, on his side on the blanket in front of a fire that was not much more than embers. She tossed her carry sack aside, laid down with him, and curled into him with a hand on his waist.

As the fire continued to wane, the little mammal crept into the dim light and sat, green eyes on the pair.

"Food time, Fuzz," Cara whispered, dug into her bag, and tossed a piece of meat to it. As they lay quietly, it came up and sat on its haunches in front of Rodani to nibble on its meal. When it ate, it let Cara pet it and stroke the soft fur.

And to her surprise, it curled up near their heads and went to sleep.

SIXTEEN

"How are you doing with the new words, aisu?"

Rodani fumbled with the growing set of vocabulary cards in his lap. He flexed his swollen fingers and pursed his lips. "Well enough...until you test me," he admitted.

"Am I such a terrible taskmaster?"

"Or I am a lazy student."

"I'm so glad your wound is getting better." They sat side by side on the sand in the sun, just outside the edge of trees that covered most of their island.

He inspected his hand and arm. In two weeks, the terrible swelling had gone down by about half, though his grip was still less than perfect. "Guild instructors taught that it would, years ago. I am fortunate they were correct."

"Fortunate too, that it hasn't rained in two weeks. Let's hope that continues for a bit."

He glanced at Cara with a slight smile. "I climbed to the bottom branch the first weekend, and to the third branch last weekend. I hope to make it up to the hammock this time."

"Don't fall. Please. If you break a leg, I can't carry you."

"What would you do if I did?"

"Gods. It would depend on how badly. If the bone were sticking out, I doubt I could do anything. Otherwise, I'd wrap it as tight as I could in the hopes you could make it into the boat. Then hope that your town wouldn't capture me when I brought you there."

"If I made it into the boat, likely I could drive myself," Rodani mused.

"Let's not let that happen. Okay?"

^Yes, dear.^

Shocked for a second, Cara burst out in laughter, rocking side to side and then sputtering to a stop. "I didn't know you memorized that one."

"I have not forgotten, my mate."

The giggles took a minute to subside. It had been too long since she'd had a good laugh. She nuzzled Rodani's arm, then continued to stitch her current design.

"Our little furry hunter is getting bolder, aisu."

"Yes?"

"Fuzz let me touch him several times, and almost let me pick him up."

"I think he is young," Rodani said. "Otherwise, would he not be less brave? More frightened?"

"I would think so. It's kind of nice having him around. I hope he stays."

"We continue feeding him, he will stay."

***

To their west, beyond the shoreline, Davad stuffed his boating shoes into a sack. The windows of their snug cabin were open to the summer breezes, and the sun reflected off the seashells that had been strewn outside the front of their door.

Merelin glanced at him. "Where are you going?"

He smiled, reassuring his anxious and expectant fiancée. "I have an errand." He kissed her on the forehead. "Don't worry. I'll be back before it's born."

"Not funny, Dav."

"Then I have five more months to come up with something better, don't I?"

Merelin sighed. "I know you love that boat more than you love me."

"Not quite." He hugged her to him. "I don't have to clean out your bottom or scrape the barnacles off your back."

She shoved him away in mock anger. "G'wan," she said, chuckling.

Davad cast off and headed his boat away from the docks, east toward the islands. The sun shone in his eyes, and the sea breezes blew curls away from his face. He loved the sea, the open vistas, the calm, and the danger.

Waves tumbled under the boat as it rode. Now, now he would find out what was up with his sister, what secrets she was keeping from her family. Playing each weekend with Jonie's band, disappearing each week. Did she know she was talked about? The busybodies in town had more than once cornered him for information, Suraya foremost among them.

One, two, three, four islands passed by. A low line of trees appeared on the horizon. He veered right in his approach.

Cara stitched another piece of thread into the fabric in her hand. One of their blankets protected her skin from the ever-present sand on the beach.

Rodani sat beside her. Driftwood chips landed in his lap and lay scattered around his legs as he carved. She tossed him simple questions in Cene'l, which he answered with simple words. Sparkles of light reflected on the waves in front of them. Cara squinted against the glare and stretched her cramping fingers.

A spot appeared on the horizon to her left. It resolved into a sail. She watched it a little suspiciously, as the day's fishing boats had already safely passed by them. When the sail didn't seem to be heading to sea, she tapped Rodani on the thigh.

"Aisu, boat."

He watched for a few careful minutes. "Human."

"You should hide. Try the hammock."

He rose. "I will stay back in the trees."

"Aisu, if you have to leave the trees to protect me, you'll have to leave me and go back north again. It's probably not any danger to me."

Rodani made no reply. He crept back into the trees, near but not up into the hammock.

The boat pulled onto the sand of the cove. A familiar form jumped out and walked her way.

Cara rose to greet her favorite brother. ^What in the world are you doing here?^

^Took the question out of my mouth, sis.^ Feigning nonchalance, he regarded her with a steady gaze and stepped up to her. ^Why are *you* here?^

^How did you find me?^

^I followed you,^ he told her.

^I haven't even been out today.^

^Sunday morning.^

^Why for all the gods' sake?^

^Curiosity.^

Cara crossed her arms and returned Davad's steady gaze.

Davad waved to the blanket. ^Let's sit.^

Protesting, she thought, would make him more suspicious. She sat, wrapping her arms around her knees.

^Kimi has asked about you. Suraya, too. The dock supervisor wonders why you disappear with Ama and Dae's boat every Sunday, and bring it back every Friday. I wondered why you disappear, too.^

^I like it here. It's peaceful. No one bothering me. No dirty looks. No lewd ones, either.^

^So you sit on this spit of land with no food and water five days a week, just to avoid people who shouldn't matter to you?^

Silence rose between them.

^No answer?^

^None should be necessary, Dav.^

^Cara, those aliens did *something* to you. Don't tell me they didn't. You can trust me, you know.^

^How much can I trust you?^ She shifted to look at him. ^Where do you draw the line?^

^Which line?^

^The one where you can't keep a secret.^

^Is there a war coming?^

Her eyes widened. ^Not at all, that I know of. Of course I was a nobody there, just as I'm a nobody here.^

^Then what did happen? Something made you change so much that nearly everyone has said something to me about it.^

^Dav, there are reasons secrets need to be kept.^

^You don't trust me.^ The hurt bled through his words, and into Cara's heart.

^Dammit, it's more complicated than that.^

^Try me. I've got time.^

^And if someone wormed it out of you?^

^They won't.^

She waited, tight-lipped and frozen on the blanket.

^Trust me. I want to know what's wrong with you. What happened up there.^

^Absolute trust?^ she shot back. ^Life-ruining trust? There's a life on the line.^

^Who's life?^ Davad grabbed her arm. ^You're in danger? Here? At home?^

^No!^ *Calm. Be calm.* ^Not me. Absolute trust?^

^Yesss.^ He waited out another silence. ^Cara.^

She ached to tell him. The burden of secret-keeping lay heavily on her mind, and the guilt would kill her if it turned out badly. It might also kill the man she loved. She'd already been forced by circumstance to tell one other person. But she did trust this brother, the only sibling besides Kimi who didn't judge her. She wondered if he would, now.

Making her decision, she lowered the barriers she'd hid behind for weeks. ^I'll do you one better.^ She waved her hand behind her.

Seconds passed. A tall form appeared at the tree line. Stopped. Then walked onto the sand. Sat down at Cara's side.

Davad watched, mouth open in utter disbelief. His wide eyes traveled from Cara's face to the face of the alien next to her, who in turned watched him in stiff silence.

"Rodani," Cara said in Selandi, "this is my brother, Davad." She switched to Cene'l, ^Davad, this is my husband, Rodani.^

Rodani's pupils narrowed. "You trust this brother?"

"Yes. Very much."

Davad found his voice, and it was filled with incredulity. ^Husband?^

^Yes. We fell in love in Barridan. He was my guardian.^

^Love? Impossible.^

^Nope. And when they sent me home, I had to leave him behind. That's why I cried so much.^

The two men stared at each other, as much in curiosity as suspicion.

^Well,^ Davad drawled, ^tell him I said welcome to the family.^

Cara interpreted his words. Rodani replied, bowing his head.

^He says, 'I thank you for your welcome.' Try not to stare so much.^

Davad grimaced. He knew what the Selandu looked like ever since he began selling them fish from southern waters, and buying and selling trade goods. His sister had made that possible by teaching him a little of their language. But this...*this* was several steps beyond. *This*, was personal.

^Is he gonna hit me?^

^No. It's just discourteous.^ Cara smiled. ^You know, I've already had this conversation with someone else.^

Davad planted his fists on his hips, despite the fact that he was sitting cross-legged. ^Who'd you tell before you told me?^

^Uh, Nick found out. Accidentally.^

Davad scratched his forehead. ^Okay, I can see him keeping a secret. So how did this,^ he waved his hand between the two of them, ^happen?^

^Just about the same way it does with anybody else.^

^So you married an assassin.^

^A guardian, Dav. He protects. If he needs to kill to do that, he can.^

^So he protected you while you were there.^

^Yeah. Almost at the cost of his life. What was it? Four or five times?^

Again, disbelief filled Davad's face. ^Someone tried to kill you five times?^

^Six Selandu, with two being crafters, and four guardians.^

^Well...tell him thank you.^

She turned to Rodani. "Davad thanks you for protecting me in Barridan."

"My duty, kia."

Davad leaned back on his hands. ^So,^ he glanced at the two of them, ^is he *really* your husband?^

Cara drew her eyebrows together and cocked her head.

^You know, in *that* way?^

She grinned and ducked her head, shook it side to side. ^Yes, in that way.^

^I didn't know that was possible.^

^I didn't either. But Rodani had an idea it was. Rumors from the guardians who deal with Menachem and Andrew.^

^That must have been a trip and a half.^

Cara laughed out loud. She took Rodani's hand in hers. ^Oh, it was. And a very interesting one.^

^Does Menachem know? Andrew?^

^Nope. And I had to work to keep it a secret.^

^What would they do if they found out?^

^I don't know, and I don't want to know. Even more, I don't want them to know he's here, in the south.^

^They won't get it from me. What happened to his arm?^

^Death's head bite.^

Davad's eyes grew wide. ^Why isn't he dead?^

^Luck of the species.^

^You need to be careful coming and going. If I found you, others can, too,^ he said, worried.

Cara looked down at the sand. ^I know. The only thing that seems workable is to come and go at different times. Leave in a slightly different direction, maybe.^

Davad glanced at the sun. ^I should go back.^

^How's Merelin?^

Davad smiled fondly. ^Well, and getting bigger.^ He shook his head. ^She doesn't like me being too far away from her for too long.^ He got up and brushed sand off his legs.

^You'll keep our secret, right?^ Cara cocked an eyebrow. ^Right?^

^Sure. You've had enough trouble over the years. I don't need to add to it.^

Cara's shoulders slumped, and some of the tension in her gut disappeared. ^You're a good man, you know that?^

^And what will you do for me in return?^

^Just don't ask me to babysit.^

Davad laughed and nodded to them both before turning back to his boat.

SEVENTEEN

It wasn't likely to be a good day. Cara opened the door of The Wet Bar and almost didn't go in. Voices were raised in argument behind the long bar top. Nick's voice was immediately recognizable, but it took a moment for Cara to remember the other one.

Dottie, Nick's ex-wife, stood facing him with a bottle in her hand. "I know what I'm doing. Stop harping on me."

Nick scratched his head. A pained expression covered his face. "I'm not harping, Dot. I'm trying to explain—"

"You've explained enough. I get it. Go on and run away to the aliens. Run away from your kids, your livelihood, your patrons. It's what you've been waiting for." She turned away and continued placing bottles on the back wall.

Nick glanced at Cara in the doorway, then strode up the stairs and out of sight.

Cara started toward the bar top. *You can do this. You've faced worse.* "Dottie?" she said as she got close. "I'm sorry to bother you. I know you're busy."

Dottie glanced over her shoulder. "I know what you want. The answer's no."

"May I ask why? I can pay you."

"My son needs the room."

"There are cabins for singles."

"Which you could easily rent. Or buy, with all those coins tossed at your feet." Dottie sniffed in disdain. Her opinion of Cara's dancing wasn't a secret.

Calm, she heard in Rodani's voice. "I don't need something seven days a week. Just two."

"You got your answer."

Well, it wasn't unexpected. "Good luck with the bar."

"I won't need it."

Cara headed to the door. Behind her, footsteps clomped down the stairs. She went out, holding the door for Nick. "Gods, I envy you," she said.

Nick hung his head and took a deep breath, almost as if he was about to jump off a cliff.

Somehow, she found a smile for him. "Dottie, or Himadi?"

"I got what I needed for the sale of the bar." Another breath. "How did you feel when you climbed into that boat to go north?"

"Petrified and exhilarated."

Nick's mouth widened into a smile or anxious grimace. "That fits."

"Keep your patience. Keep your courtesy. Keep your flash cards handy." She patted him on the back. "You'll do fine. I'll miss you," she added.

In a quick move, he hugged her and let go. "Keep that husband safe," he whispered.

"I'll try."

Soon, he was out of sight, off toward the docks and the new life she'd helped him make. A fierce ache enveloped her, a desire to follow so strong as to make her take a few steps in that direction. But what of Rodani? What kind of reception could he get after abandoning Barridan so abruptly? He carried way too many scars already. And what would Andrew say if she showed up there? Nothing good, she was sure.

Face your reality, fem, not your dreams.

Dejected, Cara made her way around to the wheelwright's shop, where she purchased a small cart to carry her drums. Hauling it behind her, she went back to the bar and took her drums out of the shed, then began pulling it down the street. Where could she put them? Her father's lab didn't have room, and he was already hiding her trunk. Menachem wouldn't want them at the CSC. She didn't want to be in Gerry's debt, so he was out. NO to Ama's house. Davad might, but Merelin wouldn't want them there with a baby on the way.

One more place she could try. She walked north, away from the bar and toward the river. A small house sat among other small houses, those meant for families. Families were most important here, of course. More than nearly anything else this side of the border. More babies. More babies. Get married. Get to producing. Keep the species alive. Didn't matter that they already existed on at least two other planets. Nope, they had to do it here, too, regardless of how many people they made miserable.

She dropped the cart handle and stepped onto the porch. Knocked. Waited.

A face peered out from the doorway and smiled. "Cara! Welcome, stranger."

"Hi, Emmie. I'm sorry I haven't been around much."

"What's new? Come on in." Cara's sister pushed on the door. A small baby cried inside.

"That Nick's?" Cara asked.

"Yeah. Did you know he's gone now? Gone up north."

"And that's why I'm here."

"Oh? Do tell." Emmie waved at the nearest chair, then picked the baby up, sat, and put him to her breast. The ear-splitting wails faded mercifully.

Another, younger, woman appeared in the back doorway. "Cara?"

"Kimi!" Cara got up and threw her arms around her youngest sister. "I didn't know you were here."

"Visiting and helping." Kimi glanced at Emmie. "Not only on Ama's orders."

The three women shared a family chuckle. "I won't take much time," Cara said. "I was wondering if I could ask a very small favor."

Another smile from Emmie. "Ready to babysit?"

"Gods, no. Maybe a small payment instead?"

"What do you need?"

"Just a place to store my drums during the week. I thought you might allow me to keep them on your porch."

"What happened to keeping them at the bar?"

Mild disgust spread across Cara's face. "Nick sold the bar to Dottie. One of her sons needs the room. I don't know anyone else who might be willing."

Kimi leaned forward. "I can."

"Where?"

"In my room."

"No. I don't want to give Ama any reason to bitch at you."

Kimi sagged.

Emmie jiggled the baby in her arms. "That's tough. Where will you live?"

"Oh, I have a little camp outside somewhere. I don't want to leave the drums there."

"Why not?"

"Too much trouble. Too little security. At least here they won't get stolen."

"Where is this camp?"

Cara waved her hand. "Just out—away from people. Please? I'll pay you a little bit for the space."

Emmie smiled wryly. "Someday, someone's gonna figure you out."

"Nah. I'm not worth that kind of effort."

"Cara!" Kimi shook her finger, a reminder of their mother she didn't want. "That's not right. Don't think that way."

Emmie glanced at that same finger. "Where will you stay on the weekends if not the bar?"

"The hostel, I guess."

"Ugh. You sure? You can still sleep here."

"Thanks, Emmie. I appreciate it. But I really don't want to babysit."

"What have you got against babies? You did alright with your sibs."

"Yeah!" said Kimi, one of those selfsame siblings.

"Maybe that's why," Cara replied. "I had my fill of them before I had any of my own."

"It's not so bad when they're yours. It's different."

"The screams, the crying, the puking, the dirty diapers, the mess, the chaos, the toys, the kid battles, the time, the—"

Emmie held up a hand. "Okay, okay, it's up to you."

"Not what Ama says," Cara replied morosely.

"And when did you ever listen to what she says?"

"Just because I don't listen doesn't mean I don't hear."

Emmie's gaze wandered the room. "Point."

"So, I can store them here?"

"Sure. Why not."

Cara stood. "Kimi, will you get the smaller one?"

"'Kay."

Together, the two sisters, the grown and not-yet-grown, hustle the drums around back and onto the porch. One-handed, Emmie moves a few things aside.

"Thanks again, Emmie. Here." Cara pulled a half-copper out of a pocket. "I'll be back before dusk to pick them up for tonight."

Kimi followed Cara away from the house. "Cara, can we talk?"

Cara regarded her youngest sister, noting the serious face. "What's up, kidlet?"

Kimi stayed silent for a bit as they walked toward a bench on the river. She stuffed her hands in her pockets. "How did you survive all those years? With Ama?"

"Is it that bad?"

"Yeah, and getting worse."

They sat side by side, staring out at the water. "She's getting worse, or you are?"

"Both. Her worse is making me worse."

"In what way? Or should I say 'ways'?"

Kimi took a deep breath and began to spew. "You saw what happened when I went to watch you play. Whatever I do for the house or for the rest of the family, it's never enough. There's always something I forgot or didn't do right. I have no spare time. If I try to take some for myself, I'm slacking. I'm lazy. I'm supposed to pick a career and also look around for a husband to have a bunch of kids with. She just pushes and pushes and never stops."

"It's who she is, Kimi. Some is her inner nature. Some probably came from Papaw."

"Ugh. I vaguely remember him. And wish I didn't." Kimi kicked a convenient lump of dirt. "But how did you survive her?"

"I kept my mouth shut and my head down as much as I could and swallowed her punishments—excuse me...*discipline*—and counted the seconds until I could get away. I'd sneak out at night and practice dancing. I'd go to Mamaw's and craft with her. Ama didn't really approve of the amount of time I spent there, but she let it ride because it was her own mother."

"I don't have any place to go, and it's like she keeps me prisoner."

"Well, there are times to keep your head down and keep moving forward, and times to stand tall and hold your ground. Wisdom is knowing when to do which."

Kimi waved a hand in the air, as if shooing away insects. "How will I know?"

"Best I can say, is look at the cost of not obeying, and decide if you're willing to pay it."

"I can't pay. I'm a servant. An unpaid one."

Cara grinned at her. "I didn't mean money. You do have a roof over your head and food to eat. Clothes. That's why you don't get paid."

"You sound like her," Kimi grumbled.

"No. I've just been away long enough that I can see some of her side. You still need a life outside of chores and responsibilities."

"Can I stay at your camp? Live there with you?"

"Do you think she wouldn't come looking for you? Who else would she get to do all her housework for her?"

"She can afford to pay for a maid."

"Yeah, but that would offend her high and mighty sensibilities."

"Thbpthbpthbp."

Cara glanced at her. "Those raspberries sound pretty bitter."

"Gettin' that way."

"Where would you go, if you could? And what could you do to earn a living?"

"I don't know."

"Can you help Dae?"

"Already asked. He said no."

"Help Davad? Help your other siblings?"

"No one wants to get on Ama's bad side."

"Seamstress? Cook? Bookkeeper? Teacher? Crafter?"

"That's just it, Cara. I don't even know what I want!"

"Shopkeeper? Goat herder? Gardener?"

Kimi smacked her fists together and swore. "I don't know. And if she never lets me loose, how can I figure it out?"

"Calm down, kidlet. What do you do in your spare time?"

Kimi threw her hands up. "What spare time?"

"Steal a few minutes here and there. Especially when she's in the clinic. Take time during her errands to talk to other adults. Ask about jobs and skills. See who says what."

Kimi stayed silent for a little while. She shifted on her feet. "Why doesn't Dae do anything about all this?"

"I think he just wants to keep the peace."

"For himself."

Then, it was Cara's turn for silence. "Yeah."

"You sure I can't stay with you?"

"I'm sure."

"Why?"

"Because I need to get away, too."

"Why can't we get away together?"

"Someday maybe I can explain."

***

One more stop. One more unhappy choice. One more door opened, this one a weather-beaten, pathetic excuse for an entrance rather than the well-crafted, heavy door of the bar. A middle-aged man stood behind the counter. A leer meant to be a smile crept onto his face as she entered the hostel.

"Cara! My favorite person. Welcome, welcome."

His attempt at hospitality fell as flat as Kimi's bread loaves. Cara approached with more than trepidation in mind. His presence produced the same aura of creepiness as his lodgings did.

"Thanks, Joel. I just need a room on weekend nights. Second floor, if you have one."

"Got one right here." He reached for a key. "Two coppers a night."

She stopped her advance. "That's high."

"Sliding scale, my dear. I'm sure you have plenty of coins to spare."

The implication in his words made her fume inside. She nearly turned away. But sleeping on the beach at night was one more step downward, and too close to homelessness for her comfort. She drew a few coins out of a pocket and gave him what he asked for, thankful that her Selandu coin belt remained hidden under her clothes.

He handed her the key. "Room 6."

Tired already, she climbed the stairs and unlocked the door. She looked around, trying to see it as Rodani might have. Bed, sheet, tiny table, tinier lantern. No facilities, of course. That was at the end of the hall. Flimsy shutters barely covered the window. Not even a threadbare rug covered the floor. The bed looked clean, at least. That was all she really needed.

At the end of the night's performance, Cara looked around for Graeme. He hadn't been at his usual position near the bar's entrance. She missed his watchfulness, the closest thing she had to a sense of security with Rodani out in the trees. Then, she saw Mack.

He hovered in the shadows just beyond the bakery, a brooding presence that made her gut clench.

Why didn't Graeme tell her he was free again? She should have been forewarned! *Ignore him. Ignore him.* Cara put her drums in the cart behind the stage, then walked into the bar. A few stragglers sat, slumped over tables. Cara approached the bar top, where Chucko washed glasses and mugs. Nearby, Dottie totted up the night's take. They both ignored her.

"The crowd was lively tonight," she offered. The silence beat against her eardrums. *Gods, this was awkward.* She tried again. "Nick always had a coin or two for me for bringing in more patrons since I returned."

Dottie shoved the cash drawer closed with a bang. Her eyes flashed. "Do I look like Nick?"

Cara backed off, humiliation in every line of her body. She dared a glance at Chucko, who gave her a look like he was already dying by inches. She mimed taking a bite of a sandwich.

"Kitchen's closed. Sorry."

Cara nodded and went next door to buy a pastry from Shandar while he was still open. "Have you seen Graeme, today?"

Shandar wiped his hands on his smock before scooping her coin off the counter. "Word is he went north. Same place as Nick, but a few days ago."

"Oh, gods." This was a complication she didn't need.

"Please don't speak that way in front of me."

One of Suraya's brothers. She'd forgotten. "I'm sorry." She inclined her head and unrolled her fingers, a Selandu gesture he probably didn't recognize. "Thank you for telling me."

Feeling both bereft and anxious, Cara rolled her cart to Emmie's house as quickly as she could. She stowed her drums, left the cart, and scurried off to the hostel. Good thing it wasn't as far south as the stage. She still kept her hand on the baton Rodani had given her, just in case. Her nerves thrummed with fear as she walked down the middle of the streets. Her weekend dread wasn't going to go away now, in daylight or in dark.

Her room was pitch-black, but at least the door had been locked. She felt her way to the mini lantern on the side table and lit it. No one jumped out at her; the room was too small to hide in. She double-checked the door lock, extended the baton, turned off the lantern, then slumped down on the narrow bed.

Her body felt torn between exhaustion and agitation. She rocked forward and back, gaining nothing but empty comfort. Change was good, she told herself. Change was opportunity. Despite the words, she didn't see any. Just life disruptions that hovered around her temples and rattled her equanimity. She needed Rodani's calm. *Kimasa's robe,* he so often said. The memory brought a quick smile. She breathed deeply for a handful of minutes in an attempt to empty her mind. But every time she did, another thought crept in, another embarrassment from her past, another preoccupation with her future—and Rodani's. She gave it up as a bad job and settled into the mattress. At least he was healing. At least that was one worry she could let go of.

She'd relaxed into a drowse when the sound of creaking wood came through her window. Instantly alert, Cara grabbed her baton and waited, heart pounding against her ribs. Something rasped against the outside wall. She crept to the side of the window, flattening herself against the wall. The worthless shutters moved aside by an unseen hand. Cara shivered in anticipation, in dread. Fingers appeared on the window ledge. By the crescent moon, she counted them. *Five.*

Be brave, like Rodani, she told herself. Find it. Feel it.

The top of a head appeared, rising upward from below the sill. Cara clenched the baton in her fists. *Wait,* she told herself. If he fell outside the building, she had no proof of ill intent. No proof of danger or the need for self-defense.

The head bent forward, and shoulders filled the opening. Mack's face was outlined in moonlight. She heard his foot scrabble for purchase, then stop. *A little farther*, she urged him silently. *Just a little more.*

When his body was halfway in and an arm reached for the floor, she struck, battering his back and broad shoulders, his arm and hand.

He roared in pain. Cara screamed in unison, more in rage than fear. When he reared up and reached for her, she bashed his head. He went limp, half in and half out of her window.

Soon, shouting came from outside, on the street. Lights flashed past her window, illuminating the hanging legs and feet. Someone banged on her door and rattled the knob. "Cara!"

Recognizing Joel's voice, she opened the door. He ran in, followed by two others. "Light the lantern," he shouted. As she did, voices rang up from below. "Somebody get the sheriff." "Who is that?" "Whose room is that?" "What the wide deep was he doing up there?"

Cara sat down on the bed and let the chaos swirl around her. Now, she could shake. Now, she could worry what the consequences might be. Would she go to jail? It wasn't likely, but wasn't impossible. Reputations mattered, and hers wasn't the most sterling among her people.

Rodani! Had he heard me scream? He'd be frantic! Shit! The 'com's in my carry sack, and with all these people about, I can't contact him. What to do? Where to go?

While others dealt with Mack, she scrabbled for the 'com and stuffed it inside her halter, then grabbed Joel's arm. "Going to the bathroom," she told him. He stared at her wide-eyed as she ran out. Once in the toilet, she turned the 'com on and whispered. "Aisu. Aisu."

"Where are you?" came the hissed reply. "I heard a scream. Was that you?"

"Yes, but I'm okay. Not hurt." She tried not to babble into his ears. "Stay where you are, please. Don't try to find me. Stay safe. I have to talk to a bunch of people now, and I won't have time for you for a while. Be calm."

"Temi's gibbering demons, Cara!"

"I fought him, aisu. I beat him with the baton. I won. Stay there! Promise me," she begged.

His voice bled through, deep with force. "You come find me the moment you can."

"I will. It may be morning before I do."

Voices in the hall called for her. "I have to go, aisu."

"Go."

She hid the 'com back in her halter and opened the door to the hall. Chief Sheriff "Berg" Heisberg, Graeme's boss, met her halfway.

"What the hell happened here?"

Cara put her hand on her head. "Looks pretty obvious to me, Sheriff. Did you see who was hanging out my window?"

"Why was he there?"

"He was climbing in."

"Who knocked him out?"

"I did."

"Why?"

Cara froze, uncomprehending. "Wait a minute. Wait just a minute. I'm not having this conversation without witnesses." She strode past him into her hostel room. Three more people had crowded in, two men and a woman. Mack's body lay crumpled on the floor.

Ricardo, the town's weaver, grabbed the man next to him. "Go tell Dr. Liz we're bringing her a patient. Wake her up if you have to!"

The man scrambled to obey, rushing out the door.

Cara snagged her notebook and began to scribble down the names of the people milling around. She leaned out the window. "Who's down there? Give me your names, please. We're going to need you as witnesses." Five people gave their names. Two slunk away into the shadows.

Ricardo leaned out afterward. "We need a couple of strong men up here to carry Mack to the clinic. Two volunteers, please."

As he turned back to the room, Cara put her hands on his arms. He, at least, seemed to be thinking rationally. "Ricardo, does what you see here make sense? That this was self-defense?"

He studied her face a moment and then glanced at Mack's body and the window. "Seems to be, yeah."

"Will you try to explain it to the sheriff? Because I don't think he sees it. I don't think he sees what happened here."

"Alright."

"Can you remind the other witnesses about Mack stalking me, and trying to kidnap me, and what his intentions probably were tonight?" He hesitated. "Please. Think of Rosalinda. Think of your daughters."

Ricardo pulled his arms out of her hands gently. "You made your point."

Two men came in. One stripped the sheet from Cara's bed and laid it on the floor. Together, the two moved Mack onto it and carried him off to her mother's.

Chief Berg tucked his hands into his belt. "You gotta come with me, Cara."

"Am I under arrest?"

Berg glowered at her. "You think you ought to be?"

"No. It was self-defense. Can't you interview me here?"

"Let's follow the rules, instead of ignoring them."

She pursed her lips. "I think I just got dinged."

As Berg went to the door, Cara made a face at Ricardo, a high sign of his promise. He nodded and shuffled the other people out the door for Cara to lock up. All the witnesses followed them to the sheriff's offices and congregated in the waiting room.

The chairs in the chief's office weren't the most comfortable things she'd sat on. But the atmosphere added to her discomfort. Rules had been set down 75 years ago. Relatively enlightened rules, and Cara believed she'd squeaked under them tonight. Barely. But things could still go wrong.

"Tell it to me straight."

"I need to start at the beginning."

He sat, pen at the ready.

"It started when people found out I was going north, to live with the Selandu for a while...." She explained the basics and then worked her way up to the current time. "Do you have Graeme's report of a few weeks ago, when Mack grabbed me?"

"I read it. I'll pull it again."

"Please. Because it shows intent and a pattern. That's important."

"Don't tell me my job."

"Sorry. It just seems obvious he wasn't climbing in to invite me for caffee."

"That all?"

"I think so."

Berg held his hand out. "Give me the weapon."

Cara passed the baton to him, now closed up.

He looked it over. "Where'd you get it?"

"In Barridan."

"Why?"

She waved her fingers, minimizing. "I had extra time on my hands. My guardian let me play with it. Let me keep it when I came back."

Berg whipped it forward. It stayed closed.

"Harder," Cara suggested.

A second try extended the baton. Berg slapped it against his palm.

"Do a lot of damage with this if you're not careful."

"Mack wanted to do a lot of damage to me. A. Lot," she said pointedly.

Berg laid it on his desk. "I'm going to have to confiscate it."

Her eyes went wide. "It's my protection!"

"Mack's not going anywhere," he said under lowered brows. "Not for a while."

"And what about his pals? What will they do to me when they find out? You're leaving me defenseless!"

"Don't exaggerate."

Now Cara pounded her forehead with the meat of her palms. "I'm not!"

He tapped his fingers on the desk, twitched his lips, and regarded her with some mix of frustration and sympathy. "You can have it back tomorrow."

"Before I perform?"

"Yeah."

"Thank you," she said, heartfelt. "...We done?"

"For now."

Cara nodded, bypassed the witnesses with nothing but a dip of her head and a quick thanks, and stepped outside, supremely relieved. *Now what?* she thought. There was no one in the shadows that she could see. Where was Rodani? Had he seen her come here? Or was he further south?

She slipped around the corner to the east, nearest the trees, and flattened herself against the building. *Aha.* Her 'com went off inside her halter. She pulled it out. "Aisu?"

"Straight ahead," came the instruction.

Warily, she advanced through a couple of home gardens and up to the trees. Her nerves were still ramped to high from Mack's treachery. And Rodani would not be happy. When one painful issue passed, another popped up to take its place. She wasn't looking forward to listening to him.

His form emerged from the shadows as she worked her way inward. He stood still and quiet in the dark, waiting. But she couldn't call it *patient*. She knew better.

"Aisu," she greeted him. "Before you speak, I'd like to thank you very much for giving me the baton, and for pushing me to practice, and for making sure I took it with me. You were correct." She held her hand out to him. "And now, I'm even more aware of how serious the situation could be, even if it is my home." When he didn't move, she dropped her hand to her side. "Does that make anything better?"

"Explain what occurred, kia. Then I may answer you."

She told him what happened, minimizing where she could without outright lying. It didn't make her feel good inside, but neither did their angry confrontations. "I need to sit." She searched the ground without a light. "Do you have a blanket here?"

"Behind me."

When she walked around him, he made a guild full-body turn to keep her in sight. Again, her heart began to race in fear of the unknown. "Please, aisu."

"Please to what, Cara? Make your words clear."

Oh, boy. She could feel the heat from his tone of voice. "I know that movement. I know what it means." She flopped down on the blanket, already exhausted.

"I am surprised you saw it in the dark."

"Are you going to sit down?"

"How long are we to remain at odds on this subject?"

Aaaand he didn't sit. *Oh boy, doubled.* "To not feel dishonored by breaking my promise to the other musicians, I would have to tell them why I'm leaving the group. That would make four people who know about you. That's four too many, Rodani. I don't want to chance it."

"Then what other chances do you take in place of that one?"

"Whatever makes sense to me at the time. And that's where we have difficulties. Because 'makes sense' is different in every culture."

"Rather than focusing on learned discourse, let us focus on facts closer to hand."

Finally, he sat. Finally, Cara could take a deep breath with the assumption he was ready to listen, not command obedience.

"You are making a choice, kia. Between money and promises made to your companions, and your safety. I—"

"And to you, safety is everything. I understand that. To me, it's important, but not to the exclusion of all else."

Under the darkness, under the branches and leaves, Rodani sat in silence. Beyond the trees, the surf crashed against its sandy shore.

"And has the danger passed?"

"From Mack, for a while, yes. Similar to when he was in jail. But he has friends."

"And are these friends also a danger?"

"I don't know. Before tonight, I would have said 'not as much'. But now that I've hurt him, I don't know how they'll react. The bonds of rage and hatred are strong."

"^Jail^. ^Friends^. ^Hatred^. My understanding of your words is less than I would wish."

"Then keep asking questions."

"Will these friends hurt you?"

"I don't know."

His voice rose, along with the agitation in his hands. "How do you expect me to be willing to accept this?"

"Shhh," she admonished him, patting her hands in the air. "Consider it compensation for all the times you prevented me from doing what I wanted in Barridan because of safety."

"Because I could not let you be unsafe in my own home, I must let you be unsafe in yours?"

At her wit's end, Cara curled down into a ball, arms covering her head—worthless, paper-thin armor for protecting her skull from the wall she was beating it against. Who was in the right here? Who was wrong? And how badly? How far kwould she let him push her? How far could he be pushed? *Not much farther*, was her fear.

"Let's see what today brings," she said, sitting up. "And tonight. I'll get the baton back before I play. Then, hopefully, I'll know how badly Mack is hurt and have a better idea of what danger his friends may be."

Silence filled her ears as she waited for his next pointed, too-accurate question.

"Can you sleep in the jail? Behind those bars?"

Holy tsunami. Could she? Berg probably wouldn't let her, but, "I'll ask."

***

Dr. Liz opened the door of the waiting room and inspected the two men who sat slumped in uncomfortable chairs. Their muttered conversation stopped in mid-sentence.

"Mr. Cornyn?"

The older of the two men stood up, slouching in the unusual necessity of showing respect to a woman. "Yeah? How is he?"

"Your son has been hit on the back of the head, but he's regained consciousness," she began in the crisp voice of medical authority. "He has several large bruises on his back, shoulders, and upper arms. They should be monitored, but I don't believe any will cause lasting harm. The bigger worry is that the blow to his head has caused double vision." She motioned behind her with a wave of her hand. "I am going to keep him here for 24 hours, at least, to watch for improvement."

"Can I see him?"

"For a few minutes only." Liz ushered him into the hallway behind her. "Second door on the left."

"Doctor Liz?"

She turned back to the much younger man. "Deputy?"

Adam Roberts slipped his hands into his pockets. "He'll be here all day tomorrow?"

"Yes, as I said."

"I'll need to interview him. Is there a good or bad time to come back?"

"Not really. I can't predict when he might be sleeping."

Adam hesitated, too new at his avocation to be comfortable with uncomfortable questions. "How close did he come to dying?"

"A blow to the head can cause anything from a mild headache to almost instantaneous death, depending on where it was hit, the weapon used, and the strength of the hit. Mack wasn't in mortal danger. But that's because he was lucky."

He nodded. "Thank you."

Liz shut the waiting room door, only to hear raised voices from behind another one.

"What the hell were you thinking, crawling in a woman's window at midnight? You're an idiot! Didn't you learn anything from me? You don't control a woman by threatening to rape her."

A quiet murmur replied to the accusations.

"You don't convince her with fear. Not at first. You change her mind by telling her what she needs to hear."

Another murmur, frustration in a slew of unintelligible words.

"Then you keep trying. Giving up is cowardly, and I didn't raise my sons to be cowards."

Liz shook her head. *Down through the generations*, she thought. *It just doesn't stop.*

***

Word had traveled fast around town. Every place she walked into went silent, every person she walked past glanced at her, or stared outright. At first, it was unnerving. Then came the anger. What did they expect? For her to run, only to face it again another night? To give in to him, as if she deserved the pain and degradation he wanted to give her? Not going to happen. She held her head high.

"Cara!"

Recognizing the voice, Cara turned and waited. Kimi ran up the sidewalk toward her, dodging pedestrians with adolescent ease.

"Cara, everyone's talking about you! Even Ama."

"Wait, wait. Let's talk somewhere else."

"I can't stay. I have to get back." Kimi grabbed her arm. "Are you okay?"

"Yeah."

"You sure?"

"Yes, kidlet. I'm sure."

"Ama was called into surgery in the middle of the night for some man. They said you beat him up. Did you?"

"He was going to hurt me, Kimi. Badly. I defended myself. And in the process, yes, I hurt him. Did he survive?"

"Yeah. Really banged up, though."

Cara stared into her sister's wide eyes. "Good. He deserved it. Walk with me?"

"Not very far. Ama, remember. Where are you going?"

"Sheriff's."

"Why?"

"To get my weapon back."

"Weapon?"

"It saved my life."

Kimi remained quiet on the short walk. Sheriff Berg met them as they came through the doors, the baton in his hand. Cara looked at it, and at him, waiting for him to hand it over. After a stern look of his own, he did.

"I spoke to the judge, gave him my report. You scraped by on self-defense, but there was talk of excessive force. You need to be careful."

"So do the people who try to attack me, sheriff. Right?"

"Heed what I said. Maybe you should stop dancing."

Frustration and defiance filled Cara's face. *This*, this was Barridan all over again. Blame those just trying to live their lives, not those who took offense at what wasn't their business. Not those who used violence to punish innocent people living those lives.

"Cara," Berg said into that face. "Be safe, not sorry."

Calm, kia, she told herself. She inclined her head. "Thank you for the advice."

Kimi followed her out, and Cara led her into the woods for just a little way. "This," she said, waving the closed baton, "is my weapon." With a sharp wave of her arm, the baton extended.

Kimi gaped at the sudden transformation.

Cara gripped the baton and let the rage of injustice steel her muscles. "Watch." With a massive swing, she hit the trunk of the nearest tree. Bark flew out, and the baton rebounded to the side. She hit again and again in the same spot, then moved to a limb and hit downward. She put every bit of emotion she could into her swings, pounding the limb with the same viciousness she felt last night. Then she turned to Kimi and held out the baton.

"Here. You try."

"Uhh," Kimi folded her arms. "You sure?"

"Yes." Cara pulled Kimi's arm out and planted the grip in her hand. "Pretend the tree is Ama at her worst. Get mad at it."

Supremely unsure, Kimi regarded the baton like a sea snake that might bite.

"Go on."

Kimi swung and tapped the side of the tree.

"You can do better. Again."

She swung harder.

"Again. Here." Cara brought Kimi's arm back to her shoulder. "Now swing. Smack it."

The strike was still not much more than a tap.

"Where's your anger? Do it again. Get mad at Ama. At me. At the world." She stood behind her sister, grabbed the fist that held the baton with both hands, and swung it against the tree trunk.

It hit and rebounded with enough power to make Kimi gasp.

"See? Makes you feel strong, doesn't it? Makes you feel a little more in control. Now, do it yourself."

Kimi swung.

"No, you can't go out," Cara chanted. "Swing. No, you can't dress like that. Swing. No, you can't like that boy. Swing! No, you didn't cook it right! Swing! No, you didn't clean that right! Swing!"

Kimi battered the tree trunk until she was almost in tears.

"Enough, enough." Cara took the baton out of her hand and pulled her into a hug. "You've got it. You've got it figured. You're getting an idea of just what you can accomplish when you have to." She caressed her sister's hair. "Don't be afraid of your anger. Use it. Channel it."

Kimi pulled away from the hug. "I gotta go."

Cara followed her back toward the rows of cabins that brushed the edges of the woods. "Now it's my turn to ask. Are you okay?"

Kimi stopped her headlong rush. "Yeah." She looked around. "Yeah."

***

Gods, what a day. And night. She stared at the steps that led up to the back of the stage. Did she have enough energy for this? Maybe the crowd would buoy her. She heaved the drums and her stool onto the stage, then walked forward.

James and Jonie stepped back, leaving her alone at the front of the stage. She looked out over the crowd and took a deep breath, but it did little for the tension in her gut.

"I'd like to mention two things before we begin." She glanced at the bar. "When Nick was here, he understood that my dancing brought a slightly larger crowd." A few people clapped and cheered, to which Cara bowed. "In thanks for those additional thirsty patrons, he would offer me a coin or two at the end of each performance," she nodded to James and Jonie, "which, of course, I shared. Now that he's moved to Himadi House, north of the hills, we're no longer receiving that small portion of extra income. It was refused." She took a deep breath. "I hope you know how much we appreciate the coins tossed on stage. But if any of you might have," she waved her fingers, "just a little extra you could share with us, sometimes, it would be very much appreciated.

"Also, some of you know what almost happened to me last night. And what I had to do to prevent it. I haven't slept, I've hardly eaten." With effort, she brightened her tone a little. "As always, we'll do our best to entertain you. I just don't know how many dances I'll be able to manage tonight. I'll do what I can. And we thank you for whatever encouragement and understanding you can offer us during a difficult time. And now," she said with a smile and a wave to the pair behind her, "please clap for our masters of voice and fingers."

She took her seat and raised her drumsticks to wait for James' signal. As she did, she heard boos from the back of the crowd.

James and Jonie ignored them. Then again, those boos weren't directed at the pair, but at her. She drummed through them, under them, past them. Their verbal displeasure tapered off for a few songs but erupted again as Cara got up to dance.

You're in Barridan, fem. Rodani is sitting there, watching you raptly, waiting to put his warm hands on you afterward. Do this. Do it like you always do.

The first lump of something flew past her, bouncing onto the stage between her feet and James'. A second something hit the edge of her skirt, ending up in front of her drums as it rolled to a stop.

James stopped playing, dropping his hands to his side. With the music gone, Cara also stopped. James glanced back at the trash that had landed near her drums. The audience went mute. Their swaying and clapping faded in the face of James' contained fury.

"If this is how we're going to be treated, then maybe it isn't a good idea to continue to play tonight. Or," he paused for effect, glaring out at the edge of the crowd, "maybe some of you can teach these gentlemen better manners."

Several people in the crowd shifted, looking around. For what, Cara wasn't sure. Questions? Consensus? An ally in whatever they thought to do? Humans in crowds could be dangerous, and violence was a slippery slope.

A handful of men approached Mack's gang at the edges of the spectators. Words were exchanged and gestures thrown about. Cara couldn't hear them and, to be honest with herself, really didn't want to. After a few minutes, James restarted his song, and Cara went back to her dance.

At the end of the performance, Cara approached James. "Thank you. Really."

"Welcome. They insult you, they insult us."

Behind him, Jonie pursed her lips and glared out at the dispersing crowd. But she kept her frustrations inside. Something else Cara didn't need to hear, she was sure.

"You going to be safe walking back?" James asked.

"I hope so. My usual watchers went north."

He leaned over the edge of the stage and spoke to a few people still there, then turned back. "We'll walk you."

They gathered around her and escorted her to her sister's, then back to the hostel. Joel gave them a good once-over as they trooped up the stairs en masse. Cara unlocked her door and turned.

"Thank you so much. Every one of you, and those who confronted Mack's gang, too. You all give me courage."

They mumbled replies and then headed back down the hall. Cara locked her door and collapsed on the bed. Laying the baton to the side, she pulled out her 'com and checked that it was on broadcast from channel 9. Not too far a signal, but not so close that Rodani wouldn't catch it. She waited a bit, listening for footsteps, for rasps, clinks, or thumps, sounds that nature didn't normally make. Nothing intruded on her senses, and Cara began to relax. She kept the mini lantern off, and settled at the window to watch for possible watchers. To her unpracticed eye, there was nothing to be seen.

The 'com whispered. "Kia."

She pressed a button. "Aisu."

"Come out. Bring your belongings. We go home."

"Ninety-nine."

EIGHTEEN

Languid in afterglow, Cara nestled into Rodani's side. His arm curved around her shoulder to pull her closer. The breeze was warm on her skin, the sea calm to her ears.

"If there were ever a reason to believe in a goddess, aisu, this would be why."

He turned his head toward her. "Sela brings you your crests?"

It provoked a chuckle. "No. You do the work for that. You should get the credit." She ran her hand down the length of his chest. "Does Temi have anything to do with crests?"

Rodani tapped her arm with his fingers. "That was never a thought of mine." He stared down over his lower body. "I would suppose he would induce Sela's crests. I do not know about yours."

"I wonder what Sela's crests feel like. Better than mine, do you think?"

Now he laughed, his chest heaving in quick spasms. "Au, kia, the images! Kimasa would be aghast at your thoughts." He bent his head and kissed her hair. "Maybe that is what causes thunder."

"No, that would be Temi's growls. Like yours, but much louder."

"Do you disapprove of my sounds?" he asked, rather plaintively.

"Gods, no, Rodani. I love them." She ran her hand over his pelvic orifice. "They make me shiver."

Rodani sucked in a breath. "Too soon, kia." He removed her errant hand and held it so that his pelvic muscles would cease twitching, not to mention his ear tips.

Most of the rain had stopped, but a few sprinkles still fell onto the tarp that covered their hammock.

Now that the frenetic activity had stopped, Fuzz crept out from his hiding place near the trunk and wandered onto the branch above their heads. He sat on his haunches, curled his tail around his feet, and licked the rain from his fur, then stared at them in anticipation.

"Do you have food handy, aisu?"

"A few nibbles." He reached around behind him and opened a sack, and gave a couple morsels to Cara.

"I'm going to have to start carrying some around." She pursed her lips and made a ticking sound. The red-brown furball crept forward and took it from her fingertips. She brushed his pelt and slipped her fingers under his belly to lift him. His eyes widened, but stayed in place as she laid him on her chest.

"Au," Rodani whispered.

Cara grinned at him, careful not to show her teeth. Who knew what Fuzz would consider an act of aggression? He let her stroke his back for a little while before he scampered off on a branch.

"Success," she whispered, then sighed. "I wish I could lie here longer, but I need the facilities."

"Latrine," he corrected with a smile in his voice.

^Yes, dear.^

Cara grabbed her clothes bag and sidled, naked, onto the branch. Two people in a hammock never left enough room to comfortably change clothes or dress. It was all they could do to undress in it—usually in the frantic haste of passion. Rodani was probably enjoying the view she gave him, anyway. She climbed down a newly made ladder he'd built and attached to the limb and moved over to the next section. The bark was wet. Another climb down, another move. When her clothes sack got caught on a twig, she yanked at it and lost her footing.

She let out a yelp, clutched at the limb in front of her, and toppled. She hit the ground with a grunt. As she began to check in with her body, she heard Rodani scrambling down the tree above her.

"Cara! Cara!" He landed next to her in a crouch in the wet leaves. "Are you hurt?"

"Uhh, my shoulder, I think," she said, shifting in the leaves. "I think I hit it on the way down." She grimaced. "I...watered myself."

He grabbed the nearest clean rag and handed it to her. "Can you sit up?"

"Help me."

Between the two of them, she was able to sit. "Does your shoulder move?" Rodani asked, concern written over his face.

Cara bent over in an effort to wipe down her thighs but stopped. "I'm afraid to try very hard. It hurts."

"How much?"

She tested it again. "Kind of a lot."

"Contradictions again. Physician?"

She huddled, still skyclad in the leaves. "I think I'd better."

Rodani pulled a haphazard choice of clothes out of her bag to help her dress. The shoulder proved a problem, though. He climbed back up to the hammock and brought down some of his own clothes. One of his shirts covered both her chest and her sore arm.

He looked her up and down. "Shades of Barridan," he joked lightly.

"Dammit," she said with the memory. "Why do I always have to fall?"

"At least you did not land on rocks." He held his hand out toward the cove. "I will help you climb in."

After much wincing in pain and cursing, Cara seated herself on the bench in his boat.

"Will you see your mother?"

"No! There's another physician at the south end of town, near the stage. Head there."

Despite the calm seas, the ride was bumpy and aggravating. Cara swore up and down to be more careful, less negligent or slipshod. *Stupid, Cara. Idiot. Fool.* Then, *Shut up, brain.*

Rodani carried her through the water and into the sea grass and sand that bordered it. When he got to dry land, he set her down. "You can manage?"

"Yeah. Thanks."

***

Bethamy walked into the office and found Suraya where she expected her to be—at her desk, writing. "Guess who I just saw?"

Suraya scribbled a few more words before looking up. "Who?"

"Cara."

Confusion spread across her face. "In the middle of the week? Where?"

"Heading toward Doc Shen's office. She was holding her arm. I think she's hurt."

Suraya grabbed her pen and paper, pushed them in a bag, and hustled out. "Thanks," she called over her shoulder. Bethamy just shook her head.

Suraya hopped up on the nearest sidewalk and took it south, thankful that the town had agreed to build them. Too many childhood years were spent with muddied shoes and wet socks.

Wednesday, the streets were wet, she thought. Would that be a good first line for another chapter? How did Cara get hurt? Would it make a good story? At least if she's walking, it sounds like she'll be okay.

Her sandals slapped against the wooden slats, and occasional sprinkles dampened her long black hair, like crystals forming among the strands. Other people were venturing back out from homes and shops after the midday rainfall.

Doc Shen's clinic sat on the corner of Fourth Street, far enough west of The Wet Rag bar and the stage to not let his patients' ears be too badly inundated twice a week. Suraya pulled open the door and scraped her sandals against the welcome mat. "Someone said Cara's here."

The receptionist frowned. "Who's here and who isn't is private, Suraya."

"Oh, she won't mind. Can I talk to her?"

"If she's here, she's with the doctor right now. So no, you couldn't."

"That's okay. I'll wait." She took a chair in the waiting room and willed herself to patience. It wasn't one of her better traits. Dogged determination was common for her, which suited her chosen profession like she was born to it.

It wasn't too long before someone walked into the receptionist's area from another door. Dr. Shen bent over the admin's shoulder and muttered an instruction.

"Dr. Shen." Suraya got up and walked to the window. "I'd really like to talk to Cara. Will she be okay?"

"You're not family, Suraya."

"Have you notified anyone in her family?"

"No."

"I could do that for you."

"She will be capable of doing that herself."

"Would you at least ask her if she'll talk to me?"

226

Dr. Shen straightened and crossed his arms. His eyes narrowed. "She is in pain and needs quiet. I suggest you wait until she's discharged."

"When will that be?"

"Later."

Suraya pursed her lips and nodded. "Fine."

Out the door again, she stole around to the back of the clinic. Windows partitioned the wall at regular intervals. She tiptoed past them, checking for open shutters. *Silly. But I might get lucky.*

Further on, she did hear a voice. Cara.

And a faint reply.

And it wasn't Cene'l they were speaking. Suraya walked closer.

"The physician said I shouldn't play or dance this weekend." Cara spoke in a lowered tone, as if she didn't want to be overheard. "It'll still be hurting and could postpone the healing."

"That does not displease me, kia."

"Well, I'll have to go over to Jonie's shop and tell her I won't be there. I can't just not let them know."

What in all the otherworldly gods was she hearing? Suraya edged up to the open shutters and leaned in.

"I will wait. Do not spend too many hours talking."

"You should be pleased I have other people to talk to besides you, aisu."

^Touché,^ came the reply after a moment.

Cara chortled.

That was a native Selandi speaker. Of the male variety. Was he in the room with her? He couldn't be. No Selandu was allowed south of the border!

Suraya peered in. Cara sat in a chair with her back to the window. She was alone. One arm was in a sling. The other held a small silvery rectangle a little bigger than her palm. It was held to her mouth.

"How much pain do you carry?" the man said.

"Some. But I can manage."

"Smoke?"

"Yeah. That'll be good. Do you have enough?"

"Yes."

Smoke? An image of her father's pipe smoking came to Suraya's mind. *This makes no sense.*

"I'm gonna rest a bit, aisu. I'll call again after I talk to Jonie." Cara paused. ^I love you.^

The statement shocked Suraya to her bones. As did the reply.

"And I am yours."

Cara got up and turned to lie down on the clinic bed.

Suraya ducked down and held her breath, hoping she hadn't been seen. Her mind reeled with all that she had heard...and what it might mean.

The ^I love you^ was obvious. But who was the man? And where in all the gods' name was he? Could that little radio-thing broadcast all the way to the other side of the hills? What was it? What in the ever-loving space dark was going on?

Suraya wandered over the sidewalks in a daze, her feet tripping on an errant board, her eyes not on the people she passed. Cara loves a Selandu man. Cara loves a Selandu man! And he had replied in kind? "I am yours," seemed pretty clear. Holy sunspots and solar flares! It isn't believable. It isn't!

But.

Suraya rounded a corner and sat on a bench outside the candy store across from Jonie's shop. How many times had she—and others—told Cara she was different since returning from Barridan? Could that be the answer? Could it all come down to a man? An alien man? A man she had to leave behind and could only talk to through some hand radio?

Does the CSC know? If Cara is so intent on keeping it quiet, surely she didn't tell Menachem. Suraya's mind went back to her interview with Cara in the CSC.

And then the drawings she'd gotten a glimpse of.

Holy Brahma.

***

A while later, Cara woke to the alarm she'd set on the 'com. It took her a second to remember where she was, but a stab of pain did the trick. She climbed out of the clinic's bed and gathered her wits. Jonie in her shop. Rodani in his boat. The smoke umbrella. Man, she was looking forward to that, and her husband's soothing presence at her side.

She thanked Dr. Chen on the way out. "I'll be careful," she said to his expected warning.

Jonie's shop wasn't too far away, but the pain made it seem longer. Eyes on the ground, she stepped into the shop and wiped her feet.

"Jonie?"

"Cara?" The tailor pushed her way through the racks of clothes she'd made. "What are you doing here in the middle of the week?" She stopped. "What happened?"

"I wasn't careful enough." Cara waved her hand disparagingly, with a twist to her mouth. "Fell. Stupid. Listen, Doc Shen said I shouldn't play this weekend. I'm sorry."

Jonie looked her over. "I guess so. We'll cope."

"I'm really sorry."

"We made it seven months without you. We'll manage one weekend."

Cara ducked her head. "Thanks."

"What's with that baggy dress-type thing you've got on?"

She looked down at Rodani's shirt. "I brought it home from Barridan."

"Where are you staying?"

Another wave of her hand. "Maybe with Emmie. Or Ama; I can survive her a night or two."

Jonie raised her eyebrows. "You sure about that?"

Cara laughed. "Yeah, I think so."

"Okay. I'll tell James."

"Pass on my sorry, please."

"I will."

Cara left the shop, only to meet Suraya crossing the street.

"No stories today, Su."

"How did you get hurt?"

"I fell."

"Did you trip?"

"Something like that."

"What happened?"

"Not today. I have to go." She stepped off the sidewalk.

"Where?"

"You've asked that before. A hideaway doesn't hide me away if people know about it."

"You were never a recluse, Cara."

"I value my privacy." She switched to Selandi as she walked past. "Please honor it."

"I wish I knew what you were afraid of."

Aching, tired, frustrated, Cara shot back. "Who said I was afraid? I'm in pain, and I need to lie down."

"You know you can trust me."

Cara spun to face her. "Will you leave me the fuck alone?"

Suraya's expression folded into shock and mortification.

Cara waved her unencumbered hand between them. "That was uncalled for. You didn't...quite...deserve that."

"Okay. Okay." Suraya raised her hands in surrender. "I'm sorry. And sorry you're hurt."

"I'm sorry, too. Pain makes me bitchy."

"You gonna be okay? Alone?"

Cara squeezed her eyes shut. "Yessss." She turned away.

"Take care."

Rodani, she thought as she walked. *Smoke. Peace and quiet.* But would she be able to climb to the hammock? *No.* Well, she'd stay on the ground like she did when Rodani was sick.

When she hit the line of trees, she pulled out the 'com. "Aisu."

"Kia."

"Pick me up?"

"Ready."

"Minute. I have to place my feet carefully."

"Wait. I will walk you down."

"I'll meet you halfway. Shoreline is the worst."

More than halfway, she thought, as he came into view. Rodani's long legs were useful beyond eye candy and copulation. She managed a smile as he held out an arm to lean on.

"Were you followed?"

"Oh, gods, Rodani. I don't think so."

When they reached the boat nestled in sea grass, he picked her up and set her in it. He climbed in, and they motored off.

Just inside the tree line, Suraya plopped down on the wet grass and forgot how to breathe, her thoughts spinning.

What in the world do I do here? Does anyone else know? Who, if anyone, is owed the truth? Cara would be in so much trouble if the authorities found out. Oh, this explains so much! Her change in attitude, her disappearing every week, her hesitation about discussing her guardians, even, maybe, her temper. Is that what he was, a guardian? He wasn't dressed in black. Or was he an artist, or a meek and mild bookkeeper type? He didn't sound dangerous over that radio.

Then she remembered Cara's story of the knives. *His?* Suraya got up and made her way north through the trees, hiding the wet patch on her pants until she could turn west to her cabin.

I know what it's like to be in love. I don't want to ruin it for her, so I'm not going to. Hell with rules and regulations.

But guilt shadowed her. Given her family dynamics and the rules she was raised with, it was more difficult than she thought to hide her knowledge. Good thing her brothers didn't know. And Mack and his gang? That could be deadly. *Would be*, she amended.

But oh, what a story she could tell! *I hope I get to tell it one day.*

Then it hit her, and she stopped, just halted right there in the street. Was this why Cara was sent home? Was this what caused the rift in Barridan? The violence that ended her stay? Or had they hidden it, as they were doing now? Good gods of the wide deep.

Where were they staying? What did they do for the rain? What about food? What did the man do for his supplies? Did he travel back to Selandan for food, clothing, medicines?

So many questions. So many she wanted to ask. Ached to ask, but judging from today, there was no way Cara would answer. No wonder she kept her mouth shut. No wonder she needed privacy! Shame piled onto the guilt Suraya was feeling. She had pushed Cara far past her comfort zone by her own frustrations and need to know, causing them both pain.

It was time to reevaluate some things.

***

Mack paced his living room. Back and forth, back and forth. No little cabin for him, but a real house, bought with the sweat and energy from transporting goods around Glaniad and its outlying farms. Even as far as Lordstown on occasion. No bending over a lab counter to play with plants, no being stuck at the back of a shop counting coins and bagging junk, no herding goats, no cataloging useless, leftover rubbish from a worthless, damaged spaceship. Just hard work of the physical kind, the kind only a real man could accomplish. Work that women couldn't do. Work that roughened hands, built muscles, and gave a satisfaction that no brainwork gave.

The back of his head still carried a lump from that infuriating woman's attack. But the headache only appeared when he drank. That was another repercussion he could lay at Cara's feet: forcing him away from his favorite pastime.

Damn the bitch anyway.

Stefan, his little brother, swallowed another mouthful of brew and belched. He shifted in his chair. "Spit it out, Mackie. You're going to set fire to your shoes if you keep this up."

Mack glared at him and at Clark in the corner, his sole lifelong friend. The only man aside from his brother who understood what was in him, what drove his desire to conquer and control.

"I could've had her. I know it. If she'd just listen, dammit."

Clark laughed. "When does a woman ever listen?"

"I know what she needs. What every bitch needs. I've seen her choose idiots for lovers, then acting all heartbroken when they mistreat her. She doesn't see what's in front of her, what I can give her."

He kicked the nearest table leg, upending a cup of watered-down ale to splash on the floor.

Stefan took another mouthful, nearly emptying his second bottle of the night. He reached for another. "What you need is a way to hold her attention for a longer time. Some way to keep her focused on you. Give you time to convince her."

"That's what I was going to try at the hostel."

"No. Too many other people to hear her when she yells and cries like a little girl. You need privacy."

"What are you suggesting? That I chain her up? That won't make her open her legs for me."

"Nothing wrong with rape," Clark offered. "Every slut has that fantasy. She'd love it, even while she cried and begged."

Mack stared out his southern window toward the crowded part of town. Toward The Wet Rag bar. "I don't want her running to the sheriffs, telling lies, making me out to be the bad guy."

"So don't let her run."

"I don't want a prisoner, Clark. I want someone who is willing to stay with me. To wait on me, cook for me, fuck me when I want."

"You could keep her at my cabin, and I'd stay here," Clark offered. "Mine's isolated enough."

"I'd still have to tie her down."

"You could keep her drunk," Stefan suggested. "She wouldn't be able to run away, especially from Clark's. She might not cook very well, but she'd be fuckable."

Mack thought for a moment. "She might get used to me that way. Get her familiar with my lifestyle, my needs, then bring her here."

Clark nodded enthusiastically. "Sure. All you need is time. And a hard dick," he said, laughing. Stefan joined in, appreciating the good joke.

"That's not a problem. The problem is I know how hard-headed she is." He went back to pacing.

"You know," Stefan began, "you can come on strong, but you don't have much subtlety. You're kinda lacking in charm. Why don't you let me talk to her?"

Mack spun around to face his brother. "You touch her, I'll slice it off."

Stefan raised his hands in mock surrender. "I know better, brother. Besides, I've got my eye on her sister."

"Kimi? A kid?"

"No." An expression of disgust crossed his face. "She's cute, but I'm no cradle robber. I'm watching Teria."

"What do you want with a dumpy girl with a little hellion at her feet?"

"Wouldn't you like to know?"

Mack waved away the discussion of anyone that wasn't Cara and went back to wearing down the wood floor.

"So, you want me to talk to her? I can coax her into the bar after the band finishes."

Mack sighed and rubbed the knot on the back of his head. "You can try."

"Smackin'!" Stefan raised his bottle for a toast.

Clark scratched his ample belly and slipped his shoes off. "You know, there might be another way."

Mack toed the spilled beer on the floor. Dammit, he needed a woman to clean up the place. "What?"

"You heard of that crazy woman south of town? The one who brews potions?"

"The witch?" Mack laughed. "I'm surprised no one's burned her at the stake yet."

Stefan chuckled in sympathy. "We're too civilized for that."

"Well, it wouldn't hurt to ask her about love potions. Or better, sex potions." Mack smiled at his own cutting-edge snark.

"Those are old wives' tales, dimwit."

"So," Clark replied, "she's an old wife. Maybe she knows somethin' we don't."

Mack grimaced, but nodded his head. "Sure. Go ahead." He checked the overturned glass for any remnants of his drink. "I'm going to talk to Davad."

***

Back in a corner of the repository, the weather station flickered to life.

NINETEEN

"How do you feel today, aisu?"

"Better, I thank you. And your shoulder?"

She rotated it gingerly. "A little less sore." She handed him a bowl of stew from the pot on the fire. "Yesterday was the second time you spent all day sleeping. Is it from the death's head?"

Rodani took a spoonful and blew on it. "Yes. It is an unfortunate effect of the venom."

"Oh," she said, reevaluating. "How long does it last?"

"It seems to depend on many things. Weeks, at least."

"You can rest this weekend, instead of following me to town."

"No." His voice went deep.

"Ki'oto, you are stubborn."

He eyed her over the spoon at his mouth. "And you just now realize that?"

It provoked a laugh. Cara pointed at his uncovered legs. "I like that you're wearing shorts."

Rodani glanced down. "My pants were becoming ragged."

"Mmmm. Touchable." She reached for his thigh. Rodani tapped her fingers lightly with his spoon, a wry grin and raised eyebrow taking away the sting.

She pouted. "Awwww."

"You will run out of time for the tasks you said you must do, kia, if we take time to play."

"Then keep me in mind for when we return."

He rolled his eyes. "When do I not?"

"How much varigestra do you have left?"

"More than enough, I believe."

"Good." She winked at him. "Will you clean up?"

"Yes."

"Then kiss me before I go."

Their lips met, then their gaze. It warmed Cara to her toes as she walked to her boat.

One missed weekend was all she would allow herself. Whitecaps ruffled the waves, spilling lacy foam. Cara headed for the docks with an aching shoulder and dour attitude. She wished fervently she could've stayed with Rodani. But breaking promises always made her feel wrong somehow, as if she'd let everybody down and needed to do penance. She hated the feeling.

The waves were up today, dashing themselves against the front and sides of her boat as she sped westward. The whitecaps arched at the tops of waves further inward than she had seen them.

Storm coming. Great. Maybe I won't get to play tonight after all. Good reason to go back to my husband instead. She guided the boat toward the south end of the docks and pulled into the slip where she usually moored.

Davad walked up to her as she stepped out. "You just now coming in? Where are you going to stay for the duration?" He bent his head to whisper. "Where is your husband going?"

Cara looked up at him in surprise. His face was full of anxiety. "What do you mean?"

"Didn't you hear the weather report when you were here last weekend?" Davad spread his arms in exasperation. "They've been talking about it all week."

Cara spun around to look at the sky, and the surf. "I wasn't here last week. I hurt myself and couldn't play. What weather report?"

Davad's jaw dropped. "Sis, there's a Cat 3 hurricane a few hours away!" He waved at the elongated clouds moving shoreward. "Don't you see the rain bands? Everyone's preparing!" He gestured inland. "Are you going to stay with Ama? Merelin's already there."

Panic flooded her. "Rodani!" Cara ran back and unroped her boat as Davad followed, confused.

"What are you doing?"

Her hands shook, and her shoulder's pain fled behind the frenzy in her brain. She threw the rope into the boat and started to climb in. Davad grabbed her arm.

"Cara, what the hell? You can't go back out."

She turned around, fury in her face and a hiss in her voice. "I'm not leaving my husband on an island two feet above sea level to ride out a hurricane!" Yanking her arm out of his grip, she climbed back into the boat and started the motor.

"Where are you gonna go?"

She backed out, spun the boat, and took off the way she'd just come. The rising waves wanted to push her back to shore, but she fought them with maniacal fear.

Ohgodsohgods. Rodani! Where can we go? Not to town. Not to Soldan. They were stuck between a surf and a seawall just as much today as they were last week, or last month.

South. Gotta go south. Somewhere between Glaniad and Lordstown? And where would they land? *Shitshitshitshit.* On their island, that hammock wouldn't survive 120 mph winds, let alone what the storm surge would do to their camp. But where could they go onshore that was any better?

And how far could they get in a few hours? The wind direction would help them, not hinder. But the waves! How bad would they be? She'd never been on the sea in a bad storm, only sheltering in homes. *Damned if you do and damned if you don't.*

The caves. The caves beyond Lordstown! Could they make it? How many years had it been since Davad had taken her to visit them?

Cara pulled out her 'com as she drove the boat eastward through choppy waves. "Aisu! Aisu! Pick up!"

"Kia," came the quick reply.

"There's a terrible storm on the way!" Panic made her voice crack. "We have to leave the island. Now! Pack up everything we can't replace. I'm coming back to help."

There was a pause on the other end. "Where do we go?"

"I'll tell you when I get there. Get the hammock down! Pack everything you can."

Another pause made her want to scream. "Ninety-nine."

By the time she moored and ran to their camp, several precious minutes had passed. Sacks lay haphazardly on the ground while Rodani rolled up the hammock's cover.

"We have less than three hours before it hits," she said, running up to him. "And we still have to get where we're going."

"Where is that?"

"We have two options." She pointed west. "I go home," she pointed northwest, "and you go to your safe town, or we both go south, together."

Rodani shoved the hammock into a large bag. "What is in the south?"

"Caves. Caves in the cliffs."

He stopped to consider. "We can get in them? With our belongings?"

"One of them is open to the water, and we climb up to a shelf. I remember it. I just have to recognize it when we get there."

"How powerful is this storm?"

Agitated, Cara waved at the sacks and hopped on the balls of her feet. "Bad enough to drive the rain sideways and topple trees."

Rodani glanced toward the cove, then back at Cara. "We take my boat."

"Okay. Survive together, or die together."

Rodani climbed their tree and began untying the hammock. As he looked down, he saw Cara run into the trees with the cage.

"What do you do?" he called down.

"I want to find Fuzz!"

And she disappeared into windswept trees and bushes. Rodani climbed down, hurriedly folded the hammock, then stowed it and the covering in his boat. He met Cara on the way back, the cage heavy in her hand.

He took it from her, slogged through the rising storm surge, and placed the cowering animal beside their bags, then ran to grab the last of their belongings.

"We have to go, Rodani!"

"We have three hours."

"Two, mostly. And the sea will only get rougher. Please!"

One more trip, and Rodani's boat was filled.

"What of yours?" he asked.

"It'll have to take its chances, aisu."

Rodani helped Cara into the boat and backed it out of the cove. The waves were rising as the pair headed south.

With nothing to do and no way to help, Cara fretted and wrung her hands while Rodani battled the surf. A rain band passed overhead, spattering them with just enough rain to add some physical misery to their already stressful predicament. It stopped for a while, then restarted with a heavier downpour.

After far too long an anxious wait, Cara pointed toward shore. "You can see the cliffs beginning. They'll get taller soon and go a long way. You should get closer."

Rodani bent down to speak to her as the waves rocked the boat. "How do you know the correct cave? What does it look like?"

"I'm not sure I can describe it. I'll just have to go by sight and see if something looks familiar."

Rodani's expression wasn't pleasant, but there was nothing else for it. The wind was rising, whipping their hair in tandem and pushing the boat closer to shore.

"There's the first cave." Cara pointed to a dark, irregular hole in the cliffside.

"Do you have any idea how far your cave is?"

Cara staggered sideways as a particularly tall wave hit them broadside. She grabbed for the railing in front of her.

"Ware!" Rodani called out. "Hold on!"

"Five or ten minutes, I hope," she shouted back.

Two more cave openings went by before Cara called out again. "There it is!"

"You are certain?" He had to shout over the howling winds.

"Yes! I recognize the shape."

Rodani steered closer, heading almost due west. The rain hardened into a steady drumming that dripped into their eyes.

"Quick! Don't pass it!"

"Narrow," he judged the opening through squinting eyes.

"Turn more! The wind's going to push us against it."

Rodani followed her directive. The boat neared the opening, then the bow smacked the edge of the rock face.

"More power!" she shouted.

The whole of the left side scraped the rocks as Rodani maneuvered the boat inside.

The cave widened a little, with a height of thirty or forty feet. A rough stairway of stones rose up the left side of the cave. Rodani steered the boat to its base, away from the cave opening with its higher waves. Even there in the corner, the waves were still tall enough to make any movement unsteady. But Rodani wrapped a length of rope around an outcropping of rock and crawled onto the bow of the boat.

"Pass the sacks to me."

"Fuzz first, please," she replied, hefting the cage up on the boat's prow. Rodani took it from her and placed it carefully against the cave wall.

The wind was increasing into a steady moan as Cara passed their meager belongings over to him. He tossed the unbreakables onto the rocks above the water line and carried the few others off the bow. The rocks were slippery, and more than once Rodani lost his balance. Cara screamed a warning that was swept away in the wind before it reached his ears. She crawled onto the bow as it rocked and dipped. If she fell off, she'd be broken against the rocks.

Rodani slithered back and pulled her off the boat into his arms. In a few careful steps, they were safe.

Marginally.

"What is up there?" Rodani asked, his gaze following the line of steps.

"A ledge where we can sit." She waved at the sacks at their feet. "We need to move these up. The water's gonna keep rising."

They carried the cage and sacks higher by ones and twos, resting them against the wall in a line to the top. Rodani picked two to place at the head of the line. With the light of the sun covered by storm clouds, they made their way up the rest of the rocks. Spray from the growing waves, helped along by the storm surge, blasted them with water that tried to pull them off the rough steps. On hands and knees, they crawled onto the ledge at the top of the cave.

Below them, the boat jolted and banged against the rocks. Every wave created a swell of water that burst against the west wall at their feet. Cold, wet rocks hugged their backs. Ten feet above their heads, the cave's ceiling dripped water onto their hair and down inside their shirts. Wet and bedraggled as the rest of them, Fuzz huddled in his cage.

"Was there any word on how long this one will last?" Rodani asked.

"I didn't take time to find out. I should have." She rested her head against his upper arm. "I'm sorry."

Rodani looked back and forth to either side of their shelf. "There is room to lie down, kia."

She copied his glances. "Are you sure?"

"Yes, if we lay on our sides and I hold you."

The rock shelf was hard and unyielding, but Cara didn't relish sitting in a wet crouch until evening—or longer. "Okay."

"Put your back against the wall."

She lay down on her side and wiggled backwards until she was firmly wedged. Rodani lay down in front of her and wrapped his left arm over her. They closed their eyes against the drips from above and the splashes from below. But nothing stopped the roar of the wind, the crash of the waves below them, and the knocking of the boat against the rocks.

It was probably no more than two hours or so, but seemed longer when Cara heard a sharp crack. She felt Rodani jerk and shift in her arms, then yelp in fright. As she opened her eyes, large blocks of rock tumbled from underneath his shoulders and chest, falling into the water below and leaving him hanging unsupported off the ledge. Eyes wide, he lifted his upper body and clutched at her, unbalanced. Cara grabbed at his jacket with fumbling hands as her own head hung down unsupported. "Aisu!"

Fighting not to follow the rocks into the deadly sea below, Rodani bumped and shifted his weight farther toward the south wall beyond his feet. Pebbles rained down from the ledge and from the wall as he grasped at any bit of rock that jutted out. Cara moved with and against him as he hauled his long body toward stability, toward safety. Breathing heavily, he stopped after a few feet and stared at Cara in fright and agitation.

"Oh, my gods," she whispered, an oath barely heard over the crashing waves. He looked back to where he'd been resting, now an open space at the end of the shelf. He leaned toward Cara and clutched at her body, closing his eyes and gasping into her hair.

"Are you hurt?" she asked.

"Du."

"I don't know if we're still safe here."

He took a deep breath. "Nor do I."

***

Davad strode away from the docks, his thoughts whirling as much as the tree limbs in the storm winds. *What in the name of the great sea god was she going to do?* He knew why she ran back. *But where could they go? Maybe he'd return to his own people until the storm passes. Cara could come home. Ama would let her stay for a while, as long as she pulled her weight. There was going to be plenty to do both before and after the storm.* He quickened his pace. *Ama wanted some of the vegetables pulled from the garden before it hit, and the goats needed penned up. Dae would handle boarding the windows, and Ama would lock up her surgery.*

Unfortunately, there was nothing he could do for his boat except triple-tie it. He could only hope.

Once his pre-storm tasks were done and he'd calmed Merelin as much as he could, he checked the attic for his sister. It was empty. He walked outside to see if his father needed any last-minute help.

"Have you seen Cara?" he asked.

Dae looked down from the last window. "No. I don't even know where she is. Last I heard, she was staying at the hostel, where Mack pulled his stunt."

Should he even say anything? What good would it do? His family was worried enough about the inevitable storm damage. To add Cara to the mix would just bring out complaints, worry, and tempers, depending on who was speaking. Maybe it was best just to keep his mouth shut. It's not like he wasn't used to doing that. Growing up listening to Ama and Cara rage at each other was more than enough to create the habit of keeping his thoughts to himself.

But he worried.

Ama stormed into the house and swept through the rooms, making sure all was where it should be. "Kimi, did you pack everyone's clothes in waterproof bags?"

"Yes, Ama."

"Alan, did you put towels between the dishes and glasses in their boxes?"

"Yes."

"Are they packed behind the tables?

"Yes."

"Chairs tied to the table?"

"Yes."

"Teria, did you fill the water barrel and cover the kindling out back?"

"Yes, Ama."

Liz fisted her hips. "Davad, go over to Emmie's and see if they need any help."

"We don't have much time, Ama," he ventured into the midst of her absolute authority.

"That's why you go now. Don't dawdle."

Davad sighed heavily and pushed his way out the door. The wind was already picking up, and the sky was sprinkling again. He ran the few blocks to his oldest sister's home.

"Ama wants to know if you're okay," he said when Emmie opened the door.

"About as well as we're going to get."

"Got something you can climb on if the surge gets this far?"

Emmie shifted her baby from one hip to another. "We can get up to the attic, and Dag sharpened the axe if we need to get onto the roof."

"That's not likely, at least."

"We can hope."

"Okay. Just needed to check. Be careful."

"Thanks. We'll be alright."

Davad ran back to the family home and checked in again with Merelin. He never knew, since her pregnancy hormones had started rampaging, whether she'd laugh, cry, or verbally attack in any given circumstance. But she and Teria were curled up on the couch together, talking in whispers. He walked back out and studied the sky. Maybe he had time to go by the repository for a weather update.

He ran toward the building, and climbed the steps to the doors. It was a good thing his great-grands had constructed it with a half-story beneath the first floor. No one wanted their irreplaceables flooded. Sallah, the repository's archivist, was still there, staring at the weather station's screen.

"Any updates?" he asked.

"It's moving fairly quickly," she said. "About twenty-five miles an hour. It won't have time to destroy us. I worry more for the wind than the rain."

"Any idea on the height of the storm surge?"

"Middling. The ship's computer gauges it at about seven feet, given the tide schedule. By the time it gets up here, *if* it gets here, it won't be more than a foot or two."

"How long are you going to stay here?"

She eyed him coolly. "I'm not leaving."

He tapped her arm. "What would we do without you?" he teased, then turned for the door. "Oh yeah," he said over his shoulder. "Make sure the 'corder stays dry. I don't think Cara could survive without it."

Sallah shook her head, smiling grimly.

By the time he got back home, the rain was beginning to pour down. He grabbed the door handle, but the door wouldn't budge. "Hey!" he shouted, banging on it.

Alan opened it and frowned. "You'd better stay here. Ama won't want you dripping all over the rugs and floor." He shut the door behind his older brother and returned to the living room.

"Merelin?"

"Yes, baby," came the reply.

"Can you bring me some dry clothes?"

His fiancée rounded the dividing wall and looked him over. "Geez, Dav, did you go swimming?"

"Yeah," he said, removing his sopping shirt. "In the middle of the street."

"Just a min."

She returned in short order with a set of clothes taken from the carry sack they'd brought from their cabin. He doffed his wet things and dropped them by the door, then slipped the dry ones on before anyone else could invade his privacy.

The living room was full with family, except for Emmie and Cara. Every seat was taken, and Kimi sat on the floor. Davad took the place on the couch that Merelin had saved for him. The rain pounded against the walls of the house.

"Davad, where's Cara?" Kimi asked.

He clenched his jaws and looked across the room, away from her. "I'm not sure. But I'm sure she's safe. She's not stupid."

The reassurance seemed to satisfy her. She fiddled with a cloth and thread in her lap, but the light was too dim to stitch. Their father stretched out his legs and slid down in his chair until the base of his head hit the chair back.

"Plants gonna be okay, Dae?" Davad asked.

"Hope so. I think so."

The wind increased to a howl outside the house. "What have you been working on?" Davad continued.

"Pain relief."

"Man, I hope that goes well."

Liam pursed his lips. "You and everyone else."

Liz spoke up. "Did you know that the lower pressure of a hurricane can start labor in pregnant women?" She looked around to see who, among her brood, would find the knowledge as fascinating as she did.

Merelin grabbed Davad's hand and put her other one on her four-month pregnancy bulge. "That can't be right, Ama."

"I don't think you have to worry, Merelin. It's only those near term who seem to be affected."

Merelin leaned her head on Davad's shoulder. "Next time, please add your caveats at the beginning, not at the end. This whole nine months is stressful enough without misunderstandings adding to it."

Kimi looked at Merelin and grimaced in sympathy at her mother's thoughtlessness.

Lightning flashed, and a boom of thunder startled every single body in the room. The rain was a constant drumroll in their ears. The hours passed in stories and silence, worry and wonder.

***

Cara craned her neck to see around the ledge they laid on. "There's that little place in the corner we could sit."

A larger wave splashed upward and onto their already wet bodies, dousing them with salty froth.

"We should at least move down to the other wall," Rodani told her.

"Okay."

They scooted and bumped their way until Rodani's feet touched the south wall. Face to chest, they lay and hugged each other tightly, silent, each digesting the death he had barely missed. Time crept onward.

After a while, after they had begun to relax somewhat, the raging wind stopped abruptly, its volume dropping to a whisper. Rodani opened his eyes and rolled partway toward the cave opening, acutely aware of the edge of the ledge under his back. The rain had stopped.

"I should check the boat," he said.

Cara gripped the sides of his shirt. "No! You can't."

"Why? It is quiet."

"That's got to be the eye of the storm. You can't go down there. You don't know how long the calm will last!" She shook her fists, yanking at his shirt. "Don't."

He leaned up against her again. "You have been correct so far, kia. I will heed your warning."

"Thank you." She let out the breath she'd been holding. "Enjoy the quiet while we have it." *Gods, let this storm pass. Quickly.*

Inside his cage, Fuzz began to trill in the silence. "Oh, baby," Cara crooned as she swiveled to look. "I can't let you out yet. I'm sorry." He blinked at her and pawed at his whiskers in agitation, then scraped the bottom of the cage with his claws.

In way too short a time the other side of the eyewall hit with a ferocious howl. The waves that had died down smashed again and again against the rock ledge where they lay. When another hour had passed, water began to drip, then run from a hole in the ceiling over their feet, and then pour down as it enlarged. Their bags that sat among the steps began to soak up the running water, and it began to pool under Cara's and Rodani's lower bodies. Rodani sat up to check the corner nook. It wasn't dry, but being slightly higher, it didn't hold a pool of water, either.

"The corner may be less uncomfortable," he told Cara. "I suggest we move."

They crawled into the cramped space, no longer able to lie down. They sat together, face to face and legs intertwined, their upper bodies resting against each other. The spray was lighter, but not gone. The roof over their head still leaked just beyond them. The wind still buffeted their eardrums with a constant and painful roaring. There was no help for it and nothing to be said. They waited.

Finally, after an interminable and uncomfortable eternity, the wind died down and the raging waves ceased to splash them. Rodani looked down at the water and out into the slice of sky that could be seen through the cave's opening. He sat on his rear at the top of the steps and scooted downward toward the waterline as Cara watched.

He pulled on the ropes that had miraculously held the boat in place. He inspected the outer edges of the craft, then climbed in and tried to start the engine. It came to life with a stutter, then settled down into a steady vibration. He shut it off and climbed back up on hands and knees.

"What next?" he asked.

Cara thought for a minute, looking around—and up. "We should get to the surface and see what's there. At the very least, we should dry our clothes in the sun. But I doubt we could climb the cliffs from the beach. I don't want to try. They're too tall." She glanced back up. "Do you think you could get through that hole? See where it leads?"

Rodani reached up and pounded at the edges of the ragged hole with his knife, enlarging it. He tried to climb up, but had nothing to stand on. He tried again, putting his non-slip shoes on the few protruding rocks in the wall. Some of the dirt at the hole's rim gave way, but some held. With more effort, he pulled himself up and out of the cave.

"What do you see?" she called upward.

"Trees, both standing and fallen. Grass. A stream washing over its banks. And the edge of a cliff."

"Before we bring the sacks up, do you want to listen for human sounds? I don't know how far we moved past Lordstown."

"If you are willing to wait down there."

"I can manage. Walk north." As Rodani's steps faded away, she thought they might yet have to leave by boat. She waited, trying to get her anxious gut to unclench. What did their island look like now? How had it fared? And Glaniad? How many boats were smashed? How badly were the docks damaged? How many roofs lost and floors muddied with sand, dirt, driftwood, and seaweed? She had no idea how high the storm surge had gotten, whether it had overtopped the sandy dune that sat between shore and town.

They would have to stay here at least a few days—to dry out, rest, and collect their wits. But she felt guilty that she wasn't there to help clean up the mess that was sure to have invaded her hometown. She wondered, too, about Soldan and Rodani's safe town. Had they been hit? Had they known? Did they have their own weather station to warn them, or did the CSC pass on any warnings?

Breathe, fem. One step at a time. She began to get restless, not knowing how far Rodani would scout or how much time had passed. She studied the steps below her, but didn't really want to attempt the slippery climb down. Not when it wasn't necessary. Not without her husband nearby. For lack of anything else to do, she pulled out a strip of meat and fed it to Fuzz, still wet, still cowering in his cage.

Eventually, she heard the sounds of footsteps. Rodani called down to her.

"I neither saw nor heard any humans, kia. But that is no proof."

She stood up. "I think that will do for now. Thank you. Do you want me to pass the sacks to you?"

"Yes." He knelt down and lowered his arm. One by one Cara passed them upward. The cage was almost more than she could manage. But Rodani grabbed it and hauled it up. With that task finished, she held her hands over her head and looked up at him.

"Study the wall for footholds, kia. Likely, you will need them."

She lowered her arms and examined the wall. "Okay, I think."

Arms again raised, he grasped her wrists and pulled. "Shit," she swore as her shoulder complained. She planted the toes of her shoes on the jutting rocks and pushed up. More swearing escaped her mouth as Rodani continued to pull. Head, chest, abdomen, thighs. Rodani drew her upward onto the wet grass and puddles of rainwater. She flopped over and held her upper arm, grimacing in pain. "Memories of the waterfall, aisu."

"I am sorry, kia. Rest a while."

Cara shook her head. "You were the one who didn't have the energy to move, yesterday. I'll help." She rose a bit unsteadily, then helped him unpack, one-handed.

Being taller, Rodani laid their clothes out on the branches of nearby trees while Cara unloaded the rest. "Thank the dark gods for waterproof packs," she said as she pulled out her notebook and stitching. "At least a few things stayed dry."

They cleared away brush and tree limbs to build a fire. Unfortunately, everything was too wet to catch. "Well, we still have some travel food," Cara said as she stared at the pile of damp twigs. "You should rest, too, aisu."

"When there is something dry to rest on."

They sat in companionable silence, enjoying the quiet instead of hours of pounding and wailing. Rodani tossed a bit of dried meat on the ground and let Fuzz out of his cage. He sniffed it, chomped, and ran off into the underbrush.

"What did you think of the hurricane?" Cara asked.

Rodani unclipped his hair and ran his fingers through the long, tangled strands. "Exhilarating, but not something I wish to repeat."

"I almost lost you. Again."

Rodani closed his eyes and ducked his head. "Temi can blast those loose rocks into the cold depths of hell."

She mustered a quiet chuckle. "Agreed. I don't think I've ever seen you so frightened."

He turned his head to her. "Is that a rebuke?"

Cara reared back in surprise. "No! You had a right to be! And I was every bit as scared as you." She climbed to her knees and wrapped her good arm around his neck. "Gods, if you had fallen... Aisu, I don't ever want to live without you."

He pulled her wet body onto his equally wet lap and held her.

What was left of the late afternoon passed while they wandered about, exploring their near environs. Small fish swam in the stream, sun-ripened berries clung to bushes, small mammals skittered away into the grasses or down into holes as they walked by. Birds soared overhead. Cara recognized a patch of edible tubers they could harvest.

Rodani found a tree near the stream that would do for the hammock, and dragged that sack upward into the limbs.

"Are you sure you need to do that?" she called up into the leaves. "We don't have to stay here long."

"Yes, we will," came the reply.

"Why?"

No answer filtered down. Cara checked their clothes. They were damp, but not dripping. She sighed.

Within a short time, Rodani climbed down. "Kia, we must talk."

Cara turned to him in surprise. "About what?"

Rodani pulled out one of the mats they'd used on the island, and laid it on the ground. "Sit, please."

Mystified and not a little worried, she sat.

Rodani knelt down in front of her. "I do not wish to go back to Glaniad."

Her eyes went wide. "Why? I have to."

"You do not."

"Rodani, my family needs help. The town needs help to repair the damage from the storm."

"There are more than enough people to do that work."

Her mouth remained open, like a fish desperate for oxygen. "I have to go back and play. I made promises. I don't want to break them. Again," she emphasized.

He looked away. "No."

"What do you mean, no? James and Jonie need me."

"Cara, you have enemies there, and I cannot protect you from them. And no one else there will do even a half-decent duty for your safety. No."

Her heart rate began to rise. She threw out her hands, palms up. "I doubt very much Mack is going to chance me beating him up again. And when his gang made threatening noises that one time, the crowd stood up for me." She took a deep breath. "I'm going back."

Rodani stood up and made a quarter turn away from her.

"Cara, I am about to do to you what you did to me in Barridan."

"And what is that?" Cara's tone rose and fell in overt fear.

"Tender an ultimatum."

"What?" The word shot from her mouth, short and hesitant, followed by rapid breaths.

Rodani turned back to face her. "If you need so badly to return to your town, even while in danger, you may go. But you will go alone. I will not follow. What I will do is stay here for a time to see if you return to me. If you do, we will continue forward together. If you do not, I will return to my homeland. I cannot sit and wait while you are handed appalling threats. I cannot stand aside as you are stalked, assaulted, and attacked when I cannot defend you and your sheh-riffs refuse to. The need to protect what and who I cherish is in my bones and blood. It was there before I ever moved to Barridan. My double-bond only multiplied it."

He put his fists on his hips, a gesture she'd never seen. "I left behind nearly everything I earned in life and everyone I know to be here with you. I turned away from my paths and promises. Will you do the same for me? Please have the courtesy to tell me, when you have decided." His gaze bored a hole in her soul.

Cara looked away, speechless as she rarely was. This had struck like a bolt of lightning, swift and electric and utterly unexpected. She covered her mouth with her hands, and swallowed the lump in her throat. "Rodani," she said slowly, "I can't leave you. You're my mate. My ^husband^. We belong together."

"That is my wish too, kia, or I would not be here. But I will not take you back into danger. Now," he continued, his arms at his side, "if you wish me to go back and kill him so that you can return safely, then tell me so."

Shocked anew at Rodani's blatantly violent offer, Cara rocked back and forth on the mat, her chin tucked to her chest. He waited out her silence.

"My heart says yes, but my ethics say no, Rodani."

"Which wins?"

"Can I have a day or two to think?" she asked, looking up at him. At the remote, closed-off expression she hadn't seen in months. A chill rolled down her body.

"As long as we stay here, you need not even answer. If you wish to return, *with me*, you will have to tell me to kill him and, afterward, accept without judgment that I have committed another cold kill." He looked down at her from his great height, with the deadly knowledge and skills he wore like armor. "Can you do that?"

She sighed heavily, needing a release from the tension in her gut. "I won't say yes unless I can. That, I can promise."

"That is acceptable."

Rodani sat down again, no nearer to her than before, but no farther. *Waiting,* she thought, for her to say something else. Something human. Something that probably wouldn't make sense to his Selandu brain.

"I don't want to send you out as an assassin, Rodani. It's one thing to kill in the midst of battle, like at Barridan. It's a whole 'nother universe to tell you to take someone's life who isn't trying to kill me."

"Then you agree we will stay here?"

She leaned her forehead on her fists. "Unless I change my mind for some reason, yes."

Another, longer silence filled the space between them. Rodani sat still, reserved in Selandu patience. Cara rocked and wrung her hands.

"I didn't know you were so unhappy. Why did you give me the ultimatum?"

"I could do no else, kia. I had nearly reached my limit. As you gave one for Ikemi's safety months ago, so I did for you."

"You're an adult. He was a child."

"Kia," he linked his hands in his lap. "There were...problems in my childhood family. I do not wish to discuss them. But they are the reason why I am so protective. As I must adjust to your very strong emotions, so must you adjust to my very strong protectiveness."

Cara rubbed her scarred palms together. "Aisu, when there is something in a mate's past...that interferes with their life together, it's something that should be discussed. If it affects you so badly, I should at least know something about it. Enough to help you. Enough for us to work through the problem. That's what bonded mates do for each other."

"We have worked through the problem," he countered.

"But I'm not pleased with it. I don't really want to accept it. I don't want to leave that part of my life behind. I want both my town and you."

"As I did mine. But I turned my back on it to follow you."

"What happened in your childhood?"

"I have stated my wishes, Cara."

Finally, finally she looked into his face. "I'm sorry for whatever happened."

He glanced away. "You need not be. It is long past."

"But if Selandu minds are anything like human minds, the past stays with you, and still affects you. Like with your protectiveness. That's stayed."

He said no more, so Cara let it go. At least they had survived the bombshell he'd dropped. But she could never look Jonie in the face again. And Kimi? And Davad? Could she get word to them she was alive?

***

Later that afternoon, when nature had spent her fury, Davad made his way back to shore. Trees lay in tumbles. Broken slats of sidewalk blocked his path. The separate pieces of the Glaniad docks floated in a jumble near—and onto—the beach. Boats, both those afloat and those half-drowned in the water, crowded the docks. A few had been pushed onto land. He searched for his own and, to his grateful amazement, found it floating upright several yards offshore.

Thank the sea gods, he thought. With a baby on the way, he was in no position to buy and outfit another fishing boat. His livelihood depended on it, and he was well aware of the dangers and delights of the ocean that fed and clothed him. He walked to the harbormaster's hut.

"Anything I can do?"

The harbormaster waved at the storage shed. "Help the others put the docks back in order, first. When that's done, take one of these skiffs and see how many boats you can bring 'round."

"Aye aye."

He worked until dusk began to fall, then drove his own boat near the shore to look for other boats that had been pushed south. He counted four, then froze at the wheel. A fifth boat lay in the water, its port side submerged. He throttled down, drifting closer to what he recognized in horror.

His parents' boat. The boat Cara had fled in, back to rescue her alien husband. Back into the arms of the hurricane.

Slowly Davad maneuvered up to the ruined craft. There was nothing in it whatsoever. He circled it, looking into the water for bodies.

There were none that he could see. Of course, he thought with his stomach in knots, bodies could be washed miles down the coast or out to sea. The former might produce a noisome, decaying answer in the days to come. The latter would forever leave a black hole in his life. He sat and stared at the catastrophe in front of him as the sun sank into the horizon.

"I'll come back," he said to himself, "in the morning. And pull it home."

He docked his boat in the twilight and made his way back to his parents' house. But this time, he walked past the garden and knocked on the door of his father's lab.

"Come in."

Davad stepped into the crowded room and slid into the only open chair, across from Liam at his desk.

"What put that on your face?" his father asked. "Did your boat sink?"

"No, she's fine."

Liam waited. "And?" he said, when nothing else was forthcoming.

"Dae," Davad shoved a few things out of the way and leaned his forearms on the desk. "Did you know Cara was borrowing your boat?"

Liam leaned back to regard his only biological son. "No."

"She was."

"And?" he repeated his prompt.

Davad took a deep breath. "I found it a bit south of here, in the water, half-submerged." He paused. "No one was in it."

"You mean Cara took it out and didn't return it before the storm?"

"Yeah."

"Why would she do that? She has her own ways; we all know that. But that doesn't sound like her."

Davad interleaved his fingers and clenched them tightly. "Dae, I met Cara at the docks when I went down to tie my own boat up. She was coming in to dock. I told her a storm was coming. She hadn't known about it."

"Why? It was on everybody's lips for days beforehand."

"She'd been...away. Living on one of the islands."

"So... she docked the boat and took shelter somewhere before the storm hit."

Davad closed his eyes. He didn't want to see his father's expression. "No. She jumped back in the boat and took off, back toward the islands."

There was no sound from across the table for several seconds. Davad kept his eyes shut.

"She left again?" Dismay flooded his father's voice. "Why?"

Davad opened his mouth then closed it again. His heart thumped in his chest, and breaths were hard to come by.

His father watched him fight an unseen foe. "Will you please tell me what's going on?"

"Dae, you have to promise you won't tell anyone."

"I have to know what I'm agreeing to, son."

"And I have to have a promise."

Liam bent his head and rubbed his nose. His gaze wandered over the bottles, vials, planters, and sacks of plants, living and dead, that cluttered his desktop. He blinked in rapid succession, then stared.

"All right, you have my word."

Davad straightened in his chair, and opened his eyes. "Cara was living on one of the islands with a man. With her husband."

"Her what?"

"Husband."

"Who?"

"An alien. A Selandu."

Liam's face fell into confusion. "What rock did you hit your head on?"

"I met him, Dae. I went out there one time, out to the island. She introduced me to him and translated between us so that we could say a few things to each other."

"Assuming I believe you, which I'm not sure I do, what does that mean?"

He must not want to go there, Davad thought. *I don't blame him.*

"It means she went back to the island to rescue him, instead of leaving him there to ride out the storm by himself, not knowing it was coming."

"Where did they go? North? Across the border?"

"If they got in a boat, they would have almost certainly been blown south. How far they might have gotten, I have no clue." He looked down at his clasped hands. "But I saw your boat. If that was what they were in, they didn't get very far."

Now, the silence stretched into minutes. Davad glanced up into his father's face, his expression mirroring Davad's own terror.

"No," Liam finally spoke. "*No.* Not my little bit. Not her."

"I'm sorry, Dae. I really am."

When his father lapsed back into quiet, Davad got up to leave.

"Wait."

He reseated himself.

"Tell me about this husband."

Well, he'd broken his promise to Cara already. What more damage could he do? "She met him in Barridan. He's one of those assassins. Always dressed in black. Lotta weapons. He was guarding her there, spent time with her every day." Davad spread his hands. "They fell in love."

"Word is, they don't even understand the term *love*. Or *friend*."

Davad shook his head. "Well, whatever they call it, it happened. She was happier at that moment than I've seen her since she got back from that place. In fact, happier than I think I've ever seen her."

Liam palmed his forehead and ran his fingers up into his thinning hair. "What do we do? Send out a search party?"

"If they both survived, and they're found, I assume he'll either be imprisoned here, or sent back home. I don't know that he deserves either one."

Liam stared back at Davad, eyes wide and angry. "So, we just forget her? Let it go?"

"The only other thing that comes to mind is if I search up and down the coast by boat for any sign of them. But it's just two people, Dae, and miles and hours of coastline. They could easily hide where I couldn't find them unless I walked the shores for days or weeks. And they have good reason to hide." Davad pursed his lips in frustration. "What are the chances?"

"She played every weekend. Right?"

"Yeah."

"Maybe she'll come back. With him. Hide on the island again. Are you the only one who knew where they were?"

"I think so. But she told me Nick had also found out about her husband. She didn't say how, and she didn't say he knew where they stayed."

"The bartender? Go ask him what he knows."

"That bartender is now living in the north," Davad said, morose. "In that new house where both species live. I forgot its name, but Nick's not around to ask."

"You could ask Menachem to use the CSC's radio and contact Nick."

"I don't trust them not to eavesdrop. I don't think Menachem would approve. He might make trouble."

"I don't know what else to do," Liam said dejectedly.

"Well, if she's dead, it doesn't matter. If she's not, we have time to think of something else."

"Okay. I think."

Davad got up again and turned for the door.

"Thanks for telling me," his father said.

He couldn't muster a smile. "Sure."

That night in their cabin, Davad refused to answer Merelin's queries on his mood. He only pulled her close and held her tight.

The cleanup took days, but it could have been a lot worse. Back aching, Davad straightened up from the pail of hot glue he'd been stirring. He'd learned the technique for making it from his dae's father. If it wasn't made right, the glue would dissolve, and cracks and holes would appear in the boat's hull. Disaster always followed.

As he looked around, he noticed a broad form walking toward him with a purpose in his stride. *Speaking of disasters,* he thought worriedly. *Patience,* he wished himself. *Curb your desire to finish the job your sister started.*

Mack strolled up and looked around at the industry going on all over the docks. "I'd like to talk to you," he said without preamble.

I can guess what. "About?"

"Cara."

Davad bent to resume stirring. "I can't help you, Mack."

"You haven't even heard what I want to say." Frustration seeped into Mack's voice.

"Fine." He straightened. "What do you want to say?"

"I want you to give me ideas on what I can say to Cara to convince her to give me a try. Every time I approach her, she blows me off. I've got a lot to offer, you know. And I deserve a chance."

Good gods, where do I begin? Or do I begin at all? "Mack, you do realize that nobody *deserves* a chance at a woman, right? You have to earn it. And what earns a woman's affection is a little different for each one."

"That's what I'm asking you," Mack protested. "I need you to tell me what to say to make her want me."

"It doesn't work like that. You can't just walk up and say some magic words to get her into bed."

Mack tucked his thumbs in his belt. "Then what does work?"

Davad scratched his head and wiped the sweat that was running down his cheek. "Respect. Patience. Caring about her as a person, not as an object you want to use for your own libido."

"There's nothing wrong about my sex drive!"

"I didn't say there was, and I wouldn't know either way. It's your attitude and your actions, Mack."

"I reassure her. Lots of times."

"And she doesn't believe you, because your words and your actions don't match."

"What do you mean?"

Davad shifted his footing as the docks rocked with a large wave. "I'm not a psychologist, Mack. You need to talk to a professional."

"I don't need any sucking head doc!"

He shook his head. "I'm sorry. I can't help you. And even if I could, I won't. Because you don't have her best interests at heart."

Mack glared at him in a towering rage. "Fuck you!" He stomped off the docks and up the path to town.

Nothing like proving the truth of my words, Davad thought. I'm almost glad Cara disappeared.

Almost.

TWENTY

"I haven't seen Fuzz lately," Cara said. "Have you?" She switched thread colors on her needle, and moved to a different spot on the fabric.

"I have not."

A collection of sticks, larger and smaller, sat piled on the blanket in front of Rodani. He turned one in his hand, inspecting the carving that ran up and down the length. Pursing his lips in dissatisfaction, he laid it to his side and picked up another, one from a different species of tree.

"I hope he returns," she continued. "I miss him."

Rodani glanced at her. "More than Davad? Or your sister..."

"Kimi." She shrugged her shoulders and stared at her stitching, not really seeing it. "No. But I can't cuddle them and feed them scraps."

Rodani studied the new stick. "You could cuddle and feed me."

"Again?" Cara asked, laughing. "That reminds me. I need to peel those tubers for dinner. Have you cleaned the fish you caught?"

"Yes. And I tire of fish, already."

"We could search for Lordstown, see how far away it is."

Rodani considered. "That might mean an overnight stay."

"But it might be worth it."

***

A week to the day after the hurricane, Suraya stood outside The Wet Rag bar and watched the crowd. It wasn't Mack she was looking for, or his gang. It wasn't the gathering townsfolk she was studying. She was waiting to see if a certain long-haired drummer showed up on stage. Cara's arm should have been healed enough by now.

Maybe her shoulder still hurt? Maybe that's why she hadn't shown for the post-storm clean up. Tongues had wagged about that social blunder. Nobody was supposed to skirt the responsibility. Even the oldsters shuffled down the streets, picking up bits of trash. If you could walk, you helped. Even one-armed, Cara should have at least made an attempt.

James stood on the stage, tuning his guitar. Jonie walked back and forth, watching the increasingly loud spectators with a hard look in her eye. She turned to her husband with a look that could murder a saint. James just shrugged his shoulders and strummed a chord.

"Looks like it's just us, tonight," he told the crowd. "Sorry about that."

"We want dances, too!" someone shouted.

"Well, maybe she'll show up." He nodded to Jonie, who began to sing.

Inside the bar, Mack slammed his empty glass onto the table. His head was already pounding, and it was all because of that damned woman. "Where the fuck is she?"

At his right elbow, Stefan grinned. "Maybe she's playing hard to get," he teased.

"Screw that. She's showed up every other weekend, why not this one?"

"She missed the one before the storm, too."

"Did you talk to Davad?" Clark asked.

"Yeah, that was a worthless effort."

"Why?"

"He just blamed it all on me. Cocksucker. Managed to knock up one woman and thinks he knows everything about 'em all."

"Did you rough him up?"

"No. I hurt him, and I'll never have a chance at Cara. She'll never believe he deserved it."

"And of course, I never got the chance to talk to her—seeing she's not around." Stefan waved at the new barmaid, lifting his empty glass, then looked across at Clark. "Did you talk to the old witch?"

"Yeah. Said she doesn't sell to men, only women."

"Whaaat?"

"Typical female. Only cares about her own kind."

"Bitch."

"You got it."

Stefan eyed his brother. "You know, Cara's dad messes with potions and stuff. He might listen."

"Not to me. Or to you. He'll be too suspicious."

"Clark?"

He took a man-sized gulp of ale. "What would I say?"

Stefan winked at the barmaid as she set his next drink in front of him, then frowned when she ignored him. "Say you have an aunt who needs something to calm down."

"What would that be?"

"What's that thing women go through when they get old?" Mack asked. "When they turn all bitchy?"

"Menopause," Clark said.

"There you go. Perfect excuse."

"I don't want to talk about that with somebody," Clark replied, disgust dripping from his voice. "Besides, why wouldn't she be the one asking? Why me?"

"Because she's being too much of a bitch to want to, that's why. You say you'd be doing her a solid. Just being a good nephew, you know?" Mack smiled at his own brilliance.

"Maybe." Clark shook his head. "I'll think about it."

They all stared into their drinks as the ideas lagged.

"I know." Stefan held up a finger and turned to Mack. "Did you ever think of suing her?"

"I climbed in her window, man."

"But you never hurt her! She hurt you, instead, with no warning and no good reason."

"Yeah," Clark chimed in. "Talk to Sheriff Berg about it."

"I don't think sheriffs do anything with lawsuits. They just put people behind bars."

"Talk to a lawyer."

"And how would I pay him?"

"Umm..."

"Yeah."

***

Late the next afternoon, Suraya walked up to a cabin she knew well and knocked on the door. She hoped he was home from fishing by now.

Davad opened the door.

"You got a minute? Can we talk?"

He glanced back at his fiancée, who was eyeing the pair suspiciously. "For a few, sure."

"Let's walk down to the bar."

Arms crossed, Merelin walked toward the door. "Anything you need to say to him, you can say right here, Suraya."

Davad held up one finger and turned around to Merelin, coaxing her back into the room. "Linnie, my love," he whispered, "there is no reason for your jealousy. Su is my past. You are my present and future." He ran a hand down her cheek, and a thumb across her lips. "Let it go, for your peace of mind, and mine."

Her expression softened just a bit, but there was no smile to be found in it. "You can still talk out in the yard."

"If it will make you feel better."

"And if your dinner gets cold, you can eat it that way."

Davad smiled. "I won't be that long." He walked out to meet Suraya, pulling the door shut behind him.

Suraya had her arms crossed and a frown on her face to match Merelin's. "What?" she spat. "She think I'm here to steal you away or something?"

Davad knew better than to dive into that kind of conversation. "What's up?"

Suraya looked around the yard. "Have you seen Cara since the storm?"

His stomach clenched in response, but he kept his face composed. "No."

"Any idea where she is?"

"No."

"Aren't you worried about her?"

"She's pulled disappearing acts before. I assume she found some other place to shelter."

Suraya spread her hands. "She didn't show up to play last night."

"At all?"

"No. Jonie was ticked, and the crowd was pretty disappointed, too. And I heard James grumbling about her."

"Well, she'll have to face them when she reappears."

Suraya shook her head. "Have you searched for them?"

Davad stilled. *Them? What did she know?* "Them?" he asked, verifying the unexpected word.

She paced a few steps in either direction, agitated. "Dav, do you know anything about what she's been up to since she returned?"

"Not my business."

"You two used to be close. Did she tell you anything about her time there? Why she came back so unhappy?"

"Very little. She's been pretty closed-mouth about it."

Suraya stopped in front of him, eyes fixed on his face. "She's been living somewhere, away from town. Every Sunday she'd disappear, and every Friday she'd come back to play."

"And? She likes her privacy. Always has."

"I think I know where she was staying. Davad, I don't know how to drive a boat. Can you take me out to the islands?"

"Why? If she's out there, she wants to be left alone."

"How could she have stayed there during the storm? And if she didn't, where did she go? And if she went somewhere, why didn't she come back?"

"Storms kill, Su."

Her eyes went wide, her voice faltered. "What do you mean?"

Now Davad turned away. "I found her boat after the storm. Our parents' boat that she'd been using."

"Go on," she whispered.

"It was tipped on its side south of town, in the reeds near shore. Empty." He turned back and met her gaze.

"Noo," she moaned, ducking her head. "Nooo." She looked back at him. "Did you search?"

"For bodies, yeah. For about an hour south. Nothing."

"Did you search by boat, or walk the beaches?"

"Boat. But I skimmed the shore."

"What are we going to do?" she asked, voice rising in panic.

"What is there to do?" he countered.

Suraya clutched her arms across her chest. "If she's dead, he is, too."

Davad waited a beat, for emphasis. "Probably. Unless he fled north."

Her mouth dropped open as his words hit her. "You knew? How?"

"I followed her to the island one time. Met him." Davad dug the toe of his shoe into the dirt. "We exchanged a few words. How did you find out?"

She gazed off into the distance. "I found her at Dr. Shen's office a few weeks ago, mid-week when she's usually never around. I hid when I overheard her talking to someone on a handheld radio. Someone who was a native Selandi speaker and sounded like a man. I heard her say 'I love you' to him." She licked her lips and bit down on the bottom one, thinking back to that day. "I followed her to the shoreline, hiding in the trees. The man took her back to his boat and drove off, east. I never saw them again."

"What boat were they in? Ama's?"

She shook her head. "It wasn't a style I recognized."

"Then they might have gotten away in his boat, not hers."

"We should find them."

"If they're alive, they don't want to be found, Suraya. And we don't even know if they are. Or where they might have landed." He waved his hand, brushing away any hint of surety. "They could be anywhere. Or their bodies could be."

"We should check their island, Davad. You know which one it is. I don't."

"I already did. There was nothing left but a flooded latrine." Now he rubbed his forehead, pensive. "One thing I do believe, is that they would have stayed together. When I spoke to Cara on the docks that morning, she was adamant about not leaving him behind. For their sake, let it go."

Suraya bent her head in prayer. "God grant them rest."

Back inside his cabin, Davad gave Merelin a hug. "See? No problem."

"What did she want?"

"To ask about Cara."

"Why?"

"She's disappeared again. Typical Cara." He forced out a chuckle to distract her, and left his arm around her shoulder. "Let's eat."

***

Kimi leaned up against the kitchen table. The potato in her hand and the ones resting in front of her were being watered in tears.

She was supposed to have dinner ready by now. Ama would be home soon. *Angry mother again* was not a scene she wanted to endure tonight. She'd lived through too many already, but other things kept crowding into her head instead of cooking. Her sleeve was already wrinkled and damp from her eyes. She didn't want to think about what her nose left behind in the same place.

She'd visited Emmie this afternoon and found that Cara hadn't picked up her drums over the weekend. No one had seen or heard from her. Emmie had tried to reassure her, but the words had slipped through her ears without being processed.

The front door thumped shut, and footsteps came toward her. She didn't look up. Didn't need to. She knew well what her mother's expression would be.

"Where is dinner, Kimi?"

She sniffed mightily, noisily. "Meat's in the pot."

"Why are you crying? Is that why you're still peeling vegetables when it should all be done by now?"

Kimi bit her lip to keep angry words inside, but the effort to suppress them made her sob harder.

"Is it time for your red tide?"

She shook her head, then wiped her eyes again.

"Well, I don't see any reason for you to be dripping tears all over our dinner. Stop." Her mother headed upstairs to do whatever she did when she got home.

Kimi swore under her breath. Did the woman not see? Not care that she had a daughter missing? What kind of mother can feed and clothe her children but have no empathy for them? How could she take so much care with her patients and none for those who waited at home?

She hacked at the potato skins with angry slashes, hurrying through the process with frantic abandon. Get out! She had to get out of this house!

Before too long, she had a pile of cubes. She scooped them up and dumped them in the pot to cook with the goat meat, then washed her hands and face. She fled out the front door as her father came in the back from his lab.

"Kimi?" he called to her departing form.

Silent, she charged down the block then stopped in her tracks, lost inside her head and nowhere to go for answers. She didn't want to go back to the house. Emmie was busy feeding her own kids, whose antics would make sure nobody had a decent conversation around them. She had another brother, Gavin. But he'd moved out into the hinterland, probably for the same reason she herself wanted to. Davad was the only reasonable adult left. She didn't much like his fiancée, but right now, Kimi didn't give a flip. She headed in the direction of the docks where their cabin sat at the northeast corner of town.

She knocked on the door, hoping Davad would be the one to answer it. Tears were threatening to fall again, and she didn't want to chance any teasing Merelin might deliver.

But Merelin opened the door. "Yes?"

"Can I speak to Davad, please, Merelin?"

"We're not finished eating."

Kimi hung her head, feeling like the helpless teenager she was. "Please?"

"Who is it, Linnie?"

Davad appeared behind, and raised his eyebrows when he saw who was at the door. "Excuse me, love." He glided past Merelin and walked outside.

"What's up?"

His gentle demeanor opened up her waterworks. She covered her reddened face with her hands and tried to speak. Hiccups and gasps interrupted every other word.

"Let's go for a walk, Kimi." He turned to Merelin, who was still guarding the door. "I'll be back."

Davad led her east, over the grassy expanse that separated the town's edge from the docks at the base of the dune.

"I didn't bring a kerchief."

She tried to smile. It didn't get very far. They stopped near the edge of the dune's slope toward the sea.

"Want to try again?"

Kimi took several breaths. "I went over to Emmie's today. She said Cara hadn't been by to get her drums since two weeks before the storm. She said she'd asked around, but no one had seen her. That's three weeks, three weeks when Cara should have shown up and hasn't.

"I waited for her to come to the house before the storm, but she didn't. Nobody else said anything, so I didn't. But...nobody's talking, Davad. Nobody's mentioned she's missing. Why?"

"I don't know."

"You haven't heard from her either? I thought at least she'd talk to you! Why wouldn't she come home before the storm? If she's staying somewhere, alone, she needed shelter."

"I can't speak for her, Kimi. I don't know what's in her head."

"Where else would she go?"

Davad shrugged. "Maybe she went north."

"Why would she do that? They don't want her!"

"It was just a thought."

"You don't know where she was living?"

"No." But when you lie, even for a good reason, it still stings.

"I hope she didn't get hurt."

"Me, too."

"Who's hurt?" said a voice.

They both turned to see Gerry walking their way.

"Nobody that we know of," Davad said.

"Who were you talking about?"

"No one."

Kimi's face filled with righteous anger. "I don't want to talk to you. You threw her out! Go away!"

Gerry ignored her and kept his focus on Davad. "What's happened?"

"Nothing I want to discuss with you."

He stepped closer to the pair. "I love your sister. If something's wrong, I want to know."

Davad raised his chin, unmoved by the drummer's declaration. "You're not the only person asking me questions. I won't discuss her with you any more than I did with that sea scum, Mack."

"I heard what he did, and I would never threaten her like that. He deserved what he got, and more."

"You still hurt her," Kimi yelled.

"Sometimes love hurts, kid. She hurt me, too."

Kimi stalked off, swearing words she'd never let her mother hear.

The men watched her stomp away. Gerry turned back. "Now that she's gone, what can you tell me?"

Davad stared into his eyes. "Man to man, huh? Well, this man could be just as pissed as Kimi that you kicked her out when she didn't have any place to go." He crossed his arms. "You deserve to be kept in the dark."

"C'mon, Davad. You have to know what unrequited love feels like. What it does to you."

"It doesn't turn you into an asshole, Gerry."

***

Cara and Rodani stood just inside the edge of a forest, one heavy with undergrowth. As Rodani had been without a debilitating episode since they fled the storm, they had spent nearly three hours this day hiking north from their new camp in an attempt to find Lordstown. It had finally appeared through the trees.

Hardly different from Glaniad, it sported small cabins, huts, and one- and two-story houses and shops. She saw a main street, but the rest of it looked jumbled—as if the buildings had sprung up haphazardly like mushrooms after a rain. A few men strolled among them, but no women that she could see.

"Aisu, what are they going to think if I just walk out of the woods like this?"

"They are your people, kia. What will they think?"

She pointed her finger and waved it. "I know. I'm scouting the forest for new herbs for my father. They should know who he is, and it will make sense. Hmmm."

"Kia?" he prompted after a moment's silence.

"I wonder if I can sell any of my needlework here?"

He tilted his head. "Something to think about. Do you have your list?"

She patted the pocket in her shorts. ^Yep.^

"It still surprises me," he said with some humor, "how many words you have for a simple assent."

Cara laughed softly. "And you only have one, aisu. How boring." She took a deep breath. "Well, here I go."

Cara walked a little way east before turning north. She entered the town at its southeast corner, if you could call four cabins facing four different directions a corner.

She worked her way west for a couple of minutes until she reached what she thought was Lordstown's main street. Before she could turn the corner, a young man stepped out of a house and stared at her as if he'd never seen a woman before. He even turned to watch her as she walked by, with no attempt at disguising his blatant interest.

Cara rounded the corner and began inspecting the shops that lined the first street. There were no sidewalks. By the time she reached the third shop, a woman ran out, grabbed her, and pulled her inside. Protesting, Cara fought to retrieve her arm from the shopkeeper. Instead, she was inundated with a barrage of questions.

"Who are you? Where are you from? Why do you walk around dressed like that? Don't you know better? Who taught you your morals?"

Cara pried the woman's fingers from her arm and looked her over. Ankle length skirt, long-sleeved blouse that even in the summer heat was buttoned up to the chin, hair pulled back into a severe bun that even an unmated Selandu would approve of.

"What's your name?" she continued. "Why are you here? Don't you know what Preacher will do to you if he sees you looking like that?" She pulled at the skimpy t-shirt that Cara wore. "Have you no shame? Here." Pulling Cara toward the back of the shop, she opened a box and held out a long skirt nearly identical to the one she herself was wearing. A tunic followed. "Put them on before someone catches you."

A bit mystified, Cara slipped the skirt over her shorts and tied it at her waist. The tunic billowed loosely over the top half of her body, except where it stretched against her generous breasts. She plucked at the cloth, uncomfortable with the odd-fitting garment.

The shopkeeper planted her hands on her hips. "At least now you can be out in public without trouble." She looked Cara down and back up again. "Have you paid your respects to our Lord at the chapel yet?"

"Uhh," Cara dithered, confused. "No, why should I?"

The woman stiffened in arrogant shock. "You have to. Everyone does, at least once a day. And every visitor goes first thing, as soon as they arrive. Go. Shoo." She flapped her hands in front of Cara.

"Wait, please. Do you have a grocery or market here?"

"Of course, sister. It's farther down the street. But don't forget, chapel first."

Bemused, ears full of vague warnings, Cara thanked the woman and left her shop. She had, of course, no intention of bowing and scraping before some random god in some random chapel. She'd had her fill of religious pressures in Barridan. She headed for the market.

With soap, toothpowder, needlework thread, dried meat, fresh veggies, and fruits, the walk back to their camp was going to be heavy and long. But at least Rodani would carry the better part of it.

She wandered past the shelves and bins, checking each item against her long-term future in the area. She found a pair of sandals that fit, with the thought of saving her somewhat worn shoes for rougher weather. She also scooped up another notebook. Between her life with Rodani in Barridan and her life with him in the south, she was running out of blank pages.

She found some thread and picked up several skeins, wishing forlornly that they had brighter colors in stock. Everything seemed a little dim, or washed out here. Or maybe it was just her mood...

Home without Rodani, or here with him. There wasn't really a choice, but she hated having to make the choice that was no choice. It still rankled, even as she understood his stance on the matter.

Compromise, she chided herself.

The cashier behind the counter added up her purchases. "One silver, three copper," she quoted.

"Do you have an extra sack?"

"Quarter copper," she added, flopping a cloth bag on the counter.

Cara passed over the money, which the cashier inspected carefully. Cara wondered what the woman would have done if she'd handed a few Selandu coins to her. Probably have a conniption fit. Cara smirked.

"I take it you're new here," the woman remarked as she bagged Cara's items.

"Yeah. I'm just searching the forest for new plants to bring to my father. He's a botanist. He's busy, so I'm doing him the favor."

"Be sure to go by the chapel and pay your respects."

Cara put her hand on the sack. "I'm curious why that's so important."

The cashier regarded her quizzically, as if the question had never entered her mind. *Maybe it hadn't*, Cara thought.

"We all pay respects to our Lord above. It's not only required, it's an honor to exalt Him. The Lord watches over us and keeps us safe."

"So, nobody was injured or died in the hurricane?"

"There were two deaths."

Cara pouted her lips. "Guess he didn't keep everybody safe."

The woman's face drew into anger. "Now you blaspheme? He has a plan for each of us."

Cara raised her hand, palm out. "My mistake. Have a bright day. Thank you." She carried the two sacks out into the street and headed for the forest. She didn't walk straight for Rodani's location in case anyone was watching.

Past a few trees, Rodani popped out of the shadows. Cara passed the heavier sack to him, grateful for his strength and his willingness to share their burdens. They butted heads a little too often for her comfort, but his attentiveness to her needs—not to mention his loving attentions—made every day worthwhile.

Hours later, she staggered into camp behind him, dropped the sacks, and flopped onto the blanket, moaning. "I hope it'll be a while before we have to do that again."

Rodani cracked a smile. "It will depend on how quickly we both tire of eating fish."

She huffed in bad humor.

"Did you find your red tide supplies?"

"Yes, fortunately."

Rodani pulled out his notebook and wrote in the date.

"What are you doing?"

"Keeping track of your tides."

The corners of her mouth drew down in a mock grimace. "Why?"

"To anticipate your moods, kia. Then I do not waste time wondering."

"Oh, good gods."

Rodani smiled and kissed the palm of her hand. "And how did you come by those clothes?"

"Ugh. I was so tired, I ignored them." She stripped them off and flung them away from the blanket. "The first woman I talked to told me I couldn't walk around in what I was wearing and made me put them on. Said I'd get in trouble by somebody named 'Preacher.' She said his name like the words should be capitalized or written across the sky with fireworks. I guess he's the human equivalent of Kimasa or something. Somebody religious, in any case. The woman said I had to go to their ^chapel^, which is like a smaller Enclave, and pray to their god. Said I was required to do it."

"And did you?"

She looked him in the eye and smiled. "What do you think?"

He returned the look in full measure. "Either you ignored the order completely, or you gave her a lecture on the value and efficacy of science versus superstition."

Cara laughed out loud. "I do miss debating Iraimin and Kimasa."

"Because you always assumed you won."

"Didn't I?"

"I am quite certain they simply thought you misinformed and misguided, and retreated to formulate further arguments."

Cara sat up and looked off into the distance. "We had some fun in Barridan, didn't we?... Until it all fell apart."

"Change is the only constant, kia."

She leaned her head into his shoulder. "And there's that wisdom again."

TWENTY-ONE

Suraya scribbled the final words to her latest article, stabbing the last period with an emphatic thunk of her pen. It worried her that she was losing interest in her everyday job, with its everyday topics. Two weeks past the storm, she was tired of writing about the cleanup's progress, and what was still missing. And the need for more sheriffs to replace the two who went to Himadi House, the slow decline of The Wet Rag bar under Dottie's mismanagement (helped along by Cara's absence), the latest failure of Prof. Liam's pain relief research results, the necessity of building more boats to replace those lost in the hurricane, and a possible looming insect infestation of the caffee plants.

Cara's disappearance still nagged her brain in its idle moments, despite the fact that no one else mentions her anymore. "It won't sell, Suraya. Pay attention to what's under your nose," her boss says.

Maybe she should change careers. But what else was she good at? Nothing.

"That was an awfully big sigh. I could hear it from across the room."

Suraya grimaced at Bethamy, who seemed perfectly content to organize and update the community message board. Not everyone had an obsession, she reminded herself. Obsessions were like a bad rash. The more you scratched them, the more they bothered you. Liam, she thought, needed to develop a salve for the brain. It really was sad that almost all of the medications brought down from the ship hadn't lasted more than a couple of years.

Bethamy piped up again. "Are you ever going to write a feature about that preacher in Lordstown?"

"He's hours away," Suraya pointed out. Frustration colored her voice. "Who would care..." A tendril of thought squirmed through her mind. Slowly, it wrapped itself into a speck of an idea and lodged in her forebrain.

If there's any chance Cara is alive, she's in the south. Even Davad admitted that much. Where else would she get her supplies except in Lordstown?

"Paolo?" she called for her boss.

"Yow," he replied from inside his office.

She stuck her head in the door. "Has Bethamy said anything to you about doing a story on that Lordstown preacher? She's mentioned it to me twice. I thought it might be worth something, as well as get our minds off our own problems."

"Write up a précis for me."

Suraya returned to her desk. "What do you know about this guy, Beth?"

"He's a real old-fashioned fire-breather, I heard." Bethamy took a sip of her caffee, now gone lukewarm. "Like right out of history cubes."

"In what ways?"

"He makes the rules based on whatever he believes his god says to him. Forces everyone to obey them. Preaches against immorality—whatever he thinks that is—and demands that women subjugate themselves to their fathers or husbands."

"Good gods in space, Beth. What century was he born in? That's an atrocious way to live."

"Some people like it."

"And what happens to those who don't?"

Bethamy set her caffee cup down with exaggerated care. "I hesitate to guess."

Suraya pulled another piece of paper from her desk. "Maybe I can find out."

Three days later, she handed a full silver to Davad for a two-hour boat ride to Lordstown. It was his day off from fishing. Her carry sacks sat on the bottom of the boat near her feet. She wondered idly if Merelin had put up a fuss about the trip and had demanded to come along. Fortunately, she hadn't.

"Do you know much about the town?" Suraya asked.

"Not very."

"You don't trade with them?"

274

"No. What was left of the people who survived the River War came here afterwards. They're big on self-sufficiency for some related reason, I think. I only trade with the Selandu."

"But they have an inn, right?"

Davad glanced at her for a moment. "You're staying there four days, and you don't know if you'll have a room to sleep in?"

"I just assumed they would. They're a human town, after all."

Glaniad's docks shrunk to pinpoints behind them as they sped south.

"Have you heard anything—uh!" she gasped as they hit a big wave, "—about this preacher they have?"

"Vaguely," Davad answered. His hands on the wheel were never still, his eyes always scanning the horizon. Despite his relatively young age, he was a respected seaman and pilot.

"What have you heard?"

"He sort of runs the place, is what I heard. Like a mayor or something."

"Anything else?"

"Nope."

Suraya tried to enjoy the 360-degree view, but the salt spray in her face and the constantly bumpy ride soured the trip. She was a landlubber and refused to be ashamed of it. *Did Cara and her husband pass this way? Did they see these shores as they ran from danger? Where would they have gone?*

Eventually, Lordstown's docks came into view. Davad berthed the boat into a slip and roped it tightly to a post. "To your door service," he quipped.

"Four days, right? Monday, midday."

"I'll be here. Hopefully, you will, too."

Suraya gazed upward at the low cliffs that lined the beach. A stairway led upward at an angle parallel to the cliff face. "I don't expect any danger, Dav. Thanks a bunch." She grabbed her carry sacks and let him steady her exit as she climbed out.

First things first. She looked both ways down the docks for a hut or office, finding it on the northern end. She made her way to the tiny building as Davad backed out behind her.

"Dockmaster?" She leaned into the doorway.

He turned at the summons. His sun-wrinkled face was half-covered by a long, scraggly beard, as if he had studied images of sailors from centuries ago and decided to imitate them. He looked her up and down. "Yes?"

"Sorry to bother you, but I'm visiting the town for a few days. Is there an inn or hostel I can stay at?"

He gestured upward. "Southeast end of town, just off the main street."

Suraya smiled here best, determined to ingratiate herself with everyone she met. It was a necessary talent for a journalist that she'd tried to master. Sometimes it even worked. "Thank you. I appreciate it."

He turned back to his desk without a word.

The steps were a challenge with the burdens she carried. But she made it, out of breath and ready for a cool glass of tea. She headed left, then right after passing four curiously oriented cabins. No town planner, she guessed.

At least the inn was recognizable as such. "Rooms to let" sounded like a really old-time term to her ears. She pushed open the door with her shoulder and walked toward the desk. The man behind it widened his eyes as she neared.

"I'd like a room for three nights, please." Another smile. She hoped it didn't look too forced. The man was staring at her like she had three heads, and one of them was breathing fire.

"Three coppers."

She handed them to him, and took the key. "Thanks."

"Young woman," he said sharply, "you'd better change your clothes before you go back outside."

She thought for a moment, but her mind went blank. "Why?"

"That is not at all appropriate attire for your kind."

She almost called him out on his choice of words, but held back. No sense in starting off on the wrong foot. "This is all the type of clothes I have."

The clerk shook his head at the idiocy of northerners. "There's a place three doors down on the left. Shopkeeper'll find you something that's not so indecent."

Indecent? She felt insulted. *Since when?* Then Bethamy's description came back to mind. Well, she'd better find this shop. She

276

unlocked the door to her room and left the sacks behind, taking only pen, notebook, and money.

Third shop on the left. She didn't even have to check inside when she got to the door. A woman ran out screeching, and dragged her in.

"You can't wear that here! For the Lord's sake, cover up that skin. What did your mother teach you, anyway?" The woman plucked a full-length skirt from a rack and pushed it into Suraya's hands. "Put this on. Shame on you for dressing like that." She pulled out a tunic and held it up to Suraya's body, waiting while she wrapped the skirt around her. "This next."

Suraya held it out, eyebrow raised.

"Here, here," the shopkeeper complained in a clipped voice. She balled the hem in her fists and dragged it over Suraya's head. "You're not the only northerner I've had to dress in proper clothing lately. You know that? Someone else came waltzing in here weeks ago, dressed just as scandalously as you. I had to cover her up, too. Don't you girls know how to dress?"

In an instant, all thought of clothes fled from Suraya's mind. "What did she look like? About my height but pale skin? Dark blue eyes?"

"Maybe she did. I don't remember."

"Did she have really long brown hair held back with a clip?"

"Now that, I do recall." The woman stood back to give a once-over to Suraya's new clothes. "Looked like she'd never cut it in her life." She cocked her head. "Sort of like yours, actually."

"Did she say where she was going to do her shopping?"

"All I heard her mention was the market."

"Thanks!"

"The chapel is over that way." She pointed behind her. "You have to go there, first."

"I do?"

"You sound like her, too. All visitors have to pay their respects to the Lord in His house. Get you gone."

Suraya retraced her steps, and found her way to the chapel. Unremarkable in its simplicity, the façade held nothing but an unadorned sign while the inside held the typical accouterments of one more incarnation of Christianity among the tens of thousands that had existed before it. A rough-hewn cross hung from the far wall and long empty benches filled the intervening space.

A little unnerved, Suraya crept forward into this unfamiliar abode. Her own religion was older than this one, and met her needs better. But, she reminded herself, she had a story to write. People to interview.

"Hello?" she called out into the empty room.

The scrape of a chair on wood alerted her. A man stepped out of a side room she hadn't noticed. He was tall and thin, with a humped back that gave him a predatory stance. His face however, lined and worn with age, showed nothing but a contemplative expression.

"Welcome, my dusky daughter." He placed his palms together. "What can the Lord do for you?"

Dusky? Suraya flipped through the dictionary stored in her head. More than one definition came to mind. *Which one did he mean?*

"Ah, I'm visiting from Glaniad. We have heard of your beneficence, and your influence in Lordstown. I was wondering if you had a little time to talk with me."

He stepped closer, toward the first of the benches. "I am always willing to discuss our Lord with a stranger, my child. But for what purpose do you seek Him?"

"I'm a journalist, Mr.—"

"Just call me Preacher. It's what I do in the service to our Lord and his chapel. What does the news business need with me?"

"My boss, who collects and coordinates the town news, believes you to be a worthy story for our readers. You might use the opportunity to spread your word."

"The Lord's word," he corrected her. "I have visited your town in the past, daughter, and found little reception. The few I have preached to I found unrepenting. They aren't ready to hear God's word."

Suraya bent her head. "I'm sorry for the disappointment you found. Sometimes, the written word will make its way forward more easily than a verbal sermon."

His lips thinned into a line, wary. "Perhaps."

"How did you convert your people, Preacher? It must have taken a long time."

"I preach the truth. The truth that all men know in their hearts, even when they ignore it." He sat on the bench, facing her. "Sometimes calling up the truth is enough, but more often, it must be helped along with education and laws. I have used all three, all for the glory of God."

"What happened to the people who didn't submit? Who didn't—or couldn't—believe your truth?"

"Those who do not shelter under the canopy of faith are shunned," he said bluntly. "And if they disobey the laws of the land, they are punished."

"May I ask how?"

"Incarceration and reeducation, usually."

"How many left town?"

The preacher studied her out of the corner of his eye. "Few. And they are not missed."

She didn't like the look he was giving her. There was danger beneath it; it crawled up her nerves. "I understand. Thank you." She took a deep breath and tried to unclench her gut. "Are there any written lessons you might have that I could read?"

"The best teaching is face-to-face. Spoken word to listening ears. The Lord speaks with more than just the written word. He flows forth from the face, the hands, the body."

"I see." Grab a person's emotions, and the rationalizing tags along behind. *Oh, that technique's never misused or abused.*

"Have you had any other visitors from Glaniad recently?"

"No. It's unusual for anyone to come nearer than the docks."

Hmmm. "When is your next sermon?"

"Sunday, as always, my child. The Lord's Day. That has not changed in thousands of years."

"May I listen? I won't intrude."

The preacher rose from the bench. "You would be welcome."

Suraya left the chapel at a sedate walk. Fleeing felt too cowardly. She found a bench outside of a shop and sat down to make notes. *Whoa, what a trip that was.*

On the surface, it was no more than a calm sea. But below? Denizens of the deep. Gnarly creatures with fangs and tails that whipped reality into a froth. He was so completely sure of himself and his beliefs. Jail the unbelievers? Bully them behind bars with proselytizing until they caved in? He made it sound so normal. So *right*. So *moral*. There was a reason certain types of beliefs were called seductive.

Maybe she should just write her story, but keep it hidden. *Sorry, Paolo. I couldn't get enough people talking to make a decent exposé.* Probably for the best, anyway.

She moved onward in the search for evidence of her quarry.

***

"I miss music," Cara lamented as she plucked the leaves off the stem of a pepper bush she'd found.

"It is unfortunate," Rodani replied, tugging on his fishing pole, "that you cannot have it here."

She sniffed. "Sallah would tie me in knots if I had."

Rodani yanked on the pole and pulled a wriggling fish out of the stream. "Sallah?"

"She runs the repository, where I borrowed the 'corder and sewing machine."

He mumbled an acknowledgment before quickly gutting the fish, thanking the goddess he wasn't sure he believed in for the bounty.

"We could sing," she ventured into the quiet.

"I am sorry, kia," he told her as he baited the string. "I have forgotten the words to the songs. It has been too long."

"And that's unfortunate, too."

Their supplies of food from the town were diminishing despite the attempts to stretch them out. Cara looked over the small mound morosely. "I'll go searching around for anything that looks like a vegetable, aisu. See what I can find."

"Yes, you should, and so should I. You are thinner than you were, and it concerns me."

"I'm well enough."

"You need to eat more."

"But you need it more than me. You were injured, and I wasn't. And you're half-again my height and three times my weight. I won't let you damage your health for me."

"Nor I you, kia."

"Then we go hunting and gathering. Yes?"

"We should buy some traps," he said. "I should have purchased some in Endolan the last time I was there. But it did not seem necessary at the time."

"Times change," she grumped.

Rodani reached over and pulled her to him, kissing the top of her head. "We should be used to that by now."

She wrapped her arms around his waist and held on. "Comfort?" he asked.

"I'll never turn that down."

He picked her up and held her to his chest, then kissed her lips. "There is more than one type of comfort, yes?"

"Search, first."

He plopped her down on her feet. "As you wish." He tapped her mating clip, a mild romantic tease she'd learned in Barridan.

The forest spread out in dappled sunshine. Cara had already become familiar with some of the landmark trees and bushes around their camp. She wandered farther, searching new ground for anything promising, digging here and there. But nothing plump or appetizing showed up for her efforts.

Along one sandy strip, she saw a row of bushes with needles instead of leaves. The needles grew somewhat large at the base of the bush and became much smaller at the top. Curious, she inspected one. It seemed to be hollow, with a drop of liquid at the tip. *Useful, maybe,* she thought. *Somehow.*

As she walked farther, a familiar bush appeared in front of her, something she'd seen around home. *Yes.* Ripe berries hung in clusters from the stems of the bush. She slipped Rodani's knife into its sheath and pulled open the bag she'd carried. "Lots, lots, enough for both of us, lots," she chanted, pulling the berries off their stems. The bush held more, and she promised herself she'd come back a second time.

Cara walked back to camp with a hand cupped full and a bulging sack. "Look what I found." She knelt down beside Rodani, who leaned over and inspected the mound of burgundy berries that lay within.

"How do they taste?"

"Try one."

He eyed her with a curve to his mouth. "And they are not poisonous?"

"If I can eat them, you should be able to," was her droll reply.

He picked one at random and popped it into his mouth. In a moment, he collapsed on the blanket, eyes shut.

"Aisu!"

He opened his eyes and gazed up at her astonished expression, smiling.

"You!" Cara threw the berries all over him and smacked his chest. He sat up and brushed away any berry still stuck to his shirt.

"Too obvious, kia?" His smile curled into something more than humor.

"Sure, unless you want me to die of fright."

He leaned forward and kissed her, then held a berry to her lips. She accepted it with just enough delay to reprove him without words. He winked in response.

"You're in rare form today, aisu. I could almost say you're human."

"Au, now you offend me."

They shared smiles in harmony and polished off a goodly portion of the berries one by one, taking turns feeding each other. It was a charming type of intimacy they hadn't shared before, and it warmed Cara's romantic heart. When they finished, they got up to wash their berry-stained hands. She returned to the blanket with the towel.

Rodani sat a little behind her as she finished drying her hands. But before she was done, he took the towel from her and laid it in the grass. He wrapped his arm around her waist and pulled her down to the blanket, pupils pulsing slowly.

"Something on your mind, my mate?"

"Yes," he whispered, stroking her hair and cheek. "I believe there is." He moved her closer to the edge of the blanket.

Cara relaxed in cheerful anticipation. His intense and devoted lovemaking rarely missed its mark, and she cherished their joinings with everything her heart and body could give him.

He peeled off her clothing piece by piece, then made quick work of his own. He lay down beside her and ran his hand down her arm, moving it above her head.

Suddenly, she felt metal on her wrist. Something clanked and held. Almost before she could react, the other wrist was caught.

Rodani's pupils pulsed faster. He brought his hand near her breasts.

282

Cara's heartbeat exploded in panic as she realized what he'd done. She wrenched her hands in the cuffs and rolled her body back and forth, interrupting her husband's attempts to caress. "Let me go, Rodani!"

He laid his hand gently on her mouth. "Peace, kia. There is no harm here." He reached out again.

"Don't do this! Dammit, let me go!" She kicked out with her feet and fought the cuffs' tight grips. The blanket wrinkled beneath her and shifted sand onto its edges. "Let me go! I'm serious, Rodani. I can't do this!"

"You can," he said softly. "This is naught but a game that some play in the guild. Calm, kia. Calm." He ran his hand down her furiously rocking body. "Tsss. Be still. Pretend. Enjoy."

"Why won't you listen to me?" She wrenched her hands in the cuffs, scraping her wrists painfully on the metal. As anger turned to fear, her eyes began to fill with tears. "I don't want this! Stop!"

"Enjoy the game, kia. I know how to pleasure you."

Eyes squeezed shut, she let out a scream, loud and long and full of the rage of madness.

Rodani reared back, eyes wide and pupils round as full moons. He uncuffed one hand. Cara was already rolling away as he reached for the other one. When he had freed her, she ran full tilt for the stream and collapsed onto her knees in its cold embrace. Bent double, she stuck her face in the water with her arms crossed over her chest, shaking. The cold slowly bled away her panic, but it morphed into outrage and humiliation. She lifted her head just enough to see the water ripple. She scooped it up and splashed it over her face and hair. Her chest still heaved as adrenaline coursed through her blood and into her clenched muscles. She rocked forward and backward, her arms once again across her body, unable to keep still.

Leaves crunched under a set of footsteps. They came closer. Cara shut her eyes and let the water flow past.

"Kia?" Rodani's voice was soft, carrying no anger she could hear. That was best, as she carried enough for the both of them. "Kia, what happened to you?"

She turned her head away, still rocking. "What do you think happened?" she spat.

Rodani took his time answering. "You misunderstood my attentions, I believe, the game I wished us to play."

She looked toward him while avoiding his face. "How can I know your intentions if you don't say anything?" Temper wormed its way through her words as she fought to unclench her fists. No, she wouldn't hit him. That was a path she didn't want to walk.

"But I told you."

"After you locked me up! After! Not before!" Her heart was racing again, her breaths shallow.

"I meant you no harm."

"It's not what you meant," she said, hitting the water in front of her and splashing his knees. "It's what you did."

"What did I do except try to soothe you and allay your distress so that we could enjoy the tryst?"

"You locked me up before you ever said a *word*, Rodani! You can't *do* that!"

"I meant it to be a surprise."

Cara ran her hands into her hair and gripped the strands. "Obviously, I missed teaching you a few things."

"I am abjectly sorrowed, ki'tana. I did not know you would react so strongly."

She closed her eyes and tried to calm her breathing.

"I hope you will forgive me."

Silence stretched between them, raw and painful, wide and deep. Only the trickling stream made any sound. *Breathe, fem. Just...breathe.*

Cautiously, Rodani ventured into the quiet. "Why did you react the way you did?"

Cara took an audible breath and let it out. "Because I can't stand to be held against my will. I guess I thought you knew that after our first fight in Barridan."

"I never thought to equate the two."

"Whether you did or didn't," she said heatedly, "you should never have tried to play..." she flapped her hands in agitation, looking for a word, "strange games without asking me first. It's offensive and frightening."

Rodani held his hand out in a mute plea. "If I had known your reaction beforehand, I would not have."

"Don't ever."

"What part of it frightened you?"

She took another deep breath, tired of the dialogue but well aware of its necessity. "What I said. Being held so that I can't get away."

"You would not have needed to get away," he said softly. "I meant only pleasure."

"Rodani," she said, gathering her thoughts, "remember in Barridan when you defended me against Kusik in the inquiry about my hands?"

"Yes."

"You said you'd learned that ignorance in humans causes fear, and fear causes rash actions. Do you remember that?"

He sat with his own thoughts for a moment, hands resting in his unclothed lap. "Yes, I see that." He looked over at her. "But I still do not understand the root of your fear. Did you truly think I would hurt you?"

"No. I was hardly thinking at all, let alone thinking of what you were trying to do."

"Then from whence came your fear?"

"I don't know."

Rodani got up and moved closer to her, right to the forward edge of the water, where she could see him easily. "It came from somewhere, kia." He paused. "Who hurt you?" He looked straight at her, straight into her soul. "Who held you down and did not let go?" His words provoked a darkly veiled fear; a fear trapped so deeply in her mind that she couldn't look at it. She shook her fists in the air, unable to hit anything but herself. "I don't know!"

"How can you not know?" he asked, with only sympathy in his tone.

"Because I don't have any memories. Just the fear, by itself."

"Can those types of memories truly be hidden in your mind?"

"I don't know what types you mean, Rodani. But yes, they can."

"I would find that person if I could, kia," he said softly. "And I would make them hurt."

She shook her head roughly. "It wouldn't fix anything. Besides. I don't even know if there *is* a reason behind my panic."

"A fear of that strength? I would."

"Our brains are different, remember?"

Rodani ran his hand through the water that flowed between them. "True." He rose to his feet. "I will bring you a towel."

Cara bent her head toward the water. A breath caught in her throat and shivered inside her chest. *Build a wall, fem. Block whatever's down there. Keep it there.*

When Rodani returned with the towel, she climbed out and wrapped herself in it.

He sat down on the blanket at the far end, and waited with a courteously patient expression on his face. His clothes still lay in a pile to the side.

She eyed his location on the blanket and the distance he left her to fill as she pleased. She chose a spot where they could easily talk, but not touch. She wasn't ready for that. She threw off the towel and slipped the long Selandu shirt on, then waited to see if he would speak. And he did.

"You did desire me at first, yes? I did not mistake that?"

"No, you got that part right." Her mouth turned downward. "You weren't forcing me to join with you."

"That is a reassurance I wish I did not need," he said quietly.

Surprised, she studied his expression. "You're not a rapist, aisu. You have too much honor. And I wouldn't be with you if I thought you were."

"Have you...ever had that reaction before?"

She let out a puff of air. "No one else ever took me quite so far down that path before."

He looked out over the cliff, into an evening sky shot with pink. "You truly have no memories of any dire incidents?"

She shook her head. "None."

"Possibly, that is the better alternative."

"In some ways. But it sure leaves blank spots in understanding myself."

"I believe I would rather have the blanks."

Something seeped through his words. Cara turned to look at him, but Rodani resolutely gazed out over the distant water, mouth closed and face masked.

"Are you sure you don't want to talk about yours?"

He didn't answer.

"Aisu, I know nothing about the biology of the Selandu brain. But I know some about ours. Maybe I can help you understand some of your own pain."

"What pain?" he asked in a deep voice, staring at the horizon in front of him.

She shook her head. "Please don't try to hide it from me, aisu. I can see little bits of it. Hear a tiny portion of it. You're good at hiding it. But I would like, eventually, to earn enough of your trust so that you feel safe telling me."

He turned his head aside, staring over the ground past the blanket they shared.

"When we're hurt in childhood," Cara offered, "from abuse or neglect, it damages our brains. To try to protect us from it, our brains—" she shrugged her shoulders—"shut down our emotions about what happened and hide them in our minds. And because those emotions are so strong, they come out in adulthood in unhealthy ways. Like drinking or eating too much. Or focusing too much on joining—like Serano seems to do.

"That hidden pain very often comes out in terrible anger. Some people throw their pain on others. Other people keep that pain so deeply hidden they become sad and withdrawn all their lives, and some of them throw themselves off a cliff rather than feel that pain."

Rodani turned his head her way, not quite looking at her, but it was obvious he was listening.

"I'm never going to demand that you tell me things you don't want to, aisu. But I do know, in my people, that pain hidden away doesn't heal. It stays in your mind and has ways to make your adult life even harder than the world can make it."

Rodani stirred on the blanket. "Is this what you spoke of in Barridan? When we were coming back from getting the nuts for Shisa?"

She nodded.

"And that child pain is what makes you rain? When I say or do something that reminds you of when you were young?"

"Exactly. And of course, it also comes out in anger sometimes. But I know how hurtful that is, so I try not to do it. Now," she took his hand and shook it gently, "how does your childhood pain come out as an adult? Can you tell me? Will you tell me?"

He went still and gazed down at their hands on his leg, thinking. "The only confidence I will offer at this time," he said carefully, "is that the reason I honor Kimasa to the level I do is because she helped me when I was accepted into Barridan."

Cara leaned forward in excitement. "She helped you heal? Oh, that's wonderful! Someday I'd like to hear how she helped you. What worked for you. Someday... Aisu," she said softly, rubbing the top of his hand with her thumb, "did you run away from home?"

He turned his head sharply with a tight focus on his face. "Why do you say that?"

"Iraimin told me you came to Barridan at an earlier age than most."

He returned his gaze to the horizon and a calm sea. "Yes," he admitted, spitting out the word like it soured in his mouth.

She tapped her fingers on his hand. "Yes, you arrived early? Or yes, you ran away?"

His lips thinned, and his fingers clenched on hers. "Both. And I will say no more now."

"Alright," she said in an attempt to soothe. "I'll honor your decision. I will say two small things, though, and then I'll stop. One," she pointed to his crooked little finger. "I'll bet that this occurred in your childhood."

Rodani glanced down at the defective appendage as if seeing it for the first time. Then he looked away.

"Two," Cara continued, "I would bet that your issues with Ikemi are based on your childhood. And that's all I'll say now. Except—" She raised up and planted a kiss on his cheek. ^I love you.^

They sat, hand in hand, staring out to sea.

After several minutes, Rodani began to rub his legs. "How do you fare, kia?"

"I'm calm enough. As long as you discuss your intentions first, before you try anything so different with me again."

He reached over and removed the clip from her hair, holding it long enough to allow her to take it back if she wished to refuse. When she didn't, he gently set it aside and lay back on the blanket. Behind his head, he fumbled for the cuffs that still hung in place and snapped one over his right wrist. Then he watched her, on high alert to see what she might do. When she didn't move, he held his free hand out to her. "Maybe a turn of the saddle would help you understand my intentions, ki'tana."

Eyes wide, Cara leaned away from him, from what he seemed to be offering. "No. Hell no."

"Why? You need not ask my permission."

"I don't ride you as well as you ride me. We both know that."

"Then use your hands. Or other parts of your body."

She looked away, annoyed at her embarrassment. "I don't know if I can make you crest that way."

"Then, tease me, kia." He smiled. "I can make you beg. Can you do the same to me?"

Holy shit. Now what? "You had plenty of opportunities to learn to, Rodani. What can I do here, like a child at her first lesson?"

"What any child does. Play. Learn the pleasure of having full control." He held the cuff out. "This is my gift to you. And my apology."

She put her palms to her forehead. "Rodani, I've never done this. I don't... My mind is blank. I don't know what to do."

He laughed.

How could he feel humor, she wondered, half-chained to a log?

"Be a scientist, kia. Experiment. Take all the time you need." He shook the empty cuff. "Here."

Anger began to rise again. "Shouldn't you at least find out if I can get you out of the first one, a'tem? If I can't, you lay here while you die of thirst."

The smile dimmed but didn't go away. "A logical thought. Test your hypothesis."

With little care or courtesy, she clambered over his outstretched legs and crawled up his long body. "How?"

"Slide the button you see, then flip the loop off."

She fiddled with it, frustration stealing her crafter's agility. Finally it gave way and fell to the ground.

"And now you put it back."

She sat on her heels and studied the Mona Lisa smile on his face. "You're sure about this?"

"Yes."

"Well, I'm not." She leaned forward and replaced the cuff, then climbed over to his other side and repeated the motion. "There," she said with narrowed eyes. "Now what?"

Rodani twisted his hands, testing the cuffs. "Now, you remove your shirt."

She grabbed the bottom of it, then stopped. "I should frustrate you by refusing."

His smile widened. "Kia, I can guarantee you that my frustrations will be all the higher if I can see your beauty but cannot reach it."

Giving in to his fey mood, she stripped it off and sat beside him, hands in her lap.

"Now, as long as it does no permanent harm, do what you will with my body, my bonded mate."

Cara covered her face with her hands, her mind flooding with dismay, with shame. "I...don't think I could ever say that, aisu. Not even to you."

"Touch me," he whispered.

Cara laid her hands on her husband's abdomen, still flat after months of idle living. She drew her hands down to his muscular thighs and back up to his chest. She tickled him at the edge of his carapace, making him jerk and grin, then stretched her legs over his chest and bent down, kissing him on the forehead. She ran her fingers over his hairless face, over the flatter nose, and down to the pouting lips she loved to feel against her skin, then followed the same track with her own lips, kissing each spot. She scooted down his body as her kisses worked their way south. Neck, chest, stomach, abdomen. She thought she felt a movement from his pelvis as she rested her own sensitive parts on top of it. But its gift remained hidden.

She'd make sure that changed. Now sitting on his thighs, Cara ran her fingers over the orifice in front of her. It clenched, then loosened as her hand moved away. Again, she brushed it, and watched it respond. But his penis remained inside, diminished in size while enfolded below the ring of muscles. This she knew. This, she had seen, had learned of Rodani's eminent control over this part of his body in their many joinings. But how to tease? How to bring him to a gasping, begging peak as he had done to her so many times?

She curled downward and ran her tongue over the ring of muscles. The cuffs rattled and his hips shifted. She didn't need a book to deduce those responses. The thought made her smile. She licked again.

Rodani hissed softly. She heard the warning. The Enclave taught that mouths on private parts was a sin against their goddess, as mouths were reserved for talk and musical instruments only, the skills that separated their species from the animals from which they evolved. It was, Cara mused, one of the main reasons Rodani had gotten so talented with his hands so quickly, the other option being forbidden.

But Rodani's words remained in her head. *No permanent harm*, he had said. She meant to abide by that injunction...to the letter.

Cara ran her tongue around in circles and down the cavity as far as it would go—which wasn't far enough. Rodani was fighting his natural response as part of the tease. "Come on, aisu," she chided him. "I know you'll win this game." She placed the meat of her palm against it and pressed downward firmly, then began to massage it rhythmically. "Relax, te'oto."

His gaze was riveted on her, his pupils slowly pulsing wide, narrow, wide, narrow.

An idea floated into her head. "Aha," she whispered, and climbed off of his body. From the fire, she brought a bowl of warm water and put her hand in it. After a couple of minutes, she rested it back on his orifice and pushed downward. Rodani gasped as his penis erupted from inside, standing firm and ready. She rubbed it, drew her nails down the soft skin, and slipped it into her mouth.

"Kia!" came the rebuke.

She sat up. "No permanent harm, you said. Do what you will, you said." With a direct stare, she widened her eyes. "So, I am. Hush." Returning to her oral ministrations, she waited for another objection but got none. She released her suction and enveloped him with her other hand.

Rodani cried out, and his penis promptly disappeared back inside.

"Really?" she mused.

"That hand is cold, kia."

"Oh." She thought. "Well, now..." Rising up, she took another bowl and filled it with stream water, then brought it back next to the other side of Rodani's hips. Warm water on one side, cold water on the other. A wicked smile spread across her face.

She began to alternate with her hands, bringing his most private organ out into the air, then back into his body. Out, then in. With each slide past the ring of muscles, he took a deeper breath and moved his hips.

"How does it feel?" she asked.

"Pleasant," he managed to say.

She kept it up until the warm water cooled, refilled the bowl, and returned to his side. Rodani lay with his eyes closed, and mouth pursed shut, saluting the universe with his nether regions. She warmed her right hand again and let it roam around other places on his body, paying special attention to the area between his thighs. His penis pulsed as she ran her fingers over his urethra, which sat in a location very much like hers. She pressed firmly, then lightly up over his pelvic bone and down between his thighs, up and down, up and down. Then she warmed her hand in the bowl again, and returned to his penis. He exhaled sharply as the warmth pressed against it, and his hips began to move with the rhythm of her hand. Then, without warning, she switched hands.

"Au!"

It disappeared back inside. She glanced at his face. His pupils pulsed, and it looked like he was clenching his teeth. He was breathing faster, but said no word, only stared into her eyes.

Cold hand, warm hand, cold hand, warm hand. Every switch brought an intimate grunt from his throat, and the shaking in his body began to increase.

Cold hand, warm hand, cold hand, warm. When she looked down again, she noticed the orifice was swelling and taking on a reddish hue. She stopped. "Aisu."

Sense came into his eyes. "What?"

"Look down." She pointed with a finger. "Is this a danger?"

He took a ragged breath and studied the area. "I think not," he said, hesitant. "It does not feel the same as the hadaberi."

"Baldar is a long way away."

He closed his eyes and let his head drop back onto the blanket. "Do not stop, kia. Or better, finish me before I explode."

She dipped her hands and explored the other regions again, then returned to the main event. Each pass through the muscular opening brought a cry of pleasure from him and an incremental increase in hip thrusts.

"Au, kia. Please."

That was a beg. She worked hard not to laugh, but it bubbled inside. Cold hand, warm hand. Cold hand, warm hand. The orifice swelled more and turned a deeper red. Rodani's cries got louder.

"Temi's knives, Cara! Please." His eyes were clenched tightly now, signifying how near he was to the crest he begged for.

A little longer. A little more ache, a little more itch. A little more time before she gave up the control she found herself enjoying.

Cold hand, warm hand, cold hand, then she let the warmth linger. She squeezed and tugged at his softest skin, and rolled it between her fingers, moving toward the tip. The cuffs rattled and clanked. Rodani growled and then shouted louder than she'd ever heard. His penis erupted within her hand, coating them both with more than the usual amount of fluid as his cries continued. Then she felt a wetness beneath her. Confused, she raised up.

Rodani's bladder had let go as well, soaking the blanket he laid on.

Cara ran the back of one hand over her mouth in thought, then gently pried her other one off his flaccid organ. He grunted again then lay silent, lax on the blanket, arms still above his head and wrists encircled in his cuffs.

She waited patiently for him to open his eyes. It didn't take long. When he looked at her, she leaned forward over his abdomen. "Do you think I learned what you wanted me to learn, aisu?"

"I believe so," he admitted, slowly. Flexing his thighs underneath her, he added "I believe I learned something new, as well." He tried to raise a knee. "Let me up, please. It is cold down there."

"No. We're not done." She shifted her hips. "Or, more accurately, I'm not done."

His eyes went wide, and the stare was back.

Gazing right back at him, Cara began to caress her own body. She massaged her breasts and ran her hand down toward the hairline, running her fingers through the short, curly hair.

"Kia."

It could be a warning or a plea, and she was pleased to ignore it either way. She pushed a finger between her labia and began to rub.

Reaching further, she brought some lubrication up and began to circle the sweet spot.

"Kia, please." Rodani's voice dropped with the depth of his plea.

Her other hand circled a nipple, and she arched her back. A welcome warmth began inside her. She rubbed harder at the top of her cleft. As her hips began to sway, Rodani moved in tandem beneath her.

"Please, kia. Let me."

"No," she whispered, as an itch began to grow. "You only get to watch."

Whether he watched or not, she couldn't tell, as her own eyes were clenched tight. The itch intensified again and again as she bucked her hips. Then it burst forth in an all-enveloping rush that left her own cries to echo Rodani's earlier outbursts. The cuffs rattled and banged with his agitation at being denied the sharing he wanted.

Sated, Cara climbed off her husband and let him loose from the cuffs. He laid there a moment with a pout on his handsome face. Then he rolled and sat up, leaning forward to study his wet spot in silence.

"I hoped for the one release. This one was a surprise."

"Never knew that could happen, eh?"

"I did not." He leaned into her face. "Nor did I know you would make me beg twice."

"I'm pretty sure it was more than twice, te'oto. But I lost count."

"I am going to need a bucketful of varigestra."

She laughed at his regretful comment. "Was it the first beg, or the last one that caused it?"

"Both. But the last one was far more powerful than I thought it would be."

***

Suraya rose from the dockside bench as Davad's boat pulled into a slip. She walked out to meet him, and climbed aboard.

"Did you wait long?" he asked.

"Not too long. Thanks for picking me up."

"You paid me," he joked. "Besides, I wouldn't want anyone to be left here."

"I thought you didn't know much about the place? That's the impression I got."

294

"Settle in. I don't want to linger. You can tell me about it on the way home."

"Aye aye, Captain."

"Yeah, yeah."

Davad backed the boat out and turned for home. "Well?" he prompted.

"I think she was there."

Surprise filled his face. "Really? What makes you say so?"

"There were two women who remembered a Glaniad woman shopping in town, dressed like a whore—I mean, like a normal human, instead of like this." She brushed her hand across the ankle-length skirt.

He glanced at her dowdy clothing. "I wasn't going to say anything, but...that's not what you came down here in."

"Tell me about it," she grumped.

"And Cara?"

"That's all I heard, really. Except the first woman remembered her hair. But who else is missing? Who else would have reason to come down here and not know how to follow their stupid rules?

"I wonder," she continued, "what Cara thought of the place. I can't imagine she'd like it." She held her hand out against the wind, feeling the pressure buffet her palm. "I wonder where she is."

Suraya watched Davad as his strong arms held the wheel, his sea legs firm and steady on the deck. His face held an expression that she couldn't quite interpret. "You okay?" she asked him.

He glanced back at her. "Yeah, a little better. Now that there's a chance."

"I talked to that preacher. He's as crazy as a randy goat. —No," she said. "That's not the right word. He's...devious, twisted, and absolutely convinced of his righteousness. That's what he is." She looked out at the cliffs passing by. "I thought my brothers were bad. He's the same type, but with political and social power. Godawful scary."

"I hope Cara decides to stay away from there."

"This morning, I went to hear him preach. That first woman who remembered Cara? She mentioned to the preacher that there had been another northerner, and asked if she'd come to the chapel. He said no, and got *really* mad."

"Why?"

"That woman, the one who sold me these clothes, said everybody had to pray at that chapel at least once a day, and visitors had to, too, especially when they first arrived."

"And she didn't."

"Doesn't sound like it."

Davad shook his head. "Typical. She needs to know not to go back."

"Where do you think they'd be, Dav? Where would they hide?"

"I think you've already asked me that. I have no clue. They could be anywhere."

"Isn't there anything we can do?"

"I'm not traipsing all over hell-and-gone looking for someone who doesn't want to be found. I've got a pregnant fiancée who's impatient to get married, and a job to do."

"Yeah, I have one of those job-type things, too. But I hate just leaving them."

"So do I."

Suraya watched the cliffs pass by, getting shorter and sandier the closer they got to home. "Can you at least sail the coast on your days off?"

"Looking for what? A message carved in a cliff saying, 'Here we are'?"

"C'mon. Who knows what you might see?"

"While Merelin threatens mayhem at home."

Rage flooded through Suraya. "She needs to know she's not your only priority!"

Davad gazed out to sea, his mouth a flat line of annoyance. "You can lead a goat to water..."

TWENTY-TWO

Mack downed another bottle and tossed the empty in a recycle bin. It's the only thing he bothered with, and only because reusing the glass containers kept the cost of liquor down. They had the rest of the planet to trash at will, didn't they?

One more weekend gone, and Cara was still AWOL. It did more than anger him. He'd convinced himself she was shacking up with somebody. But he couldn't figure out who. *It wasn't that pudgy drummer. It wasn't that idiot alien-lover now permanently gone over the border somewhere.*

Or was it? She could have gone there. Why didn't he think of that before? Sure, Andy with the slant-eyes claimed he had nothing to do with her anymore, but who'd believe that? She'd slink into anybody's bed.

Except his. Outrage burned through his belly at the injustice. She belonged to him!

Mack stormed out of his house and crossed the river bridge, barging into the CSC on a mission for the truth. Some girl, drab, dull, and completely uninteresting, sat at a desk just inside. Her eyes widened at his presence. Oh, how he loved that look of fear.

"Where's Cara?" he barked.

"She's not here," the girl replied timidly.

"I don't trust you. I'm gonna search the place." As he began to walk past her, she stood up.

"You can't do that!"

An evil grin spread across his face. "Stop me."

She didn't. *Couldn't,* he bragged to himself. Nobody could, if he didn't want them to. Largely forgotten were his many short stints in jail. Those were aberrations to be ignored.

He searched every room, checking closets and tossing papers aside in mute frustration. He turned to the meek and powerless waif behind him. "Did she go north? With the others?"

"No. Andy wouldn't've let her."

"How do you know? Why not?"

The girl shrugged. "She already failed once. She didn't deserve another chance."

Mack stormed out in the same boiling temper he'd stormed in with and headed back to town. Next was one of her sisters. He banged on another door, and was gratified to see a second fearful face behind it.

"I'm looking for Cara," he said before Emmie even spoke a word.

"She doesn't live here, Mack."

"I don't care. I'm gonna find her." He pushed past, scattering her snot-nosed yard apes out of the living room.

"You can't do this!"

He ignored one more worthless protest and went room to room. Closets, under beds, even behind curtains, if they were full enough. But he found no hints of her anywhere and walked out leaving another shocked and powerless female behind.

Davad's was next. As he wasn't there, Mack pulled the same stunt on Merelin, who cowered with her arms across her belly. *As if that would protect anything*, he snorted in disdain.

After that came the doc's house. A beauty it was. He deserved a place like that. Another wide-eyed female opened the door. He recognized his brother's latest slut, but didn't remember her name. Didn't matter, anyway. He forced his way past her with the same words, the same self-important attitude he'd used before.

This one didn't follow him, she ran outside. He heard the door banging. Didn't matter, either. Let her run. He went through each room on both floors, and even checked the attic. Cluttered and empty of people, he slammed that door shut, too. Back outside, he headed for the repository.

Behind him, unnoticed, sprinted Liam with Teria trailing and in tears. They watched Mack stalk down the road. "I'm going to the sheriff's office," he told his daughter. "Hopefully, he won't come back."

Liam took a slightly different path. He wasn't a coward, but neither was he stupid.

He related his story to Chief Berg, and as he did, his son-in-law Dag walked in.

298

"You, too?" Emmie's husband asked him.

"What do you mean?"

"Mack searched my house, scaring Emmie *and* the kids. They ran out into the backyard, yelling."

Both men turned to the chief, who shook his head and pushed up from his desk. "Where was he headed?"

"Who knows?" Liam replied. "He was aiming for the center of town when I saw him."

"Alright. I'll see what we can do." Berg waved them out.

"Have you heard from Cara at all?" Dag asked.

Liam turned his head aside, trying to escape what wouldn't go away. "No."

Berg and his deputy finally ran Mack down at the bar, just in time to rescue Dottie from being trampled at the base of the stairs. Mack had already blown through the repository, the town's tiny library, and Jonie's clothing shop. There weren't many logical places left to search, but Mack had never been partial to logic—unless it was his own twisted kind.

"Come on, Mack," Berg said, pulling him away from the bartender. "Leave Dottie alone."

Mack swept the chief's hand off his shoulder. "I have to see if she's up there."

"I already told you she's not," Dottie countered. "I threw her out a month ago."

"Mack, no one has seen Cara since before the hurricane," Berg said in the smooth voice of reason he used for the drunk and disorderly. "She's not in town anymore. You need to forget this and go about your normal business."

Mack glanced up at the second floor and back down to Dottie.

"My son's up there. And you don't need to be bothering him."

"Maybe she's up there with him."

"He has better taste than that."

"Mack." Berg put his hand on the back of Mack's neck in an attempt to get him moving. "Come on."

***

The office was empty for once. Suraya laid her notes on the desk and sat down. She didn't want to write the exposé from Paolo's disinterested, too-even-handed point of view. She wanted to tell it from her own senses. The atmosphere. The not-so-veiled threats. The rules and punishments. The shunning. Danger lurked in Lordstown. Not below the surface, not an undercurrent, but a bubbling surface froth that left a nasty taste in her mouth and turned her nerves up to high.

The door opened, and Bethamy came in. "You're back. What'd you learn?"

"That I never want to live there."

"That bad, huh?" She slipped into her chair.

"Worse."

"What happened?"

"Let me get the story written, then you can read it first."

Bethamy grinned. "You're no fun."

"Neither was the trip."

By the time Suraya had a rough draft in front of her, the workday was almost over. She handed it to Bethamy to read. "I'll have to clean it up tomorrow," Suraya added. She organized her notes into facts, thoughts, and opinions and stuffed them in a folder for her drawer.

Bethamy passed the draft back to her. "It's not what Paolo wanted, is it?"

"No, but it's factual."

She scratched her head. "There's a lot more in there than just facts, fem."

"I know. But I don't see any better interpretation than the one I came up with."

"Then take out your interpretation."

"There's not much story left if I do."

***

Davad stood by as the dockhands finished emptying the holds in his boat. It was a good day, a good catch. He thought of Merelin and the kiss she'd sent him off with that morning. Maybe it would be a good night, too. He smiled to himself.

The dockmaster weighed his catch and passed over a handful of coins. He slipped them in his pocket, where they rested heavy and comfortable. Yes, a good night. Merelin would be happy with some extra, since she was beginning the nesting stage of pregnancy.

He glanced over his boat, reassuring himself that all was well, and headed up the stairs to the top of the dune. He could see his cabin from there. A welcome light shown in the window.

Before he got to the door, Merelin opened it, wearing a look that wasn't comforting. He hopped on the porch. "What?"

"Mack, is what. He barged in today without a please or thank you, looking for your sister." She backed inside the room so Davad could enter.

"Did he hurt you?"

"No. Scared me half dead. The man's a menace."

"Did he take anything?"

"No."

Davad looked around his home. "I wonder where else he searched?"

"I don't know. But I wish he'd disappear, too."

He turned to her, not quite believing what he'd heard. "Too?" he repeated, eyebrows raised, thinking of his sister.

Merelin had the grace to look chagrined. "I didn't mean it that way. Sorry."

He decided to let the insult go and transferred his pay from pocket to their cash box before sitting next to the fireplace. "Why would he search now? It's been a month."

"Who knows what goes on in his head."

Davad held his hands out. "Come sit with me."

She slid into his lap, where he patted her baby bulge affectionately.

***

Time moved on, and supplies became scarce again. Cara and Rodani gazed out of the forest's boundary, right about where they were the first time. She wasn't looking forward to the visit, but they were both tired of fish, and there was little travel food left. Rodani hoped she'd run across some hunting traps like those he'd used at the cave near Barridan. Those might keep them from needing a third trip for a while.

"Are you sure you're well enough to stay here? You had another bad day yesterday."

"I am."

Cara shook out the long skirt to get leaves and other things to drop off its bottom edge. "You know your own mind," she said, not quite sure of her own. "So, onward into the absurd, my protective mate."

Rodani patted a goodbye on her backside. "I will keep watch."

She went down the main street first, checking for any likely shops with hunting supplies. As she peered into windows and stepped across a few doorways, a certain nosy shopkeeper ran the opposite way and turned the corner toward the chapel.

She stared inside one shop. *There we go.* Inside, she found a wall of bows and three bins of arrows. In a case to her left was an array of knives. She walked past them, looking closely. But undoubtedly, her husband's guild knives were better than any she could find here.

"Can I help you find something, sister?"

The tall shopkeeper's bland expression reassured her that no trouble was near, despite her discomfort.

"I'm looking for some traps to use for small animals, please."

His expression turned to the lowered eyelids of curiosity mixed with just a bit of suspicion. "You're new here?"

Good gods, what do I do? What do they consider courteous?

She fell back on her Selandu habits and bowed her head slightly. "I travel a bit, with my husband. I hope it's not a problem."

"Where is he?"

Ooops. "He stayed with the boat. I offered to run the errand. To help him," she added, just in case. "Save him the effort."

"Doing the Lord's work."

"Of course. Do you have any traps?"

"Over here." He led her to a corner. "How many do you need?"

"Not many. Five or ten, I believe he said."

"Do you know how to use them?"

"I'm sure he does, but could you show me?"

The shopkeeper was in the middle of his explanation when they were interrupted by a commotion at the door.

"There she is," said a dimly recognized voice.

Cara turned to see the woman from her first visit, and a much older man next to her. The woman's face was stiff, and her eyes were hard.

"Preacher," said the shopkeeper, laying down the trap he'd been holding. "What may I do for the Lord today?"

The old man came closer. His eyes burned with anger, his breathing heavy. "You may take this disobedient woman to the stocks for me, Matthew."

The shopkeeper glanced from the preacher to Cara, whose confusion was turning to alarm. "Of course, Preacher." He wrapped his arms around Cara's chest and lifted her off her feet.

"What are you doing?" she said, voice rising. "Put me down."

She was ignored, and promptly carried out of the shop and back down the street. Cara squirmed in his arms and kicked her feet, which accomplished nothing but a tightening of her captor's grip.

"Let me go! I've done nothing wrong!"

"Oh, you're about to learn differently," said the woman, who was following behind. Heads poked out of doorways as they passed by before rounding the corner to the left.

Cara raked her nails across the man's hands, but that was also ignored. Knowing she was now in sight of Rodani—if he were looking, she took a deep breath and bellowed. "Put me down! Let me go!" She struggled again, with no more gain than before. There was nothing her husband could do from his hiding place, but he would be aware, and thinking.

She tried not to panic, but emotion ran rampant over her earlier calm. She pushed at his arms and held some thought of gouging at his eyes and running away. The old man wouldn't be able to catch her. But who else was watching? Who else would see her run into the forest and straight for her husband?

As they came to the last corner, the shopkeeper stopped walking. The preacher continued to a very large wooden box, and opened it. Its lid fell off the top and onto the ground behind. He pulled out a long, narrow contraption that meant nothing logical to Cara, but stoked her fear further.

It was some kind of bar that the preacher sat on the ground, horizontal, with two holes in it. He fiddled with a lock on one end and lifted half the bar up in the air. A hinge held the other side together.

Cara began to scream, fighting any way she could as the shopkeeper bent down. The preacher grabbed for her feet, earning a kick to one hand. He drew back, shocked and offended as she twisted around.

"For that, your punishment is extended."

"Punishment for what?" she shouted. The shopkeeper laid her on the ground and pulled her shins over the wooden bar before she had a chance to jump up. Another man held her feet as she continued to shout and scream. Each man's grip was painfully tight as they held her ankles inside the bottom halves of the holes. With a grim finality, the preacher brought the top half down and locked the two halves together.

"No!" She fought the heavy trap, but her ankles were caught fast, and her feet large enough to not pull free. She lay there, panting heavily, fear roiling in her head and gut. What kind of punishment was this? What the hell was wrong with these people?

A small crowd was beginning to gather. Mostly men, but the original woman stood off to the side, grinning like a jealous child watching a sibling be chastised.

The preacher began to evangelize. Cara turned her head away and shut her eyes, but could do nothing for her ears that soon filled with religious ranting. *Lord, woman, Lord, obedience, Lord grant, Lord teach, humility, acceptance, submission, Lord bless.* The words rolled on and on for what seemed like hours. Finally, he stopped preaching and spoke in a more normal tone.

"I will come by in the morning and release you. Until then, may the Lord heal your soul." He turned and left with the shopkeeper who carried her, and most of the crowd.

The woman who snitched stayed long enough to taunt her. "I told you to pray at the chapel before you did anything else. Just like any infidel, you ignored the Lord's rules. Now you pay."

Cara lay on her back, trying to comprehend the whats and the whys of her predicament. Hopefully, Rodani wouldn't do anything too rash, or let himself be captured. Hopefully, she'd be allowed to leave unhindered in the morning. Hopefully, she wouldn't pee her pants—skirt, in the meantime.

The last of the onlookers got bored and departed after a while, leaving her trapped in an uncomfortable solitude. Why didn't she go to the chapel? For the same reason she didn't let Kimasa lead her around, probably. The same lax attitude caused her to ignore many a rule that made no sense to her. But that preacher was no patient Rodani. He was much closer to Kusik. If she'd known enough last time to make that connection, today would have had a very different outcome.

By the time the sun was setting hours later, she'd peed twice and thirst was an ever-present irritation. Her back was sore from lying in one position too long, and her hips ached. She managed to sit up for a short time, but the angle of her legs caused her ankles to pinch badly against the wooden holes. She gave up and lay back down.

You'll survive. You'll survive. You spent three days with Kusik in a cave, and a couple of decades with your autocratic mother. You can do this. Maybe you'll even learn something from it, she chided herself.

She snoozed a little while after the sun set, and woke to the sight of stars overhead. At least it wasn't raining. She tried to reminisce about happy memories with Rodani. There were lots of those, but her increasing discomfort began to crowd them out.

How late was it? There was no way to tell. She'd stupidly left her 'com with Rodani in the forest. Gods, what a mistake that was. How many mistakes could one person survive in one lifetime? Oh, for a time machine. Or a crystal ball. Or a magic wand to cast spells. She shook her head against her worthless fantasies, and tried again to adjust her position to rid herself of the aches and pains.

"Tssss. Kia."

Cara gasped and stared into the dark, seeing nothing. Then a tiny light shone at her feet, held by a six-fingered hand. "Oh, gods, aisu, can you get me out?"

"Quiet."

She bit her lips and waited as impatience crawled up and down her nerves. Someone was going to check on her, and he'd be caught. Someone was going to see, and cause a ruckus. Would they bring pitchforks and torches? She'd read too many stories as a young teen. Freeing her took more time than she hoped, but eventually Rodani lifted the top half of the bar off her ankles, and helped her up.

"Run to the forest. Now."

She hobbled around first, trying to loosen up every part of her body that had kinked with inactivity. "Soon as I can."

Rodani closed the bar again. "Kia," he hissed.

"Okay, okay," she whispered. "You, too." She headed toward the tree line as fast as she could, turning only once to see if he was following her. But he was still crouched in front of the bar.

As she trotted between the first tree trunks, she heard his running footsteps. She stopped. Rodani took her arm. "This way."

He led her off to the right—west, and a short distance farther south. "Here."

"Wait." She ripped off the urine-soaked skirt and tossed it on the ground.

"No," Rodani told her, picking it up. "They may find it." He lifted her onto a sturdy branch, climbing up after her. Branch by branch, he helped her up until they were about thirty feet above the forest floor.

Cara leaned against the trunk to rest and relax, but it was easier said than done. Rodani perched farther out on the limb, eyes toward the town.

"Thank you, aisu. I don't know what would've happened in the morning."

"Why did they detain you that way?"

"As a punishment for breaking one of their stupid rules."

"Were you aware of the rule?"

That one hurt. "They told me. I didn't think it was important. I just didn't think," she said, faltering in shame.

Soon, he spoke again. "Come here. Cautiously," he added.

She scooted forward in her shorts, wondering how badly the residual smell bothered her husband's sensitive nose. Not that they could do much about it now. Rodani pointed towards the town's corner where she had lain. "What do you see?"

She shifted on her perch, trying to peer through the leaves ahead. "Some kind of light?"

"Watch."

The light grew gradually, taking on an orange hue and flickering against the dark of night.

"Is that what I think it is?"

He waited silently.

"You set that thing on fire?" Her voice rose, incredulous.

"Yes." He turned to look at her. "That is not all what I did, kia." His voice went deep, into a tone she recognized.

"What did you do?"

He paused for a moment, maybe to choose his words carefully. "I found the preacher."

***

With aching arms, Lorraine Beecher stirred the pot of stew that hung over the meager fire she'd kindled. Her family's allotment of wood, designated by Preacher, often left her with not much more than kindling before another load was allowed. It was, she reminded herself, entirely proper that he portioned the use of the land and food. After all, as their Lord's right hand (and ear), Preacher knew the best way to keep his flock on the righteous side of the Lord's law. But, if she admitted it to herself, it hurt to feed her family cold meals when they ran out.

She stretched the kinks out of her shoulders and gazed into the night. An unusual glow met her eyes. *Someone was using too much wood*, she thought. *He should be punished!* And it was her duty, as it was everyone's, to see that that happened.

Lorraine strode out the door on the Lord's errand, but came to a halt around the corner. The device that Preacher had named Isaac's Binder was on fire! She screamed for help, hardly noticing that the body of the disobedient harlot was gone.

"Preacher!" She raced west, toward his home at the back of the church.

The preacher's lowly assistant, Harvey, barreled out of his cabin door next to the church. "What's wrong, Lorraine?" he asked as a crowd began to gather.

"Where's Preacher? Isaac's Binder's on fire," she said, gasping.

"Well," Harvey looked around for a handy solution, and came up empty. "We can't disturb him, you know. We need buckets—"

Beyond them another voice erupted. "He's dead! Preacher's dead!" The voice shook in panic. "Murdered!"

Harvey fell to his knees at the word. "Help us, Lord!" he cried to the sky. He stared in shock as the town carpenter ran up, blood covering his hands. "We must pray for his soul. And pray for deliverance from this tragedy!"

***

Cara took a deep breath and let it out slowly. "You found the preacher. And?"

He looked her in the eyes. His own reflected the moonlight. "I tricked him into coming out of his house, slit his throat, and dumped his body back inside. It may be some time before he is found."

Immediate shock flooded her. *Don't hyperventilate. Don't you dare pass out.* She shouldn't even be surprised. How many times had he killed to keep her safe? But this danger wasn't fatal. *No, idiot, keep your mouth shut. Now was not the time to debate ethics.*

"You're sure it was him?" she ventured into his quiet.

"I am certain."

She fell silent and watched the flames reach higher.

"Kia," he said softly, turning his head to see her. "Speak to me, please."

What should she say? He'd rescued her. Again. Got her out of another corner she'd walked into with her inability to follow rules and proprieties. He didn't deserve to be castigated for his pervasive sense of danger and duty.

"Kia?"

Behind him, the flames shot higher.

She shook her head. "I'm not angry, if that's what you need to hear. What you did might not have been necessary, though. I don't think he deserved to die. It wasn't your decision to make. Removed from power, yes. And I don't know what kind of trouble this'll cause."

"Our camp is hours away."

"Yeah," she said with an exhale. "But it may not be far enough. It depends on how badly they take this."

Both looked out as shouting erupted from the direction of the fire.

"The show begins," said her husband, the assassin.

Another crowd was gathering in ones and twos. Someone must have thrown water on it, as the flames billowed, and smoke rose above. The shouting and running continued for a bit; then the townsfolk settled down to watch it turn to ash. It took a while.

"Aisu, they're going to come looking for me and probably for the human man I told them I was with."

Rodani turned with a quizzical look on his face.

"I thought it would be more acceptable to be a strange woman with a husband than a strange woman alone. I told them he was on a boat at the docks."

"Then that is where they will search."

"At first, yes. Then, when they find out I lied, they'll branch out. We need to be far away when that happens."

"And we return to fish and dried foods."

"I'm sorry."

TWENTY-THREE

Lars Gunnarsson sat behind his custom-made desk, which was currently awash in sheets of paper. The desk was carved with images of Thor, Loki, Yggdrasil, and plenty of thunderbolts.

He'd requisitioned it when he'd been elected mayor of Glaniad two years ago. The desk had turned out beautifully. The job of being mayor, however, turned out to be a great disappointment.

His imagination of the office had been of presiding at festivals, sitting at his desk signing important documents, with an assistant or two (young, female, and beautiful of course) always on hand to bring him coffee and chocolate, and laugh at his jokes.

The reality was far more depressing. He picked up a paper at random. "Need more sheriffs," it said. Well fine, but how do you hire more sheriffs if the only people who apply are wildly unfit? A few who could barely read ("need more teachers"), a couple who were far too frivolous to follow necessary rules and precautions, and more than a couple who had delusions of being heroes, racing to rescue damsels and beating up miscreants. And let's not even mention the occasional sociopath ("need more psychologists").

He picked up another paper ("need more papermakers"). And another. "Caffee plants imperiled by marauding insects." What in Valhalla was he supposed to do about ridding their caffee plants of swarms of insects? Did they even swarm? Or were they crawlers or burrowers? Was he supposed to walk the fields and pick them off one by one? And what would happen to his job as mayor if they lost all their caffee plants? He'd lose that, too for certain.

Bollocks was his considered opinion of it all.

As he ruminated, his only admin, middle-aged Martha who didn't laugh at his jokes, came running in.

"Mayor Lars, Mayor Lars, the mayor of Lordstown, Mr. Schultz, is on the radio, and he's white-hot angry." Martha wrung her hands, waiting for his response.

"What's he angry about?"

"I'm not quite sure. He's shouting about a woman, and a murder, and the destruction of property. I don't know what to make of it."

"What's his name again?"

"Mr. Schultz."

"Do I know him?" he mused. "Well, get your notebook and come along."

"I'm running out of paper, Mayor Lars."

He sighed and sat down in front of the contraption that he'd never fully learned. Martha reached across him and twiddled a dial or two, and flipped a couple of switches. She waved a go-ahead hand signal on front of his face.

"Mayor Schultz?" he said, leaning forward.

An agitated voice boomed out at full volume; Lars recoiled. "Mayor, we here are devastated, and it is all the fault of one of your people. My town is facing a tragedy of epic proportions, and we demand your cooperation."

Lars motioned for Martha to turn down the volume. "For what, Mayor Schultz?"

"A northern woman murdered our beloved preacher and set fire to an important object. You must find her and return her to us immediately."

"What's her name?"

"We don't know."

He glanced up at Martha, who was wearing the same confused look on her face as he was.

"How am I supposed to find and return a woman to you when neither of us knows who she is?"

"It's your job to find out, Mayor," Schultz said reprovingly.

"And how do you propose I do that? Do I look up every birth and death record for the last 70 years, see who's still alive, find out where they li—"

"I don't care how you do it. Just get it done!"

"I'll get right on it," he dissembled. "Any idea of what she looks like?"

"I was told pale skin, dark blue eyes, and really long hair. And she's in league with Satan, too."

Lars burst out laughing. "Really."

"Don't you blaspheme, Mayor!" The voice came through agitated and enraged. "There's no way she could have freed herself without help, and there was no one else around. And she must have had Satan's help to murder our exalted preacher! Our faith is rock solid and our knowledge infallible."

"Well, since you're the one with the hotline to the supernatural, maybe you should be asking them for help, not me."

"How dare you? We have a disaster, and you sit there and mock me. Shame on you, Mayor. You will pay for your sins. Find her."

The line went dead.

Lars leaned back, thinking of ways he could get out from under this one. He definitely didn't want to get involved in a rumpus with a bunch of nut jobs. He had more important things on his mind, things that could affect him. "Who do you know who's missing?"

"Well," Martha thought, "two people right off the tips of my fingers. Jim Miller, an elderly recluse who lives west of town, and Cara MacLennan."

"Have I heard of her?"

"She's one of Dr. Liz's daughters, Mayor Lars. The one who went north to live with the aliens for a while."

"She's missing?"

"Yes, for four or five weeks now."

"Then somebody has to find her," he said, "and see if she's the guilty one or not."

"There's an awful lot of land between here and Lordstown. If it is her, she could be anywhere from here to the other side of Lordstown, too. Or living on a boat."

"Put the word out, Martha. Ask for volunteers. Have them meet here at 9 a.m. two days from now."

***

Suraya was bent over her desk—again, scratching out another article on the caffee plant infestation, when a messenger girl ran into the office. She handed the journalist a hastily written note.

"From the mayor," she exclaimed.

"Thanks." Suraya opened it, and her eyes went wide as she read.

Lordstown. Blue-eyed northern woman with long hair. Preacher murdered. Arson. Need immediate distribution of article to community board and businesses to identify and track down this woman.

"Holy Vishnu."

"You gonna share?" Bethamy asked.

Suraya handed it over without comment.

Bethamy scanned the message and laid it on her desk. "Sounds like your obsession may be in deep trouble."

"I told you she's not my obsession, the Selandu are."

"Do you know where she is?"

"Nope." Suraya drew out a fresh sheet of paper and began to write.

"Guess she's not dead anymore."

But what about that Selandu man? Is he still with her? Gods, she wanted to find out. Wanted Cara to tell her what happened, how it happened, how she felt, what she thought of their future. Wanted to write the story of a lifetime. Wanted her curiosity satisfied. That was one thing she knew she and Cara shared.

By early evening, Suraya's article had spread over the watering holes and popular shops, the repository and library, the community board, medical offices, and the CSC.

***

Owen and Aaron, sailors, brothers joined at the hip, charged up the docks and headed straight for The Wet Rag.

"I still can't believe Lordstown doesn't have even one lousy bar," Owen said.

"Now that that preacher's dead, maybe they'll open one."

"Not likely. Just because he's dead doesn't mean his influence is gone."

"I'd shake the hand of the man who killed him," Aaron said, grinning.

"Woman, not man. Didn't you hear?"

"Yeah, I heard," Aaron replied. "But I'm not stupid enough to believe everything I hear. How many women you know would slit a man's throat open?"

They walked up to the bar. Owen pulled on the door. It was locked. "What the hell?"

A passerby stopped beside them. "Bar's closed 'til 5 p.m. now."

Two servings of *Why* came up.

"Because Chucko left and opened his own place. It's tiny, but it's got better hours."

"Where?"

The man gestured. "Two streets over, one street back."

Aaron clapped him on the shoulder. "Thanks, friend." He got a nod in return.

It took only a look between the brothers to reach an agreement. They followed the directions given.

Chucko's Haunt, the sign said. And the door was unlocked.

Chucko himself was behind the bar, washing and wiping. Four other early drinkers sat at tables. The brothers chose barstools.

"We're berthed and begging, friend Chucko," Owen said. "Two dark ales, please."

Chucko drew the drinks and passed them over, collecting the coins afterwards. "Did you hear the word from the mayor's office?"

"No," Aaron said. "We just got in."

"Supposedly, some northern woman killed a preacher down in Lordstown, and destroyed some famous device of theirs. The mayor down there is demanding we find her and send her back there for trial."

The brothers shared a glance and a smile. "We just sailed in from there, Chucko," Owen said. "That's not quite how it went down."

"What do you mean?"

"The story we heard on the docks is that a northern woman came to town to shop, saying her husband was staying in a boat on the docks, around where we were. She didn't follow one of the town rules, and got taken by the preacher for punishment. They locked her ankles in stocks, left her there for about twelve hours. It's pretty uncomfortable from what I've heard, but not deadly." Owen took a swig of his ale. "So, somehow, she gets loose. I don't know how. Then she kills the preacher who locked her up, and sets fire to the stocks that held her down. As far as I'm concerned, I'm glad she killed him. He was a lunatic."

"Flipped out of his mind," Aaron added. "Told everyone how to live their lives, what to wear, what not to eat, told them what priorities they should have, demanded absolute obedience to him and his god, the whole works. Had every person there under his thumb. Good riddance."

Chucko considered the new data. "Mayor Lars wants a meeting tomorrow morning of people who will go search for her."

"Don't look at me," Aaron said. "I don't even know who she is."

"People are already starting to guess." Chucko drew an ale and handed it off to another patron.

"Who?" Mack said behind them.

***

It didn't take long for Cara's name to be as equally spread as the news of the murder. As the most well-known missing person in town, and as she matched the meager description, she was the first to come to mind. Debates raged on whether she could have committed the murder or not, with most rejecting her guilt. The most common alternative was that a Lordstown citizen took advantage of the chaos to kill the preacher himself.

And no one thought Cara would get a fair trial in Lordstown.

On the second morning, Suraya went to the mayor's meeting. Only ten or twelve others were there. One sheriff's deputy, A couple of ne'er-do-wells, a tradesman or two, and a few others. Who she didn't see standing in the shadows was Clark, Mack's oldest and best friend. She stood on one side while search instructions were given. The only unusual one was that the searchers were to coordinate dockside with those from Lordstown. Visitors were now barred from the town.

***

Davad sped southward, pushing his boat to its limits.

"Why did I have to spend so many days out in deep water?" he berated himself, pounding on the wheel. "Why didn't anybody tell me that Mack left to go search? And with those idiot buddies of his? Couldn't someone stop him? He's not out to right a wrong. He's out for himself. Always is. And why, dammit, didn't I do more of the searching I started before things blew to hell-and-gone?"

The muttered self-criticism had been rattling in his brain for hours, now. Mean and destructive, it was wearing a painful groove in his mind. Torn between worry for a sister he loved and a fiancée he adored, he'd let guilt pull him off into a distracting and obsessive stretch of deep-sea fishing.

Now he may be too late.

He'd not searched this far before, for reasons that made sense at the time. But it came to him last night that Cara might have remembered, when she was running from the hurricane, the series of caves they'd visited years ago. It was pretty much his last hope. Merelin was already unhappy with his hopscotch focus of the last several weeks. She said he needed to settle down, and she was right.

But here he was.

***

Rodani sat up in the hammock, and didn't immediately climb out. His shoulders slumped a bit as he rested his elbows on his bent knees. Already the air was warm and humid, and the only food they had available was fish. Again.

"I'll make breakfast this morning, aisu," Cara told him, rubbing his back.

"My turn, kia."

"It's okay if you don't feel well today. You can do the next two mornings."

"Not necessary. I will rest on the blanket while it cooks."

"If you're sure." Cara watched him climb down and restart the fire from the banked coals, then she laid back down. Those relapses he was still having were making her nervous. He kept declining a trip to Endolan to visit a physician. Granted, it was a long way, but she understood stubbornness. She closed her eyes.

Shouted voices woke her up. Male voices.

"Freeze!" one ordered.

"Don't move!" came another.

"Tie his hands," a familiar, venom-infused voice commanded.

Oh, no. Oh, gods, no! She knew that voice. No! This is not happening!

Petrified, she leaned over the hammock. Rodani was on his knees, his arm outstretched to his side and as still as if frozen mid-motion. Surrounding him were three men, Mack and his cohorts, all holding bows, an arrow notched in each. Rodani's gaze was fixed and unmoving on Mack in front of him. Behind, Stefan began laying down his bow and reaching for a rope.

Nonononono! How did they surprise him? Was he so deeply asleep from his illness that he didn't hear? This is all my fault!

Stefan fought Rodani's motionless arm, trying to bend it to tie his wrists. Only when Mack shouted and shoved his bow closer, did Rodani allow himself to be tied.

"Where is Cara?" Mack shouted into his face. "Where is she?"

Rodani still knelt unmoving, his hands behind his back. His stare didn't waver. He knew those Cene'l words. But he was smart enough to play dumb.

Mack raved at him, shouting threats and questions her husband might not be able to interpret. "Hit him in the head!"

Stefan balled his fist and whacked Rodani behind the ear. He toppled onto his side on the blanket.

Real? Playing possum? Oh, gods, don't hurt him! Please! It was an empty entreaty, borne of desperation. There was nothing she could do except give herself up and hope they would let him go instead. But they'd never do that. They'd just have two hostages.

"I'll guard him. You two search for Cara."

"How do you know she's here?" asked Clark. "Nobody said anything about a stupid alien."

"Nobody else is around, either. He's the first breathing thing on two legs we've seen. Start looking, I said!"

The two men wandered around, flapping bushes and scuffling leaves under their feet. They stared over the cliff edge, followed the stream out of sight, but never did any of them do more than glance above their heads.

Mack walked up and kicked Rodani once, twice.

The sound made Cara want to scream and fight, just like in Barridan. But she clenched her teeth as Rodani curled inward from the blow.

"Where is Cara? Cara! You know that word, don't you?" He kicked again. "What are you doing here, anyway? You're not allowed down here."

"Mack, stop." Stefan appeared on the opposite side of the clearing. "He can't understand you."

"Did you find anything?"

"No."

"Tie his ankles. We wait. She'll show up." Mack turned away.

It took both Stefan and Clark to hold his legs and tie his ankles together. Clark straightened up and looked at him. "What's going on,

318

anyway, Mack? If he's here, and she's here... Doesn't sound right to me."

Mack's eyes went wide, and anger filled his face. He walked back again. "You got a dick, boy? Did you fuck her, or something? That why she's here? Let's see!"

The men pushed him onto his back and yanked down the front of his pants. At first, they stared in silence.

In the tree above, Cara bit her hands in an attempt not to shout, not to scream, not to call them every terrible name she ever knew.

"Look! He's got nothing but a hole!"

"No balls either."

"He's a neuter, or something."

"Maybe a robot."

All three laughed uproariously, staggering around and bending over to clutch their stomachs and slap their thighs. The hilarity went on far too long for the worth of their jokes.

Oh, aisu, I'm so sorry. You don't deserve this! I'd beat them bloody for every word and every laugh. Sometimes, she hated her species and the sick people who lived only to hurt and maim.

Rodani lay still, partially uncovered and eyes closed. Through some deep well of control, he'd managed not to react to the abuse, to the humiliation. His three captors settled on the ground nearby, and, always, one of them had his bow in hand.

More than an hour went by.

"This is boring. Let's let him go and keep looking."

"Yeah. It's Cara we came for, not him."

"We wait. Maybe we can get them both."

"We could just kill him."

"No. We might get a reward if we turn him in. I've spent enough money on this worthless search."

"I'm hungry."

"You're always hungry."

"I want a drink."

"No liquor in Lordstown, idiot." Laughter.

"Told you we should have brought some."

"No. We need to be sober to do this."

"Man, I'm gonna be so dry by the time we get home, I'll drink every bottle in Chucko's new bar."

"Wonder if he's got any women in the back?"

"Nah. He's too straitlaced to do that."

"C'mon. Let's go, Mack. We know where to come back to if no one else finds her."

"Give it another hour. Then we go."

And when that hour had crawled by, the men cut Rodani's ankle bonds, yanked him—and his pants—upright, and led him away to the north.

Cara had to wait still longer. Had to force with all her will to stay hidden for a little while more. She couldn't trust that trio not to wait out of sight or double back to catch her by surprise. But eventually, she climbed down, heart in her throat and hands shaking in grief and rage.

Remember what we talked about, fem, that we knew this might happen. She heard his words in her head. *Pack the essentials. Get to the boat.* And go where? Did he have his 'com with him? Oh, please, please. I think I can track him if he did.

Cara searched the blanket and the items the men had strewn about. And under the branch, in the leaves, his gun lay. She picked it up, and heard a noise behind her. She spun, gun out and ready. Her mouth fell open.

"Davad?"

Her brother stared at the gun in her hand. "That thing loaded?"

She dropped it on the blanket and ran to him, hugged him. "What are you doing here?"

"Same thing they were doing. Searching for you. Only difference is that I knew your husband would be with you." He looked away, embarrassed. "I'm sorry they treated him like that."

Her eyes blazed in rage. "You heard the bastards?"

"Heard and saw it all."

"Where were you?"

"I arrived right about when they did. Climbed a tree when I saw them. What do you want to do?"

Cara clenched her fingers in her hair. "Find him! Rescue him." She paced back and forth. "I think I can track him, if I can get close enough. But where will they take him?"

Davad shrugged. "They could take him to Mack's house. Clark's cabin is more isolated, though. Or they take him straight to the sheriff's office. I don't know."

"Did they come by boat? Do you know?"

"I didn't see any others besides the Selandu one in the cave. And mine."

"You saw it?"

"That's why I chose to look here. I thought you would remember that cave when you were looking for shelter from the storm."

"Did you tell anybody else you were looking here?"

"No. But I know others are looking. You can't stay here."

"I know that, now." She stared unseeing at the ground. "We talked about going somewhere else. Look, if they took him on foot or by cart or wagon, we'll beat them home if we take the boat. But if we wait, they may torture or kill him before we can find him." She started to pace again. "Aisu, aisu."

"We can't stop them when we're not there. Put that kind of stuff out of your head."

"Let me take a few more things, Dav. You'll take me home? Help me rescue him?"

"Yes, and I'll try."

She wanted more, but couldn't ask it. He had his own priorities, too.

Trying her best to be hopeful, she began to collect things. A change of clothes for each of them. The dried food that was left. The gun. His coin belt. The smoke and umbrella, the varigestra, her notebook. Where were his guild knives? Did he have his weapons belt on him? She shut her eyes and tried to bring his image to mind. No, there was no belt when they pulled down his shorts. She looked again under the log where he'd wrapped those damned cuffs of his that day. She shoved the memory away and felt around underneath the log. There. Yes.

"Davad, how much can I take with me? If necessary, can I leave a bit of it with you for a while?"

"I guess. You're not going to want to come back for the rest of it. But don't you want to hurry?"

"We discussed some of this, Dav. Rodani and I. We knew this might happen."

"What do you still need?"

"I want the hammock. He made it, and I don't want to leave it behind. I don't know if I can untie it, though. He always put it up and took it down." She began to climb the tree—carefully, remembering her previous fall. But she couldn't get it untied. She called down. "You're a sailor, Dav. Can you do something with these knots? Quickly?"

Davad grimaced but climbed up. He looked them over and worked the rope between his fingers, pushing and pulling. One by one, they gave way.

"Yes! Thanks!" She dropped the hammock down through the limbs, grabbed the sacks that had sat on other limbs, and climbed down.

"I think I'm ready."

"Then let's get the hell out of here."

"One last thing. We take the rope ladder off the cliff."

"How do we get down?"

"The storm opened up a hole into the cave. It's not easy, but we can do it. Easier down than up, at least."

"Show me the hole, first."

"Over here."

She moved aside the vine and leaf cover that Rodani had woven to hide the hole. Davad peered inside. "Okay. Get the rope and let's go."

They brought all the sacks over. Davad jumped down and took each one as Cara lowered it to him. She followed him, and they worked their way down the rock steps. Rodani's boat swayed forlornly in the water.

This time, the sacks went into Davad's bigger boat. They climbed in, and Davad maneuvered his way out of the cave entrance.

"Put this thing on full throttle, please."

"Let me drive. You think about what we'll do when we get there."

"Get where is the first question. And we'll have to do this at night."

"It's already near noon."

"Oh, gods, Davad, if they kill him, if they kill him..."

"Don't go there. Just don't."

Cara got up and stood next to him at the wheel. "Dav, if he's guarded, we're going to have to...how do we...what's...."

"Yeah, that's helpful, sis."

"I don't know if I can kill."

He swiveled his head around to stare at her. "Good point. You may have to."

"I can't ask you to do it. You have a kid on the way and a woman who loves you."

Davad rummaged through his mind. "I know someone who may help. My old friend, Erick. We'll have to ask, and he'll probably want to be paid."

"Shit. I've got some with me, but I have a little more in my trunk I brought back from Barridan. I asked Dae to hide it from Ama, and I don't know where he put it."

"I do. I helped him hide it."

"In his lab?"

"Yeah."

"But he keeps that locked."

"He's got a spare key. I can get to it. We'll have to wait until dark and hope he's in the house."

The boat rocked over wave after wave. Cara began to get nauseated. *Stress. It's no wonder.*

"So, we'll have some money and, hopefully, a helper who's good at criminal stuff. Right?" she asked.

"If all goes well."

Cara tried to breathe, tried to relax her taut muscles, tried to soothe the ball of hot anxiety that sat in her gut. It was one thing to discuss a possible catastrophe, and another thing for an actual one to smack them both down and kick them where it hurt. She never dreamed, when she started this adventure, how many kicks they'd both have to take. How many boulders rolled into their path. How often their different needs and fears would trip them up.

"If they take him to the sheriff, we can't get to him. If they take him to Mack's, I know where that is. If— What the hell am I thinking? I'm going to track him." She smacked her forehead. "I don't need to guess. I've got fuzz brain."

"How are you going to do that?"

"He carries something called a 'com. A pocket communicator. You can talk over it, and it transmits and receives info from other 'coms—and more I don't know about. If I'm lucky, I'll be able to home in on his."

"What if they take it from him?"

"I'll bet if they do, they'll keep it. A souvenir or something. Ugh." She sat down.

"What's wrong?"

"I didn't eat yet, and I'm getting seasick."

"Watch the horizon."

Finally, finally, they pulled into the Glaniad docks. Davad moored his boat at the far end. The afternoon was getting on.

"You stay here, as far out of sight as you can." Davad ordered. "I'll get your belt first."

"It's not dark."

"Cara, Dae knows about you, and knows about your husband."

"What?!" she shouted, distracted at the revelation and ignoring his shushing sound. "How?"

"I told him after you disappeared into the storm. He'll ask what I'm doing digging in your trunk, but I think he'll accept it if I say I'll tell him later."

"Good luck. Don't tell him what's happening!"

"I won't. I'll be back either way, and we'll go to Erick's." Davad climbed out onto the dock and headed up the steps, leaving Cara to curl up and wait.

And wait.

Worry and hope passed through her in waves.

Gods, would this day never end? Will I see him again? How badly will they hurt him? I need a Rodani to save Rodani!

To her surprise, Davad brought Erick back with him. Over his shoulder hung a bow with a quiver of arrows.

"Why?"

"Think, Cara. You can't go walking around town in daylight." He handed her the belt.

Cara shook her head. "I'm sorry, guys. This is hard on me. I'm not myself right now." She looked over at Erick, a short, slender man with a rigid and cool demeanor. "Thanks for helping."

"I haven't decided yet."

"What do you need to know?"

"What's expected of me."

"What did Davad tell you? I don't want to duplicate."

He stared into her eyes. "You know, I could just turn you in for the reward, and not do anything else."

Shock flew across her face.

"But," Erick continued, "Davad promised me more than the reward to help you."

She glanced at her brother, and covered her mouth with her hands. "What reward?"

"For bringing in a murderer."

"I didn't murder anyone!"

"Were you the woman who got in trouble there a couple of weeks ago?" Erick asked.

"Yeah."

Both men regarded her with expectant faces, one warm, one cool.

"I'm not discussing it," she retorted. "What's the reward?"

"Ten silver."

The shock on her face turned to pain. That would take almost everything she had. But...this was about Rodani. She'd pay. No question.

"However," Erick continued, "he also told me I might have a chance to kill Mack, or his brother. If that's true, I'll waive the fee."

Cara gathered her breath and what was left of her rational mind. "It's true. Mack, Stefan, and Clark took him from the south, and we assume, brought him here."

"Who's 'him?'"

"A man who means a lot to me."

"Why'd they take him?"

"Because they couldn't find me. Mack is a mad man, fixated on me, and he will make up plenty of reasons to hurt him."

"Where are they?"

"I won't be able to try to locate him until I can get over the dune. Then we can work closer to them and zero in."

"Fair enough. I will tell you, though, if I think I'm being played, I'm gone. And I will come after Davad for payment."

"Don't hurt him!"

"Don't fuck with me."

Tears burned in Cara's eyes, and she gritted her teeth against the rage that threatened to erupt. "They have my man. They've already hurt and humiliated *him*, and are going to hurt him more—or kill him. I want him rescued. You're welcome to kill any or all of his captors you can, just try not to hurt him—or Davad. Is that good enough?"

Erick leaned back. "Yeah."

She looked up at the sky. "It's still a little too early for me to leave the boat. I have an idea." She pulled out the 'com and held it up. "Dav, look." She pointed. "This dial you leave alone. It's set to the same frequency his should be set to. You change it, you won't get a signal. This one," she flipped a switch, "is now set to search. If it finds another 'com in range, this," she tapped a tiny lump, "will light up and if the volume is turned up, it'll make a soft beep. I turned it off for now."

"What is that?" Erick asked her, nodding to the 'com.

She explained, and handed it to Davad. "Go up top. Turn in an arc or a circle, and watch for the light to flash. If it does, we can follow it when it gets dark."

"And if it doesn't?" Erick asked.

"Lots of things. Maybe they're not back yet. Maybe it's not on the right channel. We could try changing it, but put it back on 9 when we're done. Maybe they took it and threw it away. In any case, we can still check Mack's and Clark's houses to see if anybody's there."

Davad took the 'com and headed uphill.

Cara looked at Erick. He was scary, but not the out-of-control kind that Mack was. She wasn't sure that was any better, but she wasn't going to complain now. *Just look at him as a type of guardian, huh?*

"Why do you want to kill him?" she asked Erick.

"Not my story."

"I've got my own issues with him. Tell you what," she said. "You give me your story now, and I'll tell you mine when we're done."

"Will I want to hear it?"

"You will."

They stared into each other's eyes.

"You're a weird one." Erick shifted on the captain's chair. "But I've known that for a long time."

"I can add a chapter to it when this is finished."

"What if we can't get to him?"

"Like if they took him to the sheriff?" She shook her head. "I'll pay you a silver for your trouble, and you can go back to whatever you were doing."

"What will you do?"

"I don't know. Depends on the situation."

Davad climbed back in. "No signal."

Cara rocked to and fro, unable to contain her disappointment and worry. "Don't rain. Don't rain."

"Rain?" Davad asked.

"It's what the Selandu call crying."

"They don't have a word for it?"

She smiled, a little. "They can't cry."

The sun dipped below the horizon, and the shadows grew. The men talked of inconsequentials. Cara fretted and bit at the skin on her fingers.

"Check again, will you Dav?"

He got up and out.

"Luck," she wished him, and went back to rocking, worse this time.

Erick gave her the side-eye. "Chill, fem."

She glared at him. "Is there anybody you love? Almost more than life itself?"

"Not so far."

"Get back to me when you do," she replied, curt.

Davad returned, and smiled wide. "Signal."

Cara gasped. "Holy shit! What direction?"

"West, mostly. But it still could mean either Mack's or Clark's. They're pretty much in a line."

"Dav, we've got one more worry. Stupid that I didn't think of it earlier!"

"Shut that, and tell me."

"How do we get him out of there, especially if he's hurt? Do you have a cart we can use?"

"No. Emmie's still got yours, though. Where would you take him?"

"West. No—south to get his boat back. Then he and I can decide."

"I suppose you want me to make that run again," Davad said with a frown.

"If this succeeds," she replied, still rocking, "yes, and I'll pay you for both trips."

Davad thought for a moment, drumming his fingers on the captain's chair. "I guess we can run the boat up the river, check the signal from there."

Cara let out the breath she didn't know she was holding. "Sounds good."

"Well, if we're gonna do that, we can leave now."

"Oh, please," she said, rocking harder.

"Will you calm down?"

"No."

Davad motioned Erick out of the captain's chair, reversed the boat, and headed the short distance north to the mouth of the East River. He turned into it, and began fighting the current trying to take him out to sea. "Easy, baby," he crooned. "You've got the power."

They worked their way west, slowed by the current. Detritus from the hurricane still lay in organized chaos on the banks. But Cara's eyes didn't leave the 'com in her hands. They passed Main Street, then the CSC on the right, then later a few scattered houses.

"We're coming up on Mack's."

"That's it," she whispered. "The signal's turning to match it! But now what?"

"Shit, fem, you're no good at tactics," Erick said. "We study the place from here, first."

"We won't be seen?" Cara asked.

"Look around. Do you see any lights?"

"I only want to see my man, Erick. That's all."

He tutted. "Women."

She turned to him in the dark. "I have plenty of skills you don't."

"Stop it, you two." Davad whispered at them. He took out his spyglass and held it to his eye. Erick looked over his shoulder.

"What do you see?"

"Nothing right now. No, a light just went on at the front of the house."

A whisper of voices floated over the water. They waited for something else, but what, they didn't know.

328

"Damn," Davad said. "Could it be that easy?"

Erick held out his hand. "Let me see." He looked through it. "Well, my work just got a helluva lot easier."

"What?" Cara hissed. "What?"

"Two of them just walked away. Headed toward town, it looks like."

"Going to get smashed, I'll bet," Davad guessed.

"But are they going to stay there or come back with bottles?" Cara asked. "They may not give us much time."

"She's got a point, Erick."

"Park this thing, and let's go."

They eased forward into the single dock ahead, shared by locals and the CSC. Cara checked the 'com one last time, then pocketed it. Erick grabbed his weapons. Davad pulled a knife out of his deck cabinet and held it at his side. Cara still had one of Rodani's knives, but left it hidden, resting against her coin belt around her waist.

They stole forward under the darkness, Erick leading the way. Given her mix of dread and hope, Cara forgot all the stealth techniques Rodani had taught her. She could only try to walk quietly and clench her teeth against a sudden yelp of fright.

Closer, closer.

Erick headed toward the front of the house. Cara and Davad took the back. "Would that 'com tell us what room he's in?" Davad whispered.

She pulled it out, fumbling in rising anxiety. She walked back and forth, and around both corners on that side of the house, and closer to the front. Then she went back.

"I'm pretty sure he's back here, somewhere. But it's hard to be exact."

He minced his way toward the one lit window. Cara followed behind. An external shutter covered it. Davad looked for the latch, found it, but didn't open it. He motioned Cara away.

"I can get it open, but we don't know where Mack is. We need to know what Erick's found. Stay here."

Davad stole around to the other side of the small house. Erick was on his knees in front of the main window. He motioned to Davad, who looked in. There was Mack, sitting in a chair, legs splayed out in front of him, bottle at hand. Davad nudged Erick and tilted his head.

They crept back around. Cara was trying valiantly to peer through the slatted shutter.

"Mack's in the front room in a chair, probably getting drunk. Be ready."

Ready to do what? she thought. But she stood back and let the men begin it.

Davad unlatched the shutter and opened it just enough to see in. On the floor was the body of his sister's husband. He seemed to be alive. They wouldn't have tied him to the bedposts at the floor if he were dead. But even from Davad's view, he could see cuts and bruises. Davad motioned to Cara.

She looked in, and covered her mouth with her hands.

***

Doma, a guild guardian of three years, returned from break and sat at his desk with a welcome cup of tea. *Nothing but leaves and water,* he thought with a sigh. Nights were long and often boring. It took only so many times of rousting drunk Selandu sailors from the bars for the task to lose his interest. His gaze drifted over his instruments, then held in one spot. He went back out to the night watch's desk.

"A'tem, we have a puzzle."

"Yes?" said his supervisor, who didn't bother to pull his attention from the book in front of him.

"There is at least one 'com out there, broadcasting."

The supervisor paused for a moment. "And why is that a problem?" he asked into the air between them.

"*Where* is the problem, a'tem. South of us."

"South?" The man turned to Doma with eyes narrowed in thought. "In the woods?"

"I cannot tell."

"Requisition a boat for yourself and another. You will sit on the border and tell me what you find. And tell Henado to check the near woods," he said as an afterthought.

***

The trio knelt under Mack's bedroom window. Davad spoke softly. "I'll break the glass with my knife haft. I'll immediately move aside, and Erick will shoot Mack when he comes into the room. Once he's down, I'll lift you in." He checked with both of them. "Okay?"

Erick nodded and pulled his bow off his shoulder, knocked an arrow, and waited. Davad drew his knife. "On three," he whispered. "One, two, *three*."

He shattered the glass with one blow, then banged the largest leftover piece out of its place. On the floor, Rodani startled and raised his head. Erick took Davad's place.

Even from the ground, Cara could hear the bang of the bedroom door and Mack's shout of anger. Erick let loose his arrow and drew another, just in case.

It wasn't necessary. Mack went down in a heap, only one hand moving toward the arrow stuck in his chest. Blood was already pouring out. Davad banged the rest of the shards out of the window and boosted Cara inside. She earned a few cuts, but nothing stopped her from rushing to Rodani's side.

He double-checked Mack on the floor, then back to Cara. She was desperately hacking at the ropes around his wrists. "Kia," he whispered, dazed by his illness and abuse.

"Cara, unlock the damned front door!" Davad said through the window.

She rushed out, and rushed back. The two men ran in. Davad worked on the ankle rope while Erick watched, silent and bemused. The ankle bonds fell first. Davad pushed his sister out of the way and finished her task. As he did, Cara stared at Mack. Revulsion flooded her, body and mind. *You deserve this, you bastard. Much as I hate to think it, you got what you deserve. You earned this.*

"Reap what you sow," she muttered.

Freed from his bonds, Rodani flexed his arms and legs.

"Can you walk?" She asked in Selandi.

He struggled to sit up. "I believe so."

Erick stepped back. "Shit, fem, what have you done?"

She turned to him. "You never told me *your* story."

Rodani used the bed to stand, and clenched and released his fists. But he hobbled, badly.

On the floor, eyes barely open, Mack groaned and muttered. "Cara." Blood still trickled out of his wound. Erick started toward him, knife in hand.

Rage overcame her, her heart pounding hearing her name from his lips.

"No," she spat. "Let me try," Cara said.

All three men turned to her. Erick raised his eyebrows and motioned a go-ahead. She drew her knife. Rodani's knife.

"Cara!" Rodani shouted as he reached for her arm. "Du! Du!"

She glanced down in disbelief to the arm he'd grabbed, then looked up at him. "Why?" She tried to shake her arm free, but he only tightened his grip. "After what they did to you?"

"I beg you, kia," he said, more softly, but no less intense. His gaze was riveted on her. "*Please.*"

Davad interrupted, his face stiff with tension. "We need to get gone, Cara."

Silent, she sheathed the knife and held out a palm to Erick.

Erick nodded. "Stand back," he told the pair. As Cara urged Rodani backward, Erick made a quick slice through the side of Mack's throat.

Red sputtered feebly from blood pressure nearly spent. Mack's eyes lost their focus, and his body relaxed into death.

Shaking with adrenaline, she pushed the horror away for the chance of freedom, of relief from the nightmare of Rodani's capture.

"He took my 'com," Rodani told her.

Cara ran past Mack's body into the living room. To their good fortune, it rested on the end table by his chair. She grabbed it.

Once they were outside, she pointed to the boat. "Can you get there?"

"To get away, I will. Give me time."

"Okay. But we don't know when the others will come back."

The point must have gotten across because Rodani tried to hurry but ended up caught between speed and balance.

"Guys," Cara pleaded, "can you help him walk? One on either side?"

"If you'll watch our backs," Erick said.

***

In the prow of the guild boat, Doma stared at the 'com in his hand. *How can this be?*

He motioned to his two-person crew, adding urgency to the hand signals. *Return!*

Back inside Soldan's guard station, Doma nearly ran to the watch desk. "A'tem," he said, his ear tips twitching in agitation. His superior frowned at the un-guild-like expression of nerves.

"Speak," came the command.

"A'tem—the signal—it is not from the trees," Doma said, attempting a calm he didn't feel. "It is on land." He took a heavy breath. "On the south side."

"Impossible," was the curt reply.

***

Davad and Erick each took a Selandu arm. Their speed improved, marginally. Cara turned back every other step to make sure no one else showed up.

"Cara," Erick said over his shoulder, "Mack raped my sister. She never really recovered."

Shocked at the open admission, but not really surprised, Cara looked off in the distance, heartsick. "I'm really sorry, Erick. Please give her my best, and tell her you made sure he wouldn't do it to anyone else."

"Will do. And your story?" he leaned his head toward the alien next to him.

"He was my guardian in Barridan. We fell in love."

"What's he doing here?"

"He followed me across the border after I was sent home. Neither of us wanted to be separated."

"Huh. Love is love, eh? Hey," he said. "If you didn't murder that preacher in Lordstown, did he?"

"No." The lie didn't hurt as she thought it would have weeks ago. Didn't even faze her, with all the terrors of the last day. Cara turned around as she heard Rodani stumble. *Mack is dead*, she told herself for the tenth time. *I never have to hear my name come out of that mouth again. Now, there's no chance for that mouth to have an opportunity to rat out my husband.*

But where was the right of it? The real right? Was she an accessory to murder?

Davad and Erick helped Rodani onto the dock. The next step was getting him into the boat. Davad jumped in first to lend his stability to Rodani. Between the three of them, he managed to climb over the side and down onto the bench at the back.

Cara put her hand on Erick's arm. "You can come with us, or go on."

"I'll take off." He paused for a moment. "I misjudged you a bit. I'm sorry for that."

"Thanks for what you did."

"My. Pleasure," he stated firmly, cold.

She bowed her head. "I get it."

Erick walked into the dark, and Cara climbed aboard. As Davad started the motor, Rodani leaned his upper body down flat on the bench.

She rushed to his side. "Can I help you at all?"

"Water?"

"Uh," she looked around, rummaged in her pack for the water bag. "Yes. Here."

He propped up on one elbow, drank, and passed it back.

"Dried food?" she asked.

"Du." He lay back down and closed his eyes.

Cara sat in front of him, on the floor of the boat. "Aisu, I'm so sorry. So sorry for what they did—and said."

"You found me, kia."

She felt it all coalesce, all of it welling up—the terror, the rage, the violence done. "Aisu, I'm going to rain, badly. Just rest, and let me get it out." She bent her head to his chest, leaned on his arm, and sobbed. It flooded through her in waves that tore to pieces what she'd held inside, washing the worst away.

Rodani laid his arm down her back, hand on her head. Soon they entered ocean water.

Davad called back to her, urgent.

More alarms rang in her head, shutting off the tears. "What?"

"There's a Selandu boat out here, right on the border."

Drying her eyes, Cara got up to look. They'd just left the mouth of the river, and to their left, a large boat was sitting still on the ocean waves.

"What do they want?" he asked her.

"No clue. Just head south."

Davad turned the boat and accelerated. The Selandu boat started moving.

Following them.

Cara turned around. "Rodani, there's a boat pursuing us. I think it's a patrol boat."

He sat up on the bench to look.

"Yes. It is," he said in a despondent voice. His shoulders sagged in weariness.

"Why?" she asked.

"They just crossed the border!" Davad yelled. He pushed the throttle to full power.

"They don't know who we are." She looked at Rodani. "They can't!"

"Kia, your 'com. Is it on broadcast?"

She grabbed it from her pocket. "I don't know. I used it to find you."

"Bring it to me."

He took it from her. "Yes, it is broadcasting. They must have picked up the signal."

Cara began swearing with every foul epithet she knew.

Davad shouted into the wind. "They're gaining!"

"You will not outrun them," he told Davad, with Cara interpreting. "They will catch us."

Cara turned back to her brother. "You have to go home."

"What?" He glanced at her as he fought the wheel.

"You have to get off this boat. I won't let them take you."

"What about you?"

"If they're coming for Rodani, I'm going with him."

"Shit, Cara." They stared at each other, at what she might be facing.

"Yeah. Look," she told him. "Let me take the wheel. I'll curve toward shore, and you get ready to swim. That do?"

The patrol boat gained a few yards. "Yeah." Davad steered landward at an angle.

"If they take us, we'll have to leave the boat behind," Cara said. "You can come and get it, right?"

"I'm not losing it."

"Take our belongings, too, please. Keep them somewhere." She tore through the bags, grabbing their clothes, Rodani's coin belt, and her notebook. She stuffed them in the weapons bag. "Get ready."

Davad stepped aside and slipped off his shoes.

"This close enough?"

"Yep."

Cara pulled on the wheel, and a fantail rose at the stern as the boat turned.

"Go!"

Davad leaped onto the gunwale and dived into the sea. Cara had just enough time for a glimpse of him surfacing before she angled back to deeper water.

"Kia."

"What?" She glanced back and saw the patrol boat only a short distance behind them. Selandu stood at the prow.

It took some effort for him to speak over the surrounding noise. "I am going to pretend that I am more injured than I truly am. I need you to follow my lead."

"Okay. Why?"

"It may grant us a little leeway."

^I love you, aisu.^

"And I am yours, kia. It has been a wild ride."

Her heart sank at his words. What she heard was *goodbye*. After all they'd won for themselves, after all they'd gained, the ending they'd both feared seemed to be in sight.

"Stop the boat," he told her. "Cease running. There is no sense in it."

Cara shut off the motor. Davad's boat slowed, then stopped in the water. In moments the patrol boat drew even with them. She sat down next to Rodani on the bench and waited. For the end of all she knew.

***

"Man-oh," Clark chortled as he strutted down the lane. His friend's cabin was fifty or so paces ahead, and Clark was ready for the fun and games. "I wonder how high his voice goes when he screams."

Stefan side-eyed him, then lifted his bottle and took another swig. "What you gonna do? Measure it?"

"Wish he spoke our language."

"Yeah. Mack's gonna shout her name at the weirdo 'til he's hoarse. But I don't think that'll help."

Eyes wide with a half-coherent thought, Clark raised his own bottle. "We could kidnap that journalist bitch and make her translate!"

"Sure, bud. How do you translate a scream?"

"That won't be the only thing comes out of his mouth."

Stefan climbed onto the step at his brother's door. "Then we'd have to kill her, too. You know that, right?"

Eager to begin, Clark reached past him and yanked the door open. But instead of finding Mack, the men found the overpowering smell of blood and urine.

Two paces in, Clark halted. "What the fuck?"

"Did he already kill that ugly long-hair?"

Clark slammed his bottle on the table where Mack's own brew rested. Stefan did the same and followed him toward the bedroom.

"Mack! What'd you do, man?" Clark shouted. In the doorway, he stumbled. "Oh, shit!"

***

A sailor tied the two boats together, and someone else placed a gangplank over the two mismatched sides. A man—no, a woman—dressed in guild black, walked across to Davad's boat. Two more guardians followed her across. She stood in front of the seated pair.

Without moving her head, she looked left. "Your name, a'sel?"

"Rodani."

She looked right. "And yours?"

"Cara."

Back to Rodani. "Give me your 'com."

He handed it over, hesitantly, as if it were a lifeline he was losing.

The woman checked its settings, then slipped it into one of the many pockets a guardian had. "You are in violation of human laws."

"As are you," he noted.

Ignoring the accusation, she said, "Both of you will come with me."

"I am injured," Rodani protested.

"But you will obey."

Cara grabbed the heavy bag and attempted to climb onto the gangplank with it. One of the guardians helped her up, holding on until another reached out from the patrol boat. She jumped down and turned.

It took Rodani a few tries to do the same, but soon he stood beside her. The boat curved around, heading back across the border.

Rodani folded himself down onto the deck. Cara sat behind him and guided his head into her lap as he lay down. The act radiated intimacy to the watching crew, whose expanded pupils and raised eyebrows spoke their thoughts.

"Stations," the woman called out.

Cara and Rodani were left to themselves in the center of the boat. She ran her fingers through his mussed hair, and held his hands at his shoulders. She bent down toward Rodani's face, upside down, given their positions. "If this is the end, aisu, I want you to know I have no regrets—about you, about being with you, about what you mean to me." She squeezed his hands. "I would do it all over again."

He looked up at her. "I would say the same to you, my kia."

The boat rocked on the waves, speeding north. *At least he's out of human hands,* Cara thought. *But what's ahead?* "Any idea where they're taking us?"

He paused, his eyes roaming the night sky. "Hadaman is most likely."

She tightened her hands on his. "Gods of the deep night. You ever been there?"

"No."

"Any idea what they're going to do to us?"

"I hesitate to guess. I suspect I will face some kind of punishment."

She swore some more.

"Take your ease as you can, kia. It will be some hours before we arrive."

***

Chief Berg slipped a written report into the day's folder. The window to his right showed him only darkness, and he sighed in weary resignation. With two sheriffs gone over the border, he was forced to work more hours. His failure at finding any replacements for the open positions just fed his frustrations.

Panicky voices erupted outside, rising as they neared the door. Alarmed, Berg sat up in expectation of more work to be done. He put his hand on the butt of his gun and waited.

When Stefan Cornyn strode in, with the second part of the miscreant trio right behind, Chief Berg nearly swore out loud.

"Chief! Chief! It's murder. Murder!" the pair's words stumbled over one another.

Berg realized they truly were panicked. He stood up to face them. "Details, gentlemen." *If you could call them that,* he thought. "Who's dead?"

"Mack," Clark spat.

Berg eyed them, smelling the alcohol on their breaths and clothing. "You sure?"

"Well fuck, Chief," Clark retorted. "There's blood everywhere, and his eyes were glassy. Smelled of piss. Whadda you think?"

Berg pointed to the door. "Let's go."

They walked out, the younger men agitated and jumpy. "See Chief," Stefan began, "We were walking back from Chucko's new bar, since it's closer than The Rag. And Mack was home, watching over...over..." He glanced at Clark in dawning dismay. "Ummm."

Berg rolled his eyes and scratched the back of his neck. His shoes scuffed the dirt as he walked. "Start at the beginning, Stefan."

Clark stepped in. "See, when the word went out about MacLennan, we went looking for her. Down south, like others did." He took a breath. "And we found an alien."

"An alien? Not Cara?"

"No, Chief. Really." Clark leaned toward the chief in earnest, nearly tripping over his own feet. "The fella was tall! Long hair, like they say."

Berg squinted his eyes against the flow of alcohol vapors that wafted his way. "And what does this have to do with Mack being dead?"

Clark glanced at Stefan's face, pale in the moonlight. "Well, we...kinda took him."

Berg stopped in his tracks, then started again. "Took. Him."

"Yeah."

"Let's start at the end and work backwards," the chief said. "Maybe that will make more sense." He glanced at both of them. "Because I think your drink has got you telling stories."

Shouting interrupted Suraya's thoughts, yanking her out of the tight focus she held on her writing. She left her chair and stuck her head out her cabin door into the early night.

No too far distant were three men: Sheriff Berg, and Mack's two friends, helpers in the calamities that often followed in Mack's wake. With a lantern in hand, Berg walked silently while Clark and Stefan talked over each other at a rapid pace. They waved their arms with unusual fervor, attempting to convince the leery sheriff of their truths. But one word caught Suraya's ears. *Alien.*

What? Her heart began to race. She crept, feigning nonchalance, behind one neighbor's cabin, then the next, paralleling the men in a clumsy attempt to eavesdrop.

"—Blood all over the place!"

"—Throat slashed!"

"—We know that thing was there, Sheriff. We caught him down past Lordstown, sleeping on a blanket on the ground. We waited for Cara to show up, but we never saw her."

Thrilled and frightened, Suraya skulked among the cluttered yards, following them up the river. *Lordstown? Caught him? Could it be? Had to be. Why else mention Cara?*

As Sheriff Berg neared Mack's cabin and the two witnesses hung back, Berg turned a full circle to check the surroundings. He met Suraya's gaze, along with many others who wondered at the commotion. Then, he faced forward and headed toward the cabin.

Caught. She knew it. Knew the moment their eyes met that she might be in trouble. Or at least, she hoped, only questioned. Who else besides herself and Menachem would the sheriff think might know? Should she tell Davad? He wouldn't give up his sister, or her husband. She'd bet the next week's meals he'd keep his mouth shut.

Unwilling to intrude any further, she turned for home. Ignoring the topic she'd been writing about before, she grabbed another paper and scribbled in excited haste. Lines and paragraphs appeared, barely legible, with all the ink blots and scratch-outs. But when a firm knock came from the door, she scrambled to hide her notes.

And...she wasn't surprised to find herself sitting in front of Chief Sheriff Berg's desk in the late hours of the evening. Her heart was in her throat, and all the prohibitions she held inside about lying were threatening to spew out.

"What do you know about the events at Mack's house today, Suraya?" Berg began in a deceptively mild voice.

"All I heard, Chief, was Clark and Stefan hollering out in the street about murder."

"Do you know who was murdered?"

She shrugged. "I assume it was Mack, because of where you were and who you were with."

"What did you hear about their claims?"

"That he was murdered."

He eyed her closely. "Nothing else?"

She stopped to think. Not about the question, but about how much of the truth to say. "No. I was too far away, and they were talking over each other." The stress made her throat tighten. Did he hear a change in her voice? Was that a tell?

"You and Cara are friends."

Here's a truth you can say, Su. "We are. Or were before she disappeared."

"You're a graduate of the CSC. So, I assume you're interested in the aliens."

She waited to see if he'd continue. "Is that a question?" she asked when he didn't.

"Don't get smart with me, young lady. What do you know about them?"

"Chief, it would take days to teach you all I learned about the Selandu."

"Are you aware they're not allowed south of the border?"

"Of course. That's one reason why they have the border stations placed along the Himadi Hills." Feigning cooperation, she added, "And why none of them get off the boats when they dock here."

"You haven't heard anything about one of them being here, on our lands?"

She shook her head, pursing her lips slightly. "Nope. If I did, I would have rushed to interview him. Or her."

"You haven't heard from Cara," he said, stating another assumption.

Another shake of her head. "No. I wish I did, though."

"Did you join the search?"

"No."

"Why not?"

She thought fast and came up with another truth. "I don't much like lingering in forests, Chief. I wouldn't be a very good searcher."

Berg leaned back in his chair, eyes still on her face. "You went to Lordstown a few weeks ago."

"I did."

"Why?"

"To write a story about the preacher."

"Did you hear any rumors while you were there?"

Ahh. A word I could use to hide the truth. "No, no rumors. No aliens mentioned."

"None about Cara?"

Here's a narrow path, fem. Be careful. "I didn't talk to many people. Mostly to the preacher, and the one sermon I went to. I listened to others talk."

"Why didn't you interview more?"

"They're not friendly people, Chief. They seem closed off with a very narrow view of life. Did you read my article?"

He looked away for the first time, then back. "No," he paused, "alright, you can go. I may have more questions for you. *Don't* disappear."

"Not planning to. Maybe I'll write an article about the murder, and your investigation." She smiled at his surprise. "I can interview you, yes?"

His face showed his suspicion. "Good night, Suraya."

She rose from the chair and walked into the waiting room, only to see Davad in a chair by the door, awaiting his turn. His eyes widened when he saw her.

Hardly daring to look at him, she shook her head very slowly, just a little back and forth in a warning she hoped he heeded.

Who else would Berg interview? How far would this go? Davad was the only other person she could think of who knew the truth. And if the rumors were true, where were Cara and her husband?

TWENTY-FOUR

It was still dark when the boat pulled in. The Hadaman docks were lit with lanterns, and an equally well-lit path led up to a multi-story building twice the size of Arimeso's house. A large lawn surrounded it, with smaller buildings beyond.

Guardians got them up and moving, and over the side of the patrol boat. They set Cara's bag on the ground at her feet and climbed back inside. A Selandu man in solid black stepped up to them and stopped.

"A'tem," he said to Rodani. "A'Cara." Stiff in formality, his body and voice held no hint of welcome.

"A'Temaso," each replied.

"Follow me."

With other guardians behind them, Chendal led them upward on the path to where the Council of Three, rulers of all the Selandu, made their home. The memory of Cara's short conversation with Kenimandil popped into her head. The Council had gone to a lot of trouble to bring them both here. Her fear of the unknown battled her fear of the known consequences they might have to face.

Those worries all scattered when Rodani curled downward to sit on the path. Cara crouched beside him. "A'Temaso! Is there a cart or something he can ride in?" she asked as Chendal walked back.

He looked them over dispassionately, then pulled out his 'com and requested a buggy, then said something about a chair.

It didn't take long to get to them, a two-seater pulled by a multicolored benatac. Cara and Rodani were ushered into the back seat. Chendal sat in front with the driver. In short order, they were at the doors of the government house. They were met by an attendant with a rolling chair. Rodani eased himself into it gratefully, and held out a hand and waved his fingers for Cara to give him the sack. She handed it over.

Chendal led the way. After a few corridors and a couple of corners, he stopped them in a medium-sized room with a table, a divan, and some chairs. One open double door led right. Another single door to the left and behind them stood shut.

He left them in the hands of the attendant, along with two other guardians who had come up from behind. One of them angled around to face Rodani about a dozen feet away. They stared outright at each other. Neither spoke.

Chendal came through the doorway and motioned the rolling chair forward, then stopped it at the entrance. "Now you will walk."

As Rodani got up, Chendal turned to Cara. "Leave your bag inside the door."

They went into a large room, relatively unadorned, with a trio of desks opposite them. Behind each one was a taso, two women and one man. Cara had never seen a male taso before, but she knew they existed. He just looked like a typical Selandu. None of the three were dressed any differently than what she'd seen in Barridan among the higher-ranking people. Around the room were a few more guardians and other functionaries standing at attention. All eyes seemed to be on her, or Rodani—except Chendal, who was approaching the taso on their right.

And behind him, stood a furious Shisa.

Outraged, Shisa felt anger thrum down her body, raw in every nerve. *Look at her. Look at him! Ragged. Dirty. Limping, bruised, and cut. He looks like a vagabond. Where in Sela's good name is his honor? His self-respect? How could he let himself fall to such depths? Oh, for one good chance at that—woman.* Shisa's fist clenched rhythmically. Her jaws flexed against her teeth in a heroic attempt to keep from shouting.

Blast that loud, ignorant woman, the fault of my brother's downfall! Freeze her in Temi's coldest hell and be done with her. Wipe her off the face of this planet!

Her foot began to tap on the stone floor, agitation barely masked. Dimly, she noted Chendal's glance in her direction. The rage she'd banked in Tendiman months ago just refueled itself.

She destroyed him. Just as I said she would, in Barridan. Nothing but a rotund, ugly child, and she held him in claws that no one had been able to remove. Temi blast her!

"A'ke'Taso," Chendal greeted Kenimandil, bowing. He stepped to the side to allow Rodani to come forward, Cara behind him. Rodani stopped a greater distance away, possibly in respect to her rank, possibly because both of them were ragged and dirty from their primitive living and the day's ordeal.

He pulled his hands behind his back and bowed, more deeply than Chendal had, and for a longer time. Out of her depth, Cara imitated him.

"A'ke'Taso."

"A'tem." The look she gave him was a cool appraisal. "Where is your guild clothing? Where are your weapons?"

"A'ke'Taso, that clothing is several hours south of here. My weapons are in the bag we brought. The captain of the patrol boat took my 'com, and did not return it."

"Have you renounced your guild status?"

"No, a'ke'Taso."

"But you have renounced your allegiance to Arimeso."

"A'ke'Taso," he said after a moment's hesitation, "her keso's mistreatment forced me to leave her house. But I will honor her to the end of my life."

Kenimandil's steady regard reminded Cara of Arimeso. The same unflappable demeanor, the same veiled power. This level, however, was several steps higher.

"And why were you found south of the border?"

"I chose to follow my bonded mate, a'ke'Taso. Neither of us wished to live apart."

Kenimandil's attention flickered to Cara, then back to Rodani.

"Without due regard for the laws our two species brokered? Laws which created the peace we live in?"

"It was an unfortunate consequence of my choice not to break my bond and my promises to my mate, a'ke'Taso."

She was silent for a moment...and another moment, raising the hackles on Cara's neck.

Shisa glared at the human, standing there looking like a beggar on the street. And Rodani, looking much the same. Beneath her burning rage, she felt pain for her brother. The youngest child. Harboring similar wounds to her own, with scars that would never fade.

"I am not certain," Kenimandil continued, "that I have ever heard of a guardian who was more proficient at breaking rules than you, a'tem."

Rodani bowed his head, and kept it there.

"You are to be punished. One, for leaving your house and your duty without prior notice or permission, and two, for traveling south where we are forbidden to go." Kenimandil glanced at Chendal, who came forward at the summons.

"A'tem," he said, drawing his belt from around his waist. Rodani looked over at him and began to lift his shirt.

"No," Cara whispered. Another temichi appeared at her right and drew her away.

Shisa.

"No," she said more loudly.

Shisa shook her arm. "Tsss. Silence."

Rodani pulled his shirt off and gave it into the hands of a waiting guardian.

"No, a'ke'Taso, please!" Cara begged. "He's injured. Can't you see?"

Shisa clapped her hand over Cara's mouth and pulled her close. Kenimandil ignored the outburst.

At the sound of the first strike against her beloved husband's back, Cara broke free and ran straight at Chendal. She grabbed his arm and the belt, and hung in mid-air with all her human strength.

"No, a'Temaso, please! He needs a physician! I beg you!"

Chaos erupted. Shisa sprang forward at the same time a frustrated Chendal tried to peel her off his arm.

Rodani spun around. "Kia, no!"

Shisa grabbed her around the waist and pulled. It stretched her out, lower half against Shisa's body and arms pulled horizontal with Chendal's belt wrapped in her fist.

"Hit me instead!" she cried.

"Cara, stop!" Rodani hissed, begging.

Wordless, controlled, Chendal unwrapped his belt from her fist and took a step back. Shisa carried her off to the side. He raised the belt and laid another stripe on Rodani's back.

Cara shouted into Shisa's palm and fought wildly to be released.

Temi's blasted demons, Shisa swore to herself. *Close your mouth you filthy, crazed woman! Shut up and let it be over!*

Another slash of the belt, and another stripe appeared.

Cara pulled Shisa's hand down, just far enough. "Please, a'ke'Taso! He's inj—" The hand re-covered her mouth with a painful grip.

As Chendal's punishment continued, Cara screamed behind Shisa's palm, pulling her legs up and covering her ears. Kenimandil turned to her, the animal sound coming from her an unexpected shock. Then her gaze returned to Rodani, who was not holding up well.

Cara was now hanging from Shisa's arms. In a mental agony that none of the Selandu understood, she pulled at Shisa's hand and bit down on whatever was pressing against her teeth.

Utterly offended, Shisa tossed her onto the floor. Her head hit, and silence filled the room. Only the sound of a belt hitting flesh could still be heard.

Rodani's eyes closed down, and he began to shake badly. He went down on one knee, then the other, then onto his side on the floor. "Kia," he gasped.

As Chendal slipped his belt back on, Rodani began to crawl toward Cara, motionless several feet away. But healers interrupted his attempt and lifted him onto a stretcher. He held his arm out as they carried him away. "Kia."

Chendal glanced at the ke'Taso, his partner, and the small form on the floor. He walked over and knelt down, turning her on her back. Her face was scraped, and dotted with blood on her jaw and cheekbone. She opened her eyes, looking around in alarm.

Kenimandil got up and came closer. "A'Cara?"

A look of fear filled her face. Her vision landed on the people around her, the walls, the doors. She muttered in Cene'l, with words no one around her understood.

Kenimandil and Chendal both looked at Shisa, who blanked her expression and pulled her hands behind her back.

Chendal spoke again, "A'Cara, can you hear me?"

She only lay on the floor, mute. Her expression screwed up in pain, and she pressed her palms against her temples.

Chendal turned to Shisa. "We will discuss this," he told her in no uncertain terms.

"A'Temaso," was her reply.

"Perhaps a call to Mena'hem?" Kenimandil suggested.

"Perhaps, a'ke'Taso." He turned back to the shaking human on the floor. "A'Cara?" He held out a hand.

She sat up slowly, pulling her knees to her chin. Her eyes roamed the room.

"A'Cara."

She stood, unsteady on her legs, and squinted her eyes as she fixed her gaze one by one on the people around her.

"How do you feel, a'Cara?"

Her arms drew across her body as if she were protecting herself from something, or someone. Her eyes went wide. She backed away from Chendal and Kenimandil, mute and staring.

"A'Cara, speak to me," he told her, attempting to be patient. This was not the kind of reaction from her he'd expected, though her earlier scream had not surprised him as badly as it had the others in the room. He had, after all, seen her in emotional upheavals before.

"A'Cara!" he said sharply.

Still, she searched the room, looking for what? Or whom, he wondered.

She backed away a second time. "Rodani?" she said with a quiver of panic to her voice. Her body's movements began to hitch instead of her normal smooth mobility, jerking as if she were losing some control of herself. "Rodani?" She kept moving her head, checking every face in the room.

"Cara, Rodani is in the clinic. Speak to me." He placed his palm on his chest in emphasis.

He received no response, and no change in her increasingly strange behavior.

"Cara," he said sharply.

Now she looked at him, but her eyes were wide, her mouth open, and her breathing deeper, faster. Again, she put her hands against her temples and retreated, shaky in her walk, to a couch against the far wall.

Chendal followed her until he was again standing in front of her.

^Rodani, where are you?^ Now she looked at no one, her glances grazing past everyone in uncoordinated sweeps. ^Please, aisu.^

Chendal turned to Kenimandil. "Why would she speak her own language, not ours?" he thought out loud. Returning back to her, he said, "Cara, do you understand me?"

She made no reply, but began to rock her body on the couch.

Chendal recognized the rocking motion. He'd seen it before on her study floor in Barridan. "Cara," he said with exaggerated slowness, "do you know who I am?"

Now she refused to look at him, still moving her body forward and back, wide eyes on the floor.

This was a puzzle, and he wasn't pleased with the shape of the pieces he saw. He sat next to her and gently put his hand on her arm. He knew better than anyone else in the room how reactive she could be. "Cara."

Slowly she looked up at his face, her strange, blue-colored eyes fixed on him. If he was not mistaken, it seemed she didn't even know him. Could that be?

"Cara, what is my name?" he enunciated the words carefully.

No change came to her expression, no recognition in her eyes.

Goddess above, he thought. "A'ke'Taso," he began, turning to his leader, "I believe she may have lost her knowledge of Selandi."

"Truly?" Kenimandil replied slowly, turning to stare at Shisa before coming back to the human. "That is a problem, a'Temaso. And I am not pleased."

Chendal's face closed down in anger as he switched his focus to his partner, still standing off to the side. "What have you done, tem'u?"

Nor did Shisa reply. Her eyes, too, were a little wide.

No one else in Hadaman, indeed in all of Selandan, knew the human language. Mena'hem was back in his town at the see-ess-see, and Andreh' was in residence at Himadi House. "A'ke'Taso, do you have a suggestion?" Chendal asked.

"Was she not teaching Rodani her language in Barridan?"

"Rodani?" Cara repeated, possibly filtering his name from the unknown sounds in Kenimandil's reply.

"Yes, she was. I do not know how much he learned."

"A'ke'Taso," a guardian named Tokennen stepped up from his place at the door. "I would offer to speak with him in the clinic, tell him of this turn of events, and learn what you wish to know."

"Do so."

He bowed and left the room. *Goddess above and Temi below,* Tokennen thought as he walked. It had been thirteen years since he'd last seen Rodani. Time had turned him from a youth to a grown man, but the worn and injured temichi who'd been brought here had shocked him nearly as badly as that human's unhinged reactions had.

Tokennen knew some of what had occurred at Barridan, knew that Rodani had disappeared into the night months ago, and the rumors that move had precipitated, and the search conducted. But the ke'taso was keeping her own counsel on why the pair had been brought here.

The clinic doors stood open at the opposite corner of the ke'taso's quarters in the government house. Tokennen checked in with the admin at the desk and was directed to a nearby room.

Rodani's back had been patched, and he had been turned face up for his other wounds to be tended. A healer stood at his side, palpitating the temichi's midsection. "A'tem," Tokennen said in greeting as he neared.

Rodani pried his eyes open with some effort. "A'Keso."

"Not for many a year," he replied, letting a touch of emotion bleed through his voice. "We have a problem to solve. How much of the human language do you remember?"

"A minimum. Barely conversational. Cara?" Exhausted worry was what his speech projected.

"She has lost her ability to speak Selandi, a'tem. From the blow to her head, it is thought. Can you speak to her?"

"Lost?"

Strange, Tokennen noticed, that Rodani's facial expressions were more pronounced than was wont for an adult Selandu. From pain? From what he had endured in the past year? Either was possible. *Later,* he chided himself. *If there was time.*

"She is distraught, and she seems not to recognize Chendal. She may have lost her memories, as well. I do not know."

"Temi's knives!" Rodani blurted out. "I will beat that sister of mine bloody the first chance I get."

"Calm, a'tem," the healer cautioned. "You need rest...and nourishment."

"Can you walk?" Tokennen asked him.

"He should not," the healer said.

"He is needed, a'sel. Where is the chair that he used earlier?"

The man sighed in frustration. "Behind the door to the clinic."

Tokennen walked out, and rolled it into the room. "As soon as possible, Rodani."

"And what will he wear?" was healer's acerbic reply. "The same filthy clothes he arrived in?"

Tokennen left the room again. When he came back, his arms were filled with black clothes. "I believe these will fit."

Rodani levered his way out of the sickbed and let Tokennen assist him in dressing. When they rolled out of the room, the healer followed.

The first thing Rodani saw as he shuffled into the council room was Cara against the far wall, curled up into a ball on the couch. Chendal and Kenimandil were conferring in undertones at the ke'taso's desk. Since they declined the courtesy of acknowledging his presence, he made his limping way over to her without bowing to them.

"Kia?" he spoke softly.

She unfurled and launched herself at him. He grabbed her arms before she could do too much damage to his wounds and sat her back down on the couch. Gingerly, he sat beside her. She babbled in Cene'l, the words flowing far too fast for him to decipher. He pressed two fingers against her lips and made the guild *stop* motion with his hand. He could only hope she'd remember.

Fortunately, she quieted in his presence. They held each other for a few minutes. ^How you feel?^ he asked.

She pressed her hand against her head. ^It hurts.^

^Where are we?^ he asked her.

She shook her head slowly. ^I don't know.^

At the sound of their Cene'l conversation, Chendal and Kenimandil joined them.

^Where are we?^ she asked.

"Hadaman." Rodani pointed to Chendal. ^You know him? His name?^

She followed his finger, then shook her head again. ^No.^

Rodani looked up at Chendal. "She does not recognize you."

Kenimandil spun around and pointed at Tokennen. "Call Mena'hem."

Tokennen made all haste to a side room where a comm set rested on a table. He flipped one of the switches. "A'Reiti, this is Hadaman. A'Reiti." When no one answered, he repeated the call.

"Hadaman," a young voice replied, "this is the CSC. What is your need?"

"Mena'hem, a'sel. Is he there?"

"A moment, a'tem. Is this an emergency? I'll need to wake him."

"Yes," he responded in a curt voice.

Chendal and Kenimandil crowded into the room. Rodani made haste more slowly, leaning against the door frame as he stopped.

"This is Menachem. With whom do I speak?"

Kenimandil leaned toward the table. "A'Reiti, we need your assistance."

"Of course, a'ke'Taso. What may I do?"

"If someone from the see-ess-see hit their head and lost their knowledge of Selandi, how long would this last? How long before the language returned?"

"From..." There was a pause on the line. "Lost... A'ke'Taso, this is a medical question. I don't have the answer in my hands. I'll have to ask one of our physicians. Is someone there with you?"

Kenimandil waved a hand that Menachem couldn't see. "Please do ask," she said. "And find out any other knowledge we need for this kind of injury."

"It will take the better part of an hour to find an answer, a'ke'Taso. I'll need to walk to the physician, wake her and ask, understand her answer, and return."

"Then begin, please."

"A'ke'Taso."

"Ninety-nine," Tokennen signed out.

A soft plaintive cry came from behind them. Rodani turned, only to see Cara wandering the room looking into faces, calling for him.

Chendal caught up with him as Rodani limped toward her. "That is what she was doing before you returned, a'tem."

Cara saw him heading her way, and ran to meet him, her arms out. Rodani stopped her as he had before. ^Aisu! Where were you?^ She began to babble again in her own language. He motioned her to stop, but she ignored the signal. When he put the fingers against her lips again, she did stop. She knew the latter, but not the former. He thought, *Why?*

^Where are we?^

He looked at her quizzically. "Hadaman." He glanced sideways at Chendal. "A'Temaso, she asked the same question just a short time ago. This sounds like more than language loss."

"Yes," he said, musing on the puzzle before them.

^I'm hungry, aisu. Are you?^ she asked.

Well, that was a thought. His sense of hunger had been blunted by the day's ordeal, and it was heading toward dawn. "A'Temaso, is there a meal to be found? Water, or tea? Neither of us have eaten for more than a day, nor slept since yesterday's dawn."

"Of course, a'tem. Tokennen," he prompted the other guardian.

"A'Temaso."

"Food. Human food, too," Chendal corrected himself. "Drink, no alcohol. Is the bedroom ready?"

"Yes, a'Temaso."

Tokennen left to pass the request onto the kitchens. Rodani put a hand on Cara's shoulder to turn her toward the couch. Her jaw was bruising, and her left temple and eye were red and swelling. "Where did my sister flee to?"

"Let us postpone that confrontation until we have more information, a'tem," Chendal replied.

Cara curled back onto the couch. Rodani thought to correct her improprieties of feet on furniture and rather improper sitting positions, but he found he didn't have the energy. He sat beside her, turning his body so that his shoulder met the seat back instead of the painful wounds Chendal had given him. He'd been spared the harsher punishment his transgressions had earned, and he was grateful. Possibly, Cara's shouted entreaties for lenience had moved the ke'taso. Possibly she had other, different kinds of punishments in mind for him. Or for *them*.

"Your injuries, Rodani?" Chendal prompted him.

From his place on the couch, he tossed the question. "Too numerous to count, a'Temaso, but none that should not heal."

"I am keen to hear your story."

Rodani's half-closed eyes opened up. "If I relate it now, a'Temaso, will I be called to divulge it again to the Council?"

"Likely."

His eyes closed down, giving a minor offense to the guild's highest representative, and one he hoped would be ignored. "I would ask not to tell it twice."

"One question."

"A'Temaso."

"Do you have regrets?"

It was a question he'd asked himself more than once. The answer needed no forethought. "Only for the actions of others. Not my own."

^Aisu,^ Cara said softly. ^Where are we?^

He opened his eyes, then took her hand and closed them again. "Hadaman."

Chendal rose and sought out Kenimandil at her desk. "A'ke'Taso, I am well aware of the urgency, here." He glanced back at the pair on the couch. "But they are exhausted, injured, and hungry. It may be better to let them rest for a time. So that their minds may clear, and their answers be more coherent."

Kenimandil's expression molded into one of enforced patience. "The delay does not please me, a'Temaso. But as I often find, your conclusions make sense."

Chendal lowered himself into one of the chairs before her desk. His rest, as well, had been interrupted by the call from Soldan and again by the imminent arrival of the patrol boat. He was not the only one who wondered where Rodani had gone when he fled Barridan or whether he would be found. No trace of him had ever been uncovered. Then again, he was a guardian. Well trained and even more motivated to escape Kusik's depredations and find his mate. That he had been found at all was a surprise, and where he had been found had been a greater one. But it was no surprise who was there at his side.

Being the temaso, Chendal had found more than his share of women available for whatever attentions he desired in his busy life. But he'd only met one who had been worth enfolding his bonds with and that, only for a time. None of them had been worthy of disrupting his entire world. On occasion, since Rodani's disappearance, he wondered what that felt like.

He glanced over at the unlikely pair on the couch, arms wrapped around each other and dozing in the respite.

A temporary one, he knew.

Tokennen came up behind him. "A'Temaso, the meals are ready. And the room."

"Lead them out, a'tem. See that they have what they need until the ke'taso recalls them."

"A'Temaso."

Not long after, the return call from the CSC came through. Chendal and Kenimandil hastened to answer it.

"Anywhere from little time at all to three or more days, a'ke'Taso," Menachem related. "And that will depend mostly upon how hard they were hit, and how long they lay unconscious. Brain injuries are fraught with variations of all kinds. There is even a chance for death if there is bleeding inside the skull."

Kenimandil's body stiffened, and her mouth pursed into an angry line. "A'Reiti, you are needed here. You will take the next boat north."

There was a pause at the other end, a longer one than usual. "A'ke'Taso."

Kenimandil turned to Chendal. "She must be punished."

TWENTY-FIVE

Voices outside the door woke Rodani. Cara was on the bed next to him, on her side, and turned away from him. He longed to reach for her, to hold her, but he couldn't forget she was injured as well. Would she remember his language when she woke? It disturbed him more than expected to not be able to talk normally with her. Despite—or because of—their many physical enjoyments, they depended so heavily on their ability to work out misunderstandings with discussion that he felt bereft and unsteady without. *Temi's demons, Shisa, could you not hold on to your temper?*

He shifted to get out of bed and felt the burn of his latest punishment on his back. It was a little of nothing compared to what he's endured in Tendiman, but he hoped it was the last punishment he'd face for a time. He combed his hair and pulled on a shirt, thankful they had taken time for a quick wash before retiring. He glanced at his mate. *Sleep,* he wished her.

Voices wafted through the door again, one a speaker with a human accent of the male variety. *Must be the ambassador.* He walked out into the room bright with midday sun, careful to shut the door behind him. The ambassador was rather tall for a human. His head might rise to Rodani's chin, far above the mid-chest where Cara's head would touch. He was slender, his skin and eyes were exceptionally dark, and his lips were full. His curly hair was surprisingly short for being an ambassador. Too short to wear a clip. He stood only a few feet from Chendal, deep in conversation.

Rather than interrupt, Rodani sat on the divan and watched them from a distance. However did humans come to be so varied in color? Skin, hair, eyes, it was a puzzle to him, more so having spent months in the south and seen the diversity firsthand.

"A'Temaso, I can't imagine why I'm being shut away from the knowledge I need to do my duty."

"I understand your agitation, a'Reiti," Chendal replied.

"You do know that a human can go to sleep with a head injury and cross over without ever waking up?"

Rodani froze in alarm at his words.

"It isn't common," Menachem continued, "but it's been known to happen."

Cara. He shot up from the divan, causing a bolt of fire to cross his back—which he ignored for the worse pain flooding his mind. Both men turned to look at him, which he also ignored.

Inside the room, she was lying in the same position. He shut the door, rushed to her side, and bent down.

Au, she is breathing. He could hear it, and see her chest rise and fall. He laid his hand on her cheek, feeling her warmth on his palm. His heartbeat began to lower and his brain to work again.

Cara moved her head under his hand. She turned to look at him, her dark blue eyes unfocused and somnolent. ^Aisu?^

"How do you feel, kia?"

^What?^ She looked around. ^Where are we?^

She spoke Cene'l. Anger began to rise in him, but he beat it down with his will. *She is not the cause.*

^Hadaman, kia.^ He curved his fingers inward. ^Come.^

She slipped out of bed and glanced around the room.

Rodani pulled her only other change of clothes out of her rescue bag and laid them on the bed. It wouldn't do for her to walk out in a guild shirt again. That had caused enough trouble the last time. She managed the clothing change and a trip to the facilities, but was still a bit unsteady on her feet. And she was quiet. Too quiet for any solace in his heart. He opened the door and stood aside.

"Cara!" The disapproval was evident in Menachem's voice, even to Rodani's ears. ^I wondered if it was you. How did you get here?^

"Selandi?" Chendal asked Rodani.

He let his expression flow into displeasure. "Du."

Menachem's gaze flickered between the two men and back to Cara.

^What are you doing here?^ he said in a rapid gait. ^You're not supposed to be here, and certainly not without me.^

She stood in front of him, her posture an unusual slouch.

He tried again. ^Why are you here?^

^I don't know,^ she said slowly, softly.

^What do you mean you don't know? How did you get here? Who brought you? Why are you dressed in rags? What have you done? Did you—^

When Cara hunched her shoulders and covered her ears as she had done during Rodani's punishment, Chendal interrupted. "I suggest, a'Reiti, that you ask one question at a time. She is obviously still confused."

"I need answers," the ambassador replied.

It set off another spate of anger. Rodani stepped up and pulled Menachem aside with a forceful grip on his arm. "You will not berate her, a'Reiti. You will not censure her in any way. Do you understand?"

Menachem's dark eyes opened wide at Rodani's unexpected reproach. He glanced at Chendal, who remained aloof. Rodani shook the arm in his hand. "I am giving this command, a'Reiti, not the temaso."

Menachem looked off in the distance, reconsidering the players in the room. "A'tem," he said stiffly.

After another warning shake, Rodani let go and put a soft hand on Cara's shoulder, urging her to sit. He turned back to Menachem. "One question at a time, a'Reiti. And I *will* discern the tone of your voice, make no mistake."

Another pause, another reevaluation of status. "Do you know why she is here?"

"No."

"How did she arrive?"

"By boat."

"From where?"

Rodani glanced aside in refusal, then back at the ambassador.

Menachem's lips pursed in frustration, his mouth drawn downward. ^Cara, how were you hurt?^

^I don't know.^ She looked at the divan, then sat, a dazed expression on her face.

^Do you remember anything?^

^I don't think so.^

Menachem turned to Rodani. "How long was she unconscious?"

Rodani looked at Chendal for the answer.

"Less than one minute."

"You were there when she was injured?"

"Yes."

"Will you tell me how?"

"Why does it matter?"

"At this point, a'Temaso, I'm not certain what will matter and what won't. What I don't understand is why I'm being barred from information."

Chendal took his time answering. "The ke'taso sets the limits on this situation, a'Reiti."

Menachem ground his teeth against the chiding in Chendal's voice. "And I still don't know why I'm here."

"In the case that we need interpreting." He watched Menachem unsuccessfully hide his frustration. "May I suggest you rest from your trip? You were wakened early."

"I would speak to the ke'taso first, if it wouldn't displease her."

Chendal inclined his head. "I will inquire."

Menachem glanced over at Cara leaning back on the divan, then at Rodani. "May I ask your name, a'tem?"

"Rodani," he replied. Leaning forward, he added, "and I would ask in return that you treat Cara gently."

"You know her?"

"Yes."

Menachem considered the unexpected reply. "May I know how?"

"I was her guardian in Barridan."

"You were called here when she arrived?"

Rodani tossed the question with the wave of his hand.

"Do you know why she's here?"

"I do not."

Menachem walked over to the table and pulled out a chair. "Why was she sent home from Barridan? What really happened?"

Rodani stepped sideways, keeping his body between Cara and the ambassador. "I have not been given permission to discuss that with you."

"I am the ambassador first. I have a need to know."

Rodani considered the truth behind the statement. "Nothing that happened there was her fault."

"Your reassurance is appreciated, a'Rodani. However, it tells me nothing else I need to know."

"I am sorry."

"How did she act there?"

"With honor appropriate to her culture and to ours, as she could." Rodani sat down on the divan, not too close to Cara but not too far.

"Did you have problems with her?"

"Nothing we could not solve."

"May I ask what problems?"

"Restrictions on her movements for security reasons."

Menachem raised his eyebrows. "Nothing else?"

"Yes."

"Can you request permission to discuss it with me?"

"I cannot."

"May I ask why?"

"No."

Crossing his arms, Menachem stretched out his legs and fought to contain his facial expressions. "A'tem, it is difficult for me to believe she is blameless."

Rodani had no trouble folding his expression into a cool stare. "You will not impugn her honor."

Menachem held his gaze for a few moments, the better to express his exasperation. Behind him, Chendal and Tokennen came through the main doors. Tokennen left in the opposite direction, toward the main hall.

Cara stood up and wandered the room, ending up at the doors to the balcony. She pushed against them and walked through. Immediately, Rodani got to his feet and followed her out.

Chendal strolled over to Menachem. "The ke'taso is not prepared to speak with you now, but spoke her appreciation of your presence here. Rest now?"

Menachem glanced pointedly at the closed bedroom door. "My room seems to be occupied."

Chendal waved his hand. "The next room down is available."

Menachem grabbed his bag and walked away.

"Lunch will be served soon, a'Reiti." Chendal said over his shoulder, sauntering to the balcony doors to look out. Unsurprised, he found Rodani and Cara side by side in a lounge chair, arms wrapped around each other. He mused on the nature of interspecies attraction and the perpetual need for touch. Was he satisfying this need for her alone? Or had his own been unveiled in the process? *Au, yes.* He remembered the Council meeting in Tendiman and Rodani's admittance. *Meeting her needs uncovered my own. Let them be*, he told himself. He sat on the divan and stretched out, closing his eyes.

In a short while, someone else entered the room. The tailor. Chendal rose as the man checked the room for a human. "A moment, a'sel," he said.

"A'Temaso."

He stuck his head out the balcony doors. "Rodani, there is a tailor here to measure Cara for clothing."

"A tailor?" he asked quizzically.

"By the ke'taso's orders, a'tem."

Rodani shifted Cara in his arms, waking her from a doze. "Kia." Temporarily forgetting the word for "up," he pulled her to a sit and urged her out of the chair. ^Come.^

Mercifully obedient, she followed his limping form back into the living area and over to the waiting man.

The tailor pulled out a measuring tape and lifted her arm. He measured what he needed as Cara stood mute and uncomplaining. That, if nothing else, demonstrated to Rodani the change in her from the head injury.

When he was finished, the tailor left with a bow. Tokennen took his place in the room, settling into the chair Menachem had vacated. Rodani sat beside him as Cara retreated to the divan.

"How do you fare?" Tokennen asked him.

Several replies crossed his mind before he chose the mannerly one. "Well enough, thank you."

"I hear it was quite a turmoil you precipitated."

There was no answer Rodani could give to that. He stared at his hands resting on the table.

"Was it difficult to leave Barridan?"

"Yes. But less difficult than having my bonded mate wrenched from my arms. And being abused past my endurance," he added.

"A'tem," Tokennen reproved him for his blatant honesty.

"A'Keso," was the firm reply.

"I am not, te'oto."

Rodani glanced at the middle-aged man. "You are still the keso to me. If I could, I would forget Kusik ever existed."

"I grieved much, leaving him behind to run my guild, especially knowing his antipathy for you."

"Do you know why?"

"I do not. When we argued, he would only say you were not worthy of guild training because you were a crafter. I saw the fire and ice in you. He did not...or he ignored it for his own reasons."

"When he dies, I will spit on his ashes."

Tokennen scrutinized him closely. "If you live that long."

Rodani gazed out through the balcony doors on the other side of the table. "Maybe I will take him with me."

"Then how will you spit on him?"

Rodani turned to him, and found him smiling. "I would give that honor to Cara, I suppose."

They sat in silence for a few minutes, then Tokennen spoke.

"How is the taso?"

Rodani considered. "The last I saw of her, she was still grieving Timan and adjusting to her new circumstances. It was not an easy task for her."

"Will she abide?"

"I am certain. As long as I've known her, she has always projected strength."

"That she did."

The clatter of food trays interrupted their conversation. They left the table to the servants, and Rodani stopped in front of Cara, who was again napping.

"Kia," he tapped her knee. ^Lunch.^

"You know her language," Tokennen judged as Cara rose from the divan.

"Not nearly enough."

Menachem came out of his room, and the five of them sat around the table. Rodani helped Cara into a chair that was, of course, too tall for her. Chendal sat at the head, being highest ranking. Cara then Rodani sat at his right, and Menachem, then Tokennen at his left.

"Cara should be at your other side," Menachem said, nodding to Rodani.

"Her left hand is dominant," he replied, his tone sharp.

Chastened, Menachem glanced away. "A'tem."

Dishes were passed. "Not that one, kia." Rodani took a red bowl and spoon away from her. Without a word she watched him take a serving from the bowl and pass it across to Tokennen.

Menachem set a serving plate down in front of him. "Why do you call her by that name, a'tem?"

Rodani tapped Cara's fork. By custom, they had waited for her to begin eating. But in her confusion, she'd forgotten. She took a bite, and the rest began their meal.

"May I ask again, a'tem?"

Silently, Rodani chided himself for his lapse. No one had given him a clue as to what the ambassador knew or was supposed to know. He tossed the question. "A simple term of companionship, a'Reiti."

Menachem looked doubtful—no, *distrustful*—to Rodani's eyes. Likely, the ambassador understood the intimate mode of Selandi, or at least some of it. Rodani let the ensuing conversations pass him by. Cara picked at her food.

Rodani watched her carefully, noting her lack of appetite. He slipped her fork from her lax hand, stabbed a piece of vegetable, and held it in front of her. Silently, obediently, she opened her mouth.

Rodani continued the caretaking, in between his own bites, for as long as she seemed willing.

Chendal watched, amused. "Why, Rodani?"

He glanced at the temaso in confusion. "She needs to eat, a'Temaso. We ran low on food during the later months and, unrealized by me, she went without enough food to make sure I had what my larger size needed. She lost weight." Another bite, another acceptance. "I will not let her go without again, if I can."

The meal wound down into nibbles and sips.

^Cara.^

She looked up from her half-eaten food at Menachem. Rodani felt his protective instincts rise.

^There have been some unexplained deaths in the south recently. Had you heard?^

^I don't think so.^

^There was a preacher killed.^

^What preacher?^

Rodani noted Cara's unfocused eyes, her slow speech. But he didn't understand the ambassador's words.

^In Lordstown.^

She blinked. ^Was I in Lordstown?^

Those words, Rodani knew. He sat up straighter, alert. Watchful, his gaze bounced between the two.

^Were you?^ Menachem asked, suspicion in his tone.

^I don't know. Why would I do that?^

Menachem voiced a sigh and rested his forearms on the table. Rodani relaxed, marginally, his own sigh released unheard.

When the meal was cleared, Rodani and Chendal played Tasos and Temichin. Tokennen left on his own errands, and Menachem wrote in his notebook. Cara lay down on the divan.

After a couple of hours, a man stepped out of the double doors that led to the Council audience room. "A'Rodani," he called out.

Rodani looked up from the cards in his hand.

"The ke'taso will speak to you now."

He glanced at Chendal across the table from him, but the temaso didn't acknowledge the summons. Rodani followed the man into the room. *Calm*, he bade himself. *Maybe you will learn the reason for your presence here.*

Halfway into the room, Rodani bowed as deeply as he had before.

"A'Rodani."

At the summons, he took a seat in front of Kenimandil. With a wave of her hand, she emptied the room of all other occupants.

They were alone.

"How do you fare, a'tem?"

"Improving, a'ke'Taso. I thank you."

Kenimandil sat forward in her chair, arms on her desk. Rodani didn't know whether to be heartened or disturbed by the intense focus on him.

"I received more than a handful of reports from Barridan— before you abandoned your duty."

Calm, he bade himself. *Be calm.*

"And I wish to hear of this affinity in your own words, not someone else's."

Rodani thought for a moment. "Is there any part of this you wish me to concentrate on, a'ke'Taso? Any portion of particular interest to you?"

"Begin with an overview. How and why."

Rodani took a deep breath. This was no difficulty. He'd done it more than once. In a hand of minutes, he was finished.

"I will ask you some questions, and I must have honest answers from you. In return, I offer you a guarantee of confidentiality. Do you accept?"

Do I have a choice? "Yes, a'ke'Taso."

"How well do the two of you communicate?"

"It takes a great deal of effort, a'ke'Taso, due to our differing languages, thought processes, assumption, and cultures. Even though one may ask a question that seems clear, and the other may seem to answer clearly, it is still far too easy to misunderstand. It takes more time, more energy, more patience, and many more words."

"How well do you compromise?"

Rodani paused a moment. "Well enough, once we have taken the time to communicate as best we can."

"So, you have not found any unsolvable problems?"

"I have not, a'ke'Taso. If it would not offend, I would suggest you ask her the same question. However, if she does not regain her Selandi knowledge, that might be the first unsolved."

"Do you have regrets about this affinity?"

"One may have regrets, a'ke'Taso, and still believe he made the correct decisions."

Kenimandil rolled open her palm for him to continue.

"I regret the deaths in Barridan," he said slowly, eyes lowered. "I regret leaving there after being forced to choose between my home and my bonded mate. I do not regret the affinity."

"Do you see, or otherwise sense, this affinity fading or ending in the near term?"

"No, a'ke'Taso. And I would fight to save it."

"Where were you going when you both were taken?"

"We were first going south to retrieve the boat we left behind at our camp. Then we had discussed the possibility of moving west of their town, in the Himadi foothills. But we had not decided."

"You planned to live isolated for the rest of your lives?"

"We had not directly discussed that, a'ke'Taso. It remained a possibility, but I cannot give an estimate for it. However, I would deeply regret a need for us to break the affinity." He bent his head, then raised it up. "It was painful enough to have it broken for me in Barridan. To be forced to choose to break it myself would be much worse."

"Do you plan to remain in the guild?"

"Yes, a'ke'Taso, if I am not removed from it."

"Would you object to resuming guardian duties?"

"No, a'ke'Taso, if I were allowed to remain with Cara. If I may be presumptuous, it would please us both to be allowed to remain here, assuming she regains her language skills."

"When you were in the south, did you spend much time with any other humans?"

"No real time of any worth, a'ke'Taso. We both knew it was dangerous for anyone to know I was there illegally. There were a few I met for very short periods of time."

"What did you think of the humans, both singly and as a group?"

"Singly, they were much like Selandu. Quite varied in temperament and attitude. Two were curious and respectful. Three were heinous and violent. I hesitate to describe them as a group or species, except on a few points."

"And those points are?"

"Their volatile emotions, and willingness to act upon them rather than rational thought. The extremely high mating drive of the majority of their men, as Cara related to me, may make a greater amount of sexual coercion or violence possible. To be impartial, she also assures me that there are many honorable men among them. Humans can work together for a common goal as we can, but many have a tendency toward extreme individualism."

"In what ways?"

Rodani held up a finger. "If I may have time to think..." He considered quietly, as Kenimandil waited. "Many ways, I believe, a'ke'Taso. In their speech, in the clothes they wear and the way they wear their hair, in their spiritual beliefs. I found the differences in cultures between the northern town and the southern one to be exceptionally surprising. They are very different."

"More different than Hadaman and Diregi Valley?"

"I believe so, a'ke'Taso," he said slowly. "But as I have not visited Ushando's estate, I may be mistaken. Please forgive me."

"Did you find them patient or impatient?"

"What little I saw directly, a'ke'Taso, I can only say both."

"And their intelligence?"

"Again, both. They did make it to space."

"And their honor? And her allegiance?"

"I did not spend the amount of time needed to learn of any human's honor besides Cara. Hers—leans more toward the personal. By that, I mean her allegiance is toward me and her brother, rather than her family group or her town's taso, or her species as a whole. And her honor is personal as well. She seems to have decided on her own what ethical standards she will abide by, and fight for, instead of automatically adopting those of the leaders of her people."

"And what are those standards?"

"Her standards, a'ke'Taso, can vary by situation. But generally, she will not lie, and would be deeply offended if she found that I lied to her. And as I agree with her, we have no problem on that issue. She tells me others have much fewer qualms with lying than she.

"She is, in almost all circumstances, opposed to violence in all its forms. Only when she or someone she is bonded to is directly threatened or has been hurt by someone will she resort to it.

"She requests or demands as many facts as possible before forming an opinion or making a decision. And again, after our problems in Barridan, I agree with her because decisions made on fears instead of facts can cause extremely poor decisions to be made."

"That is not too different from us, a'tem."

"Yes, but I believe there is a quantitative difference. A difference of degree, or strength."

"Continue."

"She firmly believes that many freedoms of individuals are of equal importance to societal needs. She understands the necessity of cooperation in a group for survival and safety, but she is also adamant that individuals be allowed to make many decisions and choices that may go against the group culture—until the point where it begins to threaten the safety or survival of the group directly."

"Can you elaborate? What freedoms?"

"Many, a'ke'Taso. Some we also abide by, and some we tend to restrict."

"As in?"

"As I mentioned, clothing and hair choices. Religious and spiritual choices, including the choice to believe none of them. Choices of who to associate with and give allegiance to. Choices not only of a vocation, but how many. One, five, it is very much a personal choice. I found myself very surprised when she told me my choice of both guild and craft was not only acceptable among her people, but it was somewhat common.

"Another freedom that surprised me was the freedom to criticize their leaders, in private and in public. Unless violence is threatened, there is no noticeable dishonor or punishment in the act. At most, one may induce verbal censure from others who disagree."

"Did she criticize Arimeso while in Barridan?"

"No. However, she was exceptionally critical of Kusik."

"Why?"

"For the disrespect with which he treated me, and herself. She also personally believes that the women of her people should have free choice as to whether to have children or not, and that is surprising only because most of her fellow humans are adamant that as many children as possible be born, to keep their species alive on the planet.

"I would add, though, as I mentioned the vast differences between the north and south town cultures, that Cara seemed to be easily allowed these ethical stances and freedoms much more in her northern town than she would have been in the south. From what little I know of the southern town, it is extremely restrictive in many of those things Cara professes to believe in. She would not fare well in that town."

"Does she have leadership qualities?"

Rodani let a small smile cross his face. "She certainly led me down paths I never thought to ride, a'ke'Taso. Please forgive my levity."

Kenimandil tossed his apology. "Is there anything else you wish to tell me of you, your mate, and the affinity?"

Rodani thought before answering. "I would not be parted from her, a'ke'Taso, unless I were physically prevented. I would rather we returned to the forest and the streams than be without her. I will not return to Barridan as long as Kusik abides there. I would need to speak with Cara first, but I would not be opposed to an attempt to live on another estate—if we would not be unwelcome there. I believe Cara would not find much difficulty under Farran's hand, since she has indicated an interest in and respect for science."

"Does she have skills or training for it?"

"No, a'ke'Taso. Although she might take advantage of such training if it were offered. Her father is a scientist, and her mother a master healer."

"Her level of intelligence?"

"Fairly high."

"And her emotional stability?"

"Moderate, a'ke'Taso. If you had asked me that in Barridan, I would have answered 'low.' However, after spending five months with her in her own land, where she had much more control over her own life and decisions, her emotional maturity rose noticeably. And through some unknown luck or direction, I am almost invariably able to calm her upsets and redirect her emotions into more reasoned thoughts.

"We each bring out something in the other that makes us better or more contented people, a'ke'Taso. I value that gift greatly."

Kenimandil leaned back in her chair and regarded him thoughtfully. "Your appraisals are appreciated, a'tem. You have been of great assistance."

Rodani bowed his head. "A'ke'Taso," he said, then hesitated. "May I ask?"

"No, a'tem. I must speak with Cara, and I have things to consider. Keep me apprised of her memory and language status. You may return."

Rodani limped back to the living area. Cara was still asleep on the divan. Chendal had procured an overstuffed chair, and rested in it comfortably slouched with his legs outstretched.

"The ambassador?" Rodani asked him.

"Resting."

Rodani slid into one of the table chairs. "Did he say aught about us, or the situation?"

"Nothing to mention. He may be waiting for Cara to improve."

Rodani gazed out the balcony doors and tried to relax his stiffened muscles. "I could say the same, a'Temaso."

"What will you do if she does not?"

He closed his eyes against the pain. "I am not ready to think it. I wish we could hasten the process."

"It has been less than a day, a'tem. Patience."

"I need something to occupy my mind. Or my hands. Or both."

Chendal folded his hands on his waist. "Have you seen the healers today?"

"No." He got up and inclined his head. "Thank you. If you would, please watch over Cara."

By the time he returned from the clinic, Cara was awake, and so was Menachem. They were seated on the either end of the divan, the ambassador facing her, and Cara facing outward wearing a painfully empty expression.

"Eshi'nu atamai colasa, Cara?" he asked her.

"Du," Menachem replied. "She does not."

Rodani wandered the room, at a loss for what to do. He thought to seek out Shisa, who had not put in an appearance since he returned from the clinic before dawn. But no, he wasn't ready for that confrontation. He needed to know his mate's final status first. If she did not improve... He shied away from finishing the sentence in his own mind. To be torn between the only two bonds left to him, mate and sister, was another pain he didn't need. Arimeso, bond broken. Kimasa, broken. Serano, broken. Father, broken. Mother, badly damaged. Brother, severed. It was no wonder he clung more tightly to Cara since he'd forsaken Barridan.

Eventually, dinner was brought up, but it ended as a replay of lunch. Other than his energy-draining meeting with Kenimandil, the day was a wash. He berated himself for his pessimism, reminding himself that he was—seemingly—safe among his own people instead of a captive of violent humans, and that Cara was alive and hopefully on the mend.

But there were too many unknowns. It brought to mind his last days at Barridan, not knowing whether he would survive Kusik's depredations or successfully reunite with Cara. *Abide, fool. Your hands are empty of tools and your knowledge deficient, but that is temporary. You are guild.*

Waking up in the morning brought no relief to his worries or Cara's injury. Only a set of basic clothes from the tailor for Cara. He took them and thanked him, then ushered Cara back in the bedroom. At least she hadn't forgotten how to dress herself.

Breakfast arrived, and four people took their places, with Tokennen being absent.

"What will you do today, a'tem?" Chendal asked.

Rodani tapped Cara's plate to encourage her to eat. "Walk the floor."

"You should practice your skills. You might have neglected them recently."

"Stealth and hunting skills weren't neglected. Fighting, yes."

"There were other skills you practiced too, aisu," Cara said with a smile.

Rodani turned and stared at his mate, then at Chendal, whose eyes were similarly wide. *Could it be?* His heart thudded. "Eshi'nu atamai colasa?" he asked, fearing the answer.

Her expression turned quizzical. "Sai. Of course. Why not?"

Chendal shot out of his chair, but Rodani held a hand up to stop him. "Cara, do you know where you are?"

She looked at the three people around her, then the room. She climbed down from her chair and went to the balcony doors. In a few moments she returned to her seat, unsteady on the rungs. Rodani held out a hand for her. "Hadaman?" she guessed.

"Do you remember how we got here?"

Her eyes went sharp with concentrated thought, and Rodani felt a wave of relief wash over him. *Wait, a'tem. See what happens next.*

"I'm not sure."

"What is your last memory?"

She raised her shoulders, a gesture he recognized.

"Do you remember Lordstown?"

"Yes."

"Do you remember leaving the camp with your brother?"

"In a boat?" she asked.

"Yes."

Now her eyes grew as large as everyone else's. "To—" She stared at Rodani as if seeing him for the first time. She grabbed for his arm.

"Calm, kia. Calm. Think it through."

Her expressions flew through various permutations, then her hands covered her mouth. Rodani guessed at what she was remembering, and rubbed his hand up and down her back. "Kia. What came next? Follow it forward."

She stared at her plate, then gasped and patted Rodani's back. "How badly are you hurt?" She turned and glared at Chendal with a ferocity Rodani was pleased to see. "Aisu?" she prompted him.

"I am healing. How do you feel?"

She thought for a moment. ^Okay.^ "I guess. Why are we here?"

"That is still unanswered."

"Is someone going to fill me in?" Menachem complained. "What are you remembering, Cara?"

Chendal walked out of the room with unusual haste.

"No," Rodani told her.

She rubbed her mouth and chewed on a knuckle, but didn't reply to Menachem.

"Cara," he said sharply.

Rodani put his hand on her forearm and squeezed. Not too hard, but enough to give a warning.

"Cara. Answer me!"

"I don't think I can right now, Menachem."

He stood up and leaned over the table. "You owe me, Cara. You came here without my knowledge or permission, not to mention causing me to be recalled long before my next visit was due."

"A'Reiti," Rodani interjected.

"You disobeyed the rules you promised to follow when you entered the CSC, and have caused who knows what problems I have to face in the future!"

Rodani stood up and leaned into Menachem. "A'Reiti, you will cease harassing Cara."

"You do not hold my leash, a'tem," he replied with gritted teeth. "This is a human issue."

"And you are on Selandu land, in a Selandu house, and governed by a Selandu taso who had her brought here." Rodani leaned closer. "I suggest you step back before I turn this human issue into a guild one."

The heated tableau was interrupted by Chendal's return. "What is this?" He returned to his place at the table and stood behind his chair.

"A disagreement, a'Temaso," Rodani replied. "Of the discourtesies offered to Cara now that she has regained her memories."

Chendal turned to her. "Cara, the ke'taso needs to speak with you. Is your mind clear enough to hold a conversation with her?"

"Can Rodani be with me?"

"No."

She stared at Rodani with an expression he recognized well. *Fear.* "Kimasa's robe," he said softly. "Put it on, and do not take it off until you are back with us."

Nodding, she rose.

"Do you remember where she is?" Chendal asked.

She pointed to the far double doors. "There?"

"Yes."

"Bow when you are halfway to her desk, kia. Bow low."

^Okay.^

When she walked through the doors, Rodani carried a chair over to the doorway and sat. The former occupants retreated as they had done in his meeting, and the doors were shut.

Rodani willed away his angst as best he could, given the circumstances. His keen hearing brought no words to him. Nor, as he waited, were there any raised voices. It reassured him. He assumed she would be asked similar questions as were asked of him, but betting on a taso's actions was not a profitable strategy. *Courtesy, kia. Patience. Control. Our future is yet to be in our hands, if it ever will be.*

In less time than he expected, a pair of slippered footsteps neared the door, and it opened. When the ke'taso appeared, Rodani stood at attention with his face blanked of expression.

"A'tem, come in. Be seated."

TWENTY-SIX

Rodani followed Kenimandil up to her desk and sat down next to Cara's right hand. He glanced at her, and she returned it with no expression except in her eyes. They both faced forward, silent. Waiting.

Kenimandil regarded them both with a sober look. "A'tem, a'sel, I have a problem. You may be of assistance to me. I have attempted to make the most fitting decisions that I could, given the knowledge I have. But events have thwarted me.

"I have had searchers out for you for many weeks, a'tem, but you were nowhere to be found. I could not search for a'Cara, as she was outside my sphere of command. By the grace of the goddess, the evening before yesterday, word reached me that a Selandu man and human woman were found together south of the border. After being given their identities, I ordered them brought to me immediately. You both were recognized by the temaso, and brought inside. The rest of the unfortunate circumstances of that night," she looked at Cara, "are remembered by both of you.

"A'sel'ai, the endeavor at Himadi is not progressing in a satisfactory manner. I am not placing blame on Ambassador Andreh', but the difficulties continue to surmount, despite his efforts to contain them. There are innumerable arguments, daily fights, disruptions in the progress we had hoped for the researchers, and an overall distrust between the two species.

"I thought that adding more guardians to the house might contain the turmoil, but those already there believe that is not the answer I seek. I re-read the reports of your affinity in Barridan, and thought you might be the answer I was seeking.

"I am well aware that neither of you have experience in a situation such as Himadi, but neither does anyone else. So, I am of a mind to install you, a'Cara, as the taso of Himadi House, with the assumption that you will choose Rodani as your keso. My belief is that you, together, can prove beyond misgivings, beyond distrust, that the two species can indeed live and work together in peace." She paused a moment.

"What are your thoughts?"

Shocked to the core, Cara sat wordless. Rodani sat still, waiting to see if she would find her voice. As the presumptive taso, she would be making the final decision. She drew her hands to her mouth, her eyes darting in many directions.

"A'ke'Taso," she said with her hands back in her lap. "May I please have time to think?"

"Yes. This is not a decision to take lightly."

^Understatement of the decade,^ she muttered. "I can see only far enough ahead to know that he and I would need two different discussions. One, to decide what questions to ask you first, and two, to make our decision. And we'll have to come to an agreement one way or another. Neither of us will force a decision on the other. Is it acceptable to you that we talk first, return with questions, then talk again?"

"Yes."

"When do you need the decision, a'ke'Taso?"

"Last month."

Cara chuckled, then sobered. "A future time, please?"

"Today, if possible, a'Cara. Tomorrow if necessary."

"It's evening already. I really don't know how long it will take us." She inclined her head in courtesy. "But I understand your haste."

Kenimandil opened her palm, as an entreaty or a goad, Cara couldn't tell.

"A'ke'Taso, if it would not offend—as I have no wish to ever offend you, is there a place here where Rodani and I could talk in privacy? Without being overheard?"

"Yes. Go to the anteroom and ask the temaso to lead you to the Room of Solitude. You should be comfortable there."

"Thank you, a'ke'Taso. Your courtesy for our needs is greatly appreciated." Cara glanced at Rodani, who began to rise from his chair. Thankful she didn't have to guess the courtesies, she mirrored him. Rodani opened the door for her, and motioned to Chendal as she walked out.

"The Room of Solitude, please, a'Temaso."

Chendal led them to a room several doors down the hall. It held some overstuffed chairs, cushions on the floor, a tea set, and a facility on one side. He shut the door behind them.

"Aisu," Cara said with a whisper of anxious laughter in her voice, "am I dreaming?"

Rodani pulled two of the floor cushions across from each other, and sat on one. "If you are, I am as well." He patted the cushion in front of him. "Before we speak of anything else, kia, you did well. Exceptionally well. I am proud of you."

"Thank you," she said on an exhale, and sat down. "That means a lot. I was petrified."

Rodani smiled, but his hands wandered over the cushion and down his pant legs. "I would be ashamed to admit my emotions."

"You know you don't have to hide them from me."

"Yes," he admitted softly. "What are your thoughts?"

"Remember the first time you asked me that?"

An authentic smile appeared. "Let us save that for another time."

Cara flipped her hair around and began fidgeting with it. "I'm procrastinating, aisu."

"I am aware."

She clasped her hands together and brought them to her mouth. "My first thought is I won't do it without you. Either we both get on this boat, or neither."

"Agreed. Next?"

"Questions!" she blurted. "We're supposed to be writing down questions." She threw her hands out, grasping air. "I need paper. My notebook—or yours."

"A moment." He rose and left the room, returning in a scant few minutes with his notebook in hand. "What questions do you have?"

"What happens if we say no?"

Rodani began to write. The Selandi script looked strange upside down.

Focus, fem. "If we say yes, when would we leave here?"

She continued. "Will Andrew be there to show us around?"

"Will we travel by boat or overland?"

Rodani answered that one. "By benatac, singly, likely with two more drawing a wagon. The distance is much greater to go to Soldan by boat first, then cross over."

"Okay. Is there anything we need to bring with us?"

And again, "When Andrew leaves, who will be left behind to assist us? Or are we completely on our own?"

"In what way?" Rodani asked.

"Um, knowledge of the house, and of the people, and of the problems and the solutions already tried, that kind of thing."

"Andrew should share that with us."

Cara sighed. "Yeah, but if I know Andrew, he's going to be enraged that he's being kicked out—and that I'm replacing him. He may not help at all, or he may tell us lies."

Rodani's eyebrows raised. "Truly?"

"For sure, no. Very possibly, yes. He doesn't approve of me."

"Why?"

"Because he and I had an affinity, and it didn't end well."

Now his dropped jaw joined his raised eyebrows. "And you only tell me now? Kia?"

She laughed ruefully, and waved her hands between them. "On a day-to-day basis, it never mattered, aisu. I didn't hide it to offend you. It only matters now because of the circumstance we're facing. But I don't think he'll cooperate."

"Are there any more secrets you should share now?"

"Not that I can think of." She patted his knee.

"Will I hear more later?"

"Well, you still have a few. Don't you?"

"None that matter for what we're considering."

"Then we're even. What questions do you have?"

"I am too busy writing and pondering yours, kia."

She scratched her head and picked at her nails in anxiety. "How much power will I have there?"

"As much as any taso."

"You mean life and death type power?"

"Essentially, yes."

"Over Selandu as well as humans?"

"Of course."

"Oh, the humans won't like that." *And maybe the Selandu won't either*, she thought with some dismay.

Rodani's voice deepened. "They either accept it, or you send them home, kia. There is no other option."

"Oh, gods," she said suddenly. "What happens to you and me if we fail?"

Puzzled, Rodani said, "Do you mean punishment?"

"Well, that too, but I was thinking about where we would go. Where else we could live."

"If Himadi stayed open, we might live there as well, with reduced duties. If it closes, your assumptions are as valid as mine. And I have no assumptions," he added.

"That needs an answer, Rodani. It matters to us."

"It should be asked cautiously and courteously."

"Then you ask it. You'll do it better." She rested her forehead on her fingertips, then looked up in alarm. "You will be my keso, won't you?"

He paled in embarrassment. "Assuming you say yes to the ke'taso, I would be honored."

"Good." She reached for his hands. "Help me not assume too much too quickly, aisu."

"I will endeavor."

She blew out a breath. "What other questions? How many Selandu are there? How many humans? How many guardians? What if we need more? Are more people expected, or are they all there? Do I have the right to admit more?"

"Slow your thoughts a moment, kia."

She began to rock again.

"Continue."

"What rules from the Council will I be expected to follow?"

"What will they consider a success, and how long will we have to reach it?"

"Where will we get the money to make any changes needed?"

"And, is that enough questions to allow us to make a decision?"

They paused to reflect, taking turns glancing at each other.

"Are we ready?" she asked.

"As best we can be at this moment, I believe," he admitted.

Heart in her throat, Cara knocked on the meeting room door, Rodani behind her. They were waved entry, and took the same chairs they'd sat in before.

Some questions were simple to answer. They would leave as soon as possible. Andrew would be told to orient them when they arrived, and they should ask him who his admins were. They need only bring what they brought from the south. She will have the same responsibilities and power as any taso; Rodani and others will help her know what those are, as needed. There are twelve humans and twenty-one Selandu at this date. Two guardians and two sheriffs. If they need more guardians, they contact Chendal. They have permission to ask Tokennen if he wishes to offer his allegiance and attach himself to her house.

Other questions were not so simple.

"What happens if we believe we shouldn't take this duty?"

"I could consider installing Mena'hem," Kenimandil told her, "but he does not wish it. I would rather appoint someone who accepts it freely. I might possibly find someone among my staff here, but neither of these options solves the largest problem I see—which I explained to you in the previous meeting. That is why you are here."

"Are more people of either species expected, or are they all there?"

"All those who petitioned and were accepted have arrived."

"Do I have the right to admit more?"

"You do, with one rule you must follow. They must actively work toward the betterment of your house and its priorities. No freefloaters. None who will not do necessary work."

"Are visitors allowed?"

"They are, but only temporarily. No more than two weeks, or you must return them to their homes. And remember, the more visitors you allow, the more expenses your house incurs."

"That brings up another question, a'ke'Taso, one that may seem ignorant. But I have no knowledge of how a new house would function. Where will we get the money to pay the people who are working? And money to make any additions or changes needed? To my knowledge, no one would yet be selling goods or services to other houses."

"Your house will be funded by taxes and donations. There are also gardens and fields being created for the future."

Cara inclined her head in acceptance, as she must. "That tells me a few things, a'ke'Taso. One, money will be scarce. Two, the amount of money will not be predictable. Both those say that we dare not overspend. It seems to me that while most of the researchers there should work on rebuilding technology, some should also work on items that our societies need and would be willing to purchase from us."

"Such as?"

"Medicines, unusual and interesting clothing, jewelry, and foods, wines and other spirits, and some of the technology that is recreated. Any kind of useful or beautiful items that people might wish to buy."

"That must be of secondary importance," Kenimandil said firmly. "It is not the reason Himadi was founded."

"Yes, a'ke'Taso. I understand. But eventually, if successful, it would lessen the financial burden on both countries, and possibly make Himadi self-sufficient. That also seems a worthy goal."

"It must not interfere with your primary objectives."

A breath caught in Cara's throat. "A'ke'Taso," she said haltingly, "I just had a difficult thought. What happens if a later ke'taso decides Himadi isn't worthy of the time and expense, and decides to close it down?"

"I had considered that," Kenimandil replied. "I may find a way to hold later ke'tasos to the agreement, or they may force you to be released from the use of tax funds. I am not certain at this time."

"That would be very harmful to the house, a'ke'Taso, and almost certainly make it fail if it happened."

"Yes."

Cara had to take a deep breath after that one. "What other rules will I be given from the Council?"

"Do not resign without allowing us an opportunity to find a replacement. Do not give us reason to think you are purposely harming the success of your house or failing by intent. Do not over-use house funds for your personal status or comfort, or any other use detrimental to its success. Be neither irresponsible nor corrupt."

"Understood, a'ke'Taso. I agree with all those rules. What will you consider a success to be, and how long will we be given to reach it?"

"This type of success is incremental, a'Cara. I am not certain there is a definition that will fit. Progress is what we will watch for."

"If truly necessary, may we contact you for advice or assistance?"

"Yes. I encourage you to use your inner circle as a resource first. But if their advice is insufficient, you may ask me."

"Thank you, a'ke'Taso. This next one is a difficult question, a personal one, and we have no wish to offend you. May I ask?"

"Yes."

"What happens to Rodani and me if we don't succeed?"

Kenimandil focused on her hands in front of her, thinking. "If you truly use your best efforts, accept advice, work diligently, and still fail, you would at least deserve a place where you can remain together if you still wish to. At this time, I do not know where that place would be."

Cara bowed her head. "Thank you, a'ke'Taso, for your consideration. We greatly appreciate it. We both hope that won't be necessary. If we decide to take this duty, it will be with all seriousness and diligence." She looked back up at Kenimandil's direct gaze. "Is there anything you would wish to add, or advise us of before we decide?"

"No."

Both Cara and Rodani rose and bowed. "Thank you for your patience, a'ke'Taso, and for all your answers," she said.

Alone again, face to face and knee to knee. She couldn't quite look at Rodani directly, not yet.

"Aisu, there's one question I need to ask, and it's the most difficult."

"Cease rocking, kia. Breathe."

He might have a smile on his face, but she didn't want to look. She held herself still and stared at his chest. "Can you obey me?"

He paused, either thinking or giving a warning. "Will you listen closely to my advice? Especially if I tell you it is truly important?"

"If I answer you first, will you answer me?"

"Yes."

"Then yes, I'll have to listen if I want to make good decisions."

"And I will obey you. Please remember that the consequences of your decisions will affect not only us both but the whole of Himadi House."

She took that deep breath he'd suggested. "Now that we've gotten past that sticky part, on to the next. Do you truly want to do this?"

"Will you look at me, kia?"

She glanced up at him, into the face she loved so much. He wasn't angry, he was measuring her—her attitude, her emotions.

"My answer will depend partly upon yours," he added. "Do you wish for this?"

Her lips stretched, but she didn't know if it was a grin or grimace. "You first. I answered first the last time."

Rodani did smile. "Sometimes your exactitude surpasses even mine, kia. Answering honestly, I do not wish for it. But I would accept it, honor the reasons, and do the duties needed."

"What are your wishes and not wishes?"

"We will be able to live openly and in relative comfort for as long as it lasts. But the responsibilities will be tremendous—on us both. Time, energy, tasks, patience, focus, knowledge...and lives will be in your hands. Now, your answer."

Well, that was clear. "So, we feel the same. What will push us toward an answer if we both do and don't want this?"

Rodani squeezed her hands. "More questions, first. I must ask this one: will you accept my security restrictions? Likely, you will not be able to walk the house or its environs alone."

She thought that one through. "Yes...if I can go out when I want or need to, and it's only a matter of asking you or one of your guardians to go with me. And I have one: can and will you be patient with other humans as you are with me?"

Now, it was Rodani's turn to pause. "That will depend on what they say or do, but I will certainly try. Be warned, kia, that I will not be patient with anyone disrespecting you or threatening you in any way."

Cara chuckled. "I can see that. But you'll need to give them a chance to learn. I doubt Andrew would have expected the same level of courtesy and obedience that you'll want for me."

"They will need to learn quickly."

"Some do and some don't, aisu. Your impatience will have to be on a case-by-case basis."

"We will endeavor together."

"That we will, my mate. Another one: knowing what you do about the running of a house, what tasks do you expect to do?"

"That is difficult to discern at this point," Rodani told her. "Himadi is a small house right now, and we will not have many extra professionals to assist. We both may do some of nearly everything."

"Will we be doing our own cooking, cleaning, and clothes washing, too?"

"Those are not tasks for a taso, kia. So, no. But I do not know who will."

"I don't suppose Hamman wants to leave. Would she recommend someone she trusts?"

Rodani tilted his head. "That is a useful idea. I should contact Arimeso."

"Um," she hesitated, lowering her gaze, and took his hands in hers. "Try not to be offended by this one, aisu, but...you won't become like Kusik, will you?"

He looked off to the side, mouth pursed. "I am trying not to be offended."

"So that means no?"

"Yes."

Cara started laughing, as much from stress relief as the language. "That's one of those answers I have to double-check. So you answered 'Yes, I will not become another Kusik,' right?"

"Yes. But remember, if there are punishments to be done, it will be my duty to perform them."

"But I'm the one who decides the punishment. Yes?"

"After you listen closely to my advice, yes."

"I'm not going to want to have my people of either species flogged. Will you help me find other ways to teach and discipline them and help them adjust?"

"I can only repeat the same answer—after you listen to me, first."

She brought their hands to her forehead, more overwhelmed than ever. "Can we really do this, aisu?"

"In truth," he spoke slowly, "I believe we have advantages that the ambassador did not, so we have a chance. However, what level of success or satisfaction we will find, I do not know."

"So, you trust me for this." She moved their hands down, and gazed at him.

"I trust you to stop and listen to me, as you have many times before, take in advice from others, and then make the most appropriate decision you can. Neither of us will lack for mistakes, kia."

Cara glanced over the room, and down at their clasped hands. "Every day will be different, and every situation will be different. Every problem."

"At first, very much so. Later, there may come some settling, some accommodation."

"I wonder what they'll think of us?"

Rodani gave her a side-eye look. "It sounds as if you've decided."

"I thought it sounded like we'd decided."

He put his hands on her arms and looked in her eyes. "Make the decision, kia. I default to you on this."

She started to rock, then stopped. "I believe in what the house stands for...and what they're trying to do. So, let's go."

"I will follow you."

Cara's heart dropped at his response, his acceptance, his belief in her. To have earned such a level of trust from a guardian, a loved one— it strengthened her, and terrified her as well. If she hadn't already been sitting down... "Breathe, breathe," she told herself, drawing a smile from him.

"Okay. I gotta get up. I can do this." She pushed up to her feet. Ever graceful, Rodani stood first, and held out a hand for her.

Instead, she raised her arms. He picked her up and held on as tightly as she did. When he put her down, he said, "Know, kia, that the ke'taso will expect to hear that it was your decision, not mine, or even ours. Only yours."

"Okay. Anything else I should know?"

"Not that I am aware of at this time."

When they walked back into the Council room, Chendal followed them in. He stood behind them, out of sight.

They bowed, and Kenimandil motioned them into the seats. "A'Cara?"

Breathe, fem. Be calm. "A'ke'Taso, I have decided to accept the duty you requested of me. I'll go to Himadi House."

Kenimandil's face showed no elation, no change at all that Cara could see. "And Rodani?"

"He will come with me, as my keso." *My keso! What an improbable switch! Don't smile. Don't do that anxious human smile.*

Kenimandil waved her hand at Chendal, who opened a side door for the other two Council members to enter. They took their places at their desks.

"Stand, a'Cara."

Now what? She tried not to look at Rodani, tried not to show how nervous she was. *Ignorance breeds fear,* Rodani had once said. *No need to fear here, right?*

"A'Cara," the ke'taso said, "do you accept the position of taso of Himadi House?"

"Yes, a'ke'Taso."

"Will you obey any orders from the Council that are given to you?"

"Yes, a'ke'Taso."

"Will you do your utmost to create a healthy and successful house under the principles and goals that it was created?"

"Yes, a'ke'Taso."

"Then I declare you taso of Himadi House."

Gods of the deep night protect me, she thought as she bowed deeply. When she straightened, Kenimandil turned to Rodani. "Kneel for your taso."

Without hesitation, Rodani got up and knelt in front of Cara. She glanced at Kenimandil.

"You will offer oaths to him to confirm his decision, as I did to you."

Her mind went blank for a moment. *Oaths. Oaths. Shit. What did they talk about? What did he promise? Basics, fem.*

"A'Rodani, do you consent to be my keso?"

"Yes, a'Taso."

The title shocked her to her toes. *Keep breathing! Think!* "Do you consent to obey my orders, given that I will listen to your concerns and take your advice into consideration?"

"Yes, a'Taso."

What now? Something else. Him, then me, the—the house. "Do you consent to assist me to the best of your ability to make Himadi House better, less...contentious, more successful and prosperous?" *Dammit, she was flubbing it!*

"Yes, a'Taso."

How did the ke'taso say it? No. Wing it! "Then I accept you as keso of Himadi House." She put her hand on the top of his head and stroked it, then took a step back. Rodani rose. They both turned to face Kenimandil.

"Seat yourselves." She nodded to Chendal, who opened the main door. Shisa walked in and up to the ke'taso, standing at attention at an angle between Cara and Kenimandil.

"There is one other, smaller issue, that I must ask you to answer," Kenimandil said. "Shisa must be punished for the damage she did to you. What would be your preference as to what that punishment should be?"

Another shock rippled through her. *Decide the punishment of a high-ranking guardian? Chendal's partner? Rodani's sister? No.* "A'ke'Taso, I would have wished to speak with Rodani first."

"As this is your first decision as taso—aside from choosing your keso, I am interested in hearing your own thoughts, not his."

Holy sunspots! Flogging? No! Let Rodani fight her? He'd win, but would he want to fight? My decision. My decision. "A'ke'Taso, not knowing what would be considered proper or improper, I would suggest this," she began.

"Do not suggest, a'Taso. Give her a command."

She knew her expressions were flooding her face. *No choice. Do it. Rodani will understand.* She turned to face his sister. "A'Shisa...a'tem...from this moment...until I say otherwise, you will be my servant. You will obey any lawful orders I give you to the best of your ability. You will carry the attitude and stance of a servant at all times...unless you need your guild skills to save your life, Rodani's life, or mine. Or the temaso's," she added. Cara glanced up into Shisa's face. The temichi was frozen in place, staring across the room, her eyes wide and full of fire. Cara waited for a response. When none came, she pulled a little bit of fire from her own anger. "What do you say to me?"

The room was absolutely silent. Cara couldn't see the others, but she could sense no hint of movement.

"A'tem!" Kenimandil ordered.

Shisa's exhale was the only fury she showed. "A'Taso."

"You can wait with the other guardians until I need you."

Shisa left the room—without a bow. It was the closest Cara had ever seen to a temichi stomping. *Unruffle the feathers, fem. Now.* "A'ke'Taso, I hope that I haven't offended the Council...or the guild. It was not my intention."

"You have not," Kenimandil answered. "But you have certainly surprised us."

Cara bent her head. *Show humility? A bit of arrogance? What's best?*

"I believe the two of you have plans to make and discussions to have." Kenimandil opened her palm.

"A'ke'Taso," Rodani said before Cara could rise, "if it would not offend, I have a question."

"A'Keso."

"Do you know if Ambassador Andreh' had servants in Himadi? Cara will need them."

Kenimandil glanced at Chendal, who answered.

"He did not."

"A'ke'Taso, I had a thought to ask Cara's servants from Barridan if they would consider relocating to Himadi. I request permission to contact Arimeso."

"You have it. She may burn your ears."

Rodani inclined his head in agreement. "I will suffer through it, a'ke'Taso. I thank you. I would rather not suffer with an audience, however. May I make use of the Council's equipment for privacy?"

"You may. But be quick. I have need of it myself."

"Yes, a'ke'Taso." When Rodani left his chair, Cara followed him. He said nothing until he closed the comm room door. "Kia."

She took a breath to steady herself. The change had to start sometime, somewhere. "A'Keso," she said with a half-smile. "I will be absolutely silent on the call."

Rodani blinked and regarded her soberly. What was he thinking? Rearranging his new status and hers in his mind? Wondering if he should object?

"You may hear things you do not wish to hear," he reminded her.

"So may you."

His gaze wandered the tiny room.

"Are there really things she might say," Cara continued, "that you don't want me to hear?"

"Not likely," he admitted. "But possible."

"I think it's time for you to let me in. Into some of what you kept away from me in Barridan. There may be some things I need to know for the future."

"You do not trust me to tell you what you need to know?"

Her gut clenched. "I think," she said slowly, "that what each of us needs to know is going to be very much unknown—for a long time. I think we should begin on the right path towards a more appropriate sharing of information."

He conceded with a sigh. "A'Taso. You should also know that if Kusik is in the room, he may say harmful things. About you, about me."

"I know what he is," she said darkly. She sat in the side seat, her mind firmly made up. Rodani took the main one, and dialed up the radio.

"Barridan, Barridan."

A reply came through promptly. "Barridan."

"A'tem, this is the keso, Rodani, in Hadaman. I wish to speak with the taso if she is available."

"Hold, please, a'Keso."

***

Hours away, Kusik muttered irritably as he yanked his chair away from the desk. "New ideas, they say. Better ways to see the world, Chendal told them." He sat and crossed his arms, glancing at Arimeso to his left. "Stable sweepings, is what *that* is worth," he spat out. "Two of the new knives sound so much like Rodani that it makes me shiver." He slammed his fist on his desk in a fury that had yet to subside in six months. "If the goddess could turn back the clock, I would see that worthless deviant dead instead of Timan."

Arimeso fought an internal battle of her own. Tired of her keso's complaints, long past ready to put all they'd lost from her mind, she wondered what, if anything, she should say to him. Sighing, she again offered a truth. "Your judgments and regrets change nothing, my mate. It does you ill to keep fighting what cannot be changed."

A polite knock on the taso's door interrupted the unproductive dialogue. "Yes?"

One of the new guardians stepped in. "There is a call for you, a'Taso, from Hadaman. A keso." He hesitated, looking confused and slightly alarmed. "Named Rodani."

***

The reply from Barridan took several moments, then a female voice came on the line, one Cara recognized. Even she heard the incredulity.

"Rodani?"

"I hope you are very much well, a'Taso."

"Where in all Sela's good graces have you been? And what do you mean by introducing yourself as a keso?"

Rodani leaned forward a little, forearms on the table. "A'Taso, it is a very long story. I hope to have a chance to tell you in the future. But Cara has been appointed taso of Himadi House, and I am her keso. I would wish—"

"Goddess above, Rodani. Is this truth?"

"Yes, a'Taso, on my honor."

A growl erupted through the speaker, and a raspy voice spoke. "Honor!"

Cara put her fists against her mouth and glanced at Rodani. He had blanked his face. "A'Taso," he continued, blatantly ignoring Kusik. "Ambassador Andreh' has no servants to attend him. Cara will need them. I am aware I have little right to be requesting anything of you, and I deeply regret that. But I would wish to ask if I might speak to Hamman and Deremic, to see if they would be willing to relocate to Himadi."

Kusik erupted at high volume. "You dare?" he shouted across the waves. "You abandoned your duty! You dare beg from the taso you deserted in her need? You did to your taso what your partner did to you! You are utterly—"

"Kusik!" Arimeso said sharply, cutting off the tirade. Muttering took over as Cara and Rodani glanced at each other. Then she spoke again.

"Rodani, I am somewhat surprised you did not ask for Serano."

"Au, honored taso," Rodani said with a hint of humor, "I believe Cara would veto that choice."

"There is something you should know before you ask them. It will not please you."

"My ears are empty, a'Taso."

"Hamman's daughter did not survive the birth of her child."

Rodani's eyes went wide. He bent his head and clasped his hands in front of him, silent for a moment. "I am sorrowed for all of them, a'Taso. May the goddess hold them close."

"Hamman is not the same person she was, Rodani."

He thought for a moment, sadness in his eyes. "She may welcome a change, a'Taso."

"Or she may not be capable of new duties."

"When did this happen?"

"Only two months ago. Not nearly enough time for the loss of a child, and grandchild."

"Would you ask her if she would be willing to speak to me?"

"I will ask her. And Deremic?"

"Please, yes. As well, a'Taso, if it would not offend, ask Cassig, the chef."

"Is that all?" she said, whimsy in her voice.

"A'Taso, if you please, yes. We would be most grateful. Cara and I will be working very hard to make Himadi into a functional and successful house."

"I will speak with them, and someone will return your call."

"I thank you, a'Taso." After closing the connection, he turned to Cara with a bemused expression.

They left the comm room, bowed to Kenimandil, and went back to the outer room. Cara headed for the bedroom they shared, then held the door open with a gaze that made Rodani's ears tingle. She shut the door behind him, and with a wide smile, held her arms up to him. He grabbed her and spun her around with a joy in his heart he hadn't felt since he'd held her in her parents' boat, soggy and laughing.

"Oh, gods," she whispered in his ear as he wound down. "What have we done?"

He nuzzled her. "Found a path we can follow together, kia."

"I wonder what will happen?"

"I have no gift of prophesy."

She laid her scarred palms on either side of his face. "You didn't see this coming either, did you?"

"Not even in a dream," he replied, tightening his hug.

Content for a moment, Cara ran her fingers through his hair. ^I love you.^

"You are my all." He squeezed sharply, eliciting a gasp, then set her down on her feet.

Cara glanced up into an expression on his face she hadn't seen in a while. Happy. Expectant. Pupils wide and a small smile on his lips. Overwhelmed with more than joy, she bent her head and covered her eyes. "Shit." She just stood for a moment, breathing in and out as Rodani waited. "Aisu…" she stared over at the door. "I'm going to have to grow up."

Silence. Then, "Kia?"

She clambered up onto the bed, and sat. "I'm going to have to become what Menachem and Andrew wanted me to be. What they tried to make me be."

Rodani sat down next to her, questions in his eyes. "And what is that?"

"Less reactive," she admitted. "Less emotional. More thought before I act. More…" *Fuck.* "Adult. To deal with all this responsibility," she added.

Rodani folded his arms across his chest. "I think I should not say what is sitting on my tongue."

"I think," Cara clasped her hands between her knees, "you should probably say it anyway."

"No," he decided, putting his arm over her shoulders. "But I will continue to help you."

"Thanks."

"And what of the deaths we left behind, a'Taso?" he asked quietly.

"Don't know, don't care," she told him. Then lifted a hand. "No, that's lazy. Stupid." She thought for a minute, rubbing her hands across her thighs in agitation as she rocked to and fro. "Unless…" she lowered her voice as Rodani motioned with his hands, "word comes north, I'd rather leave it behind." She clasped Rodani's hand. "Neither of us killed Mack. Thanks to you," she amended. "And no one can pin the preacher on you. Right?"

"Pin? Do you mean accuse?"

"No. Sorry. I mean *prove* anything. Prove you did it."

"I believe not. I was well concealed, though not completely hidden. And surely your brother or his friend would have said something to you. Yes?"

She sighed heavily, volubly. Too many thoughts, too many tasks, too many worries were stealing her breath, for the good as well as the bad. "I sure would think so, yes. Would Kenimandil have us—or you—removed from Himadi if she found out?"

"I believe not. She would not want her plans thwarted." He pulled his hand away slowly and glanced at the door. "We should return to the table...if it does not offend you... a'Taso," he added.

Cara waved an assent.

Out in the room, Rodani positioned Cara at the head of the table, noting with humor her diffidence. Chendal motioned to Menachem, sending him into the ke'taso's office, then took the ambassador's seat at the table.

Cara's gaze bounced between the two guardians, temaso to her left and keso to her right. She brought her fists to her mouth and stared at the table in front of them, as they were both waiting for her to say something. She felt very much out of place, awkward, and out of her depth in front of the men. "Your thoughts, a'Temaso?" she asked him.

Chendal toyed with a nearby candle, flicking his finger through the flame. "I believe the ke'taso is making a reasonable decision in appointing you, a'Taso. I do wonder if your emotions will help or hinder the situation."

Nope. Not going there. Not now. Play it cool, fem. "How often were you there?"

"Twice. Once when it first opened, once recently when the disturbances seemed to be escalating."

"Were you there long enough to see if there were mistakes being made? Something that might have reduced the friction?"

"I saw the ambassador and the guardians spending too much of their time stopping fights and mediating arguments, as well as interpreting everywhere with mixed species."

"So, he wasn't given the help he needed?"

"More than that, a'Taso. The differences between the cultures are wide and deep, and few wished to compromise. It was easier to take offense than to find common ground."

"Everyone's a Serano and no one's a Rodani."

"Essentially, though some simply chose to withdraw into their labs and studies rather than intermingle."

"Did Andrew kick anyone out? Send them home?"

"Not that I am aware," Chendal told her. "When do you leave?"

She gave Rodani a quizzical look. "Did we ask that?"

"'As soon as possible,' was her reply."

"Thank you." She turned back to Chendal. "What happened while Rodani was in the south, a'Temaso?"

The two men glanced at each other.

"I know someone was searching for Rodani," she continued. "He told me he'd heard of it."

"I believe Arimeso sent out searchers in her area, and when that failed, Soldan was requested to search as well. Then when the problems in Himadi became untenable, guild members in various locations were simply told to keep watch."

"And when the guild in Soldan heard our 'com..."

"They investigated."

"A'Keso," Tokennen stood in the entrance to the room.

Rodani turned to face him.

"Barridan."

"Excuse me a'Taso, a'Temaso." Rodani got up.

"I want to come with you," Cara said, rising.

He inclined his head, but looked away. "You may, of course, a'Taso. But I believe your time is better spent here."

Cara pursed her lips and tossed the suggestion, then sat back down. "So," she said to Chendal as Rodani left the room, "since my time is better spent with you, what would you do in Himadi if you were in my place?"

He tapped a finger on the table. "I would set down firm rules of interspecies contact, punish those who disobey, and reward those who obey."

"Andrew didn't do that?"

"I believe he tried. Either he was too inconsistent from being overworked, or too lax in his punishments."

She wondered what the answer to that was, knowing it likely she'd never find out. "What kind of rewards would most Selandu prefer?"

"It could be a purchase of alcohol, clothing, or shoes, paid for by the house."

"As long as it doesn't cost too much."

"Or a short holiday. But I have a question for you, a'Taso."

^Okay.^

"Will you allow your guild to punish?"

A quizzical expression crossed her face. "That's part of their duties, a'Temaso. So, yes."

"Some of your reactions in Barridan suggested you have an aversion to causing death." His pupils narrowed. "Can you allow your guild to kill?"

Carefully, fem. Tiptoe. "If...it's to save someone's life, yes."

"As a punishment, a'Taso," he said gravely.

She folded her arms on the table, staring at it. Thought. Considered her words. "I would have to decide that when it comes up. A'Temaso. *If* it comes up," she added.

"There should be no question."

"But in Himadi House," she replied with a side eye, "there have to be questions. Because there are two different cultures and rules for existing in them. Will you travel with us to Himadi?"

"I, at least, will accompany you, yes. And Shisa will follow your orders until she is released from them."

"Would you be willing to stay a few days?"

"Why?"

"Well, your presence might reinforce the...validity of our position there, at least with the Selandu. I'm not sure what will help with the humans. Maybe between you and Rodani and hopefully Tokennen, the humans will think twice about fighting."

"Your presence there will make no matter to them?"

"It will to some. But like Rodani in Barridan, I don't have the best reputation among my people."

"And how will you increase it?"

"By doing the best I can for them while keeping them informed of what I can do and what I can't."

"And the Selandu?" he asked slowly.

Cara frowned. "I'm not going to play favorites, a'Temaso. I need to do my best for both species. Otherwise, this isn't going to work."

Chendal leaned back in his chair. "Forgive my poor assumptions, a'Taso."

Cara smiled and patted his hand. "Of course."

The doors to the Council room opened, and Menachem strode out with rage and doom in his face.

^We need to talk, Cara.^

Cara opened her palm and pointed to Rodani's empty chair. ^Alone.^

She'd seen Menachem angry before, but this was a level beyond anything in the past. Not even his anger at having no choice but to send her to Barridan measured up to this.

"No," she told him, deepening her voice.

"Cara," he said behind clenched jaws, his fists equally clenched.

"A'Reiti, either spew what you need to or sit down, and we can talk civilly, *in Selandi*, in front of the temaso."

He leaned into her face. ^You don't give me orders.^

"A'Reiti," Chendal interrupted, "I believe it is normal protocol to be courteous to a taso."

Oh, that was a ding. Cara bit her lips to keep from smiling.

Menachem fought his expression down to arrogant annoyance. "A'Temaso, this is not a matter between reiti and taso," he spat out the word, "but between human and human."

"I believe it is both."

Kimasa's robe. Cara took a grip on her own rising emotions. "A'Reiti, please sit down. Rage won't solve anything."

Menachem yanked Rodani's chair out and sat stiffly. ^You are not capable of running Himadi House.^

"Speak Selandi, and I'll answer you."

He placed his fist on the table, barely managing not to pound it. "You are not capable. You're not trained in diplomacy, you have no patience, and very few social skills."

"And how did those very things help Andrew succeed?"

"Don't play games with me," he said with heat.

"I'm not. It was an honest question."

"Cara, I want Himadi house to be successful! I've worked toward this for years. And to see it in the hands of…"

Offended, resentful, she bared her teeth. "Of what, Ambassador? Of what? I want it to succeed, too. Not only for the two species and what they can create, but for my own personal reasons. I want *double* what you want!"

"A'Reiti. A'Taso." Chendal sliced his hand downward between them. "Cease, I beg you. Regardless of opinions, frustrations, and tempers, the ke'taso has made her decision. A'Reiti, has Ambassador Andreh' been apprised?"

Menachem angled his head away and stared at the doors to the ke'taso's office. "Yes."

"Then I am of the opinion that arguing is fruitless and a waste of time."

^Change your mind,^ Menachem told Cara in an undertone. ^Tell her you made a mistake.^

"No."

"You don't know what's at stake here! You're ignorant. Spouting all your feelings without thinking."

"Are you kidding me?" Cara's voice rose. "There's more at stake for me than either you or Andrew!"

"How can you—"

"A'Reiti." Rodani walked in, still limping. "You will refrain from provoking my taso!" Furious, he pulled his chair out with Menachem still sitting in it. He tilted it slightly. "If you wish to sit at the taso's table, you will treat her with the courtesy due her station."

Menachem slid out of the chair and stood eye to eye. "You are both making a mistake, a'tem."

"A'Keso," Cara spat. "And you will treat my ^husband^, my bonded mate, with the courtesy due his station and skills."

It hadn't dawned on him, that was certain. His jaw dropped and eyes widened as he stared at her in disbelief. ^Husband? You are out of your mind!^ He switched his attention back to Rodani, then over to Chendal for verification. The temaso regarded him steadily. "This is impossible," Menachem said.

"It is not," Chendal replied.

Menachem's face screwed up.

"Ooh, such a look of disgust," she said with a fierce smile. "I saw that in Barridan, too."

Rodani inspected the ambassador's expression and leaned into him. "You will not offend my taso and mate."

Cara tugged on his arm. "He has a right to his opinion, my keso. However, he should hide it better. I'm sure we'll see some of that in Himadi, too."

"This is what you hid from me when you came home, isn't it?" The growl in his voice ran down Cara's nerves.

"It wasn't your business, Ambassador."

"It was! It was the reason you were dismissed. Tell me I'm wrong."

Rodani spoke up. "You are mistaken, a'Reiti. Our private affinity caused the same disgust in others as it is doing in you. That same disgust and anger caused *their* violence. *They* were the cause of her return to her people. Not us."

"You lied to me."

"No, I did *not!*" Cara spat out. "I made sure of that by the words I used." She paused. "But I did hide the truth."

"Why?"

Cara waved her arm in frustration. "To avoid this exact type of confrontation. Why do *you* think I did?"

"This is ridiculous. You should never have gone there."

"And if I hadn't, Himadi wouldn't have a second chance."

Menachem planted his fists on his narrow hips. "Andrew is a better ambassador than you could ever be."

"But I don't need to be an ambassador. I only need to learn to be a taso. And I'll have good people to help me. Menachem," she said with a sigh, "Kenimandil appointed me. If you have a problem with it, go argue with her."

"I care what happens to Himadi!" he said, voice raised.

"And if you think I don't," she shot back, "you know a lot less about me than you think you do." Sick of it, sick of Menachem's worries that only fed her own, Cara turned away from him and toward the man who loved her—even if he didn't use the word. "Did you talk to Hamman?"

"Yes," Rodani replied. "They all agreed."

"The chef, too?

"Yes.

"When will they be there?"

"They will need at least three days, possibly four."

"Where is Shisa?"

"In the comm room, when I was there. Do you need her?"

"I'd like some tea, the way I like it, and a pen and some paper. Tea?" she asked Chendal.

"Yes."

She turned back to Menachem. "Tea?"

"No." His voice went low, and the syllable stretched out into a growling censure.

Rodani left to make the request. Menachem followed him.

"A'Keso," the ambassador said as they reached the doorway. Rodani turned and waited, his expression blanked. "Perhaps," Menachem began, "you would see the problems I see better than the taso would. If you know her that well, you are aware of her unconstrained emotions. Her childish nature. The fact—"

"A'Reiti," he said as his pupils constricted, "At this point in life, I believe I know her far better than you do. And," he drew out the word, "her reasons are my reasons as well. I suggest you obey the ke'taso."

Cara watched the two men closely, hoping fervently that another argument wouldn't erupt. This transition would be rough enough without the obvious disapproval of both ambassadors. She needed hope, and positive advice, not more soul-stealing criticisms.

Fortunately, Menachem seemed to have run out of argumentative courage, choosing to pace the room as Rodani left and returned without further conflict.

He sat down beside her. "How do you feel?"

Cara rested her cheek in her palm and grinned at him. "Physically or mentally?"

He smiled back at her. "Both."

"Gods, I need that smile, aisu," she said, heartfelt. "Thanks."

"And?" The smile remained.

"Uh, my face is tender, and my shoulder is sore. And I'm already tired of attitude problems. I'm sure I'll be more tired of them in Himadi." Then she looked up. "And how do you feel? You're not limping as badly. And your back?" she added, with a side-eye to Chendal.

As usual, Rodani waved it all away somehow. She wondered, sometimes, how much he truly felt, and how much he ignored by way of his guild training.

From the doorway, Tokennen called for Menachem. He rose and left the room.

Rodani watched him go, then turned back to Cara. "Kia, there is one thing you must learn quickly."

Her eyebrows shot up. "Yes?"

Rodani leaned toward her and rested his hand on her wrist. "You are a taso," he said pointedly. "A taso does not allow herself to be disrespected. Disagreed with at times, yes. But not discourtesy, not insolence. I will assist in this, as I already have. But you must be able to enforce it yourself."

"What's the best way to do that? As a taso?"

"Censure them verbally. Point out their disrespect immediately and demand that it stop. You cannot allow in Himadi what Mena'hem is doing here. It will damage your power, your ability to enforce change."

She stared down at the table, thinking. "I can see that. I agree." She looked at him. "You know it'll be hard for me."

"Which is why I will support you. But you must."

She gazed off into the distance and nodded, watching Shisa bring in a tea tray.

She set it down in front of Cara and stepped back.

"Thank you, a'tem." Cara turned to her. "I know you don't want to stand at my shoulder all day. But don't be too far away."

Shisa managed a bare minimum head shift, then walked off. She didn't look at her brother.

Menachem passed her on his way back from the comm room. He sat down at the table. "Mack is dead."

"Good," Cara said, eyebrows purposefully raised. "Somebody killed him. Thank the dark gods of space."

Menachem eyed her. "How do you know he was murdered?"

Caught. Shit. "He was too stubborn to die otherwise."

"What do you know about it?"

"I know more than just me hated him."

"And I know you had more reason to hate him."

"What's your point here, Menachem? Are you accusing me of something? Please don't. It's disrespectful." She paused. "Especially to a taso."

His eyes went wide, then narrowed.

"Ca—a'Taso," he corrected with a glance at Rodani, "Right before I left, I learned Clark and Stefan claimed they found a Selandu south of Lordstown, while they were looking for you. They claimed this Selandu killed Mack. I thought it ridiculous...until now."

Cara thought fast, her heartbeat rising. *Don't panic, fem.* "Really?" her voice rose and fell, feigning ridicule. "A Selandu murderer? In the south. And you believe them? Those drunks?" She watched as he considered her words.

"If they're lying, why that one? Why concoct that story?"

She rested her chin on her fist. "I suppose it's easier to point the finger at someone who isn't there, and should never be there, rather than someone more likely." She threw out a hand. "Send the sheriff down the wrong trail, I guess."

Menachem pursed his lips and looked away. To her surprise, he bowed to Chendal and left the room.

Cara pulled a paper toward her and sipped her tea. *First Day,* she wrote at the top. *Second Day,* she wrote in the middle, then started to think. She took a second piece of paper and wrote *Things to do* and *Things to say.* "You should make a list of your tasks, too, aisu. Oh, and have you asked Tokennen?"

"I will ask now." Rodani left the room.

Cara turned to Chendal. "Comments, a'Temaso? Advice?"

"I believe your keso is offering wise advice, a'Taso."

She took a moment, then smiled. "That's all you wish to say?"

Chendal sat back in his chair and sipped his tea. "Make it known to both species that repeat troublemakers will be dismissed and sent home. Reassure them that those not sent home will enjoy the improvements you are there to make."

"And ask them what improvements they need."

"Yes, after allowing that not all may be possible."

She nodded, adding it to one of her lists.

"I also suggest you reduce your expectations for a time. You will be extremely busy, and change is slow."

"You never told me how long you'll stay with us before you leave."

"Because I do not know. I will judge the time as it passes."

^Okay.^

"What is that word? I have heard it at least twice."

"Acceptance." She smiled at him. "You just learned your first Cene'l word." Looking down at the table, she added, "I just thought of something, a'Temaso. All the people who are born there won't be able to be sent back."

"Why?"

"Because," she looked up, still thinking, "they won't see their parents' home as their home. Himadi House will be their home. It would be like sending them back to a foreign country." She put her hand to her mouth, then drew it away. "A'Temaso, I'm going to be building a whole new culture."

Rodani came back. "He is considering it, a'Taso."

Cara took a deep breath, the better to firm up her own resolve. "How long will it take to get there?"

Rodani glanced over at Chendal for an answer.

"Two days generally," the temaso replied.

"What if I need some things at home?"

"Ask Andreh' when he returns," he offered.

Cara shook her head. "No. He won't want to help me any more than Menachem does."

"You. Are. A. Taso," Rodani said, censure in his widened eyes. "By treaty with the Council, he is required to assist you."

"Well, I can't force him from across the hills. You couldn't either, right?"

"What you will do is remind him of the treaty and his duties. They do not change simply because he is obeying a human taso. Why do you smile?"

Cara chuckled. "I'm imagining sending a temichi over the hills from Station Two to knock on the back door of the CSC. That might convince him."

Rodani lowered his brows. "I assume you jest."

"Mostly," she drew out the word. "Yes. But it would be tempting. I'll ask my father and brother for my belongings." She glanced at Rodani. "I should call the CSC now, right?"

"Yes."

"I hope Lara cooperates with me. She doesn't approve of me, either."

"Then I should make that call," Chendal offered.

Cara turned to him, shocked. "Would you? She wouldn't dare refuse you."

"I will, for your impatience as well as the ke'taso's."

"Thank you very much, a'Temaso." She turned back to her husband and pointed. "You should be on the call, too, aisu. So that she can learn your name and voice, and will know not to play games if you ever have to call from Himadi."

Chendal waved a hand. "I concur, a'Keso."

As the men left to make the call, Cara scribbled on the paper. *Notes. Lists.* She flipped it over. *Priorities. Duties.*

Who? What? When? Where? Why? And the big ones: How? and Can we afford it?

And the lists grew and grew.

Rodani and Chendal returned from the comm room to sit down.

"How did it go?" she asked.

"Well enough," Chendal replied.

Cara laid her hand lightly on his wrist. "Thank you for your help. For using your status to make this a little easier." She smiled at him, then turned to her husband. "You were able to introduce yourself? And say you'd be talking to her at other times?"

"Yes, a'Taso."

"So if Tokennen agrees, that makes five guardians at first, and then three, plus two sheriffs. That should be enough, yes?"

"Minimally." Rodani spread his hands. "I will need two each day to sit at the comm station, at least one to accompany you every time you go out into the main house, leaving me for all else. And you and I will be on 25-hour duty to intercede in any arguments and fights, plus all our other duties."

Cara turned back to Chendal. "Is there any chance of hiring one or two more guardians? Could I afford them? Do you know any you would trust to deal equally with humans and Selandu?"

"It is something to be considered, a'Taso."

She nodded. "And Rodani and I would need to speak with the accountant before that, yes?"

"I believe there is not one at Himadi."

"Oh." She made another note. "My keso," she said, "you and I may need to do some crafting to bring money into the house."

"I doubt either of us will have time, a'Taso."

She thought for a moment. "I know of one way. Or something that can be tried. I'd need a gardener or fieldworker."

"For what?"

"There are herbs, plants, that human women need, and they are often in short supply at home. If we could grow them, I think we could easily sell them."

"Why are they in short supply? Are they difficult to grow?"

"No," Cara replied with some heat. "Because two of them have to do with preventing babies from being born. And there are people, like my mother, who don't want those choices available to us. Over the years, where they grow have been hidden. Sometimes it's difficult to get them when we need them. If we grow them in Himadi, we can sell them in the south."

"Where would you get the seeds?"

"From my father. We could also try growing caffee beans. Different soils give different tastes. They might like something different to drink. Teas, also, the safe ones. And clothes! If there is a tailor or seamstress there, they could design different styles of clothes that might become popular at home."

"Au, a'Taso." Rodani teased, "you should cease saying 'at home' unless you are speaking of Himadi. It is your home now, not Glaniad."

Cara chuckled. "You're right, of course. That's a habit I'll need to change."

Tokennen hastened into the room. "A'Taso, your father."

Cara clambered down from her chair and sped across the room, Rodani following. Tokennen led her to a chair and held it out for her. Rodani stood behind her. Tokennen flipped a switch and motioned to her.

She flipped the switch in her brain to change languages. "Dae?"

At first, a pause. Then, "Cara?" came the shocked reply. "You're alive! My gods, the rumors. I thought I was supposed to talk to some alien. Are you okay?"

"Yes, I'm fine."

"I thought they were going to tell me you were hurt, or dead, or something. Do you know how worried I've been? How hard it was to not tell your mother? And Kimi! Your little sister—"

"Dae, please. I'm sorry. For you, for Kimi. I know I've shocked you. But please calm yourself. I don't want you having a heart attack."

"Then give me a minute, little bit."

"Okay."

She counted to sixty, then a little more. "Better?"

A sigh came through the speaker. "What's going on?"

"The short answer is I'm moving to Himadi House, and I need a little help from you."

"What kind of help?"

"First, I need my chest and its key sent to Himadi, as well as my belongings that Davad has. Can you get him to help you get it all on a Selandu boat?"

"I would assume so."

"Good. Next, I need red tide supplies. Would you ask my sisters to collect some—whatever they can afford to give? I don't know how much supplies Himadi has. There aren't many women there."

"Okay."

"And one last thing, please. It's also important, but doesn't have to be immediate."

"What's that?"

"The seeds or seedlings of the three plants that women need."

The speaker went silent for a moment. "All three?"

"Yes, Dae, all three. You'll know best how to package them. And, of course you'll need to label them so we'll know one from another."

"Alright. Any others?"

"I don't know yet what they've planted, the place is so new. But some vegetables, if you have them. Maybe the hops, too, since so many humans love beer."

"Can do," was his welcome reply.

Cara let her gut unclench a bit, and sighed volubly. One more task to cross off. "Thank you, Dae. I'm sorry I surprised you so badly, and sorry we interrupted your day. You'll be a big help to me. Thank Lara for me, too, please, for going to get you. I love you."

"Love you, too, little bit. Take care up there. And," he added, "you owe me an explanation someday."

"I know. Signing off." Cara looked around. On impulse, she laid a hand on Tokennen's arm. "Will you honor us by coming with us?"

His eyes widened, and he looked off into the distance.

"You're not obliged, a'tem. There is no dishonor in saying no. But you would be a great help to Rodani, which means you'll be a help to me, too."

He stared into her eyes. "I know little of humans except the ambassadors, a'Taso."

"Yes, we'll all be adjusting and learning. You won't be any less capable than we will be." She removed her hand. "Please think about it. We leave in the morning."

He bowed his head. "A'Taso." As Cara rose, he spoke again. "A'Keso."

Both she and Rodani turned to him. He motioned in guild code.

"A'Taso, if you will excuse me," Rodani said.

"Of course."

A short while later, he came back to the dining table where Cara was writing more notes and Chendal nibbled on sweets.

"What did he want?"

"Reassurance," Rodani said, sitting down, "on how to live with humans."

She sputtered in humor. "Did you convince him?"

"Yes."

"Good!" She clapped her hands. "One more task to cross off."

Dinner arrived. Menachem refused to come out, so Chendal directed the servant to his room with his portions.

Rodani took a sip of eisenico. "A'Temaso."

Chendal glanced up from his plate.

"What have you heard from Ushando?"

He considered the question, eyes on the table in front of him. "Little more than rumors, a'Keso. Why?"

"Because he is a danger to Himadi, a'Temaso. Would you disagree?"

"That is a long distance to travel for a double-handful of humans."

"Possibly. And possibly not when he finds out there is a human taso, and she is mated to her Selandu keso."

"You have a point." Chendal pursed his lips. "I will discuss this with the ke'taso and request a scouting mission."

"If he plans to attack us, we will need more than three guardians to protect the house."

Chendal laid his knife on the plate with a clank. "This will take much discussion, Rodani. Nothing will happen in haste. It is too fraught."

"So would be a successful attack, a'Temaso," Rodani argued. "What would happen to Himadi, even if Ushando left anything intact, if Cara and I were killed? Not speaking of the other humans."

"It will be discussed. That I assure you."

Rodani blanked his face.

"A'Temaso," Cara said. "With due respect for you, how soon will this discussion occur?"

Chendal regarded her. "I can only suggest to the ke'taso that it be brought to table when I return here."

"Will the guild fight for us?" she added.

"A'Taso," Rodani said, chiding her.

"It's a critical question, Rodani."

"And I will suggest leaving it in the hands of others, for now," he emphasized. "We will have a houseful of tasks to accomplish in the weeks and months ahead."

Mind full of new ideas and worries, Cara bent to her list and continued to write.

Not long after, the tailor showed up with an armful of cloth. "A'sel," he said, bowing to her.

"A'Taso," Rodani corrected him with dispatch, and began to inspect the clothing. It was all Selandu style, like the type she was wearing—but more appropriate for one of high status. Three long skirts, full blouses, plus two vests and jackets with embroidery on cuffs and collars.

"They're beautiful, a'sel," Cara told him, holding a vest up to her body. "Thank you for your excellent work."

The man bowed and left the room.

"And your clothes?" she asked Rodani.

"I will find some."

"Now, please, so I can cross another task off my list."

He inclined his head and followed the tailor out.

Cara looked around. "Where is Shisa?"

Chendal pulled out his 'com. "Tem'u."

A reply came through. "The taso requires your service."

In a moment she appeared from wherever she'd been hiding.

"Shisa, I need some kind of box or sack to hold our clothing during the trip, something to keep them clean. Can you find such a thing?"

She said no word, but bowed and left.

Cara leaned back in her chair and closed her eyes. She wanted badly to rest, to nap. But her mind was filled with a score of thoughts along with a gut full of anxiety. "What am I forgetting, a'Temaso? Is there anything you see?"

"Not at this moment, a'Taso."

"If you think of anything, please say so."

"What I think," Chendal folded his hands on the table, "is that you cannot know much more until you arrive."

"That's what worries me. I like to plan in advance."

Is there any other time to plan, besides in advance? he thought. Chendal pursed his lips in humor and chose not to remark upon her words.

"If there are things you need to do this evening," she told him, "you can do them now. I'm well enough sitting here."

"When your keso returns, a'Taso."

Was that courtesy to a taso, she wondered, *or watchfulness over an unpredictable human?* She longed to ask, but didn't want to offend him, especially when he was being so helpful. She'd learned a few things in the last year, so she kept her mouth shut.

TWENTY-EIGHT

As Cara contemplated all the items that her brother and father still held, Rodani folded the new guild clothing he'd been gifted this morning and laid them into the travel chest Shisa had found.

"Kia."

"Huh?"

"I have wondered about something."

Cara raised her eyebrows and grinned. "Well, that tells me a lot, aisu."

"Forgive me, kia. This one is not a matter for mirth."

The smile faded. ^Okay.^

Rodani sat on the edge of the bed and rested his forearms on his thighs. "Will someone assume anything about Mack's death? Anyone?"

She shook her head. "I hope not. I don't know." Shrugging, she added, "I think it won't be us. Only the two people who helped us know we were there, and I don't think they'll tell."

"But the surviving men knew I was there."

"Eeesh," she said in sudden dismay. "We can hope that no one will believe them. What proof would they have?"

"I cannot know. What I do know is that I left nothing of mine behind."

"That may have to satisfy us, aisu."

"And the preacher that I killed?"

Cara interlaced her fingers and bit her lip. "They believe I was there. The mayor offered money to anyone who captured me."

Rodani's eyes widened. "How do you know that?"

"Davad's friend told me. He said that instead of helping me, he could have handed me over to the sheriffs and taken the money."

He leaned forward in guild earnest that looked a lot like danger. "Then you can never go back, kia."

She held her hand out, palm down. "They couldn't prove it. They have no evidence that I did anything to him."

"But if they believe it, they could cause us trouble in Himadi."

"They could."

Rodani paced the floor, hands behind his back. "What of Ambassador Mena'hem?"

"That depends on what he finds out about where we were and ties the threads together."

"Will he?"

"He's smart. I don't know. But there's still no proof."

"Let us hope. Kia," he said, sitting next to her. "Do you rue the harm we did?"

That took some thought. "Yes," she replied slowly. "But I don't regret us saving each other."

Someone knocked.

Rodani opened the door.

Waiting outside of it stood Shisa, incipient mayhem in her eyes. "Rodani."

"Are you packed?" he asked in an attempt to redirect her. Then realized it wasn't working.

"I need to speak with you."

"We can speak as we travel, te'ono."

"Now."

He turned to Cara. "A moment, please, a'Taso." He stepped out of the bedroom and shut the door, knowing full well Cara would likely put her ear to it. He crossed his arms and waited.

Shisa moved up toe to toe, the better to not be overheard...and to get in his face. "Are you going to let her chain me? Are you going to allow this mockery of all that a guardian stands for?"

Though torn between two loyalties, Rodani held his ground. "It was not my decision to make you her temporary servant."

"But—"

"And," he overrode her, "it was not my decision to come here. Nor, may I add, to be storm-blown into a land of demons and their sycophants." When she voiced no reply, he continued. "As I was forced to aver so many times in Barridan, 'I obey my taso.' Shall I ruin the chance of Himadi House becoming successful by undermining her before she has had a chance to rule? And," he reminded her, "what will the ke'taso think of you if that happens?"

Shisa spun around and stepped away from her brother, and from her memories of their childhood. "I cannot believe what turmoil you

412

and she have created in so many. Harmed so many." She spun back. "How many humans died because you were there? Shall I add them to the count of the Selandu in Barridan?"

Her words slashed at him, at his heart, at his pride. But she wasn't finished. "I still cannot understand why you have chained yourself to her, as she has chained me. You should rid yourself of her, and you do not!"

Diverting the urge to hit back, Rodani bared his teeth at her. "Pleasant morn, Serano. I did not know you left Barridan," he replied with a sarcastic lilt. His eyes narrowed. "I allowed you to speak with me when I have urgent tasks. But I give you no right to so blindly judge me, or demand that I disobey my taso." His arm shot out in fury as he turned back to the door. "Do as you are told, a'tem."

After a hasty parting with the ke'taso, Cara and Rodani were ushered out into the dawn, chivied along by Kenimandil's guardians. They were met by a benatac-drawn covered wagon and four more of the harnessed beasts. Cara glanced at them warily as she was led to a grassy field beyond the doors. Workers hefted metal chests, wooden boxes, and bags into the wagon. Tokennen was deep in conversation with one of its drivers. Shisa stood to the side with arms crossed and mouth pursed shut.

"Come, a'Taso," Chendal said.

Hearing the title, Cara looked around for Kenimandil. Then Rodani guided her forward with a hand. She blushed in consternation. *This is going to take some adjustments, fem,* she chided herself.

Two benatacs had double saddles, and Rodani and Chendal helped her sit in the front seat of the tallest beast. Rodani helped her settle, and tied a carry sack with water and travel food near her shin. Chendal whispered to the animal in what looked to Cara like an attempt to settle it down. She dearly hoped this was the kind of gentle beast that Serano had coaxed her onto.

To her dismay, Rodani hefted himself onto the other benatac with a double saddle, and Chendal took the seat behind her.

"Aisu?"

Rodani glanced at her. "Cara, the temaso is the best rider here. You will do well."

Keep quiet and accept it, please, he seemed to say. Cara took a deep breath and tried to settle her gut as Chendal nudged the beast into a walk.

Ever silent, Shisa rode beside the wagon as it pulled out onto a set of tracks leading south. Rodani and Chendal rode side by side, with Tokennen falling behind, tasked with keeping a guardian's eye on any pursuit.

For his part, Rodani took turns watching for problems from the east, and Cara to his right. Beyond her, to the west, was Chendal's duty. The sun had not risen far into the sky before Cara began to fidget in the saddle.

"Kia?" he said softly. At his word, she looked over, and up, at him. "Are you well?"

She shrugged her shoulders, a human gesture he'd learned in Barridan. "It's getting a little tiring sitting in one place like this. It hurts a bit."

"Keep shifting. Find new ways to sit, new places on which to balance."

That worked for a while. Then it didn't.

***

"A'Reiti," a junior guardian called to Menachem.

He pulled his gaze away from the window and turned around. "Sai?"

"The see-ess-see wishes to speak with you, a'Reiti."

Now what? he thought uncharitably, as he headed to the comm room. The anger, disgust, and worry that had raged within him for more than a day had yet to settle. His whole life's work might fall into ruins in a year or less, and someone wants another trifling favor?

He sat where he was directed to. "Menachem."

"Ambassador!" Lara's alarmed voice punched through the speaker. "Ambassador, Sheriff Berg is here, and he demands to speak with you." She took a gasping breath and pushed on. "He won't take no for an answer, Ambassador, and I tried. He got mad at me."

"What does he want?"

"He won't even tell me. I asked. He just pushed his way in and started stomping around."

"Put him on, Lara, and take a breath." For a moment he wondered again why so many women could get so emotional. The fact that men felt the same emotions but showed them differently, never cracked the wall of his childhood teachings.

A gruff voice passed over the wires. "Menachem?"

"This is Ambassador Menachem. What can I do for you from so far away?"

"I've got news here that I can't believe, but can't disprove either. Mack Cornyn's dead and rumors are exploding, and I need an answer."

"I heard he was. Answer to what, Sheriff?"

"To why I have Mack's brother and friend telling me they captured an alien south of Lordstown, and brought him up here."

"That's prepost—" Menachem's eyes went wide. No. Rage flew through, a hot wire that left him breathless. She lied. That husband of hers lied. Chendal refused to speak of it. Kenimandil didn't mention it. Conspiracy! That's what this is. And everyone here is in on it.

"Menachem?"

The impatient voice drove thoughts of revenge out of his mind—temporarily. He took a deep breath to clear his head. "Sheriff, I've never heard of such a thing. I'll ask the people here, and I'll let you know if I learn anything."

"Fine. Over and out, or whatever you guys call it."

The line went dead.

With a fierce hold on his temper, Menachem headed for the ke'taso's office.

***

"I'm sorry, aisu. I really need to get down and walk for a short time. I'm very uncomfortable."

Rodani opened his mouth to reply, but Chendal beat him to it. "A'Taso, we really should make what haste we can. Would you prefer to sit in the wagon for the present?"

She checked in with Rodani, who inclined his head in assent.

"Then yes, please."

Chendal nudged his benatac forward and whistled to the wagon driver to stop. He pulled up next to the open end of the wagon and gave her a boost down into it as Rodani waited to offer assistance.

The hours crawled by with muttered conversations between the drivers in front and the guardians behind her. She turned and watched her man and his guild superior ride in parallel and wondered what—or who—they were discussing. Woods appeared and disappeared as they worked their way south, with two small streams interrupting the monotony.

In a while, after inspecting the outsides of the boxes and sacks around her, Cara was reduced to playing mind games to stave off a fatal case of boredom. She couldn't even add to her to-do list. It was impossible to write legibly with the way the wagon rattled and rolled. *Patience, fem,* she reminded herself. *Show some good human qualities. You're going to need them.*

With the sun high overhead, they stopped for a rest and bladder relief on a patch of ground where a small pool of water lay. Everyone emptied their bodies and refilled their water bags. Cara jogged in place for a few minutes and swung her arms around to loosen all the muscles that had tightened. But in much too short a time, Chendal called to remount.

"Can I ride with you for a while, aisu?"

Rodani glanced down at her, then made hand signals to Chendal. She kept her eyes on her mate, waiting.

He linked his fingers and lifted her up. With less grace than she wished, she maneuvered her rear into the first saddle and her feet into the stirrups.

"My bag?" she asked.

Without comment, Rodani retrieved it from the temaso's saddle. Finally, the group moved forward.

Cara contented herself with knowing her beloved husband was seated behind her, and life together was ahead of them. Precarious as it may be, she hoped it was better than living on fish and small mammals, eating around a campfire, sleeping in a swayin—

"The hammock!" she exclaimed, turning for a side view of Rodani.

His expression was a mix of confusion and humor. "Now, you think of that?"

"I just remembered aisu. I left it in the boat."

"I have hopes that it will not be needed here."

She faced forward again, somewhat reluctantly. "I'm sorry I couldn't bring it."

Rodani tickled her cheek with a spare finger, and brought his mouth to her ear. "I am certain you can find a way to apologize to me when we settle into our new bedroom."

She bent forward in silent mirth, then patted his thigh as it rested near her. As an afterthought, she left her hand there, right where anyone could see it. That kind of thing didn't matter, now. She would do what she could in Himadi to make *sure* it didn't matter. Hiding their affinity was a relic of their past, and she'd be damned if she'd carry it with her, now.

The miles wore on as the sun crossed the sky. Sandy beaches gave way to trees as they worked their way southwest. Cara switched from benatac to wagon back to benatac as riding pain pulsed in her thighs and rear.

"How much farther tonight, aisu?"

He looked to his right. "A'Temaso?"

Chendal glanced at the pair, analyzing with what he knew of humans as to the state of the new taso. "Two hours, if possible, a'Keso."

"Can you manage that, kia?"

She sighed and shifted again. "I'll do my best."

When they finally stopped near a stand of trees, Cara could only stumble and shuffle for a few minutes. She stretched her legs and swiveled her hips in an effort to undo the day's stiffness. Rodani grabbed their packs and walked to a nearby fire pit. The others began to gather and pull out food, drink, and bedrolls.

"Can I help with anything?"

Rodani pointed out a metal cook pot that their driver had pulled from the wagon. "Can you fill it? There is a stream just inside the trees."

Cara lifted the pot with some difficulty. "I couldn't carry it when it's filled." She set it back down. "But I can fill water bags and empty them into it."

Rodani tilted his head. "Yes do, please, a'Taso."

Cara grinned, discomfited at the use of her title, and went to fetch and carry.

Hot soup and a bit of wine or ale managed to erase the group's pangs of hunger after a long day.

"I will take first watch," Chendal announced. "Shisa, second. Tokennen, third."

Cara crawled into the bedroll they would share. "You don't take watch?"

Rodani slipped in beside her and curled his arm around her. "My duty is to watch you."

"What trouble am I going to be, here and now?" she said, smiling.

Rodani refused to mirror the smile. "The trouble is not you. It is what may come to you, kia."

She shifted around and looked out. "Do we expect any?"

"Expect, no. Assume, yes."

"Animals or Selandu?"

Rodani laid his fingers lightly on her mouth. "Sleep."

She puffed out a breath against them. "Are you still allowed to give me orders, now?"

He leaned his forehead toward hers. "That was a dire request, my taso. Please attend to it."

She kissed the air in front of his face and closed her eyes.

***

Morning's breakfast was a choice of cold stew or hard tack. Cara chose neither, despite Rodani's prodding. Hoisted up on benatac in front of him, her body again felt the discomfort of riding. Her stomach gifted her with another bout of nausea, as well. *Should've eaten*, she scolded herself.

"Shift your body to the four directions, kia," he reminded her.

"I do *not* know how Serano found pleasure in this."

Rodani patted her thigh. "Likely, he felt the same regarding your crafting."

"And yours?"

"And mine."

The sun rose in an autumn blue sky, and the beasts and wagons made their way over grassland, hillocks, and small streams.

"A'Temaso," Cara ventured into the quiet.

"A'Taso."

"What will we see when we get near Himadi?"

"A manor house similar to Barridan, a'Taso."

"And what will happen when we arrive?"

Chendal was silent for a moment. "One of the door guards will call for a stablehand to care for our beasts, and Ambassador Andreh' should meet us at the door. From there, it will be up to you and him."

"I'm not looking forward to that meeting."

He turned to glance at her. "Why?"

Cara debated whether to tell the truth or lie by omission. But she went with her gut. "You heard Menachem, Chendal. Andrew feels the same about me. Wild, emotional, uncontrolled, inconsistent. He'll tell me I'm not capable."

Chendal went quiet, possibly digesting the admittance. "Is this factual, or a story you devised to match your feelings?"

Rodani shot him a wide-eyed look. "A'Temaso!" he chided.

"No, aisu, he has a point." She looked over at Chendal. "I am assuming those words, based on what I know of him. But I'd be willing to bet a coin or two that I'd be right."

Chendal pursed his lips in—to Cara's eyes—an unaccustomed grin. "Shall we bet?"

Cara laughed. "No, I think I'll need those coins, a'Temaso. Something tells me that money is going to be scarce for a while."

"We will need," Rodani added, "to do what you suggested, a'Taso. Assist the Himadians with inventing that which is sellable. Tokennen tells me that most of the work now is research and toolmaking."

"They're paid, aren't they?"

"Yes, but directly from Hadaman. Himadi is not profitable yet."

"That needs to change."

As the time passed, her anticipation turned to anxiety. To break her tension, she began to sing. Softly, but not too soft for Selandu hearing.

"Kia," he admonished her.

"Join me in singing, aisu," she countered.

"Du," he said sharply.

"Aisu, my mate, today, my life and yours will change in ways I can hardly imagine. Please allow me that time to be fully human before I have to be half and half."

Chendal's voice came from her right side, carefully neutral. "Does the idea of being half human and half Selandu disturb you, a'Taso?"

Cara chuckled. "Do you wish a courteous answer or an honest one, a'Temaso?"

He took his time replying. "Honest, a'Taso."

"Then I'll say the idea of giving up half of me is a little frightening. But my hope is that I can give up more of the negative traits of humans, and gather to myself more of the positive traits of Selandu, without their negatives. But that journey, along with trying to be a taso, will be somewhat painful."

"Negative Selandu traits?" Chendal queried.

Cara leaned her head back toward her husband. "Rodani, how many times did Serano hit me in Barridan?"

"Too many, a'Taso."

"Not to mention what Shisa did to me. And, not to mention all the Temi-damned scars that cover your back." She looked to her right. "Shall I mention those that you were ordered to give him, a'Temaso? Or just keep quiet about them so that no one will be offended?"

Silence fell over the party, and the ride continued.

Before much longer, Rodani pointed ahead of them. "Do you see it?"

Cara squinted into the early afternoon sun. "Is that it?"

"It is."

"Oh man, here we go."

"No, kia. Not 'here we go,' but 'here we are,' and here we stay."

The End

The Fabric of Power
Selandu Tales 4

Rodani stood, palms on the desktop and head bent. His taso rested in bed, under the only relief he could give her now: the smoke umbrella.

Agony rolled through him. Not physical; not quite. But his emotions battered him, making him dizzy and stealing his strength.

Horror topped the list. Guilt ran a close second.

Why? Why did he send her out with another guardian instead of escorting her himself? Why did her enemies choose that moment? Could he ever forgive Tokennen for his lapse? And would Tokennen ever forgive him for the punishment he'd had to inflict?

Dimly he heard voices. The temaso arriving as he'd asked, and more quickly than expected. Then he heard another voice, one he hadn't heard in months. A tendril of hope wound through his pain like a fragile curl of smoke.

Chendal walked into the office and halted to study Rodani, his face masking his reaction to the keso's pain. Behind him stood someone Rodani thought he'd never see again. His stomach rolled and pitched. "Serano," he whispered, eyes wide.

"Tem'u," Serano responded, hesitant. He took a step forward.

It was all the invitation Rodani needed. "Tem'u," he replied, heartfelt, and pulled him into a tight embrace.

"I have missed you," Serano told him, returning the hug.

"We could have used you today," Rodani said in a hoarse voice. He let go and gazed at his old partner, not quite believing his eyes. "You might have made a difference."

"I am sorrowed that I was not here." Serano took a step back. "We may assume how your taso fares, tem'u. But what of you?"

GLOSSARY

Bolded names and words are the more important or most often use ones.

Cara MacLennan	Crafter, the lone human visitor in Barridan	CARE-uh
Rodani	Former Security Fifth; Cara's guardian and lover	row-DON-ee
ai	Suffix; plural of a noun; ex: a'tem'ai; a'sel'ai	aye
'com	Pocket communication device carried by all guardians, and occasionally by others	
'corder	Music playing device; brought down from shipboard	
a'	Prefix; honorific; formal courtesy of address	ah
a'sel	Honorific form of addressing any regular Selandu person	a-SELL
a'Selaso	Honorific form of addressing a high priestess	ah-sell-AH-so
a'Taso	Honorific form of addressing a taso directly	ah-TAH-so
a'tem	Honorific form of addressing a temichi directly	ah-TEM, as in "temp"
a'Temaso	Honorific form of addressing the head of guild guardians	ah-tem-AH-so
adashi	One who is guarded from others by a guardian	a-DASH-e
affinity	Love/sex relationship	
aisu	Cara's pet name for Rodani: "night eyes"	AYE-soo
Ahsan	Suraya's oldest brother	ah-SAHN

Alan	Cara's youngest brother, age 16	
Aldano	Pseudonym for Rodani in Endolan	All-DON-oh
Ama	Cara's name for her mother; Dr. Liz	AH-mah
Andrew Lieu	Ambassador Second; pronounced Andreh' by Selandu	Lee-ooh
Arimeso Osanin	Taso of Barridan	Air-ih-MAY-so oh-SAH-nin
au	Interjection; onomatopoeia; open-throated exclamation	As in like: ack! Or ow! Or oh!
Baldar	Physician; Master Healer	ball-dar (no emphasis), as in "dart"
Barridan	Estate that Arimeso rules; house full of crafters and artists	BEAR-ih-dahn
benatac	Large horse-like animal; toes and sharp teeth; irascible	BEN-ah-tack
'Berg' Heisberg	Chief Sheriff of Glaniad	
Bethamy	Co-worker of Suraya's	BETH-am-ee
Cassig	Cook in Barridan responsible for safely managing Cara's meals	CASS-ig
Cene'l	Human language; based on the Welsh language intermixed with English and common words from other languages	ken-EL
Chendal	Head of the Guild of Guardians; the temaso	CHEN-dahl
Chucko	Barback at The Wet Rag bar	
Clark	Friend of Mack's	

CSC	Cultural Studies Center where humans study the Selandu language and culture	
Dae	Cara's name for her father; Liam	day
Dag	Husband to Cara's sister Emmie	rhymes with rag
Darun	Guardian Council Second (m)	DARE-un
Davad	Cara's brother, age 24	DAH-vahd
Deneban	Security Twelfth (m)	DEN-eh-bun
Deremic	Cara's second servant; has some training in protection	Deh-REM-ick
Dottie	Bartender Nick's ex-wife	
du	No	dthoo; short sound, don't extend the "oo"
eisenico	Rodani's drink	aye-sen-EE-ko
Emmie	Cara's oldest sister, age 29	
Enclave	Both the area in the manor where the priestesses live and work, and the name of the group of priestesses themselves	AHN-clave
Elaine	Cara's sister, age 17	
Endolan	Small town north of Soldan where Rodani stopped for supplies and a boat	EN-dole-lan
Erick	Davad's friend and emergency helper	
erinai	Pet name for a lover or mate	ERR-in-aye
festive room	Recreation area; drinking, dancing, music, wrestling, betting.	
Gavin	Cara's brother, age 22	

gathering room	For large dinners, celebrations, punishments	
Gerry Canberry	Drummer	Gary, or Gare
Glaniad	Welsh; it means landing or touchdown, town where Cara is from	GLAHN-yadth
Graeme Wilson	Deputy sheriff	Graham
Hadaman	Capital city; north and east of Barridan, near the shore	HAH-dah-mahn
Hamman	Cara's senior servant; middle aged (f)	HAH-mun
Himadi Hills	Low hills separating Selandan (north) and Newydd Cenedyl (south)	hih-MAH-dee
Himadi House	Manor under construction on the Himadi Plateau; Selandu and humans are to live there and work together for the betterment of both species	same
Himadi Plateau	Flatlands north of the hills	same
Hurasten	Guardian Council First, leader over all of the guardians on the planet (m)	Hurr-AST-en
Ikemi	Boy who bonded with Cara in Barridan	ih-KEM-ee
Imal	Security Third (m) (deceased)	IH-mul
Iraimin	Painter; friend to Cara	ih-RAI-min, as in "rye"
James	Guitarist	
Jinai	Guardian Council Third (f)	jinn-AYE
Joel	Creepy hostel manager	
Josie	Singer, tailor	
ke	First, used as a word or an appellative	keh

Kenimandil	Taso First, head of all Selandu on world	Ken-ih-MAN-dill
keso	Security first	KAY-so
ki'tana	Little whirlwind; an affectionate nickname	kee-TAH-nah
kia	Little one (intimate mode)	KEE-uh
Kimasa	Head of the Enclave of priestesses; the selaso	kih-MAH-sah
Kimi	Cara's youngest, and favorite sister	KIM-ee
Kusik	The keso, Security First; Arimeso's husband	KOO-sick
Lanata	Security Third (f)	lah-NAH-tah
Lara	Administrative assistant to Ambassador Menachem	LAH-rah
Larisi	Serano's lover; new acolyte of the Enclave	lah-REE-zee
Litelon	A mid-adolescent stablehand, who has a crush on Cara	lih-TELL-on
Lordstown	Insular town south of Glaniad	
Mack Cornyn	Ne'er-do-well, braggart, misogynist	
Mandai	Fishmonger in Endolan	man-DIE
mate; bonded mate	Spouse; formal declaration of joined lives	
Menachem Mboto	Ambassador First; pronounced Mena'hem by Selandu	men-AH-(flegm) mm-BOH-toh as in "boat"
Merelin	Davad's pregnant fiancée	MARE-ih-lin
Misheiki	Security Seventh (m)	mish-AY-kee as in the letter "a"
Newydd Cenedyl	Land south of the hills; human lands (means "new nation")	Welsh; NEY-width KAN-a-dill

Nick Kinski	Bartender of The Wet Rag bar	
ninety-nine	Sign-off on a given command or exchange over 'com	
ono	Woman	OH-noh
oto	Man	OH-toh
Paolo	Suraya's boss of The Weekly, new items that are posted on the community board	pah-OH-lo
reiti	Ambassador	ray-EE-tee
Ricardo	Weaver	
richu	Small crustacean with pincers	REE-chew
River Samida	River where the battle was fought; also River War	sah-MEAD-ah
sai	Yes	sigh
Sallah	Keeper of the repository	SAHL-ah
Sela	Goddess of the Selandu	SELL-uh
Selandu	Species' name	seh-LAN-doo, as in "land"
Selandi	Species' language	seh-LAN-dee
selaso	Head of the Enclave; high priestess	seh-LAH-so
Serano	Security Fourth; Rodani's former guild partner	seh-RON-oh
Shandar	Baker, one of Suraya's brothers	SHAN-dar, rhymes with Stan
shigeli	Cara's alcoholic drink	shih-GAY-lee
Shisa	Chendal's guild partner; Rodani's older sister	SHEE-suh
Shurad	Riverchild; writer; tried to kill Cara in The Fabric of Honor	SURE-add
Simandil	Master healer at guild headquarters	sim-AN-dill

Smoke	Informal name for analgesic powder that is inhaled	
Soldan	Ocean-side town where boats from Newydd Cenedyl dock	SOLE-dahn
Stefan	Younger brother of Mack	
Suraya Patel	Journalist	Sue-DRAI-uh (soft 'd' sound)
taso	Head of a manor house and all its inhabitants.	TAH-so
te	Middle; middling (age, size, etc.), also youth	teh
te'oto; te'ono	Young man, male youth; young woman, female youth	teh-oto; teh-ono
tem'u	Informal name for guild partner; close companionship	TEM-oo, as in "temp"
temaso	Head of the guild of guardians (only three people in guild council are higher)	teh-MAH-so
Temi	Consort to the goddess; worshipped by guardians	TEM-ee, as in "temp"
temichi	Selandu name for a guardian	teh-MEE-chee
temichin	Plural of temichi	teh-MEE-chin
Tendiman	Town holding the Guild of Guardians' training center	TEN-dih-mahn
Teria	Cara's middle sister, age 19	tare-EE-uh
Timan	The biso, Security Second; Kusik's guild partner (deceased)	TEE-mun
Tokennen	Former keso of Barridan, now on Kenimandil's staff	Tow-KEN-nen
torac	Large ursine animal	TORE-ack
Vanu	Security Tenth (m) (deceased)	VA-new, as in "van"
varigestra	Tea leaves that when brewed, reduce the mating hormones of	Vare-ih-GEST-ruh

a Selandu man or woman;
dangerous in high quantities or
when too strongly steeped.

---

verelin	Thank you	VERE-uh-lin

J.A. Komorita is a born and raised Hoosier, who moved to Texas in her late twenties. Within two weeks, she met the man who would become her husband. They raised twin sons and a daughter. They live in a very crowded home with two cats, 1,000+ books of nearly every genre, and more art and craft supplies, completed and unfinished projects, notes, designs, and ideas than she will ever use in three lifetimes.

She would like to borrow and modify a quote from the esteemed SF author Anne McCaffrey: "My eyes are blue, my hair is grey, the rest is subject to change without notice."

* 9 7 9 8 9 9 1 1 6 1 8 4 8 *